# A Shifter's Wild Magic

Amanda Casey

Book Cover by 100 Covers

Illustrations by Amanda Casey

1st edition 2026

# Also By Amanda Casey

**Ocean Apothecary Series**

*Blue Mermaid Memories*

*Blue Reflections*

*Tidal Ancestry*

*Ocean Origins*

**Witches & Demons Series**

*A Demon's Book of Shadows*

*A Witch's Forbidden Bloom*

*A Shifter's Wild Magic*

Join Amanda's newsletter to receive a free novella!

amandacaseybooks.com

*For the creatures big and small.*

*May your magic always captivate us all.*

# Content Warning

This book contains situations and themes that include language, blood and violence, drugs and alcohol use, surviving cancer, PTSD, and explicit sexual intimacy.

# Prologue

Grinding away at the asphalt for the past hour with a jackhammer rumbling beneath my legs had my head wobbling so fiercely, I feared I might decapitate myself. The scent of tar, dirt, and sweat clogged my nose, making it difficult to breathe. My inner shadow wolf had tried and failed to sneeze.

The job demolishing the old warehouse outside of Midhaven had taken much longer than any of the guys thought. And that was saying a lot, because I was the only demon on the crew.

Other than my father, Eugene Ravenblood.

Dad had spent the mid-afternoon hours folded beneath the one lone tree that offered shade on the construction site, while the rest of us were hot and sticky with humidity from the latest heat wave. Dad's attitude toward the sweltering weather was the prime reason I preferred working third shift. I didn't have to deal with the sun beating down on my hide for one of my twelve-hour shifts.

I killed the jackhammer and tossed it aside. My father was going to get a fucking piece of my mind. I staggered over to him, claws bursting out of my steel-toed boots just to steady my footing.

I retracted them as I leveled my gaze with him. "Dad," I growled, my inner shifter getting the better of me. "You can't just sit on your ass all day, especially when I know your shadows could level this shit-hole in an instant."

Dad had propped himself beneath the trunk of the tree. He sat on the ground, sipping on his mocktail—a combination of tomato juice, jalapeños, and Dr. Pepper. How he was drinking something so nastily spicy on such a hot day (even though it was served over ice) was beyond me. Before he'd gone sober, at this time of day, he'd be guzzling down a Bloody Mary.

I stopped beside him and leaned against the tree, desperate for a moment to escape the scorching sun. Why was it this fucking hot when it wasn't even technically summer yet?

Dad kept his attention on his thermos in hand. His long reddish-brown hair was greasy with sweat. He looked as nasty as I felt.

"Zeddy, the sun is far too brutal for my Irish complexion," he protested as he stuck the straw into his mouth and slurped. "Besides, I have a hot date this evening, and I don't want to look like a cherry tomato for Cindy."

Anger flared in my gut. Hot date or not, we had a shit ton of work yet to accomplish.

His two spirit ravens, Anger and Sadness, sat atop the concrete wall our crew had slaved away all week trying to demolish. They tossed their ebony heads, frilling their tail feathers as they attempted not to overheat.

I ground my jaw. *I* was the one who should be complaining about this shitty, fiery weather, not him. My bald head had started to peel from the sunburn I'd gotten this week.

"Zed, get over here!" one of the men called from the demo site.

I left my pampered father, darting over to where the other non-demon men were struggling with a large metal pipe.

I ducked beneath the backhoe bucket that swung overhead.

*Fuck this.* I was hot and sweaty and exhausted. I didn't have another five hours to waste trying to dig this shit out of the ground. It was time to let my shadow beasts devour what was left of our demo job.

I jumped into the dirt pit as a ghoulish growl rumbled in my chest. Down here, I was out of sight from the rest of the crew, and free to shift as I pleased. My hands morphed and became a set of silver paws. I dug my claws into the dirt beside the pipe. My shadow wolf wasn't strong enough.

Shadows coiled around my forearms as I shifted again. This time, my hands took on the wide shape of grizzly bear paws.

The ground trembled as the engine roared above from the backhoe.

"Let her rip!" a man cried as he swung the large bucket over the pit where I stood.

Dirt flung into my face as the bucket hit the pipe and dislodged it from the earth.

The backhoe shifted, and a giant metal pipe came swinging for my head.

I ducked, but not fast enough.

My body bent as the pipe crashed into my arm. Tufts of fur ripped out of my back. Bones cracked.

A sickening pain knocked me on my ass. My hands shifted from bear paws back into the form of a man.

"Zed, are you all right?" the backhoe driver cried as he killed the engine.

My vision went blurry. *Fuck.*

I'd gone and ripped my arm wide open.

# 1

# Victoria

**June 10th**

Sweet fucking Hades, was it noisy and hot in my vet office. My red-tailed hawk, Francine, wouldn't stop squawking about the last egg in her nest—one that I was convinced didn't belong to her. Francine's chicks had fledged and were currently flying around town, teaching themselves how to hunt. But I didn't dare try and peep atop my filing cabinet where she was currently shooting me the crazy eyes.

I plopped in front of my desktop and brought up the local weather. It was only June, and Midhaven was set to endure a full week of a hundred-and-three-degree weather. It didn't help that the air conditioner had broken down for the third time this week. The air was muggy and made the smell of cats and dogs and a bunch of other creatures reek.

I wasn't usually bothered by the aromas, but the humidity made them ten times worse. The last thing I wanted to do was eat, but I had a few minutes to scarf down my leftovers—Mom's pesto pasta dish—for lunch.

In between bites, I grabbed my phone. Neither of my sisters had answered my SOS texts. I was going to end up closing on Friday evening, *again.* I wouldn't be able to make it to either of my after-work social engagements.

Mom was the only one who'd replied. She'd sent me multiple messages full of strings of flower emojis mixed with teacups. Knowing her, she was likely harvesting herbs like a mad woman so that she could prepare her next seasonal infusion—solstice tea. My phone kept sending out magical rays of yellow sunshine. Mom's magic was obviously heating my office, because like my two younger sisters, she was likely spending her hot, soon-to-be-summer afternoon with one of the Ravenbloods.

Mom had an actual demon boyfriend. And she wasn't being sneaky like both of my sisters had been with their Ravenbloods. Both Amon and Krim were Eugene Ravenblood's demon sons.

In other words, everyone in my immediate family was getting hot demon sex (except for perhaps my saintly witch mother) other than myself.

As I rearranged my desk, a tarot card I'd been using as a bookmark for one of my steamy romance novels fell out. I propped the card onto my desk. The Wild Card was by far the most ornate of the cards within the Three Magics Oracle Deck. The design on the card included an eye encircled by a sun. Below the eye sprouted a brilliant golden tree, its branches weaving its power into all three magics. Rooted at the base was a tiny egg, which was propped up by two supporting hands. I'd guessed for the longest time which creature that egg could belong to.

A feather came floating down and landed in my lunch.

"Can you please stop that?" I scolded Francine. She'd started to preen herself out of nervous habit because the egg she was guarding had yet to hatch.

Speaking of preening. I readjusted my top. The heat was making my scrubs stick to my curves in places that made the starchy fabric bunch. I had to cancel my manicure appointment this week due to so many staff call outs. I was also severely overdue for a new bra. I'd been trying to schedule a trip with Grace to Victoria's Secret with no luck.

Then again, finding a bra that fit my curves was not easy. *Fuck cancer.* It had gone and taken my left breast a few years ago. Cancer had put an incredible amount of strain on my marriage, which had resulted in divorce. Now I was just a middle-aged single witch who worked sixty-hour weeks at the vet clinic.

Holly Bell, my receptionist, poked her head into my office. Her face appeared as flush as I felt. Beads of sweat glistened on her forehead. "Sorry, Victoria. It looks like you might be the only vet who can close tonight."

My shoulders rose and fell as I tried not to scream. I really wanted to launch my bowl of pasta at the wall. "Of course. What's new?"

She tapped her pen across the top of her clipboard. "Honestly, I'd only trust you with these last three patients. They don't look like anything I'd trust the other vets, let alone an intern with."

While I worked with three other vets, none of them were witches like me. Holly herself was a witch, one who made her talents known with her incredible bookkeeping. She valued my skills and had labeled me as the matriarch within the vet hierarchy.

There was no magical school for veterinarian degrees. I had earned my degree alongside other non-witch vets the old-fashioned way—with blood, sweat, and so much time tending to creature patients. Witch families from the coast often sought out my specialty regarding exotic familiars. Over the years, I'd gained a reputation in other witch families for treating ferrets, felines, and of course, one of my favorite exotics—a rainbow serpent.

Canines, on the other hand, I passed on to my vet techs. I let them perform routine checkups and procedures on most domestic creatures, such as parakeets, dogs, and lizards, while I handled the rest.

Thank the goddess for Holly and her ability to pull a few magical strings when it came to my often hectic schedule. She and I had met in vet school. She was a witch who lived in Oregon, and had moved to the Midwest when her boyfriend of seven years got a job at the local hospital. We'd hit it off instantly.

The moment she dropped out of vet school, I wrangled her up and promised her a job working at my clinic the moment I opened it. We'd been inseparable as friends and working colleagues. While she worked her magic scheduling patients, I worked my magic on the plentiful familiars we had visit our clinic.

Holly set the clipboard down on my desk. "Can I get you a coffee? Cold brew, of course. By the way, you are *rocking* those red scrubs."

I ran my fingers across my temples, which were both horribly sweaty. "Thanks, it's that time of year when I feel like I need to wear a color that matches the heat. And no on the coffee. You don't need to try and appease me. This isn't your fault. I could have been better about handing out assignments last month."

I could count on my fingers the number of unique creature experiences that had ocurred at my clinic in the past month. No wonder I'd lost so many vet techs recently. The rainbow serpent fecal sampling disaster ended in so much excrement, I thought I'd walked into a multi-colored horror film. I'd lost *three* interns that day. The room was closed to be disinfected for two weeks. . .

Holly wiped the back of her hand past her forehead. "Bad news. The guy who was supposed to repair the air conditioner won't be back until Monday."

Francine squawked obnoxiously above us.

Sweat trickled down my ribcage. I had at least another hour of this hot, sweaty afternoon to endure. I *really* wanted to torture some poor intern. Then again, *my throw you in with the wolves* approach backfired on me, thus rendering me to this short-staffed situation I was in.

I grabbed the clipboard and flipped through the new patient intake forms. I still had three appointments before I could close up and leave. A few envelopes stuck out from the bottom of the paperwork. Holly delivered mail to my office every day around the noon hour. I spent so much time at the clinic, that it proved easier to have my personal mail forwarded to my work address.

"TGIF," Holly said as she slipped out of my office, fanning her face as she went.

"*TGIF*!" Francine squawked as she flapped her wings and sent a few feathers into the air.

My hand bumped into a romance novel sitting on my desk. The nitty gritty details of my favorite way to escape wasn't going to happen this month. Getting some reading done over my busy lunch break would have to wait another day. Sometimes I felt I read more than my librarian sister, Lucy. I'd started off with paranormal romance, then jumped straight into romantasy. It wasn't long before I fell in love with shifters from the paranormal genre again, and now, my latest obsession was *monsters*. The monsters in the dark romance books I read about had been my escape when I'd lost part of myself to breast cancer.

Reading about the demons and devils and monsters with horns and teeth and claws was like reclaiming a part of my femininity that had been stolen from me. I wasn't afraid of beasts, or men. What terrified me the most, was the fact that I felt like I was now half a woman.

One of the envelopes stuck out from the others in my pile of mail. The return address indicated that it was from Midhaven's Cancer Clinic. I'd gone in a few weeks ago to have my annual checkup done.

I tore open the envelope and pulled out the letter.

**Victoria Crow,**

**Please contact us as soon as possible regarding your latest breast screening. We have tried multiple times to reach you by**

**phone with no luck. We'd like you to come into the Cancer Clinic to discuss treatment options.**

# 2

# Dezmond

"*You let Pawz get hurt?*" a low growl erupted into my head.

"*Wow, glad I buried my nose into the dirt before all hell broke loose,*" followed a second voice with a howl.

"*I don't think I'm going to be showing off my claws for a while,*" a third voice grunted with a tone that sounded far more pitiful than the others.

"Guys, calm your furry tits. I'm going to be fine," I ground out as I flexed my arm. The wound had been badly stitched up by me with some fishing line, a pair of pliers, and whole lot of swearing.

After the episode at the demo site, I'd retreated to my apartment with my tail between my legs. It had taken me a good hour of trying not to grind my molars into a pulp as I sewed up my flesh. Part of what made the procedure so difficult was the size of my fingers. All of us demon Ravenblood brothers had gotten Dad's big Irish hands, but mine were much bigger than my older brothers', as I was a shifter. My joints were twice as thick, and my fingers even thicker.

What worried me was the hot, gritty sensation lurking under my skin. Even with the help of my shadow magic, my bones weren't mending properly. And my shadow beasts were all going to voice their opinions about the accident, whether I liked it or not.

"*You bet we are,*" Pawz grumbled with a clash of his claws. "*How are we supposed to help you if you let us get hurt?*"

"Dude, it was an accident. I didn't mean to injure your paw," I snapped at him.

My angry shadow bear dug his claws into my ribs. "*Next time I won't be so willing to help you out.*"

I ground my jaw. As far as I knew, I was the only brother who gave my shadows names. Amon, my oldest brother, had a multi-shadow personality like me. However, the ghoulish figures that haunted his tattoo parlor remained nameless. Krim, my brother who was a few decades older than me, had one giant hooded shadow he referred to as his *reaper.* I, on the other hand, owned three very powerful shadow beasts who manifested themselves as the three senses they represented.

Pawz was my bear, who represented touch. Jawz was my lion, who represented my ravenous taste. And Sniffer was my wolf. He could sniff out magical traces miles away. For the past year now, he'd been dead set on trying to sniff out what he referred to as my *true mate.*

Twenty-seven stitches and a whole lot of bickering from Pawz, Jawz, and Sniffer later, my flesh was mended into something that would hold up, for now. I'd sewn up flesh wounds with my teeth and floss before. I could always ask my eldest brother, Amon, to slap another tattoo over it once the scab was gone.

That's what I got for trying to shift and take a shortcut.

I stood from my seat by the window and walked toward the door that went out onto the deck. My apartment was on the upper level, with the deck hanging out into an alleyway. Downtown Midhaven wasn't super crowded. It was more of a town full of old brick buildings that had served as manufacturing plants decades ago. Out of all three of us Ravenblood brothers, I was the closest to living in what folks might call a city.

I opened the door and walked outside. The tangy aroma of trash filled my nose. A siren blared, sending a few stray cats darting over the cobblestone street. They disappeared behind dumpsters, with a few darting into the shelters I'd created for them out of old plywood and two-by-fours I'd salvaged from one of my construction jobs.

"Hey, Anchovies!" I called down to the tortie who poked her black and brown face out of the shelter. I grabbed a jar and tossed her a few of the treats Krim baked for his ghost cat named Scythe, the ultimate chewy cat treat, Bitty Bone Bites.

Anchovies darted over to the food and immediately scarfed it down. Her belly was twice as wide as the other cats swarming to share in the feast. She was expecting, and sooner or later, I'd be taking her into the animal shelter where I volunteered to have her kittens put up for adoption.

My arm throbbed the second I reached into the treat jar and tossed another handful. I would have gone to the bar to find something to drink to help numb the pain, but Krim had recently flipped Shadow Daddy's into the Blooming Mushroom Bakery. He and his witch girlfriend, Grace Crow, had recently paired off as a couple. She had been a student of his before a forbidden romance bloomed between them, and hence, destroyed the location where my band had historically performed in the evening.

A sniffing sound filled my ears. "*Don't worry. I'm going to sniff out your mate soon, whether you like it or not. Then you won't have to waste your evenings drumming.*"

I poked my finger into my ear as Sniffer's nose snuffled into my head. "Dude, get a grip. No female is going to want to be my mate with my arm looking like this."

I waved at Anchovies before retreating inside. My apartment was a fucking disaster. I hadn't cleaned in weeks. Chinese takeout boxes were stacked in the trash, and a pile of dishes were crammed into the sink.

With my arm still throbbing, I didn't feel like tidying up. And I dare not pick up my drumsticks with my arm being in this shitty mess. My snare drums all had punctures in their heads. And I was too fucking cheap to get them repaired. I'd blown them out about a month ago, when Jawz manifested out of nowhere and tried to sink his massive canines into one of my sticks.

"*I can't help myself. Your rhythm stirs up an insatiable hunger inside of me,*" Jawz grumbled into my head. His shadow lurked on my wall, where he prowled on all-fours, manifesting as a giant lion.

I grabbed my drumstick with my good arm and pointed it at him. "Save the attitude, bud. You won't be hearing any rhythms from me for a while."

With a shuddering growl, his mouth elongated, his canines growing as his beastly shadow branched up the wall behind my drums.

His mouth snapped shut, filling my apartment with plumes of green and purple smoke.

I chuckled. My shadow beasts could be such drama queens at times. Their personalities were so different. Learning to tame them in a way that still allowed them to express their wildness was a real challenge.

I set my stick back onto the broken snare. I wouldn't be able to drum, that was for certain. Telling my band that my arm was in bad shape wasn't going to be easy.

A twinge of loneliness sobered me. I'd been single for so long, I couldn't remember the last fun date I'd had. I knew I was the runt of the litter when it came to Ravenblood demon genes. Both of my older brothers were far bigger, and in some ways, *badder*, than me.

Speaking of my brothers. I'd texted both about hanging out, and neither had replied.

My phone chimed. Dad had texted me.

**Hey, Zeddy! Come over to Cindy's place.**

**Why?**

**I want you to try this new tea. Take the stone pathway around to the back of her house. I want to see how your boo boo is doing.**

**I'll be there in a few.**

I showered and changed into a new pair of clothes, some jeans with holes in the knees, and a plain white t-shirt. It was too hot for my leather biker jacket, but my boots would do. My head was sunburned from the hot day slaving away at the old warehouse amid June, so I tugged on a baseball cap with a skull and crossbones on it.

I didn't feel like taking the stairs down to my motorcycle, so I closed my eyes, and dipped into the realm of shadows known as the Summoning.

As soon as my boots hit the shadowy dimension demons used to make shortcuts between destinations in the physical world, Pawz manifested beside me. His bulky bear of a silhouette wavered ominously as I took a few steps into the inky blackness he called home.

His charcoal hair stood on end, curling out into puffs of purple smoke. "*You're lucky you didn't cause yourself more harm*," he growled as his white eyes found me. They lacked pupils and shone with brilliant intensity.

"Hey, wait up," I said as I stepped into the massive smoking pawprints he left for me to follow. His footsteps shook the ground as he took off into a run toward my motorcycle. Sometimes I thought he really housed the soul of a dog, as he always looked forward to running alongside my bike.

Two other beasts growled as they prowled from behind. Jawz and Sniffer both came up on either side of me, their shoulders scissoring at the height of my head.

"*When do we get to go hunting for witches again?*" Jawz suggested as he tossed his blackened mane into the air. His massive lion paws dwarfed my boots, making my footsteps look like they belonged to a child.

"*When you learn to keep your dong in its sheath long enough to actually kiss one,*" Sniffer howled wolfishly.

"*Hey, at least I don't go knotting every witch I want to devour,*" Jawz shot back. His muzzle crinkled, making his whiskers stand on end.

I chuckled. My lion and my wolf were the two shadow beasts who often didn't see eye-to-eye with one another when it came time to discussing the mating ritual.

As they darted ahead, they cleared the excess shadows in my path and opened my window out of the Summoning. I stepped onto the street corner, spotting my motorcycle. I swung my leg over my Harley Davidson and turned on the ignition. After I gave her a good rev, I steered her out onto the road.

Even over the rumbling noise of the engine, I could hear my shadow beasts bickering. They howled and snarled the entire way over Cindy Crow's house. By the time I parked my bike and killed the engine, I was ready to ring their furry necks and slap their muzzles.

"Hey, guys. Behave yourselves. Just because you're in the presence of a witch doesn't mean you need to make monsters out of yourselves."

At my comment, Sniffer's nose began to work, nuzzling my inner ear.

"Put that schnauzer away," I scolded him as I shoved my finger into my earhole.

Tall green hedges surrounded Cindy's lovely home. The front garden bloomed with flowers I'd never seen in my two hundred some years of life. I approached the path Dad mentioned, already spotting Pawz's massive bear prints leaving shadows on the stones. Hedges shifted as my invisible shadow beast led the way toward the backyard.

"Oh, Eugene, you *shouldn't* have!" Cindy said from around the bend.

I froze. What the fuck was I walking into?

I bustled forward as Sniffer nudged me with his shoulder. Following Pawz's massive shadow tracks, I rounded the bend and emerged into the backyard. A bubbling cauldron sat beneath a giant oak tree that had little yellow lanterns hanging off the branches. The aroma of something floral drifted on the air, instantly setting my mind at ease.

My father sat in the shade, lounging beneath a giant pink umbrella. He was hardly recognizable. He was sprawled out on a lawn chair. His feet were kicked up. A sun hat flopped sideways on his head. A cup of tea sat on a table next to him. He'd grown soft ever since he'd given up the bottle. Which, believe me, was a *good* thing. Since he'd started courting Cindy Crow, he was a changed demon.

What happened to the fierce demon I grew up with? And was that a *book* in his hand? Was my old man *reading* again?

"Zeddy, is that you?" Dad asked, his voice just as soft as the birds calling from the feeder above him. His two spirit ravens, Anger and Sadness, were being bombarded by songbirds as they tossed their feathers into the water of a bird bath.

"Yeah," I replied. "Where is Cindy? And what are you reading?"

"She just went inside to grab some more tea leaves. Her daughter, Lucy, works at the library. She brought me a super old copy of Shakespeare's Hamlet."

I chuckled. I'd forgotten how much of a fan my father was of the classics.

"To be a dick, or not be a dick, that is the question of the evening." Dad held up his teacup. "This is the tea I wanted you to try."

"How does that tea make you feel? It looks kind of wonky," I said, noting its blue color.

"As light as a feather," he replied lackadaisically as bubbles fizzed out of his cup.

While I would much rather have a sober discussion with my father than get caught up into one of his irate drunken ones, this new *tea obsession* of his had me a bit worried.

Dad squinted at my arm. "Dezmond, that looks bad. Have you gone to the doc yet?"

I sighed. He always called me *Zeddy*. Calling me my full name meant that he was being serious. But I agreed with him. I was pretty sure my arm was busted beyond repair. "No, I haven't. Do you think I should?"

"You're a shifter. I don't think you should go to a normal doctor. Cindy's eldest daughter is a vet, and I hear she's also single." He leaned forward, his brows furrowing beneath his sun hat. "Let me tell you, a witch becomes *wild* when she hasn't been with someone intimately in a while."

My stomach churned. Why did I feel like such a third wheel right now?

# 3

# Victoria

By the time I read over the letter from the hospital for what felt like the hundredth time, I was seeing stars. My lungs seized, and I forgot how to expel my breath.

**We'd like you to come into the Cancer Clinic to discuss treatment options.**

As I exhaled, nausea swelled in my stomach, threatening to cripple me. I grabbed a patient chart, forcing myself to read over the intake form. My clipboard knocked into my computer, jostling my Wild Card. I grabbed the card and quickly tucked it inside the charts. I had *three* more patients to take care of before my day was over.

*Slow breaths. In and out. No rush.*

*I can do this. Don't panic. There is no monster lurking inside of you.*

"Dr. Crow, are you all right?"

One of my vet techs stopped me with her question in the hallway. The adrenaline coursing through me did strange things to her mousy features.

I handed her two of the intake forms. "Stacey, can you and Carter take these two patients? I think they'd be good practice for you both."

She grabbed the chart from me. "Sure thing. Do you need a drink of water? Gatorade? You look pretty pale. Are you sure you're getting enough electrolytes?"

As I watched Stacey's nose and eyes pulse with the effects shock had on my vision, I felt like I might hurl. I glanced down at my last patient chart, taking note of how large my right breast looked next to the flat area that was a result of my mastectomy. The wide empty space, I'd learned to cope with.

But what if cancer took my *remaining* breast?

I rested my clipboard atop my chest, shielding myself from my greatest fear. "Water or Gatorade isn't going to quench my thirst after this week, my dear. Thank you for taking care of those for me."

I brushed past Stacey as she nodded, heading straight toward the door where my last patient for the day was waiting. Why I'd saved the worst for last was beyond me. I knew from the intake form that an *appendage laceration* was not a good sign. It would probably involve numbing agents and sutures, both of which would likely demand a lot of time.

Before entering the room where I would meet my last patient, I glanced at my reflection in the mirror hanging in the hall. My messy brown hair had been adjusted so many times, it was beginning to look like a bird nest sat atop my head. I looked so plain—so *exhausted*, another reason I was ready for this week to end.

I turned away from the mirror, focusing instead on the energies from my last patient. I could usually read the aura of the creature beyond the door before I walked inside. But after the cancer scare from the hospital, I was amazed that my magic hadn't played tricks on my ability.

I sucked in a breath and exhaled. *I can do this. One more patient to go.* I grabbed the door handle and swung the door open.

A man sat in the corner of the room. He wore a black leather biker jacket and jeans with holes in the knees. His shiny bald head hung low. Both of his arms were propped on his knees, one of which seemed to exude a dark blood-red aura.

Well, *this* was awkward. Why did this *man* have the description of the wound on my intake form?

The pulsing red light emanating from his arm told me one thing—he was absolutely wounded. While I was no empath, my magic allowed me to tap into the discomfort or illness I was dealing with. He'd suffered physical trauma to his radius, and ulna. Oh, and he'd severed some tendons, too. Why he wasn't reeling in pain was beyond me.

"Hi, I'm Dr. Victoria Crow," I said rather quickly.

He jolted upright. "Oh, sorry. Hey, doc. I'm a bit out of it."

A pair of brilliant green eyes met mine. There was something different about the green. Not goblin green, Grace's favorite color. Or moss, or viridian. The green was electric and had a tinge of wildness to it.

"Hi, I'm Dezmond, but you can call me Zed."

His voice sent a shiver through me. I shook my head. Why the odd name stuck out was beyond me. I'd seen a lot of creature owners today and the names of their creatures were often as bizarre as the species that visited my office.

I'd been so focused on his wound that I forgot why I'd even entered the room. "Where is your critter?"

His brow furrowed. "What critter?"

I arched my brow. "Well, Dezmond, you know this is a *vet* office, not a *doctor's* office, right?"

"Yeah, but," he held out his wounded arm, which looked like it had been patched up with fishing line. "I'm in a bit of a bind."

I cringed as the bones made a nasty *crunching* sound. "Couldn't you go to the emergency room?"

He shook his head. "Nope. My Pops said the only vet in town who has the magic to mend a wound like this is Doctor Victoria Crow."

Speaking of my magic. Sparks shot out of my fingertips, lighting his intake form on fire. I batted it out with my hand, then tossed my smoking clipboard onto the counter. "This has to be some sick joke. Very funny, Holly!"

What was I thinking. My receptionist staff had already gone home to enjoy their hot and humid Friday evening.

I threw up my hands. "It's not even Friday the thirteenth! What is this shit? Stress the fuck out of Vet Victoria because it's funny?"

"Doc, I—"

I folded my arms across my chest. "You know it's illegal for a vet to perform a procedure on a human, right? I don't have the proper medical license to do so."

His mouth curved into a pitiful frown as I continued to stare him down.

"So, your *Pops* told you to come see me, huh? What other secrets about me does he know?"

Dezmond climbed to his feet. "I'm sorry to have bothered you. I can just—"

"Fuck it," I said, plopping on the stool before him. "I've had the week from hell, and this isn't going to make it any worse. Sit down."

He blew out his cheeks as he lowered himself back into his seat.

I glanced at the patient profile on my clipboard. The words *ripped the shit out of my arm* had been scribbled in the wound description. "How the hell did you do this to yourself?"

"I work odd jobs, mainly construction. My buddies and I were working to remove an old drainage pipe from and old building, which slammed into me." His mouth quirked into a smile. "The lady up front said she had to pull some strings to get me in. How many hours did you work today?"

"Twelve. But that's nothing. I used to pull sixteens when I was in college working as an intern."

His eyes went wide. "Wow. And I thought *my* shifts were long."

I shrugged. "The only time I really take time off is for Halloween. It's my favorite holiday, other than Summerween."

"Summerween? Is that like Halloween in the summer?"

"I'd tell you more, but honestly, I'm so exhausted, I can barely see straight. All right. Let's see what we are dealing with."

His mouth quirked as I snapped on a pair of latex gloves. He then presented his arm to me. The skin was torn, and dried blood coated his wrist and hand, as well as the length of his forearm.

"So a *pipe* did this?" I asked.

"Yeah, and a backhoe that I wasn't looking out for," he answered as a laugh quaked in his voice.

"When did the injury occur?"

"Yesterday afternoon, just as it was starting to get really fucking hot."

I glanced up at his face. No sign of wincing warped his expression as I ran my finger over the suture. "You waited twenty-four hours before you found medical attention? And I assume you were the one who did this horrible patch job?"

"Yeah, I did. I guess I have a pretty good pain tolerance."

Something silky and dark coiled around his wrist and transferred to my hand. I blinked, and the lovely cooling sensation evaporated.

*Shadows. . .Is this guy a demon*?

I pressed my thumb onto his ulna. "Does that not hurt?"

"Not really, *oh*. But *thattttt* does."

"I was expecting a worse reaction. Any other creature I hadn't sedated first would have bit my head off."

He chuckled darkly. I couldn't help but notice how strong he was. His neck was thick and muscular. Veins snaked down his forearms.

And his hands—huge, *massive* hands. They reminded me of bear paws. Calluses lined his palms. He was definitely someone who worked a very physically demanding job.

I removed my gloves. "I need to take some X-rays. I will need to remove the sutures you've made and make new ones, but I don't want to stitch you up yet in case there are any materials embedded in the wound that I need to remove first. It will take about twenty minutes for me to take the images and develop them for viewing."

"Are you sure? I don't want to take up your Friday evening."

"It's not like I have a hot date or anything," I said, wishing I had bit my tongue before the words flew out of my mouth. The fact was, I hadn't gone out on a real date in almost a *year* now.

His eyes met mine, something dangerous burning in them. "Take your time, Vet Victoria. I'm not going anywhere. I'm just glad to finally be in your magical care."

A hot flash erupted over my body as I left the room. My ears were ringing. Had this cute, down-on-his-luck of a biker dude just *flirted* with me?

# 4
# Dezmond

Vet Victoria brought me back to a room to have X-ray images taken of my arm. Once taken, she instructed me back into the patient room where we'd first met while the images developed.

When I walked inside, I noticed a card was sitting on her clipboard. It didn't look like a poker card, but something that resembled tarot. Curious about the design, I grabbed it. Sparks shot out of the image, zapping my fingers. I withdrew my hand, startled. It must be bewitched with some kind of magic.

"*That, or you're not scenting the air properly,*" Sniffer blew a bunch of hot air into my ear. "*Do you not smell the wildness on her?*"

I glanced at the card, which was ironically named *Wild*.

I didn't need my shadow wolf manifesting in the office and scaring the shit out of the witch who was going to take care of me. As I touched the card again, the paper tingled against my skin. My senses, bound to my shadow beasts, began to align themselves as their presence retreated deep into my mind.

Taste, touch, and smell honed themselves into one demonic beast—*myself.*

As the door opened, I stuffed the Wild Card into my jacket pocket.

Victoria walked back inside. Her blue eyes swept over me, her expression worried.

"Is everything all right? Or are you gonna have to amputate my arm?" I asked.

Victoria took the X-ray film and clipped it into the light box hanging on the wall. "Your wrist and metacarpals match anatomy of, let's see, how do I say this—something that is not human."

I swallowed. "Sorry, what's a metacarpal?"

"Your *hand bones*," she answered stiffly. "They bear a similarity to well, an actual *bear*."

I tapped my fingers together.

Her eyes narrowed onto me hawk-like. "I've spent a good decade or more working with creatures from all over the world, specifically exotics. But I have *never* seen what appears to be a beast locked up inside of a man before." One of her dark eyebrows arched up her forehead. "This might be a long shot, but I'm going to assume that you aren't human—you must be a demon."

I ground my jaw. "You'd be correct about that."

Silence fell between us that was only broken by my heart trying to beat out of my chest.

Victoria folded her arms. "There is only *one* demon family I know in town, and both of my sisters are currently dating members of it." She squinted at me. "Are you a Ravenblood?"

"Yes, I am. But I swear, I didn't mean to make it seem like this was all a prank. I came to the vet instead of a normal human doctor because of, well," I pointed to the X-ray of my creature-like anatomy. "I'm the only member of the Ravenblood family who is a shifter."

Victoria's intense gaze settled onto me. "Shifter, as in a *bear*?"

"It depends," I argued. "That's my problem. I've got too many beasts all trying to shift out of me at once. Three of them, actually."

Victoria's gaze became smoky, even lustful. Had I somehow turned her on?

She opened a drawer and began to pull out different medical tools. "Shifter or not, you still have flesh and bone that we need to work on mending. There were no foreign objects embedded in your wound, so we need to get to work on patching you up correctly."

"Whoa, what's with the giant needle?" I asked.

She laughed as she sat down on the stool across from me with a syringe in hand. "Relax. I'm sure you can handle a little poke. I don't care if you have a good pain tolerance or not. First, I need to remove the sutures you made. I don't go sticking them into any creature, shifter or not, if I haven't numbed them first."

I closed my eyes as she took the shot of numbing agent and poked it into my arm. Something flashed behind my eyelids. Maybe it was adrenaline, or maybe it was her magic.

I opened my eyes. The first thing I noticed was her chest. Her cleavage looked lopsided. Did she only have one breast?

"How was that?" she asked.

"Not bad, like you said."

She grabbed a package of gauze and some disinfectant. "There, now you shouldn't feel the burn from this."

As she poured the disinfectant on my wound, it collected my dried blood and cleansed the area. More of the colorful flashes erupted into the air. It had to be her magic.

She dabbed up the area, wiping my skin clean. A calm, warming sensation enveloped my body, setting me at ease. I could sit here and have Victoria patch up my wounds over and over, as long as she was touching me.

She grabbed a pair of surgical scissors and snipped away the fishing line I'd patched my arm with. "I'll give you credit. I've seen some pretty bad patch-up jobs in my days. At least you didn't string these up too tightly."

*Click*!

The door to the back of the clinic cracked open.

*Shreeeek*!

I ducked as a bird much larger than my father's two spirit ravens came flying into the room. It perched atop the cabinet over the sink in the corner.

"Francine, really? I'm in the middle of a procedure here," she grumbled as she picked up a pack of sutures and opened them.

"Who is this?" I asked as the bird's fierce eyes dilated. It tilted its head back and forth with focused curiosity.

"My over-protective red-tailed hawk. She's all female and *very* feisty when it comes to meeting new visitors. I swear she's also part velociraptor with her talents for unlocking doors with those magical talons of hers."

*And apparently as feisty as her owner.* Well, it *was* true. Victoria's personality was as robust as she was physically—just the way I liked my women. "Don't the females get bigger than the males in most birds?"

"They do. It's because anatomically, they need more room to carry their eggs. Speaking of which. She hasn't left that thing unattended for weeks."

"What thing?"

Victoria's face twisted. "A random egg she thinks is hers, but it's not."

"How do you know it's not her egg?"

"Because it's *way* too big. There is no freaking way she could have laid it."

"Show it to me?"

A wicked smile curved her lips. "We still have at least a dozen stitches to get through first."

After Victoria patched up my arm, we walked into the room down the hall she claimed as her office. She stopped in the entryway, where Francine took to perching on her shoulder. The two females both eyed me as I cradled my now bandaged arm in my hand.

Victoria blinked, but Francine did not. I felt like I was being given the stare down.

"Have a look. Your guess is as good as mine," Victoria said.

I walked past them and into her office. A giant nest made of twigs, gauze pads, and other random medical items were jumbled inside. Sitting in the center of the nest was a purple egg speckled with green and gold flecks. "I have no idea what creature would have laid this egg. But it's pretty big. Maybe a dinousaur laid it?"

Victoria let out an exasperated sigh. "Ok, that's enough humor for the day. Party's over, pal. I want to put this week from hell behind me and go home."

My mouth watered. I wanted *so badly* to treat this witch to dinner. She was flaming hot sexy, and I wanted to get to know her better.

"*Then ask her out, you fucking idiot,*" Pawz grumbled thickly.

Instead of listening to my shadow bear, I patted the bandage on my arm. "What do I owe you for patching me up?"

Victoria slung her stethoscope onto a hook hanging from the wall. "Nothing. My receptionists have all gone home, and I'm sure the fuck not staying any later to mess around with insurance forms."

I gawked. "I can't accept this."

She set a firm hand on my shoulder and spun me in the direction of the front door. "Yes you can. Now, off you go! I'm ready to go home."

Watching Dr. Crow's gorgeous voluptuous hips sway down the hall after she promptly escorted me out of the room made my cock ache in a primal way I hadn't felt in years. In fact, I couldn't remember the last time I had four boners all competing at once to rip a hole in my pants.

I was feral. I was wild. I was untamed. I would have no witch other than Victoria as my mate. . .

I gripped my hand into a fist, straining the wound she'd spent so much careful time inspecting. My skin sizzled with the intensity of her magic. It was warm and vibrant, burning hotter than the sweltering room I was in. Victoria Crow had a remarkable gift, even for a witch. I agreed with my father—she possessed something wild and untamed that made me crazy. My brothers were all stupid for passing her up and settling for her younger sisters.

I'd struck a jackpot. But with my track record, I was sure to blow it. Unless I tamed the inner primal multi-beasts that wanted to rip out of me in a moment's notice.

As I made my way out to the parking lot, gratitude toward Dr. Crow made my body tingle. She'd gone out on a limb and stayed well beyond her closing time, all so she could take care of some bum demon's wound.

Something about the egg her hawk was guarding wasn't right. Did Victoria not see the magic sizzling off its surface? Maybe I could identify it for her?

I grabbed my phone and called my father. He picked up on the third ring. "Yo, Pops. I got a question for ya about the size and color of eggs."

"You know I like mine scrambled. I don't do any of that over-easy shit," he replied.

"No, that's not what I'm talking about. Dad, what color are a *dragon's* eggs? You used to tell stories about dragons to us as kids."

A shuffling sound made me think he'd dropped his phone. "Well, that depends. Dragons in Ireland mostly have green eggs. But I'm sure just like the rainbow, they come in all kinds of colors, isn't that right, Cindy?"

A muffled giggle sounded from the background.

I tried not to imagine what she might be giggling about. "Anyway, tell Cindy her daughter worked her magic. She patched up my arm and didn't charge me for it. You know me. I can't accept that kind of treatment without giving something back, so I thought I could try and identify the egg her red-tailed hawk was guarding at the clinic."

Dad's laughter sounded, and I knew he'd not heard a word of what I'd said.

"I'll call you later, Zeddy. Cindy's new batch of tea is now ready."

My phone went silent. I was going to find a way to pay back Dr. Crow. I reached into my coat pocket, searching for my bike keys. Sparks burned against my fingers. I tugged out the item.

*Shit. . .*

I'd accidentally stolen Victoria's Wild Card. Should I try and give it back to her? Then again, it seemed to tame the presence of my shadow beasts. Maybe I should keep it.

I held the card up to inspect the design. I couldn't help but notice how similar the color of the egg on the card looked to the egg Francine had been guarding.

# 5

# Victoria

The moment I walked into my home, I knew I was missing something. I patted my sides and searched my pockets. I must have left the Wild Card on my desk at the clinic.

I set my bag of dinner—a whopping unhealthy choice of burger and fries—down on the kitchen counter, too tired to care. The Three Magics Oracle Deck would be fine without the Wild Card for a day. A cauldron sat in the middle of my kitchen island which I'd pulled out to help me get into the mood for spooky season—Summerween. But this year, I was having doubts. Getting the letter from the cancer clinic hadn't helped my confidence.

I tucked the letter into the bottom of the stack of mail on my counter. Maybe I could forget it. I didn't *feel* any different. Maybe more fatigued, but I was pretty sure that was work-related. I didn't want to imagine facing that horrible time in my life again. Cancer was like a monster, lurking in the dark, just waiting to rear it's claws and teeth when you were least expecting it.

When I walked into my living room, the light reflecting on my ceiling startled me. It took me a few moments to realize the ghostly silver illuminations were watery reflections from my pool out back.

I'd only just set it up, thankfully so. But this week was so busy, I had little time to actually cool off and go for a swim, which I frequently did alone.

I rubbed my hand across my remaining breast. Thoughts of bikinis without any curvature on my chest seemed baffling. I'd gotten used to one boob. How would I cope with being completely flat-chested?

My phone buzzed in my pocket. I tugged it out, finding Lucy's book icon lighting up.

**Victoria, are you home?**

I groaned. Of course, my librarian sister would need me now. While my home had an open-door policy for my family, I was severely exhausted and wanted to dig into my takeout, then pass out on the sofa.

**Yes. This week butchered me.**

**I have a very big question to ask you regarding a recent life event, but I want to in person, not over text.**

**Tomorrow?**

**It's the Saturday I work at the library, but I can swing by in the afternoon. K?**

**Bring your swimsuit. Pool is up.**

**Oh I'm as white as a skeleton. But I'll tell Grace. She and her familiars love a good pool day. Her greenhouse gets really muggy this time of year.**

I scoffed. Grace's snooty hedgehog named Goblin, who had recently appointed himself as a higher-up in the bizarre hierarchy her familiars adopted, loved to pop my inner tubes with his green-colored quills. That spiky little prick had since been banned from any of my pool parties.

**We can meet tomorrow. Text me when you are available.**

Realizing I was too tired to shower, I stripped down into my bra and panties, plopped down on my sofa, and tugged a blanket over myself. As soon as I shoved my first bite of greasy food into my mouth, I was overcome with an intense feeling of loneliness.

I *wasn't* alone. I had two amazing younger witch sisters, and a brilliant witch mother, all of whom were local. The only difference was I was single and came home to an empty house. I had a strict rule. Other than Francine, I didn't allow any other magical creatures to inhabit my home.

I ran my hand over my right breast, feeling for any soreness or lumps. Thankfully, there was nothing. But that didn't mean cancer wasn't lurking beneath the surface of my skin like a monster.

One in eight women in the United States who lived to the age of seventy developed breast cancer at some point in their life. Witches were no exception. I'd fought cancer, survived, and after multiple attempts of undergoing reconstructive surgery, developed an ongoing infection that not even my magic could mend. My journey battling breast cancer had taught me one very important lesson—you can't heal if you aren't willing to give yourself grace. Realizing that my body was not willing to accept a procedure that would alter my appearance, I accepted that my chest would be forever lopsided.

But not a day went by where I wondered if being single-breasted somehow cursed me with also being single. Had Dezmond not noticed? As I closed my eyes and savored my food, Dezmond's gorgeous green eyes lit up in my mind. There was something wild about that demon, but right now, I was too tired to fantasize about him.

Saturday morning didn't come quick enough. I'd tossed and turned the night before from feathery nightmares that Francine tried to peck my eyes out. I busied myself with morning chores I'd ignored all week. Dishes, laundry, trash, mail—*so* much mail. I was surprised I had so much, being a single woman. Occasionally, I'd get something from Ben, my ex-husband, whom I'd divorced years ago. He knew never to come by, or contact me, because my phone and home was bewitched with a spell not even the worst of exes would mess with.

I huffed. My Wild Card *still* hadn't shown up.

My phone buzzed. Lucy had sent me a text.

**I have to cancel, sorry. Something came up at work. Rain check?**

Lucy's text blurred as a letter in my periphery became much more important.

I nearly spit out my coffee when I saw the return address. *Fuck.* Was I being written up by the *NVA*?

I grabbed the manila envelope from the National Vet Association and pried it open. The paperwork was more like parchment with its mottled texture and yellowish color. Just touching the ink caused my magic to flare. I unfolded the letter and read.

**Dear Dr. Victoria Crow,**

**The Paws & Claws Animal Shelter would formally like to accept your non-profit proposal. We have partnered with the NVA in acceptance of your request to rent out shelter space under one condition. Bring us the egg your red-tailed hawk has been guarding.**

**Sincerely,**
**Sloane Fox**
**Shelter Manager**

I set down the letter. My hands trembled. Hot flares of magic burst out of my fingertips, singing the edges of the paper. My mind blanked as the words *proposal* and *acceptance* muddied before me. The shelter I'd been partnering with was as understaffed as my clinic.

Had I really received an acceptance letter a year after I'd submitted my proposal?

I jumped up from my desk and batted out the flames before the entire letter went up in flames. I needed to celebrate! I grabbed my phone and typed off a text to Grace.

**Meet me at the bakery? I've got some big news to share.**

**What, are you pregnant?**

**No . . .**

**Can it wait until 1? I'm elbow deep in cupcake batter at the moment.**

**Sure, I'll be there.**

**Cool. I'll be sure to have you try out some of our new magical flavors.**

Over my lunch hour, I walked to the shop that used to be Shadow Daddy's Bar. Grace and one of Dezmond's older brothers, who also happened to be her chemistry professor, had flipped the bar and turned it into my frequent escape from the vet office over lunch. A forbidden romance bloomed between them that resulted in this marvelous little bakery I attributed to gaining at least ten pounds from over the past month since it had opened.

A giant wooden sign in the shape of a mushroom hung over the shop's entrance: **The Blooming Mushroom Bakery**

The moment I walked inside, the aroma of buttery pastries, cakes, and tarts that wrapped me into a cocoon of buttery goodness.

Grace stood behind the counter, all bubbly in her adorable green lace dress. A literal mushroom hat sat atop her head as she pulled espresso shots and served them to a group of college students. Ever since she graduated college, she'd been exceptionally extroverted. She made new friends as easily as she sprouted new magical recipes from her fingertips.

"Where is your hot chemistry professor?" I asked as I took up a seat at a table by the counter.

"Not teaching chemistry any longer," Grace replied as she sauntered over to me with two cups of espresso in her hands. "But by the way he's baking, I can tell you for certain that he's started practicing shadow alchemy again. He's in the back right now doing something with the batter I spent the morning infusing with a new batch of magical herbs from my greenhouse." She set the piping hot cups of espresso on the table and plopped down in front of me. "Well? Did you meet Krim's brother, Dezmond? Is this news about him? I really hope it is, because then I can start talking to you about how to handle his shadows when he shares them with you."

My core heated at Grace's sexual insinuation. "I *did* meet him. But that's not what I want to discuss right now." I tugged out the paperwork from my bag and set it in front of her.

Grace grabbed it and read aloud, "The Crow's Nest Vet Clinic has been approved to. . ." Her eyes went wide. "Seriously? They approved your proposal to open an adoption space for abandoned familiars? You've been working on this for how many years?"

"For as long as I've been handing off abandoned magical creatures to your greenhouse."

She beamed. "Does this mean that I'm going to have more space to you know, actually *garden*?"

I nodded. "It means I won't be sending you a new familiar to re-home every week."

She clapped her hands to her cheeks. "I can't believe this!"

I grabbed my espresso and took a heavy sip. Caffeine probably wasn't the best thing to calm all the adrenaline surging through me right now, but I didn't care. I'd felt guilty for being the older sister who'd always passed down familiar abandonees to her. Grace had always taken in the oftentimes feral creatures many witches would think twice about acquiring as a companion.

Grace grabbed her cup of espresso with trembling hands. "Sis, I'll tell you. As happy as I am right now, this news is going to spoil what Goblin has been losing his quills over for the past week. He and his mate, Wilma, have started an entire menu for the tea party they had planned for when you brought by a new batch of magical creatures."

I laughed. Goblin—Grace's hedgehog who had goblin green quills and spoke in a British accent—was apparently starting his own recruitment process for the many creatures I had surrendered over to my youngest sister.

Her eyes dropped to the letter again. "What's this about bringing them an *egg*?"

"Oh, yeah. That egg Francine has been guarding for over a month? The stupid thing won't hatch. I'm pretty sure it's a dud, so I plan on bringing it along as this Sloane person is requesting."

"Whoa, whoa, whoa. Time out. Familiar lessons 101. Do NOT get in the way of a female's maternal instinct. *You* taught me that."

"Really? It's just a fucking egg. The sooner I get rid of it, the less I'll have to deal with her constant screeching!"

Grace shook her head so fiercely that her mushroom hat flopped into her face. "I'd go and check out the shelter first. You know Francine won't leave that egg unattended if she gets any wind that someone there wants it. Trust me. She's been your familiar since you were what, *five*? She'll know if you're keeping something from her."

I sighed. I didn't want to admit it, but Grace had a sixth sense when it came to familiars. As much as I would have gladly gotten rid of that egg, she was right.

After lunch, I loaded into my purple Jeep and took off for the shelter. It was a good twenty minute drive from my home. As I pulled into the parking lot, my magic flared. Sparks shot out of my fingers and my hair.

Great. *Another fucking hot flash.* This perimenopausal shit was *so* much worse than PMS.

I climbed out of my Jeep and headed for the front door. After the flash, I felt a hollow sensation in my solar plexus. Silence pressed against my ears.

Where were all the critters?

When I visited the shelter a few months ago, I heard barking from the street. Nothing but a few birds chirped from the trees in the distance. Now I knew what my magic was reacting to—the lack of creatures was downright startling.

I walked into the shelter and approached the front desk, which was empty. That wasn't unusual, as the entire shelter was severely understaffed. The organization was basically volunteer run, except for the non-profit coordinator.

I tapped my finger on the metal bell on the desk.

A woman with a strong build, green cargo pants, and a form-fitting tank top emerged from the back. Short blond hair with pink highlights framed her angular face. "You must be Dr. Victoria Crow?"

"I am."

"I'm Sloane, the new shelter manager," she said as she threw out her hand. I took it and gave it a stiff shake. Calluses grazed my palm. Flakes of gold shimmered in her hazel eyes. A scar on her upper lip told me that she had seen some fights.

"Thank you for having me," I said, returning her firm grip with a tighter one. My gaze dropped to the fox tattoo on her muscular shoulder. "When did you take over as the new manager?"

"No, thank *you*, Dr. Crow. You're the only witch vet I know in town who could help me. I found your proposal a couple of weeks ago when I replaced Mrs. Bennett's position. She retired a month ago."

I swallowed. Mrs. Bennett had known that I was a witch for a long time, as she'd been a longtime friend of my mother's. I found it odd that she would speak about our family's magical talents with this new shelter owner. "Can I see the space you'd like to rent out?"

"Of course," Sloane said, clapping her hands together.

As we walked into the back area, I could have sworn that the fox tattoo on her arm shifted positions. Its bushy red tail had gone smooth and wrapped around the creature's dainty black legs.

I noticed the wall that used to be chain link fenced kennels had been completely opened. "Where are all of the cats and dogs?"

"The canines have all been adopted out. As for the felines, we're still working to re-home them."

"Wow, you must be incredible at your job. Over the past few years I've visited the place, I often thought I'd go deaf from the barking and hissing back here. Why are you freeing up the space?"

Sloane's mouth quirked. "The bigger creatures we're waiting for haven't arrived yet."

My stomach swooped. *Bigger creatures*? What did *that* mean?

Sloane led us into another room where the high-pitched *mews* of at least a dozen cats rang against my ears.

"By the way. How did you know that my red-tailed hawk is guarding an egg?" I asked as I walked alongside her.

Sloane stopped next to one of the kennels and faced me. Her eyes narrowed. "Your red-tailed hawk has been chosen as a surrogate mother for the time being."

"Wait a second. Francine was designated as a surrogate mother? By who?"

"As soon as you bring me the egg, I can answer more of your questions, and we can discuss the potential for this space." She leaned against one of the kennels. "Zeddy here has been pulling double shifts to take care of the last of the kitties, isn't that right?"

A shiny bald head appeared behind the chain link fence of the kennel.

My stomach swooped for some strange reason.

Dezmond threw his hand into the air and shot Sloane a middle finger. "Fuck you, Sloane. The kitties were my favorite to take care of," he ground out in a husky voice. I hadn't realized how attractive his voice sounded at my clinic. Maybe it was all the empty space in the shelter that made it sound more pronounced.

Sloane tossed her head in a flirtatious laugh. "Zeddy, you will always be one of my favorite volunteers. Always a hoot when it comes to kittens."

A twinge of jealousy rolled in my stomach. I could recognize flirtatious banter a mile away. So much for fucking a Ravenblood. He was already taken by this bad bitch who was far more attractive than me.

"Dr. Crow, take as much time as you need to examine the space. I'll be up front to further discuss the egg." Sloane spun on the heel of her black combat boot and headed down the hall before I could answer her.

The kennel door squeaked open as Dezmond emerged. "Victoria?"

I froze as his voice shook something deep inside me.

I turned to face him. *Sweet fucking goddess*. His eyes were such a gorgeous color of green. . .

"How come I've never seen you here before?" I asked, trying not to allow my voice to hitch.

Dezmond wiped the back of his head with his hand. "I'm only here in between my shifts on weekends. I normally work the graveyard shift at my construction job. But right now, due to my injury, I have some extra time off."

I noticed the wound on his arm I'd stitched up. "You really should be wearing something to cover that. It could get infected."

He chuckled. "I know, doc. But hey, do they look like they're going to scoop their own poop?" He pointed at the kittens in the corner of the kennel he'd cleaned.

I couldn't stifle my laugh if I wanted to. A loud, boisterous and probably unattractive cackle came exploding out of my mouth.

He just stared at me with his gorgeous green eyes as I tried to calm the rumble of unrestrained laughter in my chest. By the time I did, my eyes were tearing up. "I tell all my interns that if they can't pass Poop 101, they're never going to make it any animal caretaker kind of job. Your attitude would make you perfect for it."

A hopeful look overcame his face. "You're not hiring, are you?"

"No. My clinic doesn't currently have the budget to hire any new employees, even though summer is a prime time for it."

He took a step closer to me. "Oh, yeah. And the heat wave isn't letting up anytime soon. I hear it's going to be a real scorcher."

My breath hitched. Why did I feel so hot and bothered? It had to be another hot flash. Or maybe it was because Dezmond cared so much for the creatures so many people abused and neglected. That, and I finally got a good look at him. He wasn't super tall, maybe an inch or two taller than me at most. But holy fucking shit, were his arms muscular. His hands were gargantuan. He could easily grope my single breast without a problem. I couldn't stop fantasizing about what he looked like beneath his shirt.

"About that egg," he said, bringing me back to focus. "I know what creature laid it. I'll tell you when I come and get my stitches out." He held out his arm for me to see. "What do you think?"

I glanced at the sutures and noticed how quickly his skin had mended. Magic *had* to be involved. There was no other logical explanation for how quickly he was healing. "I think we are safe to move your appointment up to Monday morning."

# 6

# Dezmond

This was exactly how I *didn't* want the hot, curvy witch I was crushing on to leave me—standing with a bag of cat shit dangling from my hand. I felt like such a fucking idiot. I'd had my shot to ask her out, and I'd fucking blown it.

I tossed the bag into the trash. One of the kittens inside the kennel scrunched his face at me and let out a fierce little *mew.* I opened the kennel door. The moment I did, the mew became an angry *hiss* that quickly deflated into a head boop as he nuzzled me.

"It's not your fault, little dude," I said, tickling the chin of the kitten I so badly wanted to take home. He was getting ready to croak, and I wanted to be with him when he did. I'd given my grim reaper brother Krim his ghost cat, who had been named Buttercup in life, and was re-named by Krim in death as Scythe.

I'd fostered a lot of kittens in my days. My creature-based shadows offered them safety and companionship as they passed from the living world into the world of spirits. While I didn't personally know another demon shifter, I'd often wondered if this so called talent of mine was unique to us. Maybe I was an odd ball, but I sure the hell had a lot of compassion for the creatures that many people didn't learn to appreciate in life. The least I could do was find a proper home for them in death.

As I scratched his chin, all the possibilities I had to woo Victoria flashed through my head. For fuck's sake—we both obviously loved animals. I'd seen the paperwork on Sloane's desk before she'd mailed it to her vet clinic. The fact that Victoria had wanted to rent out this space to help find homes for misplaced familiars?

No wonder I was crushing on her so hard. She had a massive heart. As I ran my fingers through the kitten's fur, I tried to get a grip on myself. I had a track record for falling hard—dangerously so—for the women I wanted to date. But I knew this wasn't just primal attraction.

Victoria Crow had forever touched the inner shadow beasts that made up my demonic soul.

I tucked the kitten back into his kennel and closed the door. As I made my way to the front, Sloane's hushed voice turned into a yell.

She slammed down the phone and ran her fingers through her short blond hair.

I hung up the kennel keys behind the desk. "I'm done for the day."

"Thanks for all your help," she grumbled, not looking up at me.

"Is everything all right?" I asked.

"Yeah," she huffed. "Just business stuff."

I nodded and walked out the front door. Something about Sloane was off. I couldn't tell if she was a witch or not. But she definitely put off some heavy *bitch* vibes if I didn't clean the litter boxes on time. She also had a temper that flared a lot recently regarding her phone calls.

My arm was feeling good, *really* good now that I'd seen the witch who'd patched it up. I grabbed my phone from my pocket and shot off a text in the group chat with my band mates.

**Dudes, how about we meet at 3 for rehearsal?**

A string of thumb-up emojis followed.

I threw out my hands and coalesced into shadows as two massive bear paws tore into shadowy realm of the Summoning.

Moments later, my boots hit the gritty floor of our rehearsal location. Ever since Krim closed Shadow Daddy's and opened his new bake shop, my band had acquired a new practice space. The warehouse had once been an old car factory. Sometimes the acoustics echoed, but it was better than nothing. Plus, there were lots of metal scraps that I'd started to collect, as I wanted to weld together my own drum set.

I walked over to my drums and plopped down on the seat. I wanted to warm up before my other band mates arrived. My drumsticks sat in the center of the snare I usually played on. Since my injury, I hadn't practiced at all.

I grabbed one stick with my good hand. The other with my wounded one. Shadows extended from my wrists, coiling around the sticks and fastening them to my palms. I rattled off a quick rhythm, feeling for any weakness in my bones. My forearms glistened with scales as they morphed out of my skin: a morphology that until recently, was completely *new* to me. I'd sprouted fur and claws and fangs whenver my shadow beasts possessed me, but never *scales.* Who knew. Maybe I was going to meet another shadow beast personality.

I knew the song I wanted to practice. *The Dragon Within* was the name of a song my band had started to play. I'd written the tune, as it was inspired by how I'd felt about my identity. As a shifter with a multi-beast personality, I was always struggling to connect with one true unified shadow. Pawz, Jawz, and Sniffer were three primal shadow beasts who were caged inside of me, clawing at my rib cage to get out.

That was, until I'd come into possession of Victoria's *Wild Card.*

I hit circles on the snares, feeling more alive than I had in the past century. Victoria's magic had mended my flesh and bone, but she had done much more. She'd ignited a piece of my shadowy soul.

Purple smoke erupted into my periphery. Two spirit ravens shot into the air, their tail feathers breaking into plumes of coiling purple shadows. My father manifested in the far corner of the warehouse.

I stopped drumming and clutched my drumsticks in one hand. "Dad, what are you doing here?" I asked. He barely left Cindy's place if he could help it.

"To hear you play, what else? I could hear you from miles away. Your music always echoes through the Summoning for me to hear," he answered as he approached. "From the look of your arm, I'd say that Victoria worked her magic on you."

I glanced down at my forearms. The scales had disappeared. I squinted at Dad as he stopped in front of me. I was so used to seeing my father drunk when I played. Seeing him with a teacup instead of a whiskey bottle in his hand was something that would take me some getting used to.

Dad pulled up a seat and set his teacup down on the drum beside me. He wiped his neck, smearing a patch of red lipstick. Cindy was obviously having a positive influence on him. "There have been some shady folks in town I wanted to give you a heads up on."

"Shadier than the Ravenbloods?" I asked as I set my drumsticks aside.

Dad's expression remained troubled. "You know my time working for the demon council means I've dealt with a lot of spooks, but this caps all of 'em. Rumor has it that these folks are partaking in some kind of ancient ritual that I think you need to know about."

"*Ritual*? What *kind* of ritual?"

Dad's eyes brightened at my question. "Dezmond, you are my only shifter son. Have you ever wondered about the true identity of the beast who makes up your shadow?"

I shrugged. "I've put up with Pawz, Jawz, and Sniffer for so long, I've sort of gotten used to their personalities as part of myself."

Dad studied me. "What about the beast that only shows itself when you're really afraid of something?"

I chuckled. "Dad, stop pulling my leg. I'm not afraid of my shadow beasts. They're just pushy."

Dad huffed. "Want to know what I think? I think my Zeddy has gotten comfortable with Pawz, Jawz, and Sniffer, because they keep that *other* shadow beast at bay."

"So, you're telling me that I tolerate my bear, lion, and wolf because I don't want to face my fears?" I laughed. "Come on, Dad. I might be the baby demon of the family, but I'm no runt of the litter. Amon and Krim know that I'm twice as strong as them combined, even though they're bigger."

Dad chortled. "My boy, I've never doubted your sense of spirit, or your strength. But even us demons have things we're afraid of." He glanced over at Anger and Sadness, his two spirit ravens, as they preened their inky black feathers. "Besides, fear is what helps us to shape our shadows. We wouldn't have the shady personalities haunting our auras if it weren't afraid of something."

Gooseflesh rippled up my spine as I glanced over at my drumsticks. "About this ritual. Any ideas about its purpose, or who is partaking in it?"

Dad ground his jaw. "First, you need to wrap your mind around the possibility that female demons never really went extinct."

"Who said that?"

"Krim did. At least that's what his hypothesis around shadow alchemy has shown him. According to his latest studies, female demons have been using a different branch of magic to conceal themselves."

I shook my head. "But there are only *three* magics. Are you trying to tell me there is a *fourth*?"

Dad nodded. "One that has to deal with the elements and the rarest magical creatures out there—dragons."

The reverberation of my father's voice echoed into the warehouse.

*Dragons. . .*

Dad propped his elbows onto his knees and leaned toward me. "The most valuable possession a dragon owns is of course, their offspring. Not long ago, dragon eggs were fought over like gold. Once a baby dragon hatches, it will imprint on a demon or a witch, bonding them with their magic." He straightened himself on his chair. "That is, of course, if you even *believe* in dragons. They haven't been seen since the Medieval times when female demons were still around. But times are changing, and the three magics have also begun to change as well."

I ran my hand over my head, trying to comprehend everything he'd thrown my way.

Dad squinted at me. "Speaking of changes. Something about you seems different. Did you change up your facial hair?"

Sparks shot out of my jacket pocket. I reached inside and retrieved the Wild Card. "Oh, right. I accidentally swiped this tarot card from Victoria's clinic."

"A *Wild* Card, huh? What actually makes it wild?"

I shrugged. "Beats me. But ever since I took the card, my shadow beasts have been a lot tamer."

"Come to think of it, you're right. I haven't seen much of the wolf prowling around you. He's always the one sticking his nose into places it shouldn't be."

I tucked the card back into my pocket. "I plan on giving it back to Victoria come Monday. She's made an appointment with me first thing to get the sutures out of my arm."

Dad beamed. "See? I told you she'd patch you up. Now it's your turn to turn on the demon charm, if you know what I mean."

I swallowed, not wanting to admit how I was feeling about the sexy vet witch who'd done more than mend a flesh wound on my arm.

# 7

# Victoria

My whole Monday morning was consumed with another bout of hot flashes because *holy fucking shit*, of course the air conditioner had to go out at the clinic, *again*. I swore the thing must have been cursed. This time, however, I was prepared. I made sure the office had a dozen fans blowing, and a swamp cooler installed in the hallway.

Thankfully, I'd spent an hour working on intake forms and only took on what I wanted for the day—yearly checkups, and some biopsies. The only real procedure I had scheduled was removing Dezmond's stitches, which I'd scheduled for my last appointment at a whopping three in the afternoon. My interns could deal with the consequences. I wasn't going to stress myself out today.

By the time mid-afternoon rolled around, I was hyped up on three Dr. Peppers and had gotten my second wind. Dezmond would be arriving for his appointment any minute. I checked my reflection in the mirror just as I had last Friday, not knowing that an actual *demon* would be waiting for me to patch up his arm. This time, my hair wasn't tossed up in a messy bun, nor was I wearing my frumpy set of scrubs. I'd tugged on an actual vet coat, complete with the Crow's Nest logo of a red-tailed hawk.

As I straightened my jacket and teased a few strands of my hair, I puckered my lips at myself in the mirror. *Victoria. Get a grip on yourself. He's just some bum who should have gone to the minor emergency.*

I was no stranger to being *mother charity* when it came to men. Ben, my zookeeper ex and failure of a marriage, came into my life in a very similar situation. We'd met at a conference that discussed exotics, and had hooked up in my hotel after he'd claimed he couldn't afford to book his own room. He was, of course, someone who I thought at the time, cared for animals. We got engaged on a whim, and only a few months after our elopement, I'd discovered he was exploiting endangered species. I filed immediately for divorce and kicked his selfish ass out of my house.

"Victoria?"

I jumped as the male voice I'd been waiting to hear all day sounded behind me. "Hi, Dezmond. I was just preparing your room," I said, flushing hotter than I had all day.

He grinned as he extended a handful of flowers toward me. "Sorry, the ladies out front got excited, and your receptionist insisted that I head back early."

I eyed the colorful assortment of flowers in his hand, and a small animal carrier in the other. A high-pitched *mew*! erupted from the carrier.

"These are for you," he said as he thrust the bouquet into my hand. "And I brought you someone I think you might appreciate."

I took the flowers, overcome with their beauty. I couldn't remember the last time anyone had hand-delivered me a bouquet, especially one of vibrant, fire burst lilies. I inhaled their sweet aroma, then squinted at the carrier hanging from his hand. "Oh, who is this?"

"Sloane wants to get rid of him because he's sick, so I took him home with me. If he croaks, I plan on passing off his spirit to one of my brothers. But I have a feeling you'll be able to patch him up like you did me."

I opened the door to the patient room behind me. "Bring him inside and we'll see what we're dealing with."

Dezmond followed me inside and set the carrier onto the counter. Once the door closed behind me, he opened the carrier door. A scraggly-looking kitten came wobbling out.

My heart completely melted.

On any normal day, I wouldn't have thought anything different if someone brought a cute kitten into my office. But *Dezmond* brought him in, dressed up with a little orange bow decorated in skulls on his collar.

*Fuck.* Why did this have to be so adorable?

Dezmond grabbed the kitten, instantly dwarfing him in his massive, paw-like hand. "I thought about naming him Summerweenie, in honor of the holiday you like to celebrate."

"A kitten, *and* flowers?" I stammered. "Dezmond, if I didn't know any better, I would assume you were trying to date me."

"Actually, doc. I am," he replied, suddenly trapping me with that intense green gaze of his.

I dropped his patient chart onto the counter.

Summerweenie swished his tail, crinkled his nose, then let out a high-pitched *mew*!

"That is, if you'll have me," Dezmond continued, his mouth quirking as I fell further into his gorgeous stare.

I grabbed my clipboard and began to fan myself. Why was it so fucking *warm* in here? "Sorry, it's been a very hot minute since anyone has asked me on a date."

He chuckled. "I'm rusty at this too. I'm sorry if I made you feel uncomfortable."

"No, you didn't," I said rather breathily. It wasn't like I could say no to a demon who offered me a kitten *and* a bouquet of gorgeous summer flowers. I was enamored with this kindhearted and seemingly sweet younger brother of Amon's.

I snapped on a pair of latex gloves. "Before we talk about any dating business, I'd like to get these sutures out of your arm. Then we'll figure out what to do with Summerweenie."

My hands shook as I arranged the cutting utensils resting in a metal pan on the counter.

Dezmond tucked Summerweenie back into his carrier and closed the door. "That's it, little dude. We're both gonna get our checkups with Vet Victoria!"

The kitten gave another high-pitched *mew* as he nuzzled Dezmond's cheek through the carrier door. The fuzzy, warm feelings this entire encounter was having on me shook my entire focus.

I sat down in front of him with my scissors in hand. "This will only take a few minutes."

His cheeks dimpled as he offered me his arm. "So, about that egg we discussed at the shelter. Is Francine still guarding it?"

I snipped off the first suture and started on the second. "She sure is. I've still got her locked in my office."

Dezmond clenched his hand. "What if I told you that egg might belong to a dragon?"

I jolted, ripping out five sutures instead of one. "A *dragon*? Are you *kidding* me?"

He pulled his arm away and winced. "No, I'm not. I'm just glad that you didn't bring it to the shelter. About Sloane. I don't know if I'd trust her with that egg. Something about her is off, and I can't put my paw on it yet."

I glanced down at his hand. "Right, your paw." I scanned his muscular forearms, remembering back to the X-ray images I'd taken of him. "Do all demons have creature anatomy like you?"

He shook his head. "No. Some demons are born shifters, while others are not. I'm a shifter because my shadows take on the form of a beast. But my shadows don't always agree with each other on which beast is in control."

A bead of sweat trickled down my ribcage. "I'm familiar with a demon's shadows. Both of my sisters are dating your brothers, and they've dropped hints about their darker sides."

When I locked my gaze with his, I froze. There it was, that *wild* presence, lurking in his eyes as green as a jungle.

I straightened myself. "So, where is this shadow beast of yours?"

"It's not one, it's *three.* And thank fucking hell they're currently not bothering me."

"Do they usually bother you?"

He reached into his jacket pocket. "See, I accidentally stole this card from you the other day when you patched me up." He tugged my Wild Card out. "I didn't mean to steal it. It sort of just happened. I planned on giving it back to you today, but I'd like to keep it, if that's okay with you."

"Why do you want to keep it?"

"Because all three of my shadow beasts have been as tame as Summerweenie ever since I took it." He flipped the card between his thick fingers. "This card, for whatever reason, has tamed their wild streak."

The Wild Card sent out a shimmer of sparks.

"It's bewitched with magic, isn't it?" he asked.

"I'd say so. It's the only card in the deck my aunts sent me that seems to do anything magical. I usually keep it on me for good luck."

Summerweenie let out another *mew*! as he seemed to agree.

I rolled my chair across the room, opened the door, and flagged down one of my interns. "Since it's late in the day, I'll have one of my interns check him over. He looks and sounds a bit dehydrated to me. They will likely keep him overnight to pump some fluids into him."

"Sounds good to me. If you find someone to adopt him, please don't hesitate to do so. I think Krim will kill me if I try to pawn off another spirit kitty on him."

The intern entered our room and removed the carrier. With Summerweenie gone, I could return to the last bit of disinfecting Dezmond's wound.

"There, you're all good to go," I said as I snapped off my gloves and tossed them into the trash. "You can keep my Wild Card, but only under one condition," I said as I stood, my legs slightly trembling. "One of these days, I get to meet your shadow beasts and see the effects the card is having on them."

He straightened himself and tucked the Wild Card into his pocket. "Deal! Look, Victoria. I think you are amazing. I wanted to ask you out at the shelter the other day, but I got cold feet."

"Cold *paws*, you mean," I corrected him.

His mouth quirked. "Can I have your number? I'd love to take you out to dinner."

My heart jumped into my throat. *Fuck* dinner. I didn't need to wait.

Before I knew what I was doing, my lips crashed against his.

The roughness of his stubble became my new obsession, as was the wonderful taste of his mouth. A combination of mint and something citrusy filed my senses. His hand came to my waist, and I was suddenly aware of how dangerous of a situation I'd gotten myself in.

Startled by my own embarrassingly blunt horniness, I pulled away. "I'm *so* sorry. I don't know what came over me."

Dezmond's other hand planted firmly on my other hip, rooting me in place. "Why are you sorry? That was fucking *hot*."

He kissed me back until we became a tangled mess, our bodies jostling against one another.

I grabbed a handful of his jacket collar. "I've needed this for *so* fucking long."

"How fucking long," he breathed into my ear. "Tell me what you need, and I'm going to give it to you *now*, my sweet, wicked thing."

The primal tone in his voice aroused something long dormant inside of me. I forgot what it felt like to experience lust. I was consumed by the animistic urge to rip his clothes off.

He bucked his hips, and I slipped up onto the counter. My legs splayed as he pressed himself firmly against me.

"Do the doors in this room lock?" he asked.

"They do."

Shadows coiled out of his body, twisting the locks shut.

"There," he growled, his green eyes focusing on me. "Now, where were we?"

I shivered as his big wide hands worked past my knees. How badly I wanted him to caress me between my thighs. "I believe we were discussing one of your shadow beasts?"

His hands moved up my legs and settled upon my hips. "I can promise you that I'm a real animal in the bedroom. Excuse me, *vet clinic*."

I wrapped my arms around his neck. This couldn't be real. I'd read so many workplace romance novels, it had become an addiction. But no male vet, or intern had ever *fucked* me at work, even thought it had long been a fantasy of mine.

And here I was, getting it on with a demon who had *shadow beasts* locked inside of him?

His stubble grazed my neck and chest as he kissed a scorching line down my neck. "You are so fucking gorgeous, do you know that?"

"Dezmond, I—"

"Shhhhh," he whispered. "I'm going to make you see stars, Love. I'm feral for you right now."

Velvety onyx shadows enclosed me. Which of the shadow beasts he mentioned would I get to meet? Or would I be lucky enough to meet all three?

I couldn't see what kind of creature he'd shifted into, but I could touch him. His shadows felt rough, then smooth. Cool, then hot.

I closed my eyes, surrendering to his sensual touch.

"You are my mate," he growled, his voice rumbling against my thigh. "I need to taste you. Now, spread your pretty legs for me."

My mind jostled.

Did he just call me his *mate*?

His command made me relax as his shadows continued to explore my body. The sensations whirled and morphed as a beast began to manifest. My scrubs were tugged down, freeing the lower half of my body as the strong outline of a muscular back and arms lowered between my legs.

I gasped, digging my fingers into his shoulders as teeth and a tongue ran over my thigh. The sensations brought pleasure rippling over my body.

My back arched, sparks zinging out of me as Dezmond's shadows threw me into an orgasm.

# 8

# Dezmond

White sparks shot out of my jacket pocket as Victoria slid off the counter and into my arms. We stood together, her arms wrapped around my neck as we tried to regain our composure.

She pressed her face into my neck and kissed my jaw. "Dezmond. That was fucking amazing. . ."

It felt *so* good to have her hot, satiated body pressed up against me. I nuzzled her, kissing her forehead. "Are you ready for round two?"

Her hands fell to my belt, which she began to unbuckle.

My heart jumped into my throat as her fingers dipped into the denim folds of my jeans. Her soft fingers began to caress the base of my cock, which bulged to the point I thought it might explode.

"Victoria. . ." I stammered. "Please don't torture me."

*Knock, knock, knock.*

"Dr. Crow," a frantic voice called from beyond the door. "Francine has gotten out of your office. She's harassing the patients in the waiting room."

Victoria's nails grazed the base of my cock, making my entire body twitch. "She's going to have to wait! I'm still in the middle of my procedure!"

I let out a groan as she found my balls. *Sweet fucking darkness, this witch has a magical touch. . .*

An angry *shreeeeek* erupted outside the door.

Victoria made a noise that sounded even more furious.

She withdrew her hand from my pants. "Please know that blue balling you was *not* my intention," she stammered, fury and anger crackling in her voice.

"Rain check?" I suggested, not wanting to let the sexy vet witch of my dreams go.

A wicked smile parted her lips. "I can't wait to see more of your shadow beasts. How about you come over to my place this evening?"

"Deal." Victoria was a firecracker ready to explode. I couldn't wait to finish what we'd started back at her place as she'd so generously offered.

She straightened the collar on her jacket as her gaze dropped to my crotch. "I'd really hate to see you walk out of my clinic with a boner like that."

We laughed, falling into each other's arms all over again.

"About dinner," I said. "Pick you up at six? How about Chinese food? I know a good joint that I think you'll like."

She trailed her fingers beneath my jaw. "I'm sure I'll be wanting dessert afterward."

After I fastened my belt, Victoria unlocked the door and walked out into the hall. I grabbed the empty kitten carrier sitting in the hallway and held it in front of my boner. A couple of the vet techs stared at us as Victoria saw me out to the waiting room out front.

Francine sat atop the cabinet behind the receptionist desk, giving me the evil-eye as her owner tossed her hair over her shoulder. One whiff of Victoria's intoxicating scent made me want to dive between her legs and devour her all over again.

She began to write something frantically onto her clipboard and tore off the edge of a piece of paper. "We'll let you know when your kitten's blood work comes back."

I nodded, wincing as I knocked my boner into the kitten carrier and left the office.

*Holy fucking shadow balls.* I hadn't felt this turned on since my teen years when I had the testosterone of all three shadow beasts pumping through my blood. Being blue-balled was never fun. But at least I'd gotten *her* off. That was all that mattered. I didn't realize how starved for sex she was.

I unfolded the paper she'd given me. Her phone number was written next to a short message:

**Let me return the favor tonight, say 7ish?**

My cock ached just thinking about having her gorgeous body sprawled out naked across a bed. I tucked the paper into my pocket. My phone buzzed. I retrieved it, finding my brother's cupcake icon blinking at me. Why was Krim texting?

**I've got some leftover cat treats I thought you might want. They're going in the dumpster if you don't come grab them.**

The moment I walked into the bakery, I was met by a pair of pointed silver ears that flicked toward me. Krim's ghost cat, Scythe, sat in the windowsill. He followed my brother everywhere and had quickly become the Blooming Mushroom Bakery's spooky little mascot.

"Where is your owner?" I asked as I stopped next to Scythe, who was now crinkling his nose. He yowled grouchily at me. He was so accustomed to me spoiling him with treats I swiped from the shelter that if I didn't have them on me, he often gave me the silent treatment. Or worse—he slashed the tires on my bike.

Krim emerged from the back room with a platter full of mushroom-shaped cupcakes in hand. The moment he saw the cat carrier, he grunted. "I really hope that's not what I think it is."

I opened the carrier's door.

Scythe floated down from the windowsill and drifted spookily inside.

Krim's eyes went wide. "Looks like you have a stowaway. He's mad because I'm turning my bakery into a no ghost cat treat zone."

"How come?"

Scythe hissed from inside the carrier at his grumpy demon owner.

Krim shook his head as he transferred the cupcakes from his platter into one of the glass display cabinets next to my table. "That glutenous little fucker has started to train my customers to bring him food."

I snorted. "He *would* do that. Good on you, Scythey! You tell them how to treat you like a spooky marshmallow king!"

"Don't encourage him!" Krim grumbled.

Scythe pressed his ghostly white toe beans against the wall of the carrier. Five massive claws extended out of his paw, curling like scythes as he tried to establish his spooky feline dominance.

"Don't worry, little dude. I still have plans on how I'm going to turn you into a fat ghost tabby that I'll nickname Marshmallow."

"Do you have any plans for this evening?" Krim asked.

My mind bolted, fast-forwarding to seeing a naked Victoria sprawled out on her bed. "Actually, I do."

"Well, Grace has plans with a group of her girlfriends. They're going to start harvesting some of the herbs from her greenhouse. Amon and I are getting together for a thing here this evening if you want to join."

Pride filled my chest as my fantasies ran away with me. "Can't. I've got a hot date tonight."

"Oh? Who with?"

"Grace's older sister, Victoria Crow."

Krim dropped his last cupcake. It landed with a sugary *splat* on his shoe. "How did that happen?"

"Long story. I busted up my arm real bad on a job because Dad was slacking. But I can't be mad at him for long, because he was the one who suggested that I go to the vet witch in town to get patched up."

"Let me guess, he suggested that because you're a *shifter*?"

I nodded.

Krim smirked. "A vet witch and a shifter demon? That could work out. I'm going to find it hilarious if we all hook up with the Crow sisters, and our father ends up with their witch mother."

"Hey, before I dip out. I've got a question for you. Dad mentioneod that you worked as a shadow alchemist for a while, and that you might have some hypothesis around a possible *fourth* magic."

Krim's hood fell into his face, casting his feature into the shady grim reaper that he was. "It was a pretty dark time in my life. Why do you bring it up?"

I reached into my jacket pocket and tugged out the Wild Card. "See this? Apparently, it houses some kind of strange magic that helps to tame my shadow beasts. I'm wondering if it has something to do with this fourth magic you might know more about."

Krim's blue eyes narrowed onto the card. "Are there other cards?"

"Victoria mentioned a deck, but she said the Wild Card was the only one she knew of that housed any magic."

Sparks jolted out of my fingers, zapping one of the cupcakes on the table. The frosting oozed, then lit on fire.

I quickly shoved the card back into my pocket.

Krim chuckled. "I bet if you reintroduce it to the other cards, you'd discover something different."

An hour later, I left the Blooming Mushroom Bakery for home. It took a whole lot of convincing to get Scythe out of the kitty carrier, where he thought he could sneak his way back into my apartment to get fat off his cat treats. With the extra Bitty Bone Bites in the carrier, I entered Victoria's number into my phone and sent her a quick message.

**What kind of Chinese do you like? It's one of my main food groups, and I've got too much to choose from.**

**Francine has been a nightmare to deal with this afternoon, and I don't know if I'm up for being seen in public.**

My stomach pitted. She was already canceling plans before we'd even started them.

**I'll figure something out. Can I swing by your place and pick you up?**

**Sure. I live in a big purple house on the west side of town. You can't miss the magical bursts of energy it puts off.**

**I'll be there.**

A string of hearts followed my reply.

Thank the darkness. She hadn't dumped me yet. I had a few hours to shower and get myself ready for the *real* pussy I wanted to spend my evening with.

# 9

# Victoria

As soon as I sent off my text to Dezmond, I went right into my office and plopped down into my chair. There was no air conditioning in the world that could cool me down from the hot-flash I was experiencing. For the past hour, I'd busied myself in the remaining biopsies I had to process before being sent off to the lab. But my mind was anywhere but work.

I'd just had a demon go down on me right here at my clinic. . .

Holly poked her head into my office with a clipboard in hand. One of Francine's tail feathers was clipped to where a pen should be. "I think you're going to need to establish some new boundaries with your hawk. She scared three of the interns and pooped on the computer when she threw her little fit earlier."

"I'll figure something out before I leave today," I replied rather breathily.

Holly continued to observe me. "Is everything all right? You aren't having heat stroke, are you?"

"Actually, I might be," I replied, still thinking of the sinful sensations Dezmond's tongue made between my thighs.

My phone chimed. My demon had already texted me again.

**I'll be sure to have an extra ravenous appetite for you tonight.**

I texted him back one massive heart.

*Sweet fucking goddess.* I needed to get out of here, *now.* The arousal brimming through my body was either a spell, or a full-blown kundalini awakening.

After I clocked out of work for the day, I grabbed Francine's nest, including the egg she had yet to hatch, and tossed the entire thing into my Jeep. Apparently, she was just as antsy about the entire event that had happened between Dezmond and I at the clinic. I couldn't risk her squawking off some steamy gossip about the two of us hooking up to the other faculty.

As I drove down the road, Francine took to the skies above me. She flashed her red tail feathers proudly with extra flair as if to say, *hey, I know you got laid.*

I gripped the steering wheel and let my fantasies about Dezmond get the better of me. He'd pleased me without hesitation, generously so. And I had yet to meet the shadow beasts who lived inside of him.

"*Girl, don't you dare get distracted and crack my egg,*" Francine interrupted my lustful thoughts.

"*I have no intention of cracking it,*" I thought back to her. "*But why the fuck haven't you made it hatch yet?*"

*"The whole reason I went screeching out of your office was because it jumped! I think it's finally ready to hatch!"*

*"Regardless, there was no reason that you had to break up my magical fling with Dezmond today."*

*"There is no such thing as a magical fling,"* Francine corrected me. She often mixed sex with magic for some odd reason. *"You've been on a dry spell for a reason—your magic is in need of some serious cleansing."*

*"It was just oral sex. Much-needed sex that I haven't had in over a year."*

*"There is no such thing as just sex, especially with a demon. You are mates now. Once a witch has mated with a demon, she and her magic are bound to him for life."*

I clutched the wheel tightly as I pondered Francine's statement. I'd read enough fantasy romance novels with the *fated mates* trope to gather a basic understanding of what my red-tailed hawk wanted me to believe.

Moments later, I pulled into my driveway and hopped out. I tucked the egg with the blanket I'd wrapped it into my tote and carried it to the front door.

Francine flapped her wings as she flew over me.

"Stop hovering, it's annoying," I scolded her.

*"It's what mother hawks do,"* she said with that fierce sassy attitude I was starting to dislike. I just wanted my hawk to go back to the way she'd been before she'd become a crazy over-protective velociraptor over this egg.

A brilliant sheen of pink and purple turned Francine's tail feathers magenta as a solar flare lit up the evening sky.

"*Looks like your aunts are trying to convince your mother to visit them again,*" Francine squawked at me.

"That, or they are finally making an excuse to come visit her for once."

The auroras they created were often seen during the summer months, when my two aunts, Tillie and Millie, fought over trying to get my mother to visit them. They both lived on opposite coasts, and their colorful magical arguments lit up the skies of Midhaven. The lights could be seen from my house on a clear night such as tonight, where judging by the colors, I could tell that my aunts were putting up quite a fight. Millie and Tillie were twins, Millie's aura being dark, while Tillie's was light. For twins, they were complete opposites. Millie lived in Washington State and often tried to persuede my mother to visit. But the dreary skies, and cooler climate deterred her. And Tillie lived in Virginia, which according to my mother, had the snootiest of witch energies around. She didn't want to saturate her aura with the uppity magic the East Coast was known for.

I ignored the lights, making a beeline toward my home. My aunts' luminous arguments could wait. Right now, I had a mystery egg that my hawk wanted to incubate.

I pressed my key to the front door and opened it wide. "Your egg is going in one of two places. The attic, or the garage."

"*The attic is warmer. It will help the egg hatch quicker,*" Francine agreed as she fluttered after me inside and promptly perched atop my shoulder.

"All right, attic it is."

We ascended my stairs. I grabbed the door to the attic and swung it open, scattering dust and cobwebs.

I found a place atop the old bookshelf where many of my romance novels lived. I tucked the egg with the blanket into one of the empty bookshelves. "This is where you can take up your new roost."

Francine nearly clipped my cheek with her wing as she flapped over to the egg and promptly lowered herself atop it.

"Your chicks are going to wonder why you've picked a dud egg as your favorite."

"*My chicks are self-sufficient, unlike a normal red-tail's offspring,*" she said with pride.

I left her to her egg and descended the stairs into my bedroom. I needed to freshen up before Dezmond arrived. My room was a freaking *mess.* Why had I suggested that we come back to my place instead of simply going out?

It was a Monday evening. I had work the next day, so I *really* didn't want to drink. And Dezmond mentioned that he was still volunteering at the animal shelter all week. Fantasies of what could actually happen in my bedroom with those wild shadows of his wrecked my mind. Both of my younger sisters had demon boyfriends. Each had alluded to some of the intimate encounters involving their darker shadow personalities.

As far as sexual protection went, I had a stash of condoms from my failed marriage beneath my sink. And because I was so pro wait-on-babies, I also had an IUD. The last thing I wanted was an unexpected pregnancy.

I tidied up my room as quickly as I could, grabbing an armful of my dirty clothes and tossed them into my closet. I jumped into the shower, lathered myself in soap and shampoo, and teased my hair with extra conditioner. The waves had been extra rebellious ever since this horrid heat wave struck. Thank the goddess my house had air conditioning.

Panic struck me. What the hell should I wear? As I turned off the tap and grabbed a towel, my hand bumped into my vibrator. I didn't need to use it. I had Dezmond's amazing tongue, and hopefully his dick to look forward to.

My phone chimed. I grabbed it from the counter. Lucy's book-worm icon lit up on my phone.

**Can I come by? I've been hiding something from you that I can't hide any longer.**

I ground my jaw. This better not be her asking to move back in.

**Okay, but it must be quick. I've got plans this evening. Let yourself in.**

After I tugged on a pair of leggings and my bra, I revved up the hairdryer. I felt the electrical surge that was my sister's aura enter my home. Apparently, she *really* wanted to talk to me, and it couldn't wait a few moments.

As Lucy emerged in the hallway, I held up my hand. "Hold please." I curled my fingers, sending the hot air through my hair and into a bun. I wanted it extra curly for when Dezmond arrived.

Lucy jutted her left hand toward me. A giant diamond ring sparkled in the light. "Amon and I are getting married, and I want you to be my witch of honor."

I dropped my hairdryer. "What? When did *this* happen?"

"Over a month ago."

"And you're just *now* telling your older sister? Lucy, what the hell is wrong with you?"

Lucy took my hand. "I know we've been fighting. I feel like you gave me so much after I moved into your home rent free after Jason and I broke up. And I know that ever since you and Ben split, serious relationships have been a difficult topic to discuss with you."

I eyed the ring on her finger. "You're sure he's the one? I mean, I made a big mistake with the first guy I tied the knot with."

"Yes," she answered without hesitation. "Amon is someone I can see spending the rest of my life with. He's sweet and kind and incredibly creative. I've never met anyone like him." She grabbed my hand. "Did you hear me? I want you to be my witch of honor."

"What?" I stammered, dropping my brush. "I would love to!"

I grabbed Lucy and tugged her into my arms. When we released one another, we both had tears in our eyes.

"I'm so glad," Lucy said.

"Does Grace know?"

"Yeah, she does. She's known for a while now. I actually told her not long after she got out of the hospital."

"What about Mom?"

"You are the only soul I've told, other than Grace. We both know that Mom will find out on her own. I wouldn't be surprised if she's already making plans to have our aunts and cousins visit from out of town."

I began to fan my face. "Well, you outdid yourself this time. For a moment there, I thought you were going to tell me that you were pregnant or something."

Lucy laughed. "I work with kids at the library, but you know I've been on the fence about having kids of my own."

I continued to fan my face.

"Girl, why are you so flustered? I mean, other than from the news I just dropped on you."

I flustered. "I actually have a date tonight."

Lucy's eyes went wide. "Please tell me it's with the demon Grace has tried to hook you up with, Dezmond Ravenblood?"

"Yes, it's him."

Lucy beamed. "He's *really* quirky. The interactions I've had with him have been very funny. And according to Grace, he has a ferocious appetite. She and Krim have resorted to hiding certain pastries from him when he stops into the bakery."

The space between my legs pulsed as I thought back to his *appetite* at the clinic.

Lucy made a motion toward the door. "I'll get out of your hair so you can get ready for your hot date with Amon's brother." She winked. "Please tell me what his shadows are like. I can't wait to hear about them."

Giddy with fantasies, I accidentally snorted as I laughed. "I've been waiting my entire life for this kind of relationship."

Lucy hesitated before she walked over the threshold. "Oh, by the way. How did your cancer screening go?"

"Just fine, I'm in the clear!" I lied, biting my tongue.

Lucy grinned. "Good. I can't wait to go dress shopping with you!"

I straightened my bra. I didn't have time for cancer to rear its ugly head in my life again. I had too much to look forward to instead of facing that monster. Besides, I was dating a shifter who had shadow beasts who were *feral* for me.

That alone should give me a wild streak in my luck, right?

# 10
# Dezmond

My stomach was in knots, and it wasn't from the amount of cream puffs that I'd stuffed into my mouth at the bakery. As I trudged down the sidewalk toward home with the empty kitty carrier, I wished I could just stop freaking out. A witch could only be so picky about takeout. I only hoped that my hot and heavy approach at the clinic wouldn't eventually turn Victoria off. I had a history of burning through relationships before they could even get started.

Something told me that tonight wasn't just a booty call. I didn't want to fuck this up. Victoria had a special heart—one that I didn't want to ruin just because I wanted a night of animalistic sex with the curvy vet witch who'd mended my arm.

I ground my jaw. I might not have the cash flow Victoria had as a vet. What I *did* have to offer her was a good primal dicking she seemed to have gone her entire life without.

Was our meeting and attraction toward one another fate? Or a force outside my control? I'd felt the tug to her like the moon had on the ocean. Victoria had awoken something primal in me—something that once awoken in a shifter, he had very little control over.

Sure, she was a witch, and a vet witch at that. But that didn't mean that she had any experience being with a shifter in the bedroom. Some women I shared my shadow beasts with never wanted to speak to me again.

"*That's because you haven't found the right mate. She will need to accept all of us if she's to bond with you,*" Sniffer huffed into my ear. "*Just wait until you have Victoria alone at her house. I'm going to make sure that she experiences more than just my—*"

I tapped my finger against the Wild Card in my jacket pocket, and Sniffer's huffy voice quieted.

I grinned. How nice it was to silence my shadow beasts when I needed a break from them.

I glanced down at my arm. My tattoo needed to get touched up. Victoria might have mended my flesh and bones, but not my brother Amon's artwork. He owned a shop not far from where I lived called Shadow Ink's Tattoo Parlor.

As I walked into his shop, the front door chimed. The smell of ink and something musty filled my nose. I scanned the space. No sign of him.

"Yo, Amon. You have any free time this afternoon for a touch up?" I asked.

My oldest brother manifested in a plume of coiling purple smoke. Amon was taller than me by quite a few inches. His long muscular arms were covered in black tattoos of feathers and serpents. He wore a plain black t-shirt and jeans with black ink smudged all over the denim. "Only if you aren't trying to give me a kitten," he grumbled moodily. His dark hair was strewn across his face like someone from a nineties emo rock band.

"Nope. No kitty inside. Just a bunch of kitty treats from Krim's spoiled feline." I set the cat carrier full of Bitty Bone Bites down. Amon didn't own a familiar like Krim did, but that didn't mean that one day I wasn't going to dump one on him.

"What are you working on?" I asked as I walked over to his work-space.

"Just some personal projects." His shadows branched overhead as they tossed one another his paintbrushes. "Wanna see what happens when my shadows fight to express themselves?"

I chuckled. While Amon had a multi-shadow personality like myself, his shadows weren't *beasts.* They all had humanoid mani-festations and represented his separate ages. Only last year around Halloween, he'd lost his childhood shadow. Had it not been for Victoria's younger sister Lucy, he might have lost a piece of his soul to a nasty cannibalistic wendigo called the Bone Threader.

I set my hands on my hips and gazed around the room. Amon's monochromatic paintings were so emotive and powerful. Black on white would forever be one of my favorite aesthetics. I was jealous of his artistic talent. Sure, I could slam away on drums all day, but I didn't have Amon's eye for detail, or a steady hand when it came to his ink collection.

One of his ink studies was labeled *June eighteenth, eighteen six-ty-nine.* That sure put a gap in my head. Time flew by between my brothers and I. As far as our ages, I was still considered to be in my demonic sexual prime. I hadn't yet hit the century three hundred, when a demon began to have his shadows experience a sexual decline. I was two hundred and ninety-seven. Krim just hit his three hundredth and nineteenth birthday. And Amon was somewhere up there beyond us. I always forgot how old my eldest brother was.

He grabbed a towel and wiped his hands clean, then kicked his rolling chair toward me. "I have some extra time between appointments. I want to see what kind of damage you've done so I know what I'll be working with."

I flopped down on one of his chairs as he grabbed one of his tattoo pens and sat down on a stool, then rolled himself over to me.

His brow furrowed as he studied my arm. "Wow. Dad wasn't kidding. You *really* fucked yourself up. My ink is bone-deep permanent. You must have really hurt yourself this time."

"I did. Dad hooked me up with Lucy's older vet sister, Victoria. She's really good with mending a demon's boo boos."

His mouth quirked. "Boo boos, huh? Sounds like you're already soft on her. I remember Victoria. She's super sassy, isn't she?"

A chuckle escaped me. *Sassy* was an understatement. My stomach swooped just thinking about what kind of witch I might be dealing with later this evening. "Yeah, she is. You know I like my women that way."

Amon blew out his cheeks. "Well, if she's anything like Lucy, I'm sure you're going to be sharing some future stories with me." He rummaged into one of his drawers and tugged out another tattoo pen. "What creature are we going with this time? Another little dude with spikes?"

My hedgehog tattoo had been shredded from my accident, but it still had some spikes to work with.

I flexed my hand, making the muscles and the remains of the hedgehog tattoo bulge. "I want a dragon."

His thick dark brows drew up. "That's a first. Are we doing a fire-breathing kind of dragon, or something else?"

I didn't really know what kind of dragon I wanted. There were eastern and western dragons. Some had wings, and others did not. And according to Dad, they had some powerful abilities that allowed them to manipulate the elements.

I grabbed the Wild Card out of my pocket and set it down in front of him. "You see that egg at the base of the tree?"

He squinted at the card. "Yeah?"

"Draw one of those, but make it look extra scaly. And maybe have a tail poking out of it, like it's hatching?"

He smirked. "What kind of card is that?"

"A magical one."

"Obviously. Where did you get it?"

"Victoria is letting me borrow it. Ever since I've had this card, my shadow beasts are tamable. I can shut them up and actually focus."

Amon's dark eyes narrowed onto me. "You get some random magical card from a witch that has the power to tame your shadows, and you're not at all leery about it?"

"Look, are you going to give me a tattoo or not?" I pressed.

He shrugged. "Okay, whatever you say, baby bro. It's your arm, not mine. If you want to risk me drawing some symbol infused with magic onto your body, you might be dealing with some consequences."

As he busied himself with his tattoo pens and inks, I stared at the Wild Card, transfixed on its design once again. Two hands cradled the egg from which a giant tree sprouted—an egg I was convinced belonged to a dragon. "Have you ever heard of some ancient ritual that only shifter demons partake in?"

"Nope. What's it about?"

"Dad mentioned it the other day. He got all wonky and started talking about there being the possibility of a *fourth* branch of magic, and that female demons hadn't really gone extinct."

He sighed. "He's probably drinking again. I wouldn't put too much thought into his drunk ramblings. As far as I know, there are only *three* types of magic. Shadow, earth, and goddess are the only types I've ever heard of."

"Yeah, well. There *might* be some truth to what he said. I just stopped by the bakery and asked if Krim new anything about this strange ritual Dad mentioned, and he got all shady."

"Krim's shadow is a reaper. He's always been shady." Amon's eyes darted back to the Wild Card as he studied the design. "Did you show Krim this card too?"

"Yeah."

"What did he say?"

"He suggested that if I introduced the Wild Card to the deck, I'd discover that it wasn't the only card that housed any magic."

At my words, sparks shot out of the card, singing the hair on my forearm.

Amon held his tattoo pen over my arm. "Krim is the only demon who served as a shadow alchemist in our family. Maybe he has some knowledge about it. I'd trust him over Dad any day." His tattoo pen gave a high-pitched whine. "Are we giving this dragon tail spikes?"

I balled my hand into a fist. "Let's go with one that has *lots* of spikes."

He lowered his pen to my arm. "A spiky dragon it is."

The burn of his tattoo pen pierced my flesh as he dug the needle into my skin. "Speaking of the Crow Sisters. Has Dad slipped up and spilled the beans yet?" Amon asked.

"Not unless they're the kind apparently Grace has growing in her greenhouse—he once said something about them screaming?"

The pen whined as Amon dragged the needle across my skin. "Well, that's good. I thought I should mention that Lucy and I are getting married."

I shook out my head. My ears must have popped. "Wait a fat second, did you say *married*?"

He didn't look up. A few strands of his dark hair fell into his face as he continued to outline my dragon egg. "Yep."

My mouth dropped open. "Dude, you're getting *hitched*? Man, congrats!"

"Zed, hold still. . .you're going to make me fuck this up."

I tugged my arm away from him. "You can't break that kind of news when you've got a needle on someone's skin."

He was all smiles as he turned off his pen and leveled his gaze with me. "Bro, I want you to be the best demon."

"Wait, *me*? Why not Krim?"

"He's too busy with the bakery, and I'd really like it if you would do it. We want our wedding to be fun, and you are far less uptight than him. So, will you?"

"Fuck yeah, I will! I'd be honored. When is the date?"

"September nineteenth. Hopefully this sweltering heat wave shit will have died down by then. Oh, by the way. Dad mentioned something about our uncles, Liam and Oscar. They might be coming to stay for the wedding. I told him that they might need to crash at your place."

I braced myself as Amon dug the needle into my forearm again. Regardless of what the future held, I knew that in a few hours, I'd be experiencing Victoria's fiery magic once again. Maybe a little *wild* magic is what I needed to kick our relationship into overdrive. I *really* wanted her to be my date at my brother's wedding.

# 11

# Victoria

My doorbell rang a few minutes past seven. I gave myself one last look in the mirror. My nail polish was called *wild red.* I hadn't worn it since being married to Ben, and prior to having put on so much weight. My mascara was *so* overdone. And my lipstick—holy shit. Was the deep shade of mauve too much?

*He'll love it. If he doesn't, then I'll tell him to fuck off, after I've fucked him, of course.*

Bracing myself, I grabbed the door and swung it open. My breath caught. An incredibly hot green-eyed demon wearing a biker jacket with a bouquet of blood red roses in one hand, and a bag of Chinese takeout in the other, stood on my doorstep.

A whistle trilled out of his mouth as he wiped the back of his hand past his forehead. "Hot damn. You look mighty fine, Vet Victoria."

I flushed. I shouldn't be so flattered from him cat-calling me on my own doorstep. The shirt he wore made his chest muscles bunch. The only thing that could make this any more perfect would be if he had horns jutting out of his head. . .

"*Don't let your fantasies take over. Remember, you are only just getting to know him,*" Francine boasted into my thoughts.

*"I don't want to hear another peep out of you this evening, you hear me?"* I thought back to my opinionated red-tail. *"This is my date, and I plan to enjoy every scolding hot second of it."*

Francine's feathers made a ruffling sound in my head as I let Dezmond inside.

"Wow, you've got a nice place! Way bigger than my flat." His eyes darted between my kitchen and living room windows. "Dude, is that a *pool*?"

"Actually, yes."

His green eyes swept dangerously to me. "Want to skip dinner and go skinny dipping?"

"Absolutely not. I'm far too hungry to pass up good Chinese food."

He smirked. "Mark my words. I plan on getting you wet tonight, one way or another."

If I wasn't flushing before, I was now.

He ran his wide hand across his scalp. "Look, I'm going to be upfront with you. I tend to burn *real* hot at the beginning of relationships, but you burned me up hotter than a firecracker hitting the sun."

I folded my arms across my chest. "Are you regretting your choices at the clinic?"

His pupils dilated. "*Fuck* no. Heck, what I'm trying to say is, if you want me to take it slow, I can. Why don't we start with a good old-fashioned kiss on the lips, and we can see if you want more of my tongue or not?"

My belly heated as I remembered the sinful things he did with that tongue. "Deal. Why don't you settle into my place, and we can see how things go? I'm not in any rush, but I'm also not one to put on the brakes if I like someone."

He grinned that shit-eating grin that I was starting to adore. Squinting, he glanced at the silver light reflecting on my ceiling. "Is it normal for a pool to put off so much light like that?"

"Considering that my twin witch aunts gifted me the pool, I would say the lights are a source of their magic. They live on opposite coasts, and the lights are a result of their conversations with each other. They are trying to convince my mother to visit them. They have this argument every summer."

"You're joking, right?"

"Nope. My mother has a crystal ball that channels their messages sent with their auras. Millie and Tillie are twin aurora witches, so their messages come in the form of lights in the sky right over Midhaven."

"Wow, that's really cool! I wish my father talked with my uncles that way."

"How many uncles do you have?"

"Two that I know of. But Dad always makes it sound like he's got others that we don't know about. Their names are Liam and Oscar."

"Do you have cousins?"

"I think so."

"You *think* so? How do you not know if you have cousins or not?"

He shrugged. "Hey, we left Ireland a long time ago when I was just a wee lad of a demon. I don't have a whole lot of memories of my extended family like Amon and Krim do." He glanced around my home. "So, where are all the critters?"

"Oh, I get it. You think that because I'm a vet, that I'll have all kinds of creatures crawling around my place."

"Yeah, maybe I am biased. But I did imagine you'd have something meet me at the door with claws and teeth."

"Nope. Francine is the only creature I allow inside my home. I like to keep my work at work, if you know what I mean."

"By the way, where is the birdie?"

"She's upstairs tending to her egg in the attic. She has strict rules not to interrupt our evening."

"Ah, I see. I'm just glad that she didn't come swooping in to take my head off. She kept giving me the crazy eyes at your clinic."

I laughed. "Francine has been giving *everyone* the crazy eyes ever since that egg ended up in her nest."

"Are you the only Crow sister who likes critters?"

"Hell no. Grace is my youngest sister. She has a whole greenhouse full of very opinionated familiars. Apparently, the familiars who live in the greenhouse have started a magical union and won't accept any new inhabitants, unless they perform some kind of ritual."

Dezmond's eyes lit up. "Ritual, huh? I thought it was only us shifters who practiced them."

My breath hitched. Being tied up and worshiped under a blood moon by his tongue became my only focus. . .

He seemed to sense the intensity of my spontaneous fantasy. His mouth quirked, revealing two adorable dimples as he set the takeout on the kitchen table and handed me the roses. "These are for you, beautiful."

As I took the vase into my hand, magic shot out of my fingers, turning the blood-red color of the roses into an even deeper hue. "Thank you. They're lovely."

"As are you," he continued as he eyed my liquor cabinet. "Do you drink?"

I set the vase of shimmering red, purple, and black roses onto my counter. "I do. But I'm trying to cut back. Alcohol is one of the main reasons I gained so much weight after my divorce, and then the mastectomy."

His eyes dropped to my chest. "Ah, breast cancer?"

"Yes. My father actually passed from lymphoma, which is a type of bone cancer."

A pitiful look wrecked his expression. "I'm sorry you lost your old man. Just so you know, I think you are absolutely wonderful to look at, no matter what. You also smell amazing, and you feel really soft." He ran his hand across his smooth scalp. "Hey, if it makes you feel any better, I often get a bit self-conscious about my lack of hair. Don't know why, but I've been a baldie since my balls dropped."

My nipple pebbled at his compliment. *Control yourself, Victoria.*

He smiled. "I guess it's a good thing that you're taking a break from drinking. My father has given up the bottle, all thanks to your mother, Cindy."

"Yeah, about that. Do you think it's weird that our parents are you know, *dating*?"

He shrugged. "It's only weird if you want it to be. Rumor has it that a couple of our siblings are also getting cozy."

I laughed. He put my mind at ease.

He closed the space between us, and his scent of minty spice washed over me. "That's what I like about you, Victoria. You don't shy away from anything. I respect a witch who speaks her mind, above all things."

I glanced over at the stack of mail on my counter where I knew the cancer screening notice was buried. "I've had many men tell me that my bluntness turns them off. I've gotten quite used to it."

"Well, good thing I'm a demon, not a man. Believe me, we have some differences." He grabbed my hand, his green eyes capturing me. "So, I'm gonna make you a deal. For every *man* who has been a douche bag to you, this demon is going to give you an orgasm this evening."

Sparks shot out of my fingers and jolted like little fairies up his arm. "Is it common for you to offer a witch multiple orgasms on her first date?"

His eyes flashed dangerously. "With you it is," he continued, his callused fingers working over mine. "Especially now that my shadow beasts are tame, I can be the dominant demon in charge."

A card came jolting out of his jacket pocket.

He caught it mid-air as the sparks settled around us.

"How has my Wild Card been treating your shadow beasts?" I asked as he tucked the card back into his pocket.

"It's been amazing not having their claws, jaws, and noses dominating my thoughts." He grabbed his sleeve and tugged it up, revealing the spot on his arm I'd patched up. "It also inspired me to get some new ink!"

I glanced over the egg with what appeared to be a dragon tail breaking out of it. "Who gave you the tattoo?"

"My older brother, Amon, who by the way, did you get any big news from Lucy recently?"

My stomach gave a grouchy rumble. "Why don't we discuss the news over dinner?"

He grabbed the bag of takeout. "You lead the way."

A hot flash rippled up my spine as I led the way into the living room, where I sat on the sofa.

Dezmond sat next to me, his knee grazing mine as he set the bag of takeout onto the coffee table before us. "How was this news broken to you?"

I took a box and opened it, revealing a healthy portion of my favorite—chicken lo mein. "You mean the fact that our siblings got engaged and never told us?"

He opened a box too, revealing a heaping portion of fried rice. "Why were they being so secretive?"

"I have no idea. And apparently, Lucy wants me to be her witch of honor."

His eyes went wide. "Well then. It sounds like fate had us paired together, now didn't it?"

My heart thundered. "I take it that you're the best demon?"

His mouth quirked. "You betcha, baby."

I grabbed a pair of chopsticks and unwrapped them. "So, what do you actually do for a living? I know you worked on some demo job, and that you have two other brothers. One is a tattoo artist, and the other now runs a bakery with my youngest sister."

He snapped a pair of chopsticks apart and handed them to me. "I'm blue collar. Always have been. I usually work night jobs with construction when they become available. I also drum in a band that's changed its name about five times. We're currently settled on the lame name of the Nematodes."

I grabbed another pair of chopsticks and broke them apart, then handed them to him. "That's so awesome! When and where do you play?"

He dipped his chopsticks into his lo mein. "I'll let you know when we have our next gig. I hope you like heavy metal with a bit of Irish folk mixed in with it."

As we dove into our food, I let my guard down and enjoyed eating. For having such a rough appearance, Dezmond sure was a softie. I didn't feel like I needed to doll myself up with the makeup I'd put on, or two layers of mascara.

He finished his first box and started on his second. Lucy wasn't kidding about his appetite. If I ate like *he* did, I'd be three hundred pounds.

After we finished eating, Dezmond grabbed my box and chopsticks and set what I couldn't finish onto the table. He reached into his pocket and tugged out the Wild Card I'd let him borrow. "Hey, I have an idea. Why don't you perform a tarot reading on me?"

I laughed. "The only time I've actually played with the deck was a long time ago. It involved copious amounts of alcohol, and a lot of screaming."

He smiled. "Sounds like a good time. Who gave you the deck?"

"My aunts gifted me the deck, actually, back when I turned nineteen."

"So magical cards *and* a pool? They sound like some awesome aunts. Could you show the deck to me?"

"I thought you might ask to see the rest of the cards." I grabbed the wooden box sitting on the table and opened it and retrieved the stack and began to shuffle it. "It's a very simple deck. There are three primary cards that represent the three magics, Goddess, Earth, and Shadow.

"But there is only *one* Wild Card, correct?"

I nodded. "As far as I know, it's the only card in the deck that actually possesses magic."

Dezmond withdrew the Wild Card from his pocket and set it between us on the table.

I drew the top card from the deck, flipped it over, then set it beneath the Wild Card.

A creature stared up at me.

"Wow, the *Beast*? It kind of looks like me!" Dezmond said.

"The Beast is one of *three* types of shadow cards. Here, I'll show you." I cut the deck and flipped through it until I found the cards I wanted to show him, then aligned them on my table.

"Wow. Serpent, Death, and the Beast? They all seem very similar to the shadows my brothers and I all have."

I let out a yawn.

Dezmond's mouth dropped open. "I'm not boring you, am I?"

"No," I stifled another yawn. "I think I overate."

Dezmond abandoned the cards and set his hand on my leg. "I can tell you that there is a certain witch who tastes a whole lot better than this Chinese food."

I squirmed in my seat as he reached for my ankle and said, "Gimme those pretty little darlings."

I swung my legs up into his lap. I hadn't had a pedicure in over a month, but that didn't stop him from rubbing his big wide hands across my heels.

*Fuck.* I melted like butter into his affectionate touch.

"I told you. I have a lot to do to make up for you patching up my arm. I'm not going to just let you give me a freebie without letting me return the favor somehow."

"You are spoiling me."

He kissed my foot. "Just relax and enjoy it, sweetheart. We don't need to rush to the dessert part."

His words muddied in my brain as I closed my eyes. Suddenly, I didn't care about Chinese food, or even sex. I just wanted to fall into this kind of evening ritual every night and let the stress from the day melt away with him.

"Victoria?"

I jolted. I must have dozed off from his foot rub.

His green eyes locked with me. "Something is making noise upstairs," he whispered. "You don't have any ghost cats living in your home, do you? My brother has one, and he loves to haunt his attic."

Fury forced my magic to flare, sending sparks out of my fingertips. "I swear, I'm going to *kill* that bird. She knew I had a date. If she has the nerve to go and ruin it." I climbed to my feet and grabbed his hand. "Come with me. Maybe she'll get the clue if we start fucking in the stairwell."

We tore up the stairs. Magic coiled up my spine as I led the way toward the attic.

"What do you think she's so upset about?" he asked.

"No idea, but she's about to get a piece of my mind."

Feathers coiled out from under the door crack. I grabbed the door handle and swung it open.

Francine let out a terrible *shreeeek.* A fiery plume of smoke ignited her tail feathers. Flames curled beneath her as she rose into the air like a phoenix.

"Where is it? *What* is it?" I stammered as I scrambled inside the attic.

Dezmond stumbled in after me. "No idea. But wow, it smells like a fart bomb went off in here."

We backed into one another as we surveyed my dark attic. The eggy smell of sulfur filled the room.

"*It's up there,*" Francine squawked haughtily into my mind.

My hands trembled. While I wasn't usually afraid of creatures, this thing had me spooked. It was obviously quick to maneuver about, even moments after singing my hawk's tail feathers to a crisp.

Something scurried about the bookshelf where I'd tucked Francine a few hours ago to guard her egg.

A plume of flames shot into the air.

With a terrified *shreeeek*! Francine hopped from one bookshelf to another.

Dezmond grabbed me before I bolted toward the door. His hands gripped my shoulders, holding me protectively in place. "Don't move."

"What the fuck is that?" I stammered, my voice sounding just as terrified as my hawk.

He released me. He walked over to the far corner, where he crouched down and grabbed whatever it was that had spouted fire.

The creature clawed its way up the back of his neck and perched atop Dezmond's head. Purple scales covered its entire body. A long spiny tail flopped onto Dezmond's shoulder. Its eyes gave me the shivers. The colors changed from red to yellow as quickly as the vertical slits for pupils dilated. Its gaze was primal and intelligent, sending my magic into a fit of hot, rolling spasms.

This creature, if it really *was* a dragon, possessed some kind of powerful magic.

Dezmond was all grin as he turned to face me. "Little guy is scared is all."

"How do you know it's a *guy*?" I asked.

"Have a look at those dangly bits and tell me you don't agree."

He lifted the dragon's tail, revealing a patch of shiny round scales that absolutely resembled testicles.

Screw the dangly bits.

*This is a dragon…*

The creature arched his neck as his nostrils flared. Another plume of flames erupted into the air. Thank the goddess he was perched on Dezmond's bald head, because I would have ended up like my hawk.

He shot me a half-alarmed, half *this is so fucking cool* kind of look. "You take care of your hawk. I'll take him."

I walked over to my terrified hawk, where she cowered in the corner. "Come on, Francine. He's not going to burn your feathers twice."

Francine practically wilted in my arms as she folded her wings and fell into my chest.

"Stop acting so pathetic," I cooed down to her as I carried her toward the staircase. "You were the one who insisted on taking care of that egg instead of abandoning it!"

"*My feathers will grow back, right? What if my mate doesn't find me attractive any longer?*"

I laughed. My protective hawk could be such a drama mama bird at times.

# 12

# Dezmond

While Victoria got her hawk all settled, I was able to take a look at my new scaly responsibility. A low, guttural hissing sound erupted from his throat. The gassy little dragon dude was terrified, and probably needed food to settle his tummy.

Where were his parents? And what did dragon hatchlings eat? I'd fostered kittens, baby birds, and even some baby pythons in my time.

But a baby *dragon*? This was a first for me.

"Dezmond, are you coming?" Victoria called up the stairs. A furious *shreeeeek*! followed in protest from Francine.

As I descended the staircase into the light of the kitchen, the little scaly dude's scales began to change color. Their once purple iridescence became a brilliant orange before they fluctuated between red and yellow.

Victoria stood with Francine folded against her chest. Her feathered head was burrowed into her armpit. Smoke still coiled out of what remained of her tail feathers. "So, we know it breathes fire. . .that's great. I wonder what else it can do."

"*Don't let that horrid creature get any closer to me. It tried to roast me like a chicken*!" Francine screeched into both of our minds.

I tried to stifle a laugh and failed. The dragon rolled onto his back in my arms and exposed his belly to me.

"I think he's taken a liking to you," Victoria said, her brows drawing up.

I walked into the living room and grabbed one of the boxes of takeout. "I have an idea. Here little guy, want some fried rice?"

His nostrils flared, and a bright plume of flames curled out of his nose. In a fiery burst, my fried rice blackened.

I shrugged. "All right, cool. No biggie. I like mine extra crispy, anyway."

Victoria's expression twisted as she gawked at the dragon. "Well, he can't stay at my house, not with my hawk acting like this."

"I guess I'll take him with me," I said, my voice sounding distant. My stomach swooped. I felt like I was abandoning her.

"Call me tomorrow?"

"Absolutely," I replied, wishing I hadn't found the dragon to begin with. The only thing I wanted to make feel warm and cuddled and loved right now was the vet witch who'd been so good to me.

Being blue-balled by a baby dragon was not something I expected out of my evening. Should I tell my brothers about him? What about Dad? Maybe I should keep his discovery a secret for a bit.

But I couldn't keep calling him little *scaly dude.* He needed a name. As I walked down the street, he wound out of my arms and crawled up onto my shoulder, thrashing his tail as he dug his claws into my leather jacket.

The sun had set, and there wasn't much I could do with the remainder of my day. I had a couple of options on how to handle my new situation. Either I take him back to my place, or I try and figure out what to feed him.

I stopped in my tracks.

*Fuck...*

I'd left the Wild Card at Victoria's place.

I braced myself, waiting for when Pawz, Jawz, and Sniffer would fill my head with their domineering voices again. But all I heard were the little bubbly belches coming from my new baby dragon.

My phone chimed. Sloane had texted me.

**Zed, can you come and tend to the kitties tomorrow? I had a volunteer call out and we could use the support.**

As I tried to type out a reply, another stream of flames erupted out of the dragon's mouth. My phone turned into a blackened brick, similar to what had happened to my fried rice.

"Well, that settles that," I said as I pocketed my torched phone. "Hey, you can't play blow torch any time you don't like something."

A new sound rumbled in his throat that sounded like *oooorrrrc-cchhhhh*.

"*Torch*? You like that?"

He tilted his head sideways, sending little plumes of smoke out of his nostrils in what had to be some kind of *yes* in dragon.

I scratched him behind the two little horns protruding from his head. "I'm calling you Torchie, at least until you learn to control your flames, all right?"

Another guttural sound that was far too terrifying for his size rumbled in his throat.

"You know, you shouldn't have torched Francine's tail feathers. She's the familiar of the witch I'm trying to impress."

Another plume of fire erupted out of his nostrils in protest.

"Okay, sure. I'm glad we had this little chat. Maybe one day when you get a girlfriend, you won't blow hellfire out of your mouth when you want to impress her."

Torchie curved his neck back, transfixed with the moths diving in and out of the dull yellow light emitted from a lamp post. Maybe dragons were nocturnal hunters. Either way, he couldn't fly, yet. Two little nodules on his shoulders made me think that wings weren't far off from developing.

Rather than head back to Victoria's to take back the Wild Card, I continued onward toward home. I walked into my apartment and set Torchie onto one of the spare kitty beds I had sitting on the floor next to my drum set. "Just don't light my drumsticks on fire, okay?"

He curled up into a ball, setting his head onto his tail, as he promptly went to sleep.

As I took off my clothes and prepped for bed, I knew I wasn't going to get a wink of shuteye. As soon as my head hit the pillow, all I could do was imagine Victoria's soft, curvy body curled up against me.

# 13

# Victoria

So my hot date with Dezmond Ravenblood didn't work out. I spent the following morning thinking about how we could possibly pick up where we left off before the baby dragon got involved.

As I prepped a cup of coffee, Francine ruffled what had regrown of her tail feathers at me from atop my bookshelf as she preened them obsessively. "*He'll be back. Just give him some time to sort out the devil snake.*"

I couldn't stop looking at my phone. I'd texted Dezmond twice and hadn't heard anything back. A hollow sensation pitted in my stomach. What if my bird had scared him away?

What if he thought I was crazy?

Sparks shot out of my periphery.

The deck of cards remained scattered on my coffee table from the night before. The Beast Card, usually a lion-like creature, appeared more dragonic. Had playing with the cards somehow helped the baby dragon to hatch out of my attic?

I grabbed the deck and shuffled what I'd shown to Dezmond back into it, including his Wild Card, then set the stack back into its box, fearful of what other magic it might cast into the air. I took the box and set it back on my bookshelf.

Anxious about this entire situation, I grabbed my phone again. Still, no reply from Dezmond.

*Get a grip on yourself, Victoria. He went down on you and wanted to do more. You're just freaking out because your hawk is such a—*

*Tap, tap, tap.*

A fuzzy white head bobbed outside my kitchen window as two others tapped on the glass with their beaks.

"Oh look, your *real* offspring have arrived." I opened the back door and walked outside onto my backyard deck.

Francine followed, fluttering down from my bookshelf and hopping out into my yard like a mini velociraptor. She arched her wings over her head as her three chicks hopped over to where she stopped in the grass.

One of them spat out a dead rodent at her feet. "*Mom, look! I caught my first rat!*"

"*Mouse,*" Francine corrected her enthusiastic offspring. "*After the past day, I sure could use a few rats to snack on.*"

I laughed. Francine's fledglings sure knew how to spoil their mother.

As Francine grabbed the mouse with her beak and swallowed it with one gulp, my thoughts immediately went to Dezmond. What would that baby dragon eat?

"*Mother, what happened to your tail?*" one of the fledglings chirped.

Francine arched her wings over her head. "*We will not be discussing my tail any further, do you understand*?"

Her fledgling ruffled his own tail features as he took a step back from his mother.

Speaking of mothers. . .

I walked back into my kitchen as my mother's aura flared outside my home. I didn't need a doorbell to announce her arrival. Her aura burst into my house, a familiar sensation I remembered back from when I was probably ten years old.

"Good morning, dear," Mom said as she made her way into my kitchen. The scent of lavender and rose hips wafted in with her. She wore a loose-fitting floral sun dress decorated in a purple daisy pattern. Her light brown hair was tossed up into its usual bun, and her face was sun-kissed, likely from spending the early hour mornings before it got too hot tending to her garden. Tucked in her arms was a basket full of tea bags, probably from last year's harvest.

"Hi Mom. What's brought you by?" I asked as I grabbed her a coffee mug from my cabinet.

She held up her hand. "No need for coffee. I'm much too caffeinated already, love. I've brought you a batch of fresh solstice tea to kick off the summer!"

"Ah, thank you," I said, even though my mother knew that tea didn't hold near enough caffeine for me. But I loved the way the tea bags made my house smell, so I often hung them up in my window to freshen the air.

"Eugene has been very helpful in his attempts to help me prepare this batch," she said, her cheeks reddening as she scooted the basket full of tea bags toward me.

"How is everything going with Mr. Ravenblood?" I asked as I poured myself a cup of coffee.

Mom beamed. "He was so happy when he found out that you mended Zeddy's arm. I can't brag enough of my daughters as much as he brags about his demon sons. Speaking of our mingling families, I assume Lucy finally told you about her wedding?"

"Yes, she did, and she wants me to be the witch of honor. *Zeddy* told me that he's the best demon."

Mom's smile turned into a half frown. "With weddings come guests. I thought I should forewarn you, your aunts, Millie and Tillie, are coming to stay at my house for a week before the wedding."

"That's great! Are you excited?"

Mom pursed her lips, smudging her lipstick. "*Excited* is an understatement. Having three powerful witches under my roof who aren't my daughters might be a bit of a, how should I say this, magically *enlightening* experience?"

"I can agree with that."

"Your cousin Danika is too busy keeping up with her bees to visit. Apparently, they're known for producing black honey with all kinds of magic. Even though it will only be your aunts, I think we should plan on having a party, but I don't want to step on your toes when it comes to planning it, Miss witch of honor."

"Honestly, I'd love some help with planning this magical shindig. This is my busiest time of year at the clinic. Lucy hasn't given me any big hints on what her wedding theme is around. All I know is she's really fond of spooky season, so she might just be getting a Summerween-themed party."

Mom scanned my living room. "Speaking of spooky, I also wanted to ask if you still had that old deck of cards your aunts gifted you?"

I pointed to my bookshelf. "I keep them in that box. Why do you want to see the deck?"

"There is one card in particular that I am searching for," Mom said as she walked to my bookshelf and grabbed the deck out of the box I'd stored it in. Sparks fizzled out of her fingers as she shuffled the cards. "Ah, here it is—the one card that gives all the other cards their magic."

"The Wild Card," I said as Mom held the card in front of her face. "Speaking of something wild. You know that egg Francine was guarding? Well, last night, when Dezmond and I were playing with the cards, it hatched."

Mom glanced at me. "What creature escaped that egg?"

"Unless I was dreaming, a real-life dragon hatched out of it."

Mom clapped her free hand to her cheek. "You're *kidding* me, a real dragon?"

"Yes."

"Where is it now?"

"Dezmond has him."

Mom shuffled the Wild Card back into the deck. She set the cards into the box and approached me with it. "Oh, Eugene is going to be thrilled. He was just telling me about Irish dragons yesterday! This is so adorable. My daughter and Eugene's son are baby dragon foster parents? Wait until I tell him."

"Can you keep the dragon a secret for now? I really don't want to have a bunch of rumors spreading around town that we have him," I said, thinking back to Sloane.

"I will try my best, but Eugene has a way of pulling secrets out of me I've long overkept." She held up the box of cards. "Your aunts wanted to see the Three Magics Oracle Deck when they arrived. Do you mind if I borrow it?"

"It's probably a good thing that you do," I said, not wanting to know what kind of impact the wild magic in those cards might have on Francine's offspring.

Having my mother walk out of my house with the card deck somehow gave me a sense of relief. I knew the cards had some kind of influence on the baby dragon hatching. The first few hours at work flew by. I had so many new patients that I had to resort to splitting appointments between the vet techs and myself. The number of creatures coming into my clinc only reinforced why I wanted to work with the animal shelter.

As I sat down for a quick ten seconds in my office to grab a drink of water, I felt my sister's aura blow through the office. Ever since Grace started getting cozy with Dezmond's older brother, who she at times labeled as Grumpy Grim, her magical flares became much more powerful.

Holly popped into my doorway. "Your younger sister is here. And she's got something really prickly to show you."

I nearly choked. *Prickly* usually meant that I had to deal with one of my least favorite patients—a hedgehog. "Send her back."

Grace appeared in my doorway with a basket in her arms.

"I hear you have a spiky visitor?"

Grace smiled. "*Visitors* is more like it."

"Close the door and have a seat."

She set a basket down on my desk and sat in the chair across from me. The blanket inside of the basket moved as a tiny black nose poked out and sniffed.

Not one, but three noses, then five.

"Are these what I think they are?" I asked.

"You remember Goblin, my green hedgehog? Well, he and Wilma made these adorable little prickly things together a few weeks ago."

"It seems like love is in the air with all of the familiars and creatures I've had to tend to recently."

Grace clapped her hands together enthusiastically. Green sparks shot out of her fingertips and curled the ends of her pixie cut hair. "Tell my sister your names!"

One by one, the hoglets climbed out of the basket and clustered together on my desk and cried:

"*Basil*!"

"*Sage*!"

"*Rosemary*!"

"*Thyme*!"

My heart swelled. "You named them after herbs?"

Grace grabbed the basket and gave it a little shake. "Oh, where's my favorite little spiky dude?"

The last hoglet scurried out of the basket—one that was much plumper than the others, and piped, "*Mushroom*!"

Grace beamed. "If you give them a quick checkup, I'll treat you to lunch. Come by the bakery this afternoon!"

I wiped the back of my hand past my forehead. "Whew. I was scared for a moment that you were asking me to find homes for them."

"Nope. They've started a prickly little commune in my greenhouse. And if you thought Goblin's routine of eating snails with his tea was bizarre, now he and Wilma have started demanding an all-out tea cake party every Friday afternoon."

I laughed. Grace's familiars sure had themselves wrapped around her green thumb. "I'll be there around one."

Grace winked. "I can't wait to hear about your hot date with Dezmond."

Guilt plagued my gut as soon as I walked into the Blooming Mushroom Bakery. I caught a glimpse of my reflection in one of the display cases. My scrubs bunched in places that didn't make my curves look flattering at all.

I scanned the menu, desperate to try some *sugar free* options. I shouldn't be eating sugary sweets and pastries. Sure, they sold things like paninis, but I should really eat a salad—not the calorie-rich treats that Grace and her hollow legs could get away with.

Frustrated with my lack of options, I found a seat by the window and plopped down. As soon as I sat, Grace appeared from the back room. She walked over to me, carrying a giant platter of my absolute favorite thing to stuff my mouth with—cheesecake.

"We have a brand new summer tea cake platter!" Grace cried as she practically leapt across the room.

My mouth watered as she set the platter onto the table before me.

"Please don't tell me you are on one of those stupid beach diets," she said grumpily.

I reached into my purse and grabbed the spare protein bar I'd been saving. "No, but just last night, I ate enough Chinese food to feed an army."

Grace's mouth dropped. "Oh, that sounds super sexy! I bet Dezmond likes his extra spicy. Where did you both go?"

I felt something rub past my leg.

Scythe, Krim's ghost cat, came floating up to eye-level to Grace and me.

"Be gone with you, spooky little beast!" Grace teased him.

Scythe scrunched his little black nose at my sister and let out a nasty little *hiss*, then quickly turned his attention to me.

"Careful," Grace warned. "He's been a really pesky little ghost ever since Krim stopped feeding him cat treats."

Scythe stretched out his front paws, displaying a set of large hooked claws.

Grace shook her head. "Now you know where he gets his name from."

I wasn't afraid of familiars, in life, or in death. I'd not encountered many *spirit* familiars in my time being a vet, which according to Lucy, demons acquired as their own companions.

As Scythe's claws reached for me, I propped my elbows onto the table and leaned toward him. "Hey, I have a hawk who would eat you for lunch. Put those things away, or I'll summon her here to say hello."

Scythe sniffed my hand, then slowly floated toward the window and disappeared from sight.

I smirked. The spooky little feline would learn real quick that I wasn't the kind of vet to be intimidated by a set of claws, even if they were the size and shape of scythes.

I straightened myself, trying not to look at the cheesecake Grace had stabbed with a fork. "Anyway, as for the date. I asked Dezmond back to my place."

Grace tried to fork a piece of cheesecake into her mouth and missed. "And let me guess, things got steamy and shadowy *really* fast?"

I let out a sigh. "No. Our evening in didn't go as planned. Francine threw such a fit at the clinic that I had to take her and the mystery egg home. I'm still trying to digest what hatched out of it."

"Well? What was it?"

My breath caught before I answered. "A baby dragon."

Grace's mouth dropped open. "A *dragon*? Wow, I want to see it! And I get dibs on naming it! A familiar's name is so important! It holds all kinds of power when it comes to tapping into their earth magic!"

"Grace, this is a *dragon*, not a familiar," I corrected her. "It's not a common-day species that possesses earthly magic. I'm fairly certain that dragons don't only wield earth magic—they are connected to the elements."

"Elements, like water, air, and fire?"

I nodded.

"Speaking of dragons, I started taking this hot yoga class a couple of weeks ago. And holy shit! I've lost five pounds in two weeks!"

I rolled my eyes. "Like you needed to lose any weight to begin with."

She grabbed my hand. "The class is literally called *The Dragon's Breath*. It's a real workout. The instructor is really hardcore. You should come! You know we're going to have to get into shape before the wedding. We can both sweat off a few pounds!"

I glanced down at my scrubs. The rolls on my stomach weren't getting any smaller. Grace was right. If I was going to be the witch of honor, I wanted to lose a few pounds, especially if Dezmond was going to be the best demon.

# 14

# Dezmond

I'd gone to bed butt-ass naked and awoke in damp, sweaty sheets. *Fuck* this heat wave. I needed to shower and set my mind straight.

I turned on the tap and did a quick rinse in cold water. When the spray hit my head, it didn't trickle down my face like it usually did. My fingers ran through something that felt thick and wiry. . .

Panicked, I jumped out and gave myself a good look in the mirror. *No fucking way.* For the first time since my balls dropped, I ran my fingers through a thick bunch of actual *hair* that sprouted atop my head. It was strikingly similar to my father's reddish-brown color. But it was coarse and thick, the kind that women loved to stroke their fingers through.

I spiked the ends, making it stand up. "Holy fucking shit. This is awesome!" I had absolutely no idea how to tame it, let alone style it.

"*I didn't recognize you,*" Jawz said as he filled my head with the sound of his clashing teeth. "*You're a totally new demon. A new head of hair? You're making my mane look tame.*"

A shadow manifested in the mirror. Its reflection accompanied my inner shadow wolf, and the sound of his nose as it worked huffily into my ear. "*What's with the new hairdo?*"

Pawz's claws clicked across my mind as he also inspected me. "*The dragon must be responsible for this new appearance of yours.*"

Once I toweled off, I tugged on a pair of old jeans and a black T-shirt, then walked out into the main room. The cat bed at the base of my drum set was empty.

"Hey, Torchie? Where did you go?"

My drumsticks were all still there, and they weren't blackened like I thought they might be.

A bubble floated through the air, hovering in front of my face. When it popped, I almost puked. I grabbed my mouth and nose with my hand, saving myself from the putrid fumes.

My eyes watered from what had to be a gaseous explosion. More bubbles drifted in front of me. I followed them to the place where they were erupting from—Torchie.

The little dragon was laying on his side in the corner, tail curled, and mouth splayed open.

I bent down and picked him up. "Oh no, you sick little dude?"

My hair color matched the color of the scales on his shoulders. That was strange. It had only been a day since the little flamethrower had hatched, and he was already maturing?

Flames no longer erupted from his mouth, but a gurgling sound that resembled a belch. I fanned my face with my free hand as noxious fumes erupted from his mouth.

"Man, we need to get you some antacids or something. Don't worry. I know just the vet who can help you out!"

My apartment desperately needed to air out. And so did my hair. A wild idea crossed my mind as I grabbed my leather jacket. "Wanna go for a bike ride?"

Torchie was in no state to answer. If he did, I was certain that he would create some kind of explosion. I wanted to find Victoria. Maybe she could help him. She'd helped me. And the little fucker had gone and torched my phone, so texting or calling her was out of the question.

I set him in the cat bed as I tugged on my black biker boots and my leather jacket. I was half tempted to get a tiny helmet and fasten it to his head. I grabbed a backpack and tucked him inside. He curled at the bottom and poked his spiky head out. I slung the pack onto my back and walked out of my apartment to find my Harley parked on the street.

I slung my leg over the seat and gripped the handlebars. The engine revved to life. "Okay, Torchie. Here we go!"

As I gripped the throttle, my bike burst forward.

Torchie's claws dug into my back as we drove out onto the road. *Fuck*. The little devil was going to leave me some scars before the ride was over. As we picked up speed, the weather began to change. In a matter of seconds, storm clouds loomed overhead, building out of nowhere into something dangerous. A little rain wasn't going to ruin my ride today.

This was the *first* time I'd ever been on my bike and felt the wind in my hair. The sensation was odd. What other changes in my appearance would I experience? Was I reacting to Torchie's magic?

Raindrops pelted my face. As the skies opened, Torchie crawled onto my shoulder and arched his head back. He opened his mouth wide and began to drink.

As he gulped down the rainwater, I started to think. Maybe I didn't need to feed Torchie *food*. Maybe he sustained himself on something else—wind, water, and flames. Like my father had said, dragons formed magical connections with the *elements.*

As I drove toward Victoria's clinic, I slowed my bike. Torchie crawled back into my backpack, where I felt him curl against me. Someone was coming out of The Blooming Mushroom Bakery that I recognized. Victoria's younger sister hopped out of the shop with both her hands teetering with watering cans.

I steered my bike over to her and parked. "Hey, Grace. Have you seen Victoria?"

Grace doused the potted plants with a bunch of water as she glanced up at me. "Oh, yeah, you just missed her! But she was on her lunch break and had to head back to work." Her blue eyes scanned me scrutinizingly. "She said she texted you, but you never answered her."

Guilt twinged in my gut. "That's because my phone had a little accident with a scaly friend who just so happened to hatch out of her attic last night."

Her eyes went wide. "Is it true? You two hatched a *dragon*?"

Torchie let out a liquid belch from my backpack. I thumped my chest, acting like it had erupted out of my mouth. "Yeah, and he has a fiery little personality."

Grace doused the other potted plant with her remaining watering can. “I can’t wait to see him! As for my sister, if you ride quickly, you might be able to catch her before she heads back into the clinic.”

I revved my bike and swept back out onto the road. My heart skipped a beat as I spotted Victoria’s curvy figure.

“Well, if it isn’t the vet witch that I’ve been looking for.”

Victoria slowed her pace and tossed her gorgeous wavy hair over her shoulder as she shot me a death glare. “I don’t know who the fuck you are, but—”

“—Victoria, it’s me.”

She blinked a few times as she tugged down her sunglasses. “*Dezmond*?”

I killed the engine. “Hi. It's been a few hours. Do you still like me?”

“Sorry, I didn’t recognize you. I didn’t know that you rode a bike.” She glanced at my head. “Is it just me, or are you growing *hair*?”

I ran my fingers through the mass. “Yeah, and I have no fucking idea how to style it. Do you like it?”

She closed the gap between us. “I won’t know until I run my fingers through it.”

Her fingers raked over my scalp. I closed my eyes as she filled my body with the most amazing sensation that I knew other men and demons took for granted. One more tug of her nails against my scalp, and I’d be blowing firecrackers off in my pants. . .

“It’s marvelous,” she cooed into my ear. “I’d love to help you style it.”

A bubbly belch erupted out of my backpack as Torchie crawled onto my shoulder.

Victoria took a step back. "You took him on a bike ride?"

I chuckled. "I might need to start calling him Thunder Foot or something. Torchie's personality has completely changed. He no longer spews flames, but summons thunderstorms. On my drive over here, he drank at least a gallon of rainwater."

"Torchie? Is that his name now?"

As soon as I said his name, Torchie leapt into the air. Two membranous wings unfolded from his shoulders. With a *swooping* sound and a fiery belch, he swept skyward.

Victoria and I watched him do a few circles overhead, before he took off up the road.

"Um, when the hell did he learn how to fly?" she stammered.

"Just now," I answered, just as amazed at how quickly my little scaly dude was maturing. "Welp, I guess there's no option other than to go chase him down!" I reached out my hand. "Why don't you hop on and help me catch a baby dragon?"

"I've never done this before. I'm more of a Jeep girlie."

"Grab me around the center and squeeze those pretty thighs tight. We're going for a ride."

She climbed onto my bike and scooted herself close to me. The second I felt her grip my sides, my crotch was as hard as a rock. I revved the engine and took off up the street. As annoying as the little dragon had been, I had a good feeling about how he might bring out the wild side in me.

# 15

# Victoria

My entire body vibrated against Dezmond's hard back as he revved his bike and took us up the road. I had no idea where he was taking me, but I didn't really care. This was the most fun I'd had in a *long* fucking time. Who cared if I didn't make it back to the clinic for my last few patients. The interns owed me for abandoning ship the week before during the heatwave.

I gripped my arms tighter around his center. His body felt so sturdy and solid. I couldn't wait to see what he looked like under the layers of black leather. The engine was too loud and the wind too fierce for us to hold a conversation, but I was fine with that. I had a new boyfriend, didn't I? Someone I felt safe with—someone who also provided me with a wild sense of adventure.

Paved road became gravel as we left Midhaven. Groves of trees blocked off fields that were full of barley and wheat. Seeing the town transition to country somehow reminded me just how easily I'd taken for granted the simple things. I'd been a workaholic my entire adult life. I was turning thirty-six in August, and it felt like I'd plateaued in so many different areas of my life. Taking a spontaneous bike ride into the country with my hot demon boyfriend was exactly what my soul needed.

The bike sputtered as Dezmond lowered speed. We rolled to a halt in a small field surrounded by a massive grove of willow trees. An industrial brick building loomed ahead.

Dezmond killed the engine. "I saw him go flying inside the old warehouse."

I nearly toppled off the bike as he hopped off first.

He caught me as my legs gave out.

I fell into his arms, suddenly aware of how much fun I was having. I was *infatuated* with this demon. Dezmond was rough around the edges, but soft enough to take my comfort into consideration. He was ready to spring into adventure at a moment's notice—something Ben was never really comfortable experimenting with.

"How was the ride? Did you enjoy it?" he asked as he grabbed my hips.

"Entirely too much fun," I breathed. The scent of leather and his sweet minty musk had me dizzy again. I straightened myself, laughing as I noticed how wild his hair had become. I grabbed a handful of it and twisted the ends.

"Careful, you're going to spoil me with all of that caressing," he grunted.

"I take it you're not used to having your hair played with?"

He leaned forward, pinning me against his bike. His green eyes found mine, wildness flickering in them. "There are a lot of things I've done and experienced. But there are a few special things I only want to experience with you, Victoria."

His words sounded like a love song in my head. I straightened the collar on his jacket. "Careful, I just might take you up on that. By the way, how are you holding up without the Wild Card? Are your shadow beasts bugging you?"

"Actually, no. Ever since the little scaly dude hatched, they've been taking a position in the back of my mind."

"In other words, they've been less, *wild*?"

"Exactly," he replied, the dangerous look returning to his face. "And I'd be stupid to ignore the fact that I've been having a difficult time taming myself around you." He brushed his stubble across my forehead, where he planted a kiss. "So, are we a thing? I'd like us to be."

"You mean, are we dating exclusively?"

His eyes lit up. "Yeah, whatever they call it. I just want to make sure I don't go diving in horns first, only to find out that you've got someone else on the side."

My heart thundered. Did he really think I had some side thing going on with another man? The idea, while outlandish, was completely flattering. But that part of me that wanted to remain soft and vulnerable with him hardened. I'd been sweet-talked into this kind of situation before. Ben had a degree in zookeeping, and I had fallen head over heels because he had worked with rhinos and giraffes in Africa—big game I only dreamed of exploring one day.

I leveled my gaze with his. "I told you the truth about my dating life. It's been a very hot minute since I've been with anyone. And so far, I'm very fond of this summer thing we've got going on."

A look of relief came over his face. "That's good. I've been scared that I came on too quick. Look, I have a tendency to do that. Ask any of my brothers. I'm really good at going fast, but not slow. And with the summer heat and all, I had a feeling I was coming on with too much force."

My body heated. "We've already had this discussion. Who says I want a slowburn romance with you?"

His mouth quirked in the way I adored. His canines looked longer than before. "I'm okay with however fast you want us to go. But I'm warning you. Once I let one of my beasts escape my shadows, it's a little difficult to stay in control."

*Beasts* and *shadows* jumbled in my brain, creating an entirely erotic image that I desperately wanted to explore. I ran my finger along his jaw. "You're speaking to a witch who has spent a lot of working hours taking care of difficult creatures. I think I can handle them."

Dezmond's nostrils flared. "Somehow, I feel like the beast trying to shift out of me isn't like others I've experienced before. I've only started to feel his claws ever since you healed my arm."

A rustling sound from the trees made us jump.

He released my hips, and we both spun to face the warehouse. "Speaking of my arm, this is the exact spot where I injured it." He pointed across the space. "And that pipe over there? That's what brought you and I together to begin with." His jaw hardened as he glanced at me. "Do you think it was fate?"

"You mean fate, as in how we met each other?"

He held out his hand. "I guess that depends if you believe in the kind of fate I do or not."

I took his hand, relishing in his callused warmth. "Where are we going?"

"I think Torchie went this way."

In the whirlwind of the bike, Dezmond's body, and how quickly our attraction seemed to ignite, I had completely forgotten about the dragon.

We walked together into the warehouse. Broken glass crunched under my sneakers as we entered the doorway. The room was full of old rusted machinery.

"No wonder you got hurt in this place. It's just tetanus waiting to happen," I said as we continued inside.

His skin began to change in texture. What was no longer callused became leathery.

I released his hand and took a step back. "Dezmond, something is happening to you."

He glanced down at his feet. "Why am I shifting?"

His back arched. An angry groan erupted from his mouth. Fur jutted out of the collar of his biker jacket, until his body ripped out of it.

Shadows burst out of his sides, snarling and snapping at the air as they coiled around him.

Suddenly, a very large and hairy creature towered over me. A snarling muzzle curled, nostrils flaring. A pair of horns curled out from the sides of his head. Green eyes flickered with a wild intensity I had yet to see in Dezmond Ravenblood—an intensity that was both dangerous and enthralling.

# 16

# Dezmond

Victoria's aura burst in front of me like a fiery inferno. It thrashed and crackled, burning holes deep into my brain. I wasn't thinking straight. I wasn't right. The hunger I felt for her was wild and primal, rolling in my gut like a tsunami.

Instinct told me to reach for her flames and devour them before the inferno consumed me, while another voice growled, "*Tame your wildness, Demon. You could hurt your mate.*"

*Mate...*

"Dezmond, can you hear me?" Victoria asked.

Her voice shattered against my skull, breaking like waves on the shore. Even her sound worked to awaken something that had long been dormant inside of me. But *her* voice wasn't the only thing thundering in my head. The growling banter between lightning and thunder was so intense, I could barely see straight.

I lowered myself to the ground, setting my massive hands on either side of her. Claws extended. Scaled joints flexed. I inhaled her sweet, intoxicating scent—which only made me want more of her.

Victoria's scent was practically dripping from the rusty machinery that filled the warehouse. Nothing else mattered. I needed her, and her alone. If I couldn't claim her, I'd rip out of my skin.

She took a step away from me. "Dezmond, you look like a creature out of a nightmare. What's happening to you?"

I glanced down at my arms and hands. Both were covered in scales that glistened in the low light of the room. "I don't know. I've never shifted into this form before."

A crashing sound made me jump. I spun around. A massive scaly tail thrashed behind me.

"I'm not a creature, I'm a *monster,*" I stammered. "*Fuck.* How do I change out of this? How do I go back to normal?"

"*You don't change, you transform,*" the thunderous voice from before echoed in my head. "*And there will be no returning to normal.*"

I shook my head. "Do you hear them?"

"Hear who?" Victoria stammered.

"The voices that sound like a thunderstorm?"

She touched my arm. "No, I don't hear voices."

What was left of my pants ripped open as my cock hardened.

*Sweet fucking Hades.* I needed to claim her as my mate, *now.*

A blur of wings flapped in front of my face as a baby dragon descended from the sky. Torchie landed on my shoulder and belched into my face.

The thunderous voices silenced in my head.

I sneezed. Finally, I could see straight again.

My body shrank back down to a reasonable size. I picked up what remained of my shredded jeans and leather jacket and held my clothing in front of my crotch. "Well, I guess we figured out what power the little dude's belches have."

With another watery belch, Torchie spit something out of his mouth. Something hard clattered on the ground.

I bent down and picked up what appeared to be some kind of rune. A brilliant red stone had a symbol etched into it—a symbol I recognized from the Wild Card. The symbol was the inspiration for my tattoo—a *dragon egg.*

As I squeezed the stone, the tears in my leather jacket mended themselves. And the holes in my jeans from before were no longer present. Did this symbol hold some kind of magical power?

Victoria's mouth dropped open. "Are you seeing what I'm seeing?"

"The dragon egg from the Wild Card?"

She grabbed my hand. "I think we need to go find my mother. She borrowed the deck of cards from me. If there is anyone who can give us some context about the magic behind this strange symbol, it's her."

I handed her the stone.

Victoria quickly tucked it away into her bra and winked at me. "I promise I'll keep it safe until we get to my mother's place."

With a flap of his wings, Torchie swept upward and flew out of the warehouse. "*Follow your mate's advice.*"

I pushed my finger into my ear. Did that deep thundery voice come from him?

The moment I pulled my bike up in front of Cindy's home, Victoria hopped off the back and darted up the walkway. She was a witch on a mission, making it half-way up the path by the time I killed the engine.

After I parked my bike, I followed the path she took toward the back. The side gate was already open. A giggling sound erupted from the backyard.

Panic struck me. I knew that Victoria was aware that our parents were dating, but I didn't think she had actually met my father yet. What if she caught him in the middle of one of his off-color jokes? What if he wasn't wearing his clothes, and we walked into some kind of backyard flirting that would leave me scarred forever? Judging by Cindy's elated sounds, my father was obviously doing something with Victoria's mother I really didn't want to walk into unannounced.

When I rounded the corner, Cindy's magical garden appeared. Only this time, the cauldron where she brewed her tea wasn't quiet. Green bubbles popped in the air before they disappeared into the branches of the oak tree.

My father sat in a chair like he normally did when he was enjoying Cindy's tea.

Victoria stopped a few paces before Dad and tossed her dark hair over her shoulder. "Hello, you must be Eugene?"

Dad glanced up just as I stopped at her side. "And you must be the vet witch who patched up my son?"

I grabbed Victoria's hand. "Pops, this is Victoria, Cindy's eldest daughter."

"I know," he said as he glanced up from his teacup at me. "I was the one who encouraged you to go to her vet clinic, remember?"

Victoria pulled her hand away from mine and folded her arms as she shot me a flirtatious smirk. "Ah, this makes better sense now. Maybe *fate* was really just your father trying to set us up?"

My stomach swooped at her statement. I really hoped that she wouldn't write off what we had going because my father encouraged me to pursue her medical treatment. At the time, I thought the idea was crazy. But after what we'd experienced together, I wouldn't change a *thing*.

"Victoria, is that you?" Cindy asked as she appeared from behind a rose bush that had so many flowers on it, I was sure it had to be bewitched. Dad had warned me that Cindy possessed some unique magical *talents* when it came to her gardening.

"Hi, Mom," Victoria answered. "It looks like you are brewing up a fresh batch of solstice tea?"

Cindy's lips pursed into a flirtatious smile similar to what Victoria had made at me. "It's that time of year when the heat of summer does spectacular things to a witch's herbal remedies!"

I felt a certain energy erupt out of Victoria's aura. In fact, ever since I'd gone beast mode, I could feel these strange tugs and pulls spilling off her. Were these magical surges related to her emotions? If so, why was I now starting to experience them?

"*Because she is your mate, and you will learn to worship her emotions as though they were your own*," the thunderous voice echoed in my head again.

I jolted, not thinking, and swung my arm out, knocking one of the teacups into the air. It shattered against the trunk of the tree, sending yellow and orange sparks everywhere.

"Zeddy, are you okay? You look a bit rattled," Dad said, concern ringing in his voice.

Cindy set another teacup onto the table beside my father. "Not to worry, Dezmond. I have plenty of teacups to spare. Would you and Victoria like some summer solstice tea?"

"Mom, if you've brewed that tea like you have in the past, I'm pretty sure you need to give everyone a warning before you give it to them."

Dad squinted at me. "Son, am I hallucinating? What's growing on your head?"

I grabbed my hair with my fingers and spiked the ends. "Yeah, I don't really know what to say about this. Woke up this morning, and I had a whole head full of the stuff you, Krim, and Amon all take for granted."

Dad stood up and handed Cindy his cup of tea. "Okay, that might be a wee bit concerning. What other bits of your anatomy have changed?"

The seductive glance I received from Victoria was enough to set my hair on end. She'd seen the monstrous male parts from this wild new creature I'd shifted into.

A belch erupted so loudly from the trees, that I first thought I was hearing thunder. "I'm pretty sure I'm going to start calling him Belchie instead," I said as the baby dragon flapped his wings and dropped down from the sky. He perched atop the rim of the bubbling cauldron, his vibrant yellow eyes shifting to us.

Dad jolted so violently that he fell backward into his chair. "Are you kidding me? Is that a *real* dragon?"

"Everyone, this is Torchie," I said as though he was my prized mythical creature pet.

Torchie didn't seem to care that we were all staring at him. He was too busy trying to gobble down the purple bubbles that erupted out of the cauldron.

Cindy clapped her hands together. "Isn't he just adorable!"

I ran my fingers through my hair. "Long story short, Victoria and I chased the little dude down after he took flight. He took us back to the warehouse where I injured my arm."

Victoria reached into her bra and tugged out the stone Torchie had unearthed. "Mom, Dezmond and I found this stone at the warehouse. Look at the symbol and tell me what you think?"

When Cindy took the rune, sparks shot out of her fingertips, encasing the stone and making it burn bright like a piece of coal. "My word. This looks like the symbolism on the Wild Card."

"That's exactly what I thought you might say. Do you have the deck of cards I let you borrow?" Victoria asked as Cindy handed the stone to my father.

"I do," Cindy replied. " However, only your aunts know the true symbolism behind the Wild Card. It's the one card in the Three Magics Oracle Deck that gives all the other cards their magic."

Dad took the stone, but his attention was completely honed on Victoria's mother. I could already tell that my father didn't want to share Cindy with her sisters.

"Cindy, I have a question," I asked as I gave my father a swift slap on the back so he didn't look like a jealous buffoon. "Does the Wild Card give the other cards their magic, or does it awaken magic inside of them?"

Cindy's brows rose into her mossy bangs. "That's a great question. I honestly don't know how to answer that, but my sisters might know. Why do you ask?"

I shrugged. "Just curious," I replied, feeling the claws, jaws, and nose of my inner shadow beasts stirring in my mind.

The cauldron let out a gaseous *hiss*, sending a bunch of bubbles popping into the air. Torchie flapped his little wings, knocking over Cindy's tea kettle.

While Victoria and her mother tended to the tea set, Dad pulled me aside, rune in hand. Purple shadows coiled out of his thick fingers as he held it in his palm. "Zeddy, believe me. This symbol isn't only found in a deck of tarot cards witches play with." His dark eyes narrowed onto me. "This symbol dates back to when the shifter ritual was performed—one that helped to create the three magics."

My stomach knotted. "You never really gave me the details of this ritual. Where did you see this symbol before?"

Dad turned the stone, making the egg symbol dance in the sunlight. "I had access to all kinds of magical symbols and artifacts when I served on the demon council. As for the stone, it's an ancient rune called an elemental stone."

"What are elemental stones used for?" I asked.

Dad glanced over at Torchie, who was swatting bubbles with his tail as Cindy and Victoria gathered up the teacups. "To feed dragons what they crave the most—magical energies created by the elements. These stones can be used to summon dragonic beings directly from the Summoning. Dragons *love* that kind of energy—it's *food* for them. The elements are what sustain a dragon's magic."

"How are these elemental stones created? And who created them?" I asked.

Dad shrugged. "There are all kinds of folktales about how these stones are made, but the truth lies with the dragons themselves. They were the first creatures to emerge from the Summoning, so they hold the origin stories about elemental magic."

I dug my finger into my ear and gave it a twist. "Prior to Torchie finding the stone, I heard a bunch of voices."

"What kind of voices? What did they sound like?" Dad asked.

"If thunder and lightning had a conversation, that would be it," I replied. "They didn't belong to my shadow beasts. Ever since Torchie hatched out of that egg, Pawz, Jawz, and Sniffer have almost gone completely quiet."

Dad glanced up at the sky. "Sounds to me like your shadow beasts might be a bit intimidated by your new dragon. Where there is one, there are others. Dragons don't just show up alone. See, dragons are all about protection, honor, and family. Their bonds extend through generations. And they don't weaken with time—the bonds strengthen. My own father used to tell me that Ravenbloods have some elemental bonds that date back to ancient times, when dragons had their own kingdoms in Ireland."

I sighed. Dad was starting to ramble again. "Back to the ritual, Pops. Can you tell me what the symbol has to do with it?"

Dad handed the stone back to me. "I think it's best that your uncles share the details about the ritual with you. They're two shifters, after all. Which, by the way, I need to discuss Liam and Oscar's plans for visiting."

I swallowed. I'd forgotten that Amon had mentioned my uncles. "What is there to discuss?"

"The fact that they're going to be staying at your place. I want to make a good first impression on Cindy's sisters when they arrive."

My stomach did a flip. Of course my father would pawn off his family on me so he could surround himself with the witch he was wooing, along with her witch sisters. He was such a hound dog.

"When are Uncles Liam and Oscar coming?" I asked.

Dad shrugged. "Whenever the demon council lets them. Too bad they still work for the seven layers of hell. So glad those cruddy days are behind me."

"So, you're basically saying they could both just show up at my place at any time?"

"Yep!" He clapped me heartily on the back. "I gave them your address."

"Lucky me."

"As for the rune, you should take it with you. Keep it close. Its creators are sure to start speaking to you before long."

# 17

# Victoria

As Dezmond and I left my mother's garden, my phone chimed. I tugged it out of my pocket. Lucy had texted me.

**Where have you been? I need to talk with you about wedding venues. Can you meet at the bakery when you get off work today? Grace said she had something for us to sample that isn't pastries.**

I thumbed through the text. Lucy had sent me a list of a *dozen* different wedding venues she wanted to discuss.

**I can be there in ten minutes.**

"Is everything all right?" Dezmond asked as he walked next to me.

"Yeah, just my sister bugging me about wedding prep stuff. I've been a horrible witch of honor."

"Sounds about right. I'm surprised that Amon hasn't started bugging me yet." He stopped to face me. "I'm going to do some research on this rune. I didn't feel like discussing the shifting episode you witnessed at the warehouse with my Pops."

Heat rolled in my belly. I wanted to see *more* of that side of him. I had a lot of questions to ask my sisters about the specific male anatomy of their demons.

I pocketed my phone. "Well, I sort of feel like visiting our parents was not helpful at all. My mother acted like she couldn't help us with the symbolism from the Wild Card until my aunts arrived. What did your father say about the rune?"

"He just rambled on about having its creators talk to me about its purpose before long. Also, he called it an elemental stone."

"Who does he assume the creators are?" I asked, perplexed with the rune's connection with the elements.

He shrugged. "I still don't know if he was pulling my leg, or being serious. But from how he was talking, it sounds like he thinks the creators are dragons."

At Dezmond's words, a belch so unbelievably loud erupted from the backyard, sending the branches of the giant oak tree that grew over my mother's home trembling. Torchie burst into the air, his purple wings flitting like a bat overhead. He did a few circles, flicking his tail, until he promptly found a tree branch to perch upon. His nostrils flared, and burning orange embers singed a few leaves as he gazed at us in a *hurry up, let's go*, sort of way.

Dezmond's brow furrowed as he gazed up at our impatient dragon hatchling. "Wow. He's a dragon on a mission. Sure wish I had the same energy he does." He propped his hands on his hips. "You want to come adventure with me and find out who the creators of this rune are?"

My phone buzzed again. "I'd love to, but I have some wedding prep to tend to as the witch of honor. I'm going to go meet Lucy at the bakery right now."

He chuckled. "I'm sure Amon will be bugging me about being the best demon soon enough." He rummaged in his pocket. "Torchie literally torched my phone, so I can't call you. But could I swing by later on my bike and pick you up?"

My heart leapt. "Sure. Where are we going later?"

His green eyes had that wild look in them again as he tugged out the rune from his pocket. "Wherever this pretty little thing takes us. I know it's a work night for you, so I promise not to throw you into anything that will keep you out too late."

Dezmond's arms were the *only* thing I wanted to throw myself into right now—not another week's worth of patient visits.

"Stop by my house later? I don't plan to chat with my sisters for more than a couple of hours," I said.

He glanced at his bike parked on the street. "Want me to drop you off at the bakery?"

"No, but thanks. The bakery isn't far. I could use the time to stretch my legs."

Torchie let out a sound from the trees he'd not made before—it sounded more like thunder. He flapped his wings, and with a thunderous belch, swept skyward.

I laughed. "Besides, I think your dragon has some ideas on how to help you out."

He grinned. "*Our* dragon. *We* are the ones fostering him."

A chorus of belches echoed from the clouds.

His wide hand gripped my waist. He leaned in and grazed my lips with his. Sparks shot out of my fingertips. His affection caught me off guard. He kissed me tenderly, then roughly, our tongues brushing against one another.

He pulled away too soon. I was weak in the knees all over again for him.

He made his way to his bike. He gripped the handlebars and swung his leg over the seat. "Vet Victoria, mark my words. You're gonna make a wild beast out of me!"

With a rumble of the engine, my demon boyfriend took off up the street. I could have sworn I saw a giant shadowy figure hovering over him that resembled a pair of wings.

As I walked down the street toward the bakery, I thought back to what my mother had said about the Wild Card. I was frustrated that she had to rely on her sisters to help interpret the design.

I wanted to know more about Eugene's beliefs regarding the creators of the rune he called an elemental stone. What was the rune's purpose? And if dragons *did* create it, what was it created for?

Did Torchie know something about the rune that he wanted to share with us?

"*I'm just glad that horrible scaly thing isn't around any longer.*"

I glanced up, spotting my feisty hawk soaring above. "*See? I told you they'd grow back.*"

She fanned her tail feathers at me. "*They are a lot shinier than before, all thanks to your magic.*"

As Francine took off over the trees, I rounded the corner, spotting the Blooming Mushroom Bakery. A crowd of people were scattered around the front door.

Behind the bobbing sun umbrellas, I spotted Grace's polka-dotted mushroom hat.

Her hands flew into the air as she cried, "Come and gather your sample of blooming solstice tea!"

I sighed. Mom had warned me about her and Grace collaborating over their last batch of tea they'd created for the spring equinox. Her green-quilled hedgehog, Goblin, sat on what appeared to be a lemonade stand from which Grace was handing out samples. Only she wasn't selling lemonade—she was handing out little glass jars of tea leaves.

"Why is your green pincushion here?" I asked.

Goblin let out a grouchy little *hiss* before his prickly thoughts entered my mind in his most pompous of British accents, "*I'm making sure nobody takes too much. Cottagecore principle number one! Only take what you need!*"

Meanwhile, Wilma, Goblin's mate, had her five little hoglets busy shuffling through flowerpots stuffed with tea samples. I had to hand it to my youngest sister. Grace sure knew how to put her familiars to work for her.

"There you are," Lucy said as she appeared behind the crowd of customers swarming the tea leaf stand. Her bag was overflowing with books I was sure had to deal with wedding plans.

Grace waved her hand, shooing us away. "Go inside. I'll be right in as soon as we run out!"

Lucy and I walked into the bakery together and found a table by the window. I glanced around the room, remembering back when only a few months ago, the bakery was called Shadow Daddy's bar. Grace hadn't known that Dezmond's brother, and her chemistry teacher at the time, had a secret side passion—*baking.*

"Thanks for meeting with me on such short notice. I have something I wanted to run by you and Grace," Lucy said as she rummaged through her bag of books.

I was too distracted by the spooky little feline sitting next to his demon owner behind the counter. Scythe's ears twitched as Krim tossed a spare piece of dough at his cat, who quickly scarfed it down.

Krim kissed Grace on the cheek as she bustled next to him and worked her magic on the espresso machine. I thought the two were adorable together. Seeing them work so well made me wonder if Dezmond and I would ever put off that kind of vibe as a couple.

While Grace continued to pull shots, Krim made his way over to our table with a platter in his hand. He looked so yummy in his apron. "Grace wanted me to save some of these for you both to try. I hear that we're going to be catering for someone's wedding."

I eyed the *sweetest* looking mushroom cupcakes I'd ever seen—another item I shouldn't be feasting on if I wanted to fit into a bridesmaid dress in a couple of months. At the rate I was going, I'd have to go to this hot yoga class Grace had mentioned just to sweat off the pounds.

Lucy grabbed a cupcake and shoved it into her mouth. I watched enviously as she chewed, then swallowed. "These are exactly the kind of sweets that Crystal is fond of!"

"Who is Crystal?" I asked as my stomach gave a grouchy rumble.

Lucy smiled as she tugged up the sleeves on her cardigan. "I thought you might ask." She reached into her bag and tugged out a book. "Surprise! This is *my* book. *Crystal the Witch* is finally available at the library!"

I grabbed the children's book Lucy had spent the past few years working on. It had been a dream of hers to write her own magical tale about a witch who collected crystals to help others. She'd struggled to find an illustrator who could help capture the whimsical nature of the storyline. Luckily for her, she'd met Amon, whose artistic talent extended beyond that of being a tattoo artist.

Grace walked over to our table and set down our lattes. "Is this the first time you've seen Lucy's children's book, Victoria?"

"It is. I love it!"

Lucy clicked her tongue. "Do you think it's stupid to give wedding guests a copy of Crystal's story as a gift? I mean, I *wrote* it. And Amon's illustrations came to life with the help of his shadow magic."

"No, I don't think that's stupid at all!" I replied as I flipped through the pages. Amon's artwork had really brought Lucy's ideas for the story to life.

Grace sat down next to Lucy and clapped her hands together. "I think it's a marvelous idea for a librarian to do!"

Krim unloaded the remaining cupcakes onto our table. "Where is Dezmond, anyway? He usually flocks to the bakery whenever he catches any scent that we are giving out free samples to taste. Just last week, he devoured an entire cake."

I smirked. "Have you heard the news yet about what your brother and I are fostering?"

"It better not be another ghost cat," Krim grumbled. "I'm about to retire the one I'm currently spoiling."

At his words, Scythe's claws elongated, knocking a few cupcakes off the table.

"Hey, stop that!" Krim scolded his ghost tabby.

As a group of customers approached the front counter, Krim retreated to the register.

Lucy squinted at me. "What is this mysterious creature that you and Dezmond are fostering?"

"Oh, I know!" Grace interrupted. "Can I tell her?"

"She's going to find out eventually," I replied.

Grace cupped her mouth with her hand as she whispered into Lucy's ear.

Lucy's eyes went wide. "You can't be serious—a real dragon? Wow, I want to see it! Where is it now?"

"Dezmond is currently taking care of him. He named him Torchie, because he has a flammable personality," I replied.

"That's so fucking adorable!" Grace said as she took a sip of her latte.

"Dragons are considered to be elemental beings, meaning their magic influences air, water, fire, and earth," Lucy continued.

"Says what, some random book you checked out from the library?" Grace teased.

"Says the librarian witch who saved your ass when a demented mushroom sprite nearly destroyed your greenhouse."

"*You* didn't save my ass, my *magic* did. And by the way, you *did* destroy my greenhouse before those nasty mushroom sprites took over, or have you already forgotten all about the spirit tree incident?"

Lucy smirked. Sparks of magic flicked out of her fingertips as she grabbed one of the mushroom cupcakes.

I waved my hand, dispersing the argumentative magic flaring between my sisters. "Hey, cool off you two. I've had enough hot flashes to last me through the summer. I don't need any more from you."

Grace propped her chin into her hands and beamed at me. "I mean, hasn't it been a dream of yours forever to take care of a dragon? What could be better than having a hot demon boyfriend to help you take care of him?"

My stomach warmed. "By the way, I have a question for the both of you regarding your demons. When Amon or Krim use their shadows, what actually happens?"

My sisters shot each other curious glances.

"You go first," Grace suggested, her cheeks reddening.

Lucy's gaze landed on me. "Every demon is unique. Just like a witch's magic has a unique flare with the goddess, a demon's shadow is his own individual expression." She tapped her fingers together. "Has Dezmond shared his shadows with you yet?"

I wrung my hands. "No, I haven't," I lied, thinking back to the beast I'd encountered at the warehouse. I could still feel the gaze of something ancient and powerful watching me from behind the gorgeous wild green of Dezmond's eyes.

# 18

# Dezmond

The moment I took off up the road, the thunderous voice echoing in my head rumbled so loudly, it drowned out my bike engine.

"*Your father was right about one thing. He knew the origin of the ruin,*" a low, masculine voice boomed into my head. "*But there is absolutely no point in waiting for your uncles to explain the ritual to you. My mate and I will share the details of this ancient rite of passage for shifters, but only if you give us something in return.*"

I ground my jaw. The voice, if it *did* belong to a dragon, just admitted that there was more than *one* of them.

And what was he bargaining with me over? An *ancient rite of passage*?

A second more feminine-sounding voice swept into my mind. "*It shouldn't be a mystery who we are. My mate will sometimes speak over me when he's angry about something.*"

"Are you Torchie's parents?" I asked.

"*Yes,*" a unified growl erupted like a thundercloud in my head. "*Why you gave our son such a horrible name is beyond us.*"

"What are *your* names?" I asked as I took my bike into a higher gear. My knuckles bulged on the steering wheel. Purple scales formed on the back of my hands. Onyx claws extended from my fingers, curling into my palms.

*Fuck.* It was happening, *again.*

"*Give us the rune, and we will reveal our identities to you, but only under one condition. You must swear on your life that you won't allow that shifter Sloane to find our baby.*"

The words *shifter* and *Sloane* jostled in my brain.

My bike jolted. I must have hit a pothole, because my ass flew out of the seat. "What do you know about Sloane?"

"*She has long been trying to harness our magic by capturing our offspring.*"

I gripped my handlebars as tightly as I could without forcing my claws into my palms. "Look, I'm not making any deal with you until you tell me how to tame this new creature that's trying to shift out of me."

"*You are not a normal shifter, Dezmond, son of Eugene Ravenblood. Your demon bloodline originates from dragonshifters,*" the more dominant of the dragons continued. "*Take the rune north to the old grove of willow trees outside of town. You will find more answers when you arrive.*"

As quickly as the thunderous voices came, they swept out of my mind like a great wind as I drove to the edge of town. My tires kicked up dirt as the paved road transitioned to gravel and turned north. Suddenly, I became aware of how naked my back felt. Victoria should be pressed up against me enjoying this ride out into the country fields flowing with golden wheat.

A few miles up the road, I spotted the line of willow trees in the distance. Their branches were long and leafy, swaying in the humid air as I approached. When I parked my bike, everything went quiet. Not a single branch trembled in the breeze. Like the calm before a storm, the atmosphere shifted, dulling to a whisper between dancing leaves.

As I dismounted my bike and walked toward the green and brown mass of the trees, something ancient stared back at me. Its gaze made the scales on my forearms stand on end. My heart trembled to the point I thought it would rip out of my chest.

The entire grove shifted as though alive. Leaves folded over one another, creating the outline of a massive head. Yellows created the eye ridges, and darker greens flared into nostrils.

I took a step back as a dragon manifested. "Wow. For some reason, I thought you'd be real wet and stormy in appearance by the way you talked."

Another pair of nostrils flared next to the first as a second, much smaller dragon manifested beside the other. "*A dragon takes on the form of its natural surroundings. We are beasts of camouflage; our souls forged from the elements. Knowing this about us will help you when it comes time to reveal your true dragonic form.*"

I shook my head, glancing between the two. The feminine voice came from the *larger* dragon?

Foliage flared as the smaller pair of nostrils snorted. Two stumpy forearms flexed beneath the drooping branches. The lack of wings made the male look like an armadillo on steroids, with beefed-up shoulder scales that gave him a hefty amount of bulk. "*We both like our women large and curvy, don't we, Dezmond*?"

The rune flew out of my pocket as the wind gripped my jacket. A willow branch snapped out of the trees, instantly catching it.

A large yellow eye from the female opened feet away from me. It blinked a few times, making the long vertical slit for a pupil dilate as the rune hung before it. "*A dragon's primary focus is to protect those they love. The rune our son retrieved for you was one of many that Sloane has stolen from us.*"

"Why was it at the warehouse? And why is she stealing runes from you?" I asked.

The female's nostrils flared. "*Dezmond Ravenblood, you are no normal shifter. You are a dragon shifter. You should begin to treat your shadows as though they are one with us.*"

My mind blanked. *Me*? *A dragon shifter*?

The rune came flying toward me, whistling as it went.

I caught it, gripping my clawed fingers around its now pulsing symbol. A heartbeat transferred from the symbol of the egg to my hand. As the rune twisted in my palm, I realized the heartbeat wasn't one, but *two* oscillating rhythms that danced with each other. "What makes a dragon shifter so unique?"

Two massive clawed feet appeared on the tree roots before me as the female spoke again, "*Demons who are dragon shifters possess shadows that house a unique ability—to channel the elemental magic wielded by dragons. Only when a dragon shifter bonds with his mate will the power of those elements be released as wild magic.*"

"*Wild* magic, huh? So if I bond with my mate, then how does this wild magic help you?"

"*The bond between a dragon shifter and his mate opens portals between our world and yours. These portals are what keep the three magics healthy. Without the ritual, the magics practiced by demons, familiars, and witches crumble. Without the ritual, the wild nature of the three magics is powerless.*"

I tried to think of how this *portal between worlds* could benefit me at all. Sure, I'd get to help out the dragons, but what would that mean for Victoria?

Branches twisted in the breeze. "*As we've said many times before, Victoria Crow is the witch you must claim as your mate. Having our offspring hatch in the nest of her familiar was the first part of your initiation with performing the ritual.*"

"Wait a minute, you both *planned* all of this? What kind of initiation are you talking about?"

The breeze shifted in the willows as the great yellow eye from the female flashed red. "*The ritual has long been part of you, Dezmond Ravenblood. My mate and I need you to cooperate with us.*"

I folded my arms in front of my chest. "I take it that I'm not the *first* dragon shifter you've tried to convince to bond with a witch before? What's in it for me if I agree to help you two out?"

"*Willow, he's not going to buy this. You need to speak with more force,*" the male said to his mate, who hadn't taken her large yellow eye off me. Willow branches coiled around my arms and legs as she inspected me.

"*Willow* is your name?" I asked the female, while the smaller male continued to snort at me. "What do you go by, little stumpy dude?"

The snorts turned into an all-out roar as the male sent a violent bout of wind tossing the branches into my face.

The female nudged her mate with her wing, which did little to silence his temper I was sure could cause an earthquake. "*Regardless of what my mate has to say, you have a choice to make very soon. Choose to work with us, and we will generously reward you.*"

"What happens if I don't?" I asked.

Willow's eyes glassed over. "*You are the last dragon shifter in your bloodline. If you chose not to bond with her, then any and all trace of your shifter magic will vanish. With this, your family will lose its magical connection with the elements.*"

I glanced down at my hands, which were both trembling. "Nothing like putting a demon on the spot."

A hefty snort erupted from the male dragon, who still had yet to give me his name. "*Try spending the past three centuries attempting to find a dragon shifter to help you protect their offspring from other shifters who will do nothing to stop exploiting a dragon's offspring. You do not know true pain until you have lost one of your own hatchlings.*"

Willow's great yellow eye became watery. A giant tear trickled down the branches and splashed onto my arm. My tattoo of a dragon egg burned bright, glowing with the magical intensity of the rune.

Something in my chest hitched. "Wait a second. *Sloane* is responsible for exploiting your dragon eggs?"

"*She and another shifter named Maverick have been working to seal the last mated pair of the Irish Wyverns out of the Summoning for good.*"

"And how the *fuck* do they plan to do that? What is their reasoning behind all of this?"

"*Simple,*" the male grumbled as his stubby little legs stomped in the dirt. "*By finding our offspring and domesticating his magic. By doing this, a shifter can in turn, wield the power of the elements.*"

His words struck a chord deep inside of my soul. I'd felt that wild, untamed force, a creature I had yet to fully understand, attempt to rip out of me. "Why is elemental magic considered to be *wild*?"

"*Our magic is as wild and free as the earth, flames, wind, and the rain,*" Willow answered. "*Trying to tame such powerful natural forces is only destined to lead to magical destruction. Dragon shifters were given the gift of our magic from our ancestors long ago. It's up to you to honor the wild spirit of our ancestors, as well as your own if we are to protect who we love.*"

I closed my eyes, trying not to tear up from watching Willow cry. She and her mate had obviously braved all kinds of heartbreak regarding their family.

Flashes of Victoria tending to my arm played behind my eyelids. I couldn't see any reason *not* to bond with her. The attraction was there, and she was obviously someone who these dragon parents approved of enough to entrust their baby with.

"Let's say I agree to help you two out. How do I actually *bond* with her? I have no idea how this ancient ritual is supposed to play out."

"*Water has a way of telling the truth, even when our hearts refuse to show it,*" Willow answered poetically. "*Victoria has been hiding a secret he rune will help you to reveal. Your bond will emerge from this truth.*"

"*If you do not claim her soon, other wild forces from the Summoning will,*" her mate thundered, sending the rune flying into the air.

I caught it, along with a handful of brilliant golden dragon scales. "What do you want me to do with this?"

Willow's giant yellow eye blinked. "*Take the rune to your mate to initiate the bond. She has something important to share with you.*"

# 19

# Victoria

Three hours and *way* too many sugary treats later, I found my way back home. We'd barely accomplished anything around Lucy's wedding prep. My sisters were both too preoccupied with my discussion about the baby dragon and my assumptions about Dezmond's shadows.

I knew he was a shifter. He'd come to me to treat his wound because he had some powerful demonic beasts locked up inside of him. Apparently, the shadow beasts had a connection with dragons.

In an effort to distract myself, I went out onto the back deck, hopeful that Francine's fledglings would provide me with some entertainment. The sun was already dipping low on the horizon, casting the leaves on the giant oak tree a vibrant orange that reminded me of autumn.

Before I knew it, this summer heat would be transitioning into the cooler, less humid evenings, and I would be bitching less about my bra not fitting right. Maybe by autumn, I would have experienced my *second* mastectomy.

How would I look in a bridesmaid dress without *any* breasts? Would I really feel like a woman if I had to fake my curves by shoving prosthetics into my bra? The idea of that *horrified* me. How could I possibly become anything less than who I was?

I reached into a plastic container where I kept my birdseed and tossed it out into the yard. My backyard was one of the few places I knew of where birds who were both prey animals and those who fed on seed could co-exist. But that was not the truth about cancer.

Cancer cells were unique. They had forgotten how to program their own death. In other words, they didn't know how to die and instead, spread their illness.

As I tossed the birdseed out into the grass, for whatever reason, my eyes began to sting. I couldn't remember the last time I cried about this mess, let alone my own pathetic being.

One of Francine's fledglings fell out of the sky and landed on the birdseed. Clutched in its little talons was a rodent.

"All right. No more dead mice as gifts in my backyard," I said as I continued to pass out the seed to the robins flocking near me. Death was such a necessary part of life. Why couldn't a vet like me, someone who wanted to work with large carnivores who feasted on other living things to survive, understand this?

The afternoon slipped by. As I prepared an easy dinner of spaghetti and tomato sauce, (of course, more carbs I didn't need) I started to wonder if Dezmond was going to come over at all.

A sinking sensation filled my gut. *Abandonment. Rejection. Loneliness.* I hated this *not knowing* stage of our relationship. I didn't know where he wanted to take it. I knew where *I* wanted it to go, but that didn't mean anything if we weren't in agreement.

I tossed a handful of spaghetti into a stock pot of boiling water and withdrew my cutting board from the cupboard. I diced an onion and a few cloves of garlic, then tossed the ingredients into a pot. Once it was simmering in a thin layer of olive oil, I let my thoughts drift to a dark place. Like most of my internal pity parties, I thought about my failed marriage, and the dark void my life became when I discovered that I had breast cancer. . .

Eventually, I became so frustrated, I started to dice up a tomato—something that I ironically *never* added into my tomato sauce.

The knife slipped, and the blade made contact with my thumb.

"Fucking damn it!" I yelled as I drew blood.

"*Nice job.*"

I dropped the knife as a youthful male voice echoed into my head.

I rushed to the sink, instinct taking over to disinfect the cut. As I washed my blood down the drain, a grumbling sound that could have been a laugh filled my ears so loudly, I thought I might go deaf.

A pair of golden eyes gazed back at me from outside my kitchen window. I wrapped my hand in a dish towel and walked out the back door, finding a small purple dragon perched in one of the tree branches. "Torchie? Do you have any idea where Dezmond went?"

"*Dezmond is with my parents. They're not going to let him off the hook so easily. He's a very rare shifter they've been waiting to initiate.*"

"Initiate? Into what? And why are you here?"

Torchie's wings flapped a few times as he flicked his tail toward me. "*To discuss your magical talents and how they will help you bond with him.*"

My mind raced.

*Magical talents*? *Bond*? What did that mean?

Torchie's nostrils flared as he studied me. "*Have you not wondered how Dezmond healed so quickly from your touch*?"

"Not really. I figured that since he was a shifter, that maybe he just healed quicker than most of my patients." I glanced down at my hand. Blood had pooled onto the towel, but the stinging pain was no longer there. Curious to see how much damage I'd done, I peeled back the towel and held out my hand.

The cut that had been there was completely gone. . .

"How is this possible?" I asked.

"*Victoria Crow, you possess a special magical talent. But like your younger sister, Grace, you take on the pain of those who sometimes do not deserve to experience it.*"

I flexed my fingers, which were as good as new. "Yeah, sure. This has to be some kind of magical fluke."

"*Fluke, as in just like how your cancer has returned*?"

I stared at the dragon, startled at how see-through I felt. "How did you know that I was keeping my cancer a secret?"

The little dragon's tail twitched as he let out a plume of smoke from his mouth. "*A witch can never keep secrets from a dragon, especially one who possesses your unique magic.*"

I glanced down at my hand. "This doesn't make any sense. How can I heal so easily on the surface, but not *deeper*? Is this some kind of curse?"

Torchie's eyes flashed. "*Not all illnesses are the same. Your magic has been waiting to truly express itself so that it may be wild, and no longer tame.*"

My skin burned where the cut had been. Something deep and unsettling unwound my magic. I closed my eyes, but the place on my hand where I'd cut myself was still there. Like an X-ray, the cut revealed where it had been. A single red line glowed beneath the skin.

The rumbling sound of a bike engine broke my focus.

I darted through my house and opened the front door. Dezmond stood on the porch. His face was pale, and his hair was sticking straight up.

"Hi, Victoria," he said rather dryly.

"You look like you've seen a ghost."

He took a step toward me, and the scent of asphalt, something woodsy, and mint broke over me. "If ghosts are big and scaly, then yes, I saw *two* of them."

"Torchie was just here. He said that you were meeting with his parents. Is that true?"

His green eyes found mine, a grove of trees reflecting in them. "I sure did. I met them at the edge of town in an old grove of willow trees. Willow is ironically the name of his Mom. I still have no idea what his Pops' name is." He glanced up at the sky. "Where did Torchie go?"

"He was just in my backyard talking to me."

Dezmond's jaw hardened as a growl escaped him. "Little jerk. You mind if we just sit and talk for a bit? I'm beat."

"Of course," I replied. He seemed agitated. "Do you need something to drink? I've got water, beer, wine, or whiskey. Not in any particular order."

He waved his hand dismissively. "No alcohol. Just water with some good old fashioned ice cubes would be great."

Dezmond followed me inside and into my kitchen.

I grabbed the pitcher full of ice water and poured us both a glass. "Did something bad happen?"

He blew out his cheeks as I handed him a glass. "Let's go outside."

I led the way out to my back porch. Torchie had disappeared from where he'd been conversing with me in the tree.

Dezmond slumped down into the porch swing made for two and took a massive swig of his drink.

I sat next to him. "So?"

He gazed up at the sky. "Where do I start? With the fact that I'm a dragon shifter, or that there is this ancient ritual Torchie's parents want me to perform?"

My mind muddied between *dragon shifter* and *ancient rituals*, twisting in my brain like a storm. "Okay, that does sound like a lot. What do you want to dissect first? The fact that you are a dragon shifter, or this ritual?"

His hand came to mine, and I was suddenly swept up into his sweet affection. "Willow said that Sloane is a shifter. Sloane and some other shifter named Maverick have been trying to track down and exploit the magic of baby dragons."

My stomach dropped. "Is that why Sloane was after the egg?"

Dezmond nodded.

I balled my hand into a fist. "How horrible. Why are they doing this?"

"Willow's mate said that if a shifter domesticates a dragon's magic, they can in turn, wield the magical powers dragons are connected to—the *elements.*" He tugged the rune out from his pocket. "To protect their baby, Torchie's parents have been trying to convince a dragon shifter to perform a ritual with his mate."

"Well, who is your mate?"

His green eyes found mine. "Willow said there was only one mate for me. *You*, Victoria." He handed the rune to me.

As soon as I touched the rune, sparks shot out of my fingertips, catching the hummingbird feeder ablaze. The sugar water evaporated, leaving a ring of smoke in my magic's wake. I clutched the rune in my hand, which began to sweat. Everything I'd read in the paranormal romance and romantasy genres surged out of my imagination. *Mated bonds. Fated mates.* Whatever you wanted to call it, bad things happened if they didn't work out. Wars started, or plagues of illnesses were born as a consequence.

A buzzing sound broke my focus.

He reached into his pocket and pulled out a phone.

"New phone?" I asked.

"No, it's an old one I reactivated after Torchie torched my newer one." He gave the screen a quick glance before shoving it back into his pocket. "Looks like my bandmates want to get together for a gig, but they can wait." He bolted up from his seat. "You know what? I'm fucking *roasting.*" He tore his shirt over his head and began to strip.

I stared at him, completely baffled. "What are you doing?"

"Going for a dip."

"Dezmond, wait," I said, following him to the edge of my pool. "I don't know if it's a good idea."

"Why? You got sharks swimming in there?" he asked as he grabbed his belt and undid the buckle. "Why don't you stop undressing me with your eyes and actually help me shed my clothing?"

I folded my arms in front of my chest, keeping the rune in hand. "I think I'll keep watching. I'm enjoying this."

As he undid his jeans, they fell onto my deck. I loved the strip of dark hair that trailed down into his boxers.

He reached for me. Before I could retreat, he hooked me beneath my knees and pulled me into his arms.

"Put me down!" I ordered, slamming my hand into his hard chest.

A chuckle escaped him as he turned toward the pool. "I told you I was going to get you wet."

I screamed as he jumped, taking me with him into the pool. He let go of me as soon as we plunged into the water. I floundered, kicking off the bottom and shook out my hair like a wet dog.

"That's it, I'm going to kick your ass!" I yelled, water spewing out of my mouth as I searched for where he went.

I hated to admit it, but I felt a lot better.

He surfaced, tossing his soaked hair back as he floundered. "Wow, you look good when you are sopping wet," he said, swimming over to where I was preparing to climb out.

"I look like a drowned rat," I said as I reached for the ladder.

His hands gripped my hips, tugging me back against him. "No, you look like the hottest thing I've set eyes on this summer, Vet Victoria."

I spun to face him.

He set his forehead against mine. "You don't need a bikini, love. You're perfect as you are."

As his hand reached up my scrubs, and he worked his calloused thumb over the scarred remains of my left breast, my breath hitched. The taste of salt hit my tongue. It took me a moment to realize tears were streaking down my cheeks.

"Hey, sweetheart. I'm sorry. I didn't mean to be such a jerk. Did I hurt you?"

The rough quiet of his voice combined with his physical tenderness consumed me. "It's not you," I breathed, resting my forehead against his.

"Then why are you crying, love?"

Water dripped off his chin and torso, combining with my tears as they dolloped into the pool. I focused on the ripples, and how the water seemed to show what the sudden flare of my emotions couldn't. "Dezmond, I've been keeping a secret from you."

"It's okay. I can keep a secret."

"No, you don't understand," I said, grabbing his hand. "I think my breast cancer came back."

# 20

# Dezmond

The pain in Victoria's voice struck a deep mournful note in my soul. Maybe Torchie's parents had imprinted on me. Seeing Willow cry that deep, sorrowful tear had ignited something primal that went deeper than my flesh and bones. As the golden mother dragon so eloquently put it—I would experience feelings that I could only understand if I put my *mate first*. Victoria's pain was *my* pain. I would fight for her, no matter what.

Her entire body shuddered as she glanced up at me with teary eyes. "Are you mad?"

I guffawed. "*Mad*? Why would I be?"

She shrugged. "I mean, *I* would be upset if someone I was dating was keeping this kind of health secret from me."

I removed a strand of her sodden hair from her eyes. "First, you need to know something about Dezmond Ravenblood. I'm not gonna just abandon you because you have some illness that you have no control over."

She buried her face into my neck and sobbed. "I don't know what I'm going to do."

"You said that you *think* the cancer came back. Do you know for sure?"

She trembled. "I've been putting off going to the cancer clinic. They want to do tests to confirm if it spread to my right breast or not."

"Hey, it's okay. We will figure this out," I choked out, overcome with her sudden vulnerability. I wanted her to know how much I truly cared about her.

I tucked my finger beneath her chin and lifted her gaze to me. "You want to know what's funny? Torchie's momma dragon told me that you were keeping a secret from me. She said that water would likely be the element that helped reveal—wait a second." I glanced down at the light beaming up from the water. "Is something glowing?"

"Shit, I must have dropped the rune," Victoria observed as she separated from me.

"Be right back," I said as I sucked in a breath and dipped beneath the surface.

As I dove, a low, rumbling voice filled my ears through the bubbles. "*Born from water, our magic grows. Water is the element of wisdom. Water always knows the truth, even when the mouth is too afraid to speak it. Water is the truth our hearts sing with.*"

Golden light emanated from the bottom of the pool. When I grabbed the rune, bubbles exploded into my face. A scaled creature emerged, nostrils flaring, and a forked tongue thrashed out of its mouth. Sapphire blue eyes blinked at me.

The look in its eyes was completely wild. Waves crashed around the irises, spiraling like building storm clouds.

I choked, then surfaced, coughing as I broke into the air.

"Dezmond, are you okay?" Victoria said as she swam over to where I sputtered out the pool water.

"Yeah, never been better," I wheezed, squinting at the rune, wondering if the gorgeous blue dragon was still swimming beneath the water.

She squinted at it. "Hey, the rune no longer shows the symbol of an egg."

I glanced at my forearm "Neither does my tattoo. . ."

"Wha-t-t do-o-o-es tha-a-at me-e-ean?"

"Victoria, are you cold?"

She shivered. "Ye-e-e-ah."

I clutched the rune in one hand and climbed the ladder, then turned to help her up. "Let's get you into some dry clothes and get you warmed up."

We walked back into her home. Victoria turned her back to me and tore her sodden scrubs over her head.

*Fuck. . .*

Just watching her undress got me hard all over again.

She grabbed a blanket from her sofa and wrapped it around herself.

I grabbed another blanket and wrapped it around my boxers, which felt like they were going to rip in half.

She turned to face me, her hair dripping down her chest, where her lacy red bra was still in place. “Do you think the symbol changing is part of the ritual Torchie’s parents wanted us to partake in?”

I held the rune next to the tattoo on my forearm, which had the same liquid spiral that had replaced the egg. “I don’t see why not. The wild magic they mentioned is only mastered if a shifter bonds with his mate.”

She bit her bottom lip, which I desperately wanted to press my own lips to.

My stomach gave a horrible grumble, so I tucked myself into the blanket and made my way toward the kitchen. If I was going to blow her mind in the bedroom, I needed to satiate my appetite first. “You know what? I’m starved. Why don’t we eat whatever it is you’ve got cooking inside and discuss what’s been troubling you?”

She readjusted her bra as she tightened the blanket around her. “Stuffing our faces with pasta sounds like a marvelous way to warm up.” She made her way over to the stove, where the aroma of something tomatoey popped in a giant stock pot. “It’s nothing much. I’ve been craving carbs lately.

Her words struck a chord deep in my chest. My emotions felt liquid, malleable like the water we’d flirted in.

*Water is the truth our hearts sing with.*

The scent of her tears and the pool water mixed in my nostrils, combining with the sweet tang of her tomato sauce. “I’m sure we just need some food. I don’t know about you, but I’m worthless on an empty stomach.”

My cock twitched as she reached for a ladle, accidentally bumping into my front. Thank the darkness my shadow beasts weren't here, or they'd be pouncing on her. I opened up a few of her cabinets and grabbed a couple of plates.

She rummaged through a silverware drawer. "Grace warned me that you had a healthy appetite. I'm starting to see that she wasn't lying."

I chuckled. "Krim's gonna have to bake a whole lot of pastries for this wedding if he's going to keep my ravenous belly from rumbling during the best demon speech."

"Have you thought yet about what you are going to say?"

"Nope. I'm more of a spontaneous kind of guy." I grabbed one of the plates and served her a heaping portion of pasta and ladled on a bunch of tomato sauce. "How about you? Any idea about what you wanna say about the lucky couple?"

Victoria grabbed her plate. "Just how lucky Amon is to have you as a brother."

Her flattery almost made me drop my plate. "Well, your sisters sure are lucky to have you as their eldest."

I walked over to the kitchen table and set down her plate. She sat down across from me.

I spun my fork into my pasta, waiting for her to take the first bite. "Well? Now that your cancer is out in the open, do you feel better at all?"

She twisted her fork into her food, smearing the tomato sauce. "I do, oddly. I thought that if I told someone, I'd feel worse. I did the first time around. It felt like I'd never get through it."

"But you *did* get through it," I countered.

She stared down at her food. "Who says I will again?"

I got up from my spot, dragged my chair to where she sat, and promptly flopped down next to her.

She kept her focus on her plate as more tears dripped down her cheeks.

"Hey, look at me," I said, grabbing her free hand.

She let go of her fork and smudged her mascara. "Dezmond, I can't go through this again."

"You *can* go through this. I'm here *with* you."

"You don't understand. Battling cancer isn't something that you do with someone else. It hurts those around you just as badly as it does yourself."

"I'm so confused."

She glanced sideways at me pitifully. "I've been married before."

I shrugged. "*So*?"

"So, having cancer *ruined* my marriage. Ben and I fell apart shortly after he learned I had breast cancer."

A burning bundle of rage gnawed at my core. "All right, so Ben was an asshole. Do I give off the same vibes as this ex-husband of yours who obviously didn't know his own ass from his face?"

The corners of her mouth turned up into the first smile I'd seen on her all day. "No."

I chuckled. "Good. Now, the next step is telling your family."

Her shoulders seized. "I can't."

"Yes you can. You *need* to. I know your Mom and sisters all care about you. I can be there with you if that would make you feel better."

She squeezed my hand back. "Thank you. I'll consider it."

I grabbed my plate and tugged it over to where I sat. "Now, let's taste this amazing pasta so I can tell you what I learned from Torchie's parents about the ritual."

Speaking of Torchie. The little dude was perched outside on a tree branch, gazing through the window like we were a soap opera. I turned my back to him and refocused my attention on Victoria.

As I shoved the forkful of her pasta and tomato sauce into my mouth, I closed my eyes and thought back to the other day at her clinic. The scent of her arousal flooded my memory as I savored the tang of tomato against my tongue.

I dropped my fork, where it clattered onto my plate. The scales I'd seen appear on my forearms at the warehouse were appearing on my wrists again. My back felt prickly. And my forearms began to change. The fresh ink Amon had given me started to brighten as scales morphed into waves. My body began to shift, but I wasn't turning into the beasts I'd experienced. I wasn't a wolf, or a bear, or a lion.

I was shifting into a creature I'd never transformed into before—a *dragon.*

Victoria shrank as my body elongated to the point that I towered over her. I winced as my head jostled. Drywall dust confirmed that my head had made contact with the ceiling.

"Dezmond, what's causing this?" she asked, and her voice echoed so sweetly into my ears that I thought my head might explode with her intoxicating sound.

"I don't know," I growled, my voice taking on the monstrous tone it had in the warehouse.

A chair clattered onto the ground as my tail swept behind me. I lowered myself onto all fours, desperate *not* to destroy her home. "Last time this happened, Torchie found the rune and helped me to change back."

She cupped my face with her hands. "I don't *want* you to change back."

What remained of my pants was instantly gone as my beast-parts hardened.

Her fingers ran along my jaw, finding a sensitive spot behind my ears.

A whimper escaped me as she caressed my scales.

"Oh, I found the spot," she giggled. "What feels better? This, or how about, *here*?"

The more she moved those fingers, the less I could control the thrashing of my tail. She scratched behind my ears making me shiver. Was this part of the ritual? If so, was it normal to want to rip out of your skin and devour your mate in the process?

I set both of my hands on the ground beside her and inhaled her sweet, intoxicating scent. "The only thing I really want to eat right now is you, Victoria."

She grabbed my massive clawed hand and took me into the living room. When we reached the sofa, she stopped to face me. "Undress me, and this time do it with your claws."

She turned her back to me.

*Big* mistake.

All I could do was focus on her gorgeous hips and ass as she tugged at one of her bra straps. My claws made quick work of her shorts, tugging them down and ripping through her lacy black thong. "Bend over for me, my wicked thing."

Victoria propped her elbows onto the armrest of her sofa. "Please, I need you to *fuck* me."

I lowered myself to my scaly knees. She let out a moan as I flicked my forked tongue between her legs. *Sweet fucking shadow beasts.* I needed to feast on her, to make her my mate.

I grabbed her thighs. "I'm going to kiss, worship, and mark every square inch of your body. And after that, I'm going to memorize every curve, dip, and scar on your skin with my tongue."

"Dezmond, you're going to, ah—"

Her sounds became a chorus of pleas for me to make her mine. I sucked her center, rolling my tongue over the sensitive bundle of nerves as she reeled from the pleasure.

With each thrash of my tongue against her pussy, an ancient desire stirred deep in my soul. I needed to bury myself deep inside of her. I needed to lose control.

My skull felt like it was going to rip in half. Two massive horns branched out of my head, casting Victoria's trembling body into shadow as she erupted into a climax.

# 21

# Victoria

As my heart slowed, and the stars crowding my vision subsided, a giant monstrous shadow consumed my sofa. I collapsed, spent from the way he'd eaten me out from behind. When I spun to face him, Dezmond's beast form came into view. While he was still three times my size, he was no longer the giant scaly creature he'd been before he went down on me.

A dragon skull gazed back at me. Shadows billowed out of its eyes and nasal cavity.

"Dezmond?" I whispered, still woozy from my orgasm.

"Mate," he growled back, sending shadows coiling around me.

My heart fluttered as the creature's dark hollow eyes observed me. Long black fingers caressed my hips as his other hand reached for my belly.

Dezmond's morphology had shifted, *again*. Not only had he changed in size, but in structure as well. His body was no longer covered in grey scales, but in smooth grey skin. His neck and chest were thick with muscle that strung tightly over a wide ribcage. A strip of black hair tugged my eyes south of his naval.

Two *very* erect cocks sprang out of his crotch. His male anatomy reminded me of both a shark, and a snake.

"Dezmond, can you hear me?" I asked louder now that I'd finally caught my breath. Something else was watching me from behind his deep-set eyes.

This creature wasn't Dezmond. But *through* him, it came alive.

A forest reflected in its dark pupils—giant trees with gnarled black trunks and long, swaying leaves. I could hear the sorrowful sound the branches made as they swayed in the breeze.

Why was I seeing a forest full of *willow* trees in the dark gaze of this shadowy creature?

The beast lowered its head to my face. Air swept into its hollow nasal cavity as it scented me. "Witch of the wild, mate with me."

My mind raced. *Witch of the wild*? While the title might have been a pet name, it was fucking hot. I backed onto the sofa, luring the beast on top of me. Its horns seemed to grow as he knelt between my legs.

One of his massive black hands grabbed both of my wrists and pinned them over my head. The other grabbed my throat as he teased my entry with the thicker of his two cocks.

My body stretched as he thrust his hips forward, and his velvety thickness plunged into me. I became lost in the sensations as pain and pleasure blurred together.

"Faster," I breathed as undulating muscles made my body bounce. Goddess, how fucking wonderful it would feel to have this monster *break* me.

A long black tongue thrashed out of the skull as he continued to fuck me. I closed my eyes, overcome by this shadow beast's desires. The friction across my clit became too powerful for me to find pleasure any longer. I opened my eyes finding that his second cock was half-way buried into me. A knot of tissue pulsed at its thick base, forcing me to stretch painfully.

"Dezmond. . ."

"Dezmond isn't here anymore," the creature growled. "I'm your one and only mate."

Light flashed in my periphery. The rune sat on the sofa beside me, spewing water into the air. My fingers became saturated as I reached for it.

As soon as I touched the water, the shadow beast released me. His horns shrank as the monster reduced itself to the body of a naked man. He lay sprawled out on the sofa before me. I hadn't seen how cute Dezmond's bare butt was until now. He had a tattoo on one of his ass cheeks of a horned skull.

He lifted his head up, locking his green eyes with me. "Victoria? What happened?"

"We just had some wild, crazy sex. What do you remember?"

He quirked his brow. "Last thing I remember was going down on you and then blacking out." He licked his lips. "Did I at least get you off?"

"Yes, and it was phenomenal."

He crawled over and settled himself behind me. "Then get over here, love bug. I want to cuddle."

I situated myself against his hard muscular body as he tugged a blanket over us.

"You have a scratch on your shoulder. Did I hurt you?"

"No. But fuck, I'm going to be sore tomorrow."

I fell into his arms. Whatever the beastly presence was, it had gone.

As I drifted off to sleep in Dezmond's arms, I closed my eyes. Flashes of the ancient forest lit up behind my eyelids. Willow trees swayed in the wind for as far as I could see. A tall dark creature with a skull for a head gazed back at me from the shadows as it breathed, "*You are my wildness, my mate, Victoria Crow.*"

A loud thumping sound jolted me awake.

"What the hell was that?" Dezmond said as he bolted upright on the sofa.

"Definitely not Francine," I stammered. I grabbed my pink bath robe and stumbled toward the staircase, not thinking. The sound had come from above, but it sounded like it came from *beyond* the attic. Dare I say, my *roof*?

"Brrrrrr! Is it just me, or is it *freezing* in here?" Dezmond said as he tugged on what remained of his shredded jeans and followed me out the back door.

The heat from the day had been sucked away, possibly by the giant scaly beast perched atop my house.

I sucked in a breath, forgetting how to exhale.

*Holy fucking shit.* An actual full-sized *dragon* was gazing down at me.

The sheer mass of the dragon was enough to make my heart stop. Its two front feet were perched over the edge of my roof, which displayed four massive purple claws that curled around the gutters. Onyx scales shimmered with purple iridescence in my porch light. The dragon's head had to be the size of Dezmond's motorcycle. A pair of gorgeous blue eyes lit up, dilating as he lowered his head down to where I stood trembling.

The dragon's nostrils flared as a low, masculine voice echoed into my mind. "*They've definitely bonded. I can smell his magic all over her.*"

"Wow, little stumpy dude! Look at you!" Dezmond said as he brushed up behind me. "You're no longer a scaly armadillo!"

The dragon shook his giant head, sending out a set of membranous frills that made him look even larger. "*What did you think, that I couldn't take to the skies like Willow*?"

I ducked as his brilliant set of onyx wings arched over my oak tree, sending branches tossing and leaves billowing into the air. Another dragon came flying overhead, one that displayed far less mass than the onyx one perched atop my roof.

"Look! Here comes Willow now!" Dezmond cried.

Willow landed with grace in my backyard, barely disturbing the leaves in my tree. Her brilliant golden wings folded across her back and she walked across the grass and stopped beside her mate. She was so large that her head came up to his feet.

"*A scaly armadillo*?" she chuffed heartily as she tipped her snout upward. "*Drake, you must admit, Dezmond has given your earth form quite the nickname.*"

Her witty comment made my insides tremble with laughter.

"Willow, what do you mean, *earth* form?" Dezmond asked.

Willow lowered her giant head, bringing her face inches away from us. "*Right now, Drake and I are in our air forms, which gives us wings and allows us both to fly.*"

I extended my hand toward Willow's nose. "I'm sorry, I'm just so amazed at you, *wow*. Is this really happening?"

She tilted her face, allowing me to see the colorful details of her cheeks and jaw. "*I will never be shy when a witch compliments my scales.*"

The scales around her cheeks shimmered with iridescence, making her look like a giant opal. "Don't get me wrong, your son is awfully cute. But seeing a big mature dragon like you? I can barely fathom this."

Willow blinked, bringing her eyelashes down over my hand. What felt like a thousand dandelion seeds fluttered over my skin.

One of the feather-like structures tickled my nose.

A sneeze erupted out of my mouth, sending her eyelashes scattering.

I gasped, mortified at what I had done. "I am so sorry! I just sneezed away your eyelashes!"

"*Not to worry, they will regrow,*" Willow corrected me as she blinked a few times. Sure enough, a new row of beautiful white lashes sprouted from her eyelids.

Drake lowered his giant head so that his onyx scales offset the golden ones of his mate, making the pair appear like dawn embracing dusk. "*As I'm sure you now know, Dezmond is a dragon shifter. As such, he has the ability to channel the spirit of our ancestor. I will be teaching him to shift in a way that allows you to further enhance your bond with him.*"

"Where is Torchie, anyway?" Dezmond asked as he took my trembling hand. It took all my strength not to reach out and touch Willow's fluttering eyelashes as she made giant doe eyes at me.

"*Doing what all dragons his age should be doing at this time of night—feeding on midnight dew,*" Willow replied.

Drake's giant wing arched upward. Willow mimicked him. Two small stones fell into the grass.

I walked onto my lawn and grabbed one of the stones. Dezmond grabbed the other. "What do you want us to do with these?"

Drake dipped his head. "*These runes represent the two elements other than water—air and fire. You need to unlock the magic inside of them if we are going to defeat Maverick.*"

"And how are we supposed to do that?" I pressed.

Drake snorted as he lowered his wing over his mate. "*Dearest, are you sure these two have what it takes to partake in the ritual?*"

Willow snorted up at him. "*If they do not help us, then our offspring will have no choice other than to surrender his magic to Maverick.*"

Drake flapped both of his wings, creating gusts of wind that tossed the branches of my oak tree as he took off into the night.

Willow followed, creating far less of a gust of wind as she did so. Just as her golden wings disappeared on the horizon, the first rays of sunlight broke overhead. I had so many questions flooding me. I was lost to this ritual that involved dragons, the elements, and an ancient wild magic I still didn't understand.

# 22

# Dezmond

As soon as Willow's golden scales blended like a painting against the pink and orange rays of dawn, I sucked in a deep breath, overcome with emotion. Gooseflesh rippled on my arms and torso. While the shredded tatters of my jeans blew in the humid breeze, I became energized like I hadn't felt in months.

The scent of coffee jostled my focus. Victoria had already retreated into her kitchen and had started to get prepared for the day ahead of us. I glanced through the kitchen window, mesmerized by the yellow sunbeams catching in her dark wavy hair. She moved without hesitation, in her pink bathrobe, cracking eggs into a frying pan.

She glared at me through the window. "Are you going to just stand out there all morning, or are you going to help me serve breakfast?"

I scrambled inside and stopped next to the kitchen table. Her phone buzzed on the counter.

She grabbed it and jabbed her thumbs into the screen. "Apparently it's going to be a rough day at the clinic," she said, her voice frantic. "I'm sorry, but I'm going to have to head in earlier than I usually do. According to Holly, we have a bunch of new familiars coming in."

"Don't you want to discuss everything that Willow and Drake just dropped onto our plate?"

"I do. But can we talk over lunch? I'm about as confused about all of this as I am about our siblings' wedding. Maybe I can convince my mother to let me play with the deck of cards again. I have a feeling that it could be helpful when trying to interpret this ritual."

"Sounds like a plan." I flopped the last of the eggs onto her plate, giving her more than I gave myself. "How can I make it easier for you before you go in? It sounds like a hellish morning to walk into."

Victoria set her phone down. Her dark hair unfurled over her shoulder. "There are a couple of things that keep coming to mind," she said, her eyes dropping to my crotch. "I don't know about you, but I could really use a shower."

Her suggestion bunched my pants. "How does a shower for two sound?"

"Better than eating breakfast," she breathed back.

I set my plate of eggs down, walked over to where she stood, lifted her into my arms, and carried her toward the staircase.

"Put me down!" she ordered, laughing. "There is no way you're carrying my fat ass up there."

"What? You are as light as a feather. And you obviously don't know my strength."

It took me all but a few steps to carry her up to the second floor. I carried her into the bedroom and set her on the edge of her mattress. Her greedy hands worked over my chest and torso. She was *ravenous* for me. The ache in my bones to please her brought me to my knees.

As I lowered myself between her legs, she cupped my face in her hands. "Why are you so generous with me?"

Her question muddled in my brain. Was I being generous? I'd always thought that a guy's goal in the bedroom was to put his mate first.

Maybe Victoria hadn't experienced that. Maybe I had the chance to blow her mind in ways no other male ever had.

I kissed her knee, rubbing my stubble along her skin. "Are we getting wet, or tossing in the sheets?"

"Oh, I'm plenty wet," she laughed.

I slid my hand between her legs, feeling her dampness. The scent of her arousal did wild things to my brain. I took her hand and encouraged her to stand with me. "I need to see you, *all* of you."

Her cheeks flushed at my request. She turned her back to me as she whispered, "undress me."

Confusion befuddled my thoughts. Was she trying to hide her chest?

I peeled off her bathrobe, finding that she was only wearing her bra and panties. My fingers made quick work of the clasp on her blood red bra. Her skin felt so soft beneath my calluses.

My hands dropped to her waist as I buried my face into her thick wavy hair. "You are so beautiful, Victoria. Face me."

Hesitantly, she spun into my arms, so close that our bodies jostled awkwardly. She buried her face in my neck, where a soft whimper escaped her. "Please don't think I'm ugly."

Her words made my body shudder. *Ugly*?

"Sweetheart, why would I ever think that? Look at how perfect you are." I ran my hands down her shoulders as she presented herself to me.

Her chest bore the scars of cancer. Mottled dark skin ran the length of where her left breast had been. Her nipple was gone. The skin was lumpy and uneven where it had tried to heal.

My fingers brushed over her chest as I explored the softness of her flesh. "Don't ever let anyone say that you are less than perfect, my wild goddess."

Her eyes flicked up to me, and the pain swimming in them was replaced with liquid fire. The force of that wild look grabbed my heart and squeezed it tight.

*This is the woman I am falling in love with—a witch who has no idea that she is a goddess.*

"Who do I get to play with today, the beast or the demon?" she whispered as she grabbed my face and stroked my jaw with her thumbs.

I grabbed her around the waist and nuzzled her neck. All it took to make me dizzy was inhaling her intoxicating scent. "I'll let you be the one who decides who you want to tame."

Her fingers threaded through my hair. "I guess that depends on how much of a good boy you are."

What remained of my jeans shredded between us as my cock ripped out of the denim.

A wicked giggle erupted out of her as she grabbed my hard length and began to stroke from the base to the head.

*Sweet fucking wildness.*

"Where is number two?" she asked.

Her question jostled me. "Wait, two *what*?"

She kissed my jaw as she began to fondle my balls. "You don't remember having *two cocks*?"

Her phone buzzed in her bathrobe.

She let out a groan. "*Fuck*! I'm going to be late for work!"

*Late* and *work* didn't register. *Fuck* did. I still had time to please her.

As much as I wanted to get off, I wanted these few precious moments to be about her.

I took her to the bed and pinned her arms over her head. "I don't know if I can be a good boy for you right now. But I sure the fuck am going to make you cry out my name when I'm done devouring you."

She wrapped her legs around me, tugging my erection down toward her sex. "But I need you inside me."

I slid across her slick opening.

*Fuck*.

I released her hands and lowered myself atop her. I raked my teeth over her chest, gently kissing and tasting her body as I lowered myself down to the soft bunch of brown curls and nuzzled the spot.

"Dezmond," she whimpered as I licked the sensitive ball of nerves, "Please, I—"

"—I need to taste you when you come," I growled back at her.

Her phone buzzed again.

I grabbed her bathrobe and tossed it off the bed as I dipped my tongue into her.

*Holy fucking shadows...*

With each moan and growl, I fell deeper into a state of madness. There was nothing else in the world that I'd rather be feasting on. My ribcage ached as the claws of that wild beast threatened to rip out of me.

*No. This is my mate, and I'm not sharing her with you, even if she wants your cock, too.*

As I ate her pussy, I pumped my hand over myself.

"Please, Dezmond. Don't stop!"

Red sparks burst out of her hands as she came undone in my arms. Her ragged breathing filled my ears. Sweet success. I was one step closer to claiming Victoria Crow as mine.

After we spent the next few minutes showering and trying not to throw ourselves into a *round two* of hot, spontaneous sex, another buzzing sound erupted across her bedroom. This time, it came from the pocket of my shredded jeans.

I grabbed my phone. A text from my band mate, Ted.

**Your arm good enough to play this afternoon? We've got a last-minute request over at Paddyshack's Pub.**

**Name the time, and I'll be there.**

Victoria dressed in her bright red scrubs. She clipped up her still-damp hair. "See you tonight?"

I tossed my phone onto her bed and grabbed her hands. "I can't wait. I'll cook us some dinner, and we can spend the evening in together picking up where we wanted to go?"

She kissed my cheek, then my lips. I saw stars as she kissed my nose. "I can't wait to spend the evening being wild with you."

Before I headed to the pub, I swung by my apartment and changed into a new set of clothes. I still couldn't comprehend the male anatomy Victoria had become so ravenous over. What had happened to me last night that I sprung *two* hard ones and hadn't remembered it?

I pocketed the rune Willow had given me, one with the symbol of air inscribed across its mottled surface. I'd kept the rune with the water symbol buried in my jeans, afraid of what might happen if I gazed upon its magical symbol again. Water was such a vulnerable, emotive element, as the thunderous voice had echoed into my head.

*Water is the truth our hearts sing with.*

I gripped my soggy jean pocket. What if I wasn't emotionally supportive as I should be toward Victoria about her breast cancer? What if I didn't prove myself as a mate?

Victoria Crow was ill. I would do everything I could in my power to protect her from this illness that threatened her existence.

A little after eleven, I drove my bike up to Paddyshack's Pub. The moment I parked, the rune Drake had given me vibrated so violently, I thought it might jump out of my pocket. A sudden gust of wind tossed it into the air, which I caught only out of reflex. As soon as I set the rune into my jacket pocket, I spotted my band mates, Ted, and Lonnie. They carried our band equipment out of an old van parked outside the pub.

"Hey, Lonnie," I called after my buddy as I tucked the rune deeper into my pocket.

He dropped my cymbal, where it landed with a loud metallic *crash* onto the ground. "Zed, what the hell is that on your head?"

I ran my fingers through my hair and spiked it. Victoria had put some of her fruity hair product in the strands, making it stiffer than I was used to. "Yeah. It sort of happened the other day."

"Dude. Tell me what supplements you're taking. I'm already thinning up here," Lonnie said as he rubbed his hand through his dark hair.

"Hey, Nematodes!" Ted called from inside the pub. "We're going to set up in here!"

I grabbed the remaining snare drums out of the van and followed Lonnie inside. I maneuvered through the pub and caught sight of a brilliant black bird perched on the top of an old light fixture. A stocky male figure with a long reddish-brown ponytail sat at a table beneath the raven. His back faced me. His shoulders rolled forward as he muttered something under his breath about *winning*.

"Ravenblood, you fold?" a greasy-looking man who sat opposite of him asked.

Dad slammed his hand down onto the table. "I have no other option but to."

He got up from the table and walked away, slinging out a bunch of curse words as he went.

I approached him. "Dad, what the hell are you doing?"

"What does it *look* like I'm doing?" he grumbled.

I surveyed the table, where five other rough and ready-looking guys were busy fumbling with cards as they ended their round.

"So, you give up drinking only to start *gambling* instead?"

"What's a demon supposed to do to pass the time?" Dad argued.

I shrugged. "I don't know, not get addicted to other bad habits?"

Dad made a huffing sound as he rose out of his chair and clapped me on the back. "Walk with me."

I followed him over to the corner of the room, where he propped his elbow onto the bar and gave his competition a stiff look. "Zeddy, if I win this next match, I'm going to buy Cindy a ring."

My stomach dropped. "Wait a second. You're proposing to Victoria's *mother*?"

His eyes dropped greedily to my jacket pocket. "What's this? Another elemental stone?"

I dug the rune out of my pocket.

He swiped it from me.

"Hey!"

Dad made a motion with his hand toward the gambling table. "See that greasy bloke on the end? *He's* the one who's been cheating."

A man wearing a top hat sat opposite the table. One of his eyes wasn't right. It whizzed in the socket, making a horrible whining sound.

Dad tucked my rune into his pocket. "Maverick's his name. The demon council has records of him selling dragon artifacts on the shadow market. I'm going to beat his ass and win this next game."

Lonnie came up behind me and clapped his hand onto my shoulder. "Come on, Zeddy. Let's shred it. We have an hour to warm up for the show tonight."

# 23

# Victoria

The rune Willow had given me vibrated so violently, I thought it would jump out of my pocket. Maybe it was from the hot shifter sex, who knew. But *holy fucking goddess*, I was so turned on, I might have to hose off outside to prevent myself from combusting.

Twice on my drive to work, I had to pull my Jeep over to prevent my magic from short circuiting the engine. Bright red flares of my magic sizzled out of my hands every time I put my foot on the gas or turned a corner.

"*Those are normal occurrences when your mated bond kicks into action,*" a powerful female voice drifted into my mind.

My foot tapped the breaks. "*Willow*? Is that you?"

I scanned the skies, searching for her giant golden wings. Nothing but fluffy white clouds floated above.

Her voice quickly descended upon me. "*You didn't think that I'd give you the rune of flame without giving you a little guidance, now did you?*"

"I'll be honest. I have absolutely no idea what to do with it."

Another hot flash made my magic surge, sending yellow sparks dancing over the dash, through the windshield, and scattering across the hood.

Willow's warm laughter filled my head. "*Drake will be monitoring Dezmond, while I will be watching over you. A word of advice. Don't let any reptiles at your clinic near the rune.*"

I shrugged. "I'll try, but no promises."

The moment I walked into the clinic, Holly bustled over to me with five clipboards in hand. "So glad you are here. Your favorite rainbow serpent is already in room one."

"What did Rosie eat *this* time? I said as I tugged on my stethoscope and grabbed the clipboard from her.

By the time afternoon came around, my plan for the rune had basically fallen off my radar. I had so many patients needing my attention—and not enough interns to meet the demands—that I resorted to double bookings. Rosie had eaten something more obstructive than her usual lampshade. This time, she'd devoured an entire tea kettle, which would take a whole lot of laxatives to help encourage a healthy bowel movement. She was going to have to stay overnight, as it could take some time to pass such a large obstruction.

By the time I found a few moments to catch a break in my office, I noticed five new text messages on my phone. Four were from Grace, telling me the details about the hot yoga class I'd committed to going to this evening.

The fifth was from Dezmond.

I opened his message.

What are you planning on doing with your rune?

**I'm not sure yet, but I'm open to suggestions.**

I'm full of suggestions. I still can't stop thinking about you from last night, and this morning.

**Me neither. I miss you. What are your plans with your rune?**

I have a story to share with you later involving my Pops. I'm playing a gig tonight at Paddyshack's pub. Could you come out and watch me play?

**I've made plans with Grace to attend a yoga class, but I might be able to afterward.**

Holly's head popped into the room. "Hey, so the girls and I are going out for drinks tonight to celebrate the summer solstice. You wanna come with?"

I set my phone down. "I'd love to, but I've already got potentially *two* obligations this evening."

"Oh? Someone's popular. Hot date?"

I glanced at my phone. "Possibly."

"Ohhhhhh! I didn't know you were dating again. Who is he?"

"You know that guy you admitted for the arm wound a few weeks ago?"

Her eyes got real big. "Wasn't his name Dezmond?"

"Don't tell the other interns, but we have a thing going on."

Holly grinned as she reached around the corner and grabbed something. "Well then, that answers who these flowers are from." She handed me a bouquet of vibrant fireburst lilies. The orange and yellow and reds blended beautifully. I grabbed the tag hanging from the neck of the vase.

**To: Victoria, the sweetest vet I know.**

**From: Your boyfriend and the little scaly dude.**

Holly clapped her hands together. "This is great! When can we go on a double date?"

I set the bouquet down onto my desk. "As soon as we get the dragon we are fostering to develop his magic."

Holly's mouth dropped open. "Did you just say, *dragon*?"

"That egg that Francine was going bonkers over? Yeah, it was a dragon allright. It hatched in my attic the night I took it home."

Speaking of Francine. I hadn't heard her flamboyant mother-hen voice echoing in my head as of late. I wondered if she was teaching her fledglings how to hunt for creatures other than mice.

Holly clicked her tongue. "So you have plans with Dezmond. What was the other obligation today?"

"I promised Grace that I'd try out a new hot yoga class with her this evening."

As the day finally came to a close, I grabbed my phone and texted Grace.

**I brought a change of clothes. Do I need to pick you up?**

**No, just meet me there. And make sure you are super hydrated.**

I closed my office and shed my scrubs. Tugging on my tight yoga leggings only verified how ridiculously fat I was.

A purple bruise was visible on my inner thigh. I'd forgotten how rough Dezmond and I had gotten in the shower this morning. I really wanted to skip out on yoga and go see him at the pub. Seeing my muffin top through my leggings wasn't helping my confidence.

I reached into my scrubs, searching for the rune. "Shit. Where is it?"

I checked all my pockets.

*Fuck.* Had I left it in Rosie's room?

Willow had specifically told me *not* to let a reptile get near it.

"*Willow, can you hear me? I have a little problem,*" I asked with my thoughts.

Her voice didn't echo back into my head.

*Great.* Rune or not, I still had to go to a hot yoga class.

When I pulled my Jeep into the parking lot outside the yoga studio, I spotted Grace outside the door with two yoga mats curled under her arm. She looked so cute in her goblin green leggings and red polka dotted top. And of course, she was already barefooted.

I jumped out of my Jeep, nearly tripping on my flip flops.

I followed her to the front counter, regret finally taking a hold of me. "I haven't done yoga since I was probably seventeen," I said, looking at Grace's long, limber legs compared to my chunky ones. "Are you sure that jumping into a hot class is wise?"

"Hey, go hot, or go home, especially on the longest night of the year," Grace said as she paid for both of our classes.

I followed Grace into the studio classroom, which was already full of people. The air was muggy and hot.

Crowding into a room full of skinny, flexible twenty-something-year-olds. It felt like I walked into a sauna. Thankfully, Grace set our mats up at the back of the room so I could get a better view of the positions we would be folding our bodies into.

As we settled into a seated position, the door opened, and our instructor entered the room. When she walked to the front of the classroom, my stomach dropped. I recognized the fox tattoo on her arm.

*Sloane*?

She took a seat in front of everyone, folding herself onto her yoga mat. Her eyes swept over the class. Her gaze lingered for a moment when she spotted me. "I'd like to inform everyone in this class that this evening, we will have the heat turned up to honor the summer solstice. If at any reason you feel dizzy, please return into the sukhasana pose, as this is where we will begin with our breathwork."

My mind jumbled with everything Dezmond had told me. Sloane was a shifter who was exploiting Willow and Drake's offspring. The protective momma bear inside of me wanted to rake her claws across this shifter who had obviously set a trap in trying to get me to bring Torchie's egg to her. Thankfully, Francine's maternal instincts prevented me from doing so.

Grace nudged me with her arm. "Hey, close your eyes and breathe. This is yoga. You're supposed to relax!"

When I finally closed my eyes, the auras of everyone in the class lit up like candles flickering in the night. Dull hints of color glowed off the head and shoulders of every individual. While I didn't have my mother's aura-reading capabilities, I could absolutely see the energy in this room. Sloane's aura was by far the most vibrant, putting off flares of red and orange that made my own aura swell with heat.

Maybe the solstice was having an impact on my magic, or maybe it was the fact that I knew she was the enemy.

Sloane instructed us through various poses, ranging from downward facing dog, to reverse warrior pose. Grace moved fluidly with little to no problem, while I almost tripped and fell multiple times onto my face. My breathing synced with my pulse, but my mind was anything but calm. Flame burned through my body like I'd caught fire. With each new pose, my anger toward Sloane grew hotter.

Right when I thought I wouldn't be able to take any more, she instructed us to take a break by taking up a seated pose and to grab some water.

That's when I noticed the dark presence lurking behind her.

The *same* shadowy beast that had possessed Dezmond stood behind Sloane, its giant skull hanging only inches away from the tip of her head. His back was hunched, with wickedly sharp ribs splaying out near its shoulder blades.

I forced myself to exhale.

As quickly as I saw the beast, it was gone.

"Wow I am beat! You held up really well!" Grace said as she toweled off her face and neck.

"I'll meet you outside," I said as she rolled up her yoga mat. Grace left with the remainder of the group, while I stayed firmly rooted in my space. I waited for the classroom to empty before I confronted Sloane, in case the magic in our auras lashed out and hurt someone.

"Victoria, I didn't know that you were into yoga," Sloane said as she began to roll up her yoga mat. Two small black marks lit up on her forearm.

I blinked, and the strange puncture-like marks vanished.

"And I didn't know that you were hunting for dragon eggs." I said, unable to bite my tongue any longer. Sweat poured off my body. My magic sizzled and cracked, turning the drops into liquid light as they struck the ground. "I know what you are, and what you're trying to do to Willow and Drake's offspring."

Sloane's face twisted as she smirked up at me. It took me a moment to realize she wasn't even sweating. "Willow the Wyvern has spread rumors to you, hasn't she?"

"So what if she has?"

Her smirk intensified. "I'd be careful with her. She comes from a line of very dangerous Irish dragons who helped to create the last Earth Uprising."

I took a step toward her. "Leave Willow and her family alone. You have no right to exploit dragons and their magic."

She laughed. "What if I told you the elements could help you cure your cancer?"

Bile burned in my throat. I tried to swallow it down, but I choked.

Her gaze narrowed onto me. "You can tell Willow that I'm closer to finding her offspring than she thinks." The horned shadow hovered behind her as she spoke again. "As for Dezmond, I can't wait to see how you handle that ancient shadow beast once it finally rips out of him."

She spun on her heel and exited the studio, leaving me feeling hollow. The strange black marks I'd seen on her arm—what had created them?

And why did I see the shadowy creature lurking behind her? Were the marks somehow connected to it?

# 24

# Dezmond

I'd spent over an hour rattling on my drum set, trying to find a rhythm that I could sync my pulse with. Shadows tendrilled out of my wrists, making it nearly impossible to focus. Something sinister began to claw inside of me. I couldn't tell if it was Pawz or Jawz gripping their teeth and talons into my ribcage like they usually did when they wanted to prove a point about something.

Maverick sat across from my father, cutting the deck and dealing out the cards in what I assumed was a game of poker. The guy gave me the heebie jeebies. No matter how hard I tried to focus on my rhythm, his swiveling white eye found my gaze, shattering my focus.

The more I observed him, the less I wanted to be here. His right hand was completely metallic. The clinking sound of the gears rattled my ears as he dealt card after card to the men, including my father, who sat at the table.

Every once in a while, a little bout of steam would billow out of his wrist. With each strike I made, I could hear the bolts and gears in Maverick's mechanical arm clink. My drumstick slipped, cracking the rim instead of the head. Sparks shot out of Maverick's mechanical hand. His fingers brushed across a card I recognized as he flipped it over onto the table.

My tattoo burned as the symbol of the dragon egg appeared on the card.

*Fuck.*

Maybe Victoria's Oracle Deck wasn't the *only* deck that housed a Wild Card. What if there were others? And what if they, as Willow and Drake so eloquently put it, allowed Maverick to exploit elemental magic? There was so much I wanted to know about the motivation behind abusing something so powerful that was best kept wild.

"*Because he's a schmuck,*" Drake thundered into my mind with his rumbly opinion.

"*How long have you been listening to my thoughts?*" I asked.

"*For as long as your father has been gambling with the rune. He's a brave demon to go up against such a manipulative shifter. I swear to the elements, if he loses it, Willow will never forgive me for entrusting it with you.*"

My fingers gripped on my drumsticks. I was sure to splinter the fuck out of them tonight. Hell, I'd probably bust a few just by warming up.

Maverick's white eye flickered red every time I struck a certain rhythm. And a gold tooth flashed every time he grinned. Something about this shifter set fire to some spot in the back of my mind. Every time he talked, the blood pounded into my ears so loudly I could barely hear my thoughts.

As my father continued to gamble, I was able to observe Maverick do exactly what my father had accused him of doing—*cheating*. He'd wave his fat, stumpy fingers over his Wild Card, and other cards would vanish. The other blokes at the table were either blind, stupid, or under the influence of some spell not to notice.

I'd been so focused on the Wild Card that I'd failed to notice another item on the table. A creepy doll sat behind the card, seeming to guard it. The thing was lopsided and stitched together, with short, stumpy black arms and legs. The head was shrunken and bony, its features stretched with dried, blackened flesh. Sharp, equally black teeth jutted from its mouth.

One thing was for certain. I wasn't going to let Maverick take advantage of my father. I might have inherited a few bad habits from my old Pops, but being a cheating asshole wasn't one of them.

I checked my phone. Victoria never texted me back. It stung a little, knowing that I really wanted to see her again this evening.

Ted grabbed the mic and gave it a little tap. "All right, Nematodes. Let's hear it!"

Lonnie killed his guitar as Ted grabbed his microphone. As Ted sang one of his hideous warm up tunes about mutant earthworms devouring the dead, I took a moment to set down my drumsticks and walk over to where my Pops was sitting at the bar. The gentlemen at the poker table had dispersed, leaving Maverick to rake in his pile of cash and other items the group had wagered.

Dad was looking pretty dangerous with the way his veins were throbbing in his temple.

I propped my elbows onto the bar as I slid up next to him.

"You all warmed up?" Dad growled.

"I am. But Ted's another story. I wanted to check on you and see how you were doing. You look a bit glum."

Dad's shoulders slumped over as he nursed what I hoped was a virgin drink. "I'm going to tell Cindy I can't see her anymore."

I jolted. "Wait, that doesn't make any sense. Just a few moments ago, you said you were going to *propose* to her. Now you're breaking up with her?"

Dad's hands gripped tight on his drink. "She deserves a better demon that me."

Something wasn't right. Dad *never* had this little confidence, especially about a witch he was fond of. Both of his spirit ravens looked possessed. One of the two, (I never knew which was Anger or Sadness) had an eye that turned milky white.

*Fuck.*

I glanced over at Maverick, who was now playing with the creepy doll. The Wild Card was nowhere to be found. He grabbed the doll's head and tilted its neck back.

My father's head made the same movement, making his vertebrate crack.

*Double fuck.*

This creepy-ass shifter had cursed my father with some kind of voodoo magic!

I slammed my fist down onto the bar. My hand morphed, sprouting fur and claws as it shifted into a massive bear paw. "I'm stopping this fucking shit, *now.*"

Dad slumped over. When his head hit the bar, shadows burst out of his shoulders.

The bartender backed away as I let out a low, guttural growl and made my way over to the poker table.

My vision thrashed as red and black bands of magic burned through my veins. Maverick continued to sort his stash of winnings, which my rune was part of.

I set both of my paws onto the table and glared down at the top of his stupid top hat. "Hey, I have a bone to pick with you. Give me the Wild Card, you asshole. I know you're using it to fuck with my Pops."

A little puff of steam issued out of Maverick's hand. He stroked the doll's spine with his metallic finger, which made its mouth open wide. He grabbed my water rune and tossed it into the doll's mouth, which quickly gnashed its shiny black teeth shut as it gobbled it down.

Maverick's eyes swept to me. "How about we trade? I'll give you the Wild Card, but only if you give me the other rune that Drake gave you." His metallic fingers tapped across the table with a *clack, clack, clack.* "I'm quite fond of collecting runes that house elemental magic."

My spine prickled at his request. "*Fuck* you. I'm not giving you a thing." I flexed my claws on the table. "Unless you plan on handing over the Wild Card *and* the rune you stole from my Pops, I'm going to bust a claw in your cheating ass right now."

I snatched the doll away from the table and squeezed its neck. As I dug one of my claws into its center, purple smoke erupted out of its eye sockets. A horrible smell wrecked my nostrils.

The doll's mouth opened, and its black, needle-like teeth elongated.

A sharp pain struck my chest.

*Triple fuck.*

Reeling from the pain, I dropped the doll onto the table. The smell of rotting flesh confirmed that I was dealing with some very potent black magic.

Bolts and gears ground together as Maverick's metallic arm extended. Cold, vice-like fingers gripped around my neck, choking me. "Tell me where Willow's offspring is now, or the Spirit of the Wild is going to enjoy a tasty demon snack."

My mind blanked. *Spirit of the Wild*?

I dug my claws into his hand, ripping out a few of the bolts so that I could choke out a reply. "Go fuck yourself, Maverick. Willow and her family are *my* family now. You're going to need more than a Wild Card to tame my magic."

Maverick's face twisted, anger turning his already sallow skin more sunken. Flesh rotted and fell away, revealing his skull.

Before I could dig my other hand into his hand, Maverick's rotting features evaporated into a plume of smoke.

I fell forward, catching myself. That fucker disappeared like a fart in the wind, without leaving a trace.

"Hey, Zed! What happened?" Lonnie asked, offering me a hand.

Dad toppled out of his seat at the bar.

"Did your old man drank too much again?" Ted asked.

I staggered over to my father and grabbed him under the arm, while Lonnie grabbed his other. I winced as the invisible needles stung my chest and arms. "Don't worry, Pops. I'll get you home."

# 25

# Victoria

I didn't sleep a wink that night, completely heated by my interaction with Sloane. The threats she made toward Willow had my blood boiling. When I checked my phone at one in the morning, I realized that I'd left Dezmond's message about meeting at the pub unread. I felt *so* bad. I'd never gotten back to him.

Just past the crack of dawn, I sent him a text.

**Hey, sorry I never got back to you. Hot yoga wasn't what I thought it would be. Wait until I tell you about who the class instructor was.**

Moments went by. He didn't respond, so I dressed for another sure-to-be-hot day at the clinic. As I put on a pot of coffee, I busied myself with a stack of mail. I still had bills from my chemotherapy from years ago coming in.

As I flipped through my mail, I came across another letter from the cancer clinic. I sliced open the envelope with my thumbnail. I'd gotten a *second* notice warning me that I needed to make an appointment.

Flashbacks of the grueling days of my treatment played in my mind like a movie. Grace bawling her eyes out, and Lucy's cold stare melting into a terrified look that sent chills up my spine still to this day. I felt nauseous any time I thought about how my mother's aura flared when I told her I'd need to start chemo. She'd lost our father to bone cancer. I hated to think of what ran through her mind about possibly losing a daughter to another cancerous illness.

I'd gotten the notice in the dead of winter, when everything was frozen. I'd started chemo shortly after, and had endured treatments all through the spring, when I'd lost my hair. By summer, I'd gotten so weak from my treatment, that when the day came to get my mastectomy, I'd basically given up on having any hope that I'd fully recover.

After I'd gone into remission, the weight gain started. But I hadn't always been the fat Crow sister. In fact, I used to be pretty athletic. But chemo did strange things to a woman's hormones. And being a witch, finding a way to balance them again without your magic getting out of whack was nearly impossible.

My phone chimed. Lucy had texted me.

**I started a group chat with Grace because I need both of you to help with sorting some things out for the wedding venue Amon and I decided upon.**

**Where is this venue?**

**Lucy: I'll give you details this afternoon. I'm fairly certain we are going with a park. When and where can you both meet?**

**Grace: Stop by the bakery. Krim's making me share a whole new line of pastries. And I like the idea of having a wedding outside at a park!**

**I'll be there when I can after 3. Love you both.**

I pocketed my phone. Sure, I was the witch of honor. But right now, I felt like such a *loser*. I ate a quick breakfast and jumped into my Jeep. The only thing that brightened my mood was seeing Willow's golden tail dip down from the clouds as I pulled out of my driveway.

"*You need to fix your. Witches who connect with their wild side are far more successful with controling their magic.*"

"Are you saying I'm a *wild* witch?"

"*I never would have entrusted my offspring with a witch who didn't have a spark of wildness in her.*"

"No, I'm a *vet* witch. I adore wild things, but my magic is anything but wild."

Willow chuffed. "*That's because you haven't mingled your magic with the wild beast that lives inside of Dezmond.*"

By the time I arrived at the clinic, Willow's intrusive voice had silenced. My stomach was in knots. Dezmond still hadn't texted me. I began to fear the worst.

What if he'd ghosted me?

As I pulled my Jeep into the parking lot, I squinted at the flowers potted outside. The geraniums were no longer orange, but multi-colored. As I walked through the front door, the colors continued to change. My clinic had been bewitched with something I couldn't explain.

The moment I walked inside, Holly glanced up at me from behind the check-in counter. Brilliant rainbow highlights decorated her hair.

That's when everything clicked. "Rosie is responsible for this, isn't she?"

When Holly laughed, colorful sparks shot out of her computer. "Rosie hasn't pooped yet. But she's sure lit up the office with her rainbow magic."

The sound of a motorbike revved outside.

My heart jumped as my demon boyfriend limped into the clinic.

His biker jacket was torn in places. Black and blue bruises covered his neck, and one of his eyes was squinting. He set his hands onto his hips and glanced around the room. "Why the hell does this place look like Rainbow Bright blew chunks all over the walls?"

"Oh my god, Dezmond, what happened to you?" I stammered.

His good eye focused on me. "Well, hello, my pretty darlin'. I've been missing you something fierce."

I darted over to him and flung myself into his arms.

He winced when our bodies made contact, then quickly buried his face into my neck. "Easy there. I'm not going anywhere anytime soon."

I squeezed him, reeling from the roughness of his face and hardness of his body as he embraced me.

He winced, pulling away.

"What did you do, get into a fight?" I asked, feeling around his ribcage with my hands. I sensed the little pockets of my magic pooling around his center.

He chuckled, clutching his side. "I had one hell of a night. Can we go somewhere to discuss? Do you have any time to, ouch!" He winced again, "patch me up?"

Holly cleared her throat. "Victoria? Room three is open if you'd like to take your first patient back."

I grabbed his arm and took him back to the room Holly had so graciously reserved for me. I swore at times, she could read my mind before I'd even asked for her assistance.

Dezmond sat down the moment I shut the door. His breathing was sporadic. His eyes dilated.

I sat on the stool and rolled myself in front of him. "I can tell that you are in an immense amount of pain."

"Maybe just a bit," he said as he gripped his sides and grimaced.

One touch of my hand to his chest, and my magic took over. Dezmond's dark aura lit up for me. *Dozens* of pockmarks revealed themselves all over his chest and sides.

"Did you have a fight with a porcupine or something?" I asked as I continued to survey the strange puncture wounds all over his body. As I ran my fingers across one of the pock marks, I felt the end of something sharp.

He winced as I continued to feel around his arms. "Remember the name of the shifter Willow and Drake said to be on the lookout for?"

"Maverick?"

"Yeah. That fucking asshole and I got into a fight at the pub."

"How did this fight go down?"

"My Pops was there gambling. Maverick was dealing out the cards. When I was warming up on my drum set, I saw him cheating, so I went to confront his ass. Want to know what he was using in his deck? A fucking Wild Card."

I jolted. "Impossible. My mother said there is only *one* Wild Card in the Three Magics Oracle Deck."

"Victoria, I know what I saw. I swear on my shadow beasts that it was the same card you showed me from your deck."

"Where is the Wild Card now?"

Dezmond made a grunting sound. "Maverick made off with my rune with the water symbol. I sort of let Dad gamble with it. As for the Wild Card, I never got it." He patted his jacket pocket. "I still have the air rune, though."

I shrugged. "Well, you're doing better than me. One of my patients gobbled up my fire rune." As I inspected his reddening hands and arms, Sloane's arm flashed in my mind.

The strange dark marks . . .

The ancient shadowy creature lurking behind her.

I pressed my finger to his wrist. "Sloane *also* had these strange puncture-like marks on her arm."

One of Dezmond's eyebrows quirked. "When did you see Sloane?"

"Last night at hot yoga. She was the instructor. After class, I confronted her about Torchie's egg and the other dragons she's exploited." I chewed my cheek. "Then she said something about the elements being some magical remedy for my cancer."

"Do you think she was bluffing?"

"She had to be. Besides, I'm not willing to play with a cure for my cancer at the expense of Willow and Drake's family."

The mere thought of anyone exploiting *anything* from a dragon made my magic flare. I reached into my drawer and tugged out a tool I only used on patients that had been harmed by magical forces. "Hold still, this might hurt. I've had my fair share of dealing with bewitchments, but these things are nasty."

"What is that?" he asked as I held my dowsing wand—a magical tool I only used when attempting to detect curses—over his chest. Purple sparks shot out of his skin and quickly dispersed as I waved it over him.

"You've been bewitched by some kind of nasty shadow magic allright. From what I can see, they look like *shadow* needles."

"Well, Maverick *did* have a creepy voodoo doll. I wouldn't put it past him to throw a bunch of, oh, sweet mother of fucking darkness, get them out of me!"

A roar erupted out of him so loudly that If I didn't act now, he would startle patients in the nearby rooms.

He slumped over, breathing heavily. "How are we going to pull a bunch of shadow needles out of my aura?"

I set my wand down. "How about rainbows?"

He squinted at me. "What?"

"Hold on, I have an idea."

I left the room, retreating to where Rosie was in her cage. While she might not have passed the rune, she had shed an incredible amount of skin. I really didn't want to think about what it might be like to deal with a rainbow serpent's fiery poops when it came time for her to pass it.

"All right, old gal. Can I borrow some of your colorful earth magic?" I asked as I opened her cage and stared her in the face. Her yellow eyes reminded me so much of Willow's intense gaze.

An enthusiastic *hiss* filled my ears, signaling that it was okay for me to take a bit of her shed skin. I wrapped it around my wrist, closed her cage, and dipped back into the room where Dezmond was still wheezing in pain.

I returned to my seat in front of him and unraveled the skin. "Hold still. I think this might help."

Dezmond closed his eyes as I pressed Rosie's colorful skin onto his chest. His nostrils flared as the scaly pattern changed from yellow to green to vivid tones of blue and purple.

The skin sizzled, then popped. One by one, the shadow needles clung to the scales as they were extracted from Dezmond's aura.

"Ah, that's much better," he said, panting. "Where the heck did you get this colorful snakeskin from?"

"One of my patients is a rainbow serpent. And I'm fairly confident that this spontaneous flare in her magic is from her eating my rune." I set a new layer of Rosie's skin onto his chest and arm, where it instantly bound to his aura.

He grabbed my hand. "This is black magic. I could *smell* it."

"What does black magic smell like?"

"Absolute death," He nuzzled my cheek. "The only way I can get that stench out of my nose is by scenting my mate."

My body heated at his sudden affection.

He made a motion to stand. "What are we waiting for? Let's go find this Maverick guy and steal back my rune. I plan on snatching that Wild Card from him while I'm at it."

I laughed, tugging him back down by his shirt to his seat. "Dezmond Ravenblood, this Maverick guy beat you to *shit*. You need to take some time for your body to recover." I grabbed his hand and gave it a squeeze. "But good news! You're an outpatient. I'm going to suggest that someone watch over you for the next twenty-four hours."

He smiled cheekily as he squeezed my hand back. "Good thing I know of a certain witch in town who can do a magical job for me. Can I at least go hang out with my brothers? Krim said something about needing me to start prepping for Amon's bachelor party."

My stomach hollowed. I'd done nothing of the sorts for Lucy yet. "You can absolutely hang out, but no rough housing. Your aura needs time to mend, vet's orders. I've seen a lot of puncture wounds in my time. I wonder if they really aren't wounds from needles, but possibly teeth."

Dezmond squinted at his arm. "Wait a second, you think the puncture wounds were a bunch of *bite* marks?"

I shivered, thinking back to the shady beast that had manifested in my home a couple of nights ago, then again behind Sloane. "I think there might be a shadowy creature lurking around town that has ties with Maverick."

# 26

# Dezmond

As soon as Victoria mentioned *bite marks*, a light bulb went off in my head. I remembered the sharp, black, needle-like teeth from something evil that Maverick possessed.

I stood up. "Maverick had this creepy voodoo doll he used with his Wild Card. He fed my water rune to it. I think he's using the doll to exploit Willow and Drake's elemental magic."

Victoria scowled. "Creepy voodoo doll or not, you can't go picking a fight with anyone any time soon."

But I already had a plan. As soon as I ran the events past my brothers, they'd be all over this asshole quicker than a cat on a rat in a dark alleyway.

Victoria caught my arm before I could walk toward the door. "Speaking of elemental magic. Have you seen or heard Torchie or his parents at all?"

"No, I haven't. I'm starting to wonder if everything is going okay with our dragon family. Maybe they're staying on the down low now that they know Maverick is in town."

She grabbed my collar and gave it a tug. "That's it? No thank you kiss for patching you up again? I expected better from my hot demon boyfriend."

I grabbed her hips and pinned her against the table. "Unless you want me to devour you right here in this room like I did before, then expect me to save the kissing for later."

As her fingers curled into my hair, an abrupt *knock, knock, knock* on the door broke us apart.

"Victoria! Your next patient is ready!" her receptionist cried from the other side of the door.

Victoria groaned. "If I didn't have so many patients to see, I would absolutely take you up on that."

I planted a kiss on her lips instead. "What's the name of your rainbow serpent?"

"Rosie, why?"

"Tell Rosie that she better poop out that fire rune soon. We are going to need it when we go up against this Maverick guy."

I glanced down at my arm, admiring the colors of Rosie's serpent skin as I left the clinic. Only Victoria would come up with such a badass idea for a bandage. As part of my treatment, she said for me to stop by her sister's bakery and ask for one of the special pastries she swore would help with the pain.

When I walked inside the bakery, I recognized Amon's tattooed arms immediately.

He stood by the pastry display case and squinted as soon as he spotted me. "Dude, who the hell did you get your new ink from?"

I swung my arm toward him. "Victoria's rainbow serpent makes some kick-ass colors. Her name is Rosie!"

Krim came out from the back room with a platter full of pastries. "I second that. Amon, you need to up your game from the black ink you are so obsessed with."

Both of my brothers eyed me.

"Speaking of black. Do you have a black eye?" Krim asked as he set the platter down in front of my brother.

Amon grabbed one of the cupcakes decorated with miniature books and took a hefty bite. He chewed and swallowed, then offered the other half to me. "No guess that Lucy wants a bookish-themed wedding. I came by to sample the treats we're going to have at the reception."

I refused to take the cupcake and propped my arms onto the counter instead. "Cool. Well, I'm here because my sorry ass got handed to me by a creepy voodoo doll that has an appetite for demon flesh and elemental runes."

Krim and Amon both shot each other wary glances.

"You two head outside. I'll meet you there," Krim instructed.

Amon grabbed the cupcake platter and held the shop door open for me as I struggled to regain my focus.

I took up a seat at the small table beneath an umbrella.

Amon set the platter of cupcakes in front of me and folded his arms onto the table. His tattoos snaked down to his wrists, coiling into serpents as he studied me.

Grace walked out of the shop and sauntered over to Amon and I with her phone in her hands. "Victoria just texted me, saying you got in a fight with some creepy demon who looked like a steampunk Jack the Ripper at the pub last night with your father?"

I chuckled. "Yeah. Dad was gambling with him."

Amon's brow furrowed. "Dad wasn't drinking, was he?"

"No, thank Hades," I replied as I grabbed one of the cupcakes and took a bite.

Amon sighed as he rolled his eyes. "Glad to see he's picked up some other healthy habits after he kicked the bottle."

I cleared my throat, wincing. "So, for your bachelor party, I was thinking about some ideas, but I wanted to get your thoughts on them first."

"Dude, you and Dad just got attacked, and you're thinking about my bachelor party? Stop for a moment and talk to me about what happened."

Grace busied herself with stuffing the tea stand with new bags of loose leaf tea samples, but I was very aware that she was eavesdropping on our conversation. Every few moments, a prickly little hedgehog would pop out of one of the potted plants and snuff its tiny black nose at her.

Seeing the little creature made me think of Torchie. I was starting to get worried about him.

"Dad's in better shape than I am, apparently," I said, noting the string of text messages on my phone. "Apparently he's already over at Cindy's place again, enjoying the afternoon sunshine."

As Grace went back into the shop, Krim emerged. His eyes flashed red as his reaper's hood descended over his face.

He snatched my second cupcake out of my hand before I could sink my teeth into it. "Before you stuff your face. Who is this demon who attacked you and Dad?"

"His name is Maverick," I answered, wincing as my shirt brushed across my ribs. "According to Dad, and the dragons Victoria and I have met, he's some shifter who has a reputation for exploiting dragons for their elemental magic."

Amon's tattoos thrashed out of his arms as he shoved Krim's hand away and snatched up another cupcake. "Sounds like a nice guy. What's this about a voodoo doll that has an appetite for demon flesh and elemental runes?"

I held up my arm. "Victoria used one of her familiar patients to help patch up the bite marks Maverick's voodoo doll inflicted on me."

"*Bite* marks?" Amon said. "I thought voodoo dolls were paired with needles, not teeth. Let me see these marks."

"You can't," I followed. "Rosie the rainbow serpent gobbled up the rune Torchie's parents gave her. Thank darkness, because it caused her to shed her skin. Victoria used Rosie's skin to patch up a bite that felt like a thousand tiny needles digging into me."

"*I'll never let you complain about my teeth against your ribs again,*" Jawz grumbled.

"How did this fight with Maverick go down?" Amon probed, and my shadow lion withdrew into the back of my mind.

"Dad told me that he was going to back out of buying Cindy a ring. That's when I knew that Maverick was somehow manipulating him."

Both Krim and Amon's mouths dropped.

"Wait a fucking second. Dad's planning to propose to Lucy's *mom*?" Amon asked.

I nodded. "When I realized that Maverick was using a Wild Card of his own to manipulate our Pops, I confronted the asshole. That's when he went bonkers. He demanded that I tell him where Torchie was, or the Spirit of the Wild was going to enjoy a tasty demon snack. Next thing I know, it felt like I was getting stabbed all over my body."

Krim's red eyes flashed. "*Spirit of the Wild*? Dezmond, are you aware of what this creature is?"

I shook my head, *no*.

Krim's hood lowered again, casting his features in shadow. "The Spirit of the Wild is the ultimate shadow beast that only shifters can channel. It's ancient, dating back thousands of years, predating even the most primeval of shamanic rituals. The beast is so old, some say it's composed of the elements."

"Is this beast a *dragon*?" I asked.

"I can't say for certain. No shifter has ever been able to channel it without harming themselves in the process."

I ground my teeth, waiting for Jawz to grumble something snarky into my head. "That's great, glad to know there is another shadow beast out there worse than the ones I already own."

Krim's red eyes narrowed onto me. "How many of these elemental runes have the dragons given you?"

"Three, why?" I replied.

Krim's face emerged out of his hood. "Let me guess. They're named after water, air, and fire?"

"Yeah, how did you know?"

Krim flexed his hand, which had turned skeletal. "I did a lot of experimenting with alchemy when I served as a shadow alchemist for the demon council. But that was a long time ago. I can tell you what I remember—shifters were always the biggest pain in my ass. They fought over elemental runes like they were gold."

"Why did shifters fight over these runes?" I asked.

"The three primary elements are what make up the earth. Shifters would arm themselves with these elements, to protect their clans from the earth magic that familiars wield."

"You mean, Earth Uprisings?"

"That's it," Krim stammered, snapping his fingers. "Maverick is *feeding* the Spirit of the Wild elemental magic to stop an Earth Uprising from occurring, he *must* be. Do you have any of the runes on you right now?"

I reached into my pocket and withdrew the rune of air, when a light, breezy voice blew past my ear and whispered, "*Carried on the wind, our magic travels far and wide. Air is the element of movement and change. Air always knows where to go, even when the body refuses to do so. Air is the movement our souls soar with.*"

I dug my finger into my ear. "Did any of you just hear that?"

"Hear what?" Amon and Krim asked in unison.

"I just heard a voice say something about air being the breeze of change, or something like that. When I had the water rune, I also heard a voice that said something similar."

"Maybe the elements are able to speak to you through the runes," Krim said as he held out his hand. "Do you mind if I borrow your air rune and perform some tests on it? I might be able to trace any residual shadows tied to its magic, and therefore locate Maverick."

I dropped the rune into his palm. "Sure. Just don't lose it. Victoria and I are already down the other two."

Krim pocketed my rune and glanced toward Amon. "I think your brother and I are going to have a little fun with this shifter who fucked with the Ravenbloods."

Not long after I left the bakery, my phone lit up. Victoria had texted me.

**How is the inflammation?**

**It's only been a couple of hours, but it's much better.**

**I know, but I've been worried about you. I'm getting off at 3 today. Holly was able to pull some strings for me. Meet at my place?**

**Sounds good. You are a sweetheart for checking on me.**

As I rounded the corner, two massive clawed feet appeared next to the lamp-post on the corner of Main Street. I blinked a few times, trying to understand what I was observing. I stopped by the traffic light and tapped my knuckles on the metal post. "Willow, I can see your golden claws."

She shuffled her feet, sending a blast of wind that sent the old lady crossing the street's sun hat flying off. "*I'm not as good at blending in with the urban settings as I am with the natural ones.*"

I pressed the button on the light to cross the street. "Where are Torchie and Drake?"

"*Having a father-to-son conversation about what not to do when you encounter a shifter named Maverick.*" A gust of wind blew past my face. "*I smell Victoria's magic on you, as well as an, oh dear. Is that a rainbow serpent skin?*"

"Yes. Apparently one at the vet clinic devoured your fire rune. And I guess I should mention, too, that I lost the water one. And I just gave the air one to my brother that Drake gave to me."

A haughty grumble rumbled in her throat. "*I had a feeling things would go differently than planned. I've never met a demon or a witch quite like you and Victoria.*"

With a gust of wind, she took off. As the light changed, I walked across the street. I was completely bewildered that she wasn't more frustrated with me about losing my rune.

Once I arrived at Victoria's house, I found my way around back and took up a seat on the back porch.

A pair of feathered wings flit overhead. Francine landed in the nearby tree and gazed down at me with her intense eyes. Her head twisted as she studied me.

"*Where are your shadow beasts*?" she asked, her voice high and shrill.

"Ever since your witch and I, well. You know," I stammered, feeling very awkward about having this discussion with Victoria's feathered familiar.

She let out a *squaaaawwwwwk* as three other smaller hawks came flying in.

Victoria poked her head out the back door. "Francine, stop harassing my boyfriend."

"*You are officially dating now*?"

"Since when did I need your approval?" Victoria snapped.

Francine ruffled her tail feathers, "*Since I became your familiar, you wicked, witchy woman.*"

Victoria rolled her eyes at her hawk. "Dezmond, please come inside and escape the mother hen of unsolicited wisdom."

I gladly left the back porch and escaped into Victoria's home.

It took me a few seconds to take in what she was wearing next to nothing. "About that shower we never took together," I suggested.

Before I could grab her, she pounced on me.

# 27

# Victoria

As Dezmond fell back onto my sofa, I pounced on him, straddling his core. "Who do I get to play with today? The wolf, the lion, or the bear?"

"How about a *dragon*?" he suggested as he grabbed my hips.

I raked my hands greedily over his chest, wishing I could see that dark creature again. Something told me it wasn't an *if*, but a *when.*

He grazed his thumbs over the hem of my panties, teasing my clit. "I think it's time I worship you in a way I haven't yet."

My toes curled. The thought of what position he'd been saving to *worship* me in had me perplexed. I climbed off his center and helped him to stand.

In one swift movement, he curled his arms under my legs, lifted me up, and tore up the stairs to my bedroom.

As soon as my heels hit the ground, he forced me backward. My back hit the bed as he dragged me onto my mattress.

"I love the aggression," I said as he pinned one of my arms over my head. I grabbed his belt with my free hand and tugged the buckle open.

He raked his teeth past my neck as he released my arm. "Get on all fours and turn around. I can't wait to watch your gorgeous ass bounce."

I smiled up at him, refusing to let go of his belt. "Not until I've freed the beast in your pants."

Dezmond's chin jutted upward as I tugged down his jeans and boxers, releasing his hard length. His cock bounced out into the open. A bulbous knot of tissue bulged at the base.

I worked my hand from the head of his cock down to the knot, teasing this new part of his anatomy.

"*Fuck*, Victoria," he grunted, thrusting his hips as I continued to tease his throbbing member. He wasn't going to get away with giving me a fit of orgasms without me returning the favor.

"Stand up. I want to try something before we do any ass bouncing."

He did as told, standing on the edge of the bed. I kept my hand clasped around his cock as he stood before me. I continued to run my hand along his veiny shaft. I grabbed his balls, cupping them into my palm. I loved feeling his balls tighten and seeing how his entire body reacted to my attention.

I leaned back, allowing my hair to drape between his legs over the edge of the bed. With my hand still on his cock, I took one of his balls into my mouth and sucked. Dezmond's entire body shuddered as I moved to the second one.

He leaned over my body, teasing my pussy with his hand. Two of his fingers curled, arching into my G-spot as his thumb made circles over my clit. "Fuck, Victoria. *Fuck* me. I'm making you mine."

"*All of us are,*" another growl rumbled past my thigh.

As I ran my fingers along his knot and squeezed, a guttural growl erupted out of his mouth. Not one, but *three* different beasts all shifted around me. One had a wolfish snout that nuzzled my neck. The second had teeth that raked across the sensitive skin of my stomach. Two massive paws extended out of the third, a set of claws grazing my thigh as its silky shadows explored the lower half of my body.

*Fuck*. What was this wickedly wild fantasy?

"*Flip over,*" one of the beasts growled. "*I'm going to mark you.*"

"*No, I am,*" another one snapped, and I was flipped onto my side, then my belly.

"*Back that gorgeous ass up,*" a third voice demanded, which I graciously obeyed.

My face smeared into the pillows as the jostling shadow beasts tossed in my sheets. One by one, the beasts traded places with their demon, each fighting to mount me from behind. Thick penetration after forceful thrust filled me. My magic ignited, an orgasm burning through me as each one fucked me doggie style. As each of the shadow beasts claimed me, my desire for Dezmond's cock became my only focus.

"Dezmond," I breathed as my body was rocked harder into my sheets, "I want you to make me come."

A paw-like hand grabbed mine, claws gripping between my fingers against the mattress as his cock plowed into me.

"I'm feral for you." He rose to his knees, gripping my hips and pulling me back against his cock.

I gripped my sheets, feeling his knot swell at my entry. It rolled over my clit, teasing my skin and bringing my orgasm to a swell I couldn't seem to release. Sweet fucking monster cocks. His dick would be the end of me.

Pleasure burned into an insatiable heat. I was going to pass out from the sheer intensity of his knot swelling inside of me. The friction between our bodies built to a peak. My hips swayed, my body on the edge of breaking as he pounded his swelling cock into me.

"Tell me you're my mate," he grunted with each thrust.

"Dezmond, my mate, don't stop," I breathed, my face smearing against my pillow.

"*Our mate,*" one of the beasts corrected.

Fur and fangs and claws blended with the velvety shadows as Dezmond's shadow beasts all fought to claim me.

"*No, mine,*" another, far deeper voice rumbled, breaking the primal clash of the other beasts.

A whirl of heat broke over me as his claws extended, his beastly cock driving further into me. Flashes of red and white broke through my vision as Dezmond and I both released. He fell over my back, kissing my shoulders and neck as he lowered himself beside me.

We fell onto my bed, hot and sweaty and spent. I tucked myself against his hard body, my skin raw from all the amazing multi-shadow beast fucking.

As the shadow creature appeared behind my eyelids, I sucked in a breath and exhaled.

*"Set me free, and you will know what it means to be mine, Victoria Crow."*

I sat up in bed and gazed at myself in the mirror. Scratch marks lined my neck and chest from our ravenous lovemaking.

The orgasms had been so powerful that I must have passed out. Dezmond lay next to me. A satiated grin curved the corner of his lopsided mouth as he dozed.

My phone buzzed. Lucy had texted me.

**Hey, I'm coming by after work today to go over some things for the wedding. By the way, is Dezmond missing one of his shadows? Because I am fairly certain I saw something that looked like a giant shadow wolf creeping across the sidewalk when I went out for lunch today.**

I grabbed Dezmond's shoulder and gave him a shake. "Dezmond, wake up. My sister is coming over. Can you please put on some clothes?"

He didn't respond.

While I was a firecracker in bed, I knew I wasn't good enough to knock a guy out from giving him an orgasm. I raked my teeth across his ass and bit him. He didn't even flinch.

*Crap. Should I dial 9-1-1*?

My doorbell sounded.

*Shit.*

Lucy was here. I tugged on my bra and panties and draped my bathrobe over my body just as Lucy's aura blew into my home. She had a spare key as she used to live here and often let herself in unannounced.

When I dipped into my kitchen, I found her standing in front of a pile of books she'd already slung across my table.

Her blue eyes met mine. "Amon's been missing for hours. I texted Grace, and she told me that Krim is also missing. Is your demon gone too?"

Heat branched up my neck. "No. He's currently butt-ass naked and passed out on my bed."

Lucy held up her hand. "Save the shadow-twisting details for later. We don't need our demons for this discussion. Right now, I need to show you something that might be impacting our town very soon." She reached into her bag and tugged out her familiar. Grubs, her grouchy bookworm, inched across the table, pinching his little brow together as we went.

"You wanted to show me how you feed your bookworm?" I asked as Grubs inched quickly toward the book stack.

Lucy shook her head. "No. I want you to see what happens with his magic when he tries to eat a hole in one of my books."

As Grubs inched his way across the table. His little green body began to glow. The closer he inched to the stack of books, the smaller he became, until he folded in on himself and became a chrysalis.

The chrysalis trembled violently. Green sparks shot into the air as he emerged as a butterfly. As he flapped his wings, magical bursts of flame, water, and a furious gust of wind erupted out of his body.

Purple smoke issued out of the books on the table. With a fiery *poof*, the books vanished into the smoke, leaving Grubs to come inching his way out of the aftermath.

"What the hell was that all about?" I asked as I took a step back and coughed.

"His magic is backfiring," Lucy answered as she fanned her face. "It's acting like a catalyst, forcing him to metamorphose without warning. I noticed it the other day at the library. Try reading to a bunch of toddlers without them erupting into a screaming fit when an actual butterfly pops out of your book."

I laughed. "I must know, do kids actually enjoy Crystal the Witch's story?"

Lucy shot me a furious look. "Of course they do. I mean, who *wouldn't* want to read about a witch who uses crystals to help others discover their own magic?"

I stared at the place on my table where the pile of books had been. "In other words, he can't eat what he likes to snack on?"

Lucy nodded. "Not only that, but his source of food disappears. Sooner or later, he's going to get ill."

"Do you have any idea where the books went?" I asked.

"I have my assumptions, but that would require us to go on a hunt that I don't think you and I are ready for. The last time I saw a book go *poof* into thin air, it just so happened to be a grimoire. If there is anything that I learned from that book, it was that shadow magic has a direct correlation to the earth."

"Where did you learn all of this?" I asked.

"Amon took me to the shadow archives, which house an entire library that deals not only with shadows, but *elemental* magic." She reached into her bag and tugged out yet another book. Judging from the weathered spine, and the odd, earthy aroma, I assumed that it didn't come from her library.

She tossed it onto my table, where it landed with a hefty *thud*. When she flipped it open, a low, earthy groan issued out of it. Pages thrashed as what I assumed was a grimoire flipped to a place in the middle, where it suddenly stopped. Purple smoke issued out of the center as ink bled over the mottled parchment.

Symbols manifested across the pages. Images of flames, waves, rocks, and what I assumed were gusts of wind illustrated a diagram that made me think of the elements.

Lucy traced her finger over all four of the symbols, until she traced to the center, where a crystal was framed. "Earth magic is only a *fragment* of elemental magic. It is also the *binding* element. The earth supports water, air, and fire. If the earth isn't healthy enough to support the other elements, bad things occur in nature."

"Bad things, like Earth Uprising movements?"

Lucy nodded. "Exactly. All historical Earth Uprising movements have occurred when the earth magic familiars wield becomes weak. Have any of the familiars at your clinic exhibited strange changes in their magic recently?"

"One of my regulars is a rainbow serpent. She ate something I thought was what made her shed her skin."

Grubs inched his way between us, trembling slightly as he spoke, "*Listen to you witch sisters, trying to piece together what's obviously happening right under your witchy little noses.*"

Lucy scoffed. "Victoria and I aren't dumb. We can tell when a disturbance in magical energies is going on."

I glanced at my sister. "Are you saying that we're experiencing an *Earth Uprising* movement?"

"*Oh, it's well underway,*" Grubs corrected me matter-of-factly. "*The magical barrier that separates the world of the living from the Summoning has started to corrode away, all thanks to the two shifters who have come to town.*"

Lucy squinted at her bookworm. "And since when did you learn about these shifters?"

Grubs inched his way back onto his hind legs. "*Grace has a greenhouse full of familiars who have done nothing but gossip about the baby dragon they're trying to hunt down.*"

Lucy glanced at me. "Did *you* know about these shifters and this baby dragon hunt?"

"Yes. One of them is named Sloane. She is the new manager at the animal shelter I wanted to partner with. And Dezmond just told me about some guy named Maverick. He attacked him last night with some creepy shadow voodoo magic. I spent this morning pulling shadow needles out of him."

Lucy sighed. "Great. Sounds like we have a couple of shifters in town who our demon boyfriends all want to pick a fight with."

"But why would Sloane and Maverick come here?"

"Midhaven just so happens to be the best spot for an Earth Uprising to occur. There is a magical vortex here that bloomed out of the earth last fall."

"A magical vortex? *Where*?"

"Are you already forgetting about what happened at Grace's greenhouse last Halloween?"

"You mean, the spirit tree?"

Lucy made a clicking sound with her tongue. "Bingo. That's got to be where the magical energies are all surging from. The only demons who can manipulate the elemental barrier are those who are shifters, which if I'm not mistaken, Dezmond is one of them."

Grubs inched his way back onto her hand. "*I'm ready for my afternoon snack.*"

Lucy grabbed the book and tucked it back into her bag. "Let's go find Grace and see what we can do about tracking down this elemental barrier. Knowing her, she's likely at her greenhouse working her green magic to try and get information out of her familiars about the rumors they've been spreading."

# 28

# Dezmond

The warmth of Victoria's body evaporated the moment I hit a curtain of inky black shadows. Something wasn't right. We'd been tossing in her blood red sheets, having crazy animalistic shadow beast sex, and now I was in the Summoning?

I climbed to my feet. I was still completely naked. The air was muggy and thick, threatening to choke me. I'd been in a few dark, dank corridors the Summoning was known for, but nothing like this. I was surrounded by a thick never-ending blanket of onyx mist.

"Hello?"

My voice bounced off the mist. Faces morphed and twisted in the smoky wall of wherever I'd gone. Brick buildings appeared before me. Their roofs were concealed by the thick, low-hanging fog.

I paused. Figures drifted in the distance. I covered my groin, suddenly aware that others were going to see my nakedness. When I glanced down at my arms, I noticed they weren't those of a demon any longer. My hands were long and clawed, my crotch and front covered in scales. At least they covered my man parts.

People with masks lined the streets. Spirits, rather, so I assumed. Their forms were transparent, not fully fleshed out.

Were they demons, or witches? Some wore dresses, others danced with one another in suits and ties. The *clank, clank, clank* of their footsteps reminded me of the metallic sound created by Maverick's mechanical arm.

Each individual wore a mask of a creature. Some were wolves, others were bears. A few lions were mixed in there, too. As the spirits walked, the features on the masks became more grotesque. No longer furry and life-like, they became skulls with hollow eyes and rotting flesh.

I ground my jaw. What kind of crazy vortex had I fallen into? And what were these spirits all gathered for?

As I maneuvered through the crowd, one of the spirits bumped into my shoulder. Its mask fell, clattering with a horrible ear-splitting sound onto the street. The mask shattered into dozens of pieces.

I jostled sideways as spirits clawed their way toward the mask. The ripping sound of flesh and bone broke my focus. When the spirits finally left, nothing remained.

I backed away, terrified of what might happen to me if I bumped into another spirit passing through this cannibalistic parade. They were going somewhere. Might as well follow them to see if I could find my way out of this shit-hole of a place.

With each step I took, I became more acquainted with the shadow town. It was a complete mirror of Midhaven. As I walked down Main Street, I passed Amon's tattoo parlor, as well as Krim's Blooming Mushroom Bakery.

The hair on the back of my neck stood on end. What kind of creepy shadow spell was this? An underworld-equivalent of what existed on the surface?

The shop windows were full of dolls, ones that reminded me of the creepy one Maverick had brought to the pub. My sides ached just seeing the hollow eyes. My skin prickled as I remembered the shadow needles—or teeth, according to Victoria—slicing into my aura.

I spotted a top hat bouncing in the crowd.

My stomach lurched.

*Maverick.*

Something large shoved me out of the group and into an alleyway. The shadowy outline of a bear manifested before me.

"Clawz?" I stammered.

My shadow bear lowered his massive head. "*Jawz is here, too. We've been surveying the territory of this shadow vortex Maverick has trapped us in.*" He flicked his ears toward the parade of masked spirits walking down the street. "*The shadow beasts out there aren't so lucky. Maverick has separated them from their shifters.*"

"Wait a second. Are those spirits all shadow beasts owned by shifters?"

Clawz growled angrily. "*Yes. Follow me. You need to see what he's been doing to the shadow beasts. You aren't going to like it.*"

I grabbed his massive shoulder before he could lumber deeper into the alley. "Where is Sniffer?"

"*Probably sticking his nose where it shouldn't be.*"

A clinking sound made my ears ache. I glanced down at Clawz's left paw. Yellow metal shone in the dull light. His paw was mechanical, just like Maverick's hand. "Clawz, what's happened to you?"

He turned, and I followed him down the alleyway.

I dropped to my hands and ran on all-fours after him. As Clawz tore ahead, another clinking sound manifested beside me. My shadow lion appeared, his shoulders scissoring as he tried to match my pace. He gnashed his canines, and a metallic sound rumbled into my head like a horrible machine.

"Jawz," I said, slowing my pace.

He did so too, his massive black paws stopping him so I could get a good look at my inner lion.

His entire muzzle was the same yellow color as Clawz's paw. Metal had replaced his teeth and jaw.

I reached out, touching the bridge of his nose. "What is this creep doing to my shadow beasts?"

A horrible roar echoed down the alleyway.

"Clawz!" I yelled, taking off toward where I heard his roar.

As I thundered ahead, a reaper manifested to my right. "Krim?"

"Yeah," my brother answered grumpily as he floated next to me. "Amon's not far behind."

His giant skeleton hand grabbed my shoulder and forced me to stop.

"Hey, what the fuck are you doing!" I ground out. "My bear is in trouble!"

Jawz tore ahead, not slowing at all as I glared at my grim reaper brother.

Krim's bony hand held me in place before I could dart after him. "Slow the fuck down. Listen. You can't follow them. Amon and I already scoped out this place. It appears to be some kind of shadow mirage of Midhaven that Maverick is controlling."

I tore away from his hand. "I need to see what he's doing." I took off in a sprint toward where I'd heard Clawz's horrible roar. The alleyway thinned, and soon I was treading on what appeared to be golden serpents.

"Zed, wait," a voice called.

I spun, finding Amon standing next to the back door that led into his tattoo parlor. His arm tattoos were missing.

"You're my best demon," Amon said, pity making his voice sound heavy. "I don't want you to get hurt like Krim and I have."

One of the metallic snakes coiled around my foot.

I kicked it away and took off once again toward Clawz's roar.

The alley emptied into a field surrounded by trees. Willow branches drifted in the breeze. Eerie cries echoed in the air. Yellow and orange lights guided me toward a clearing.

Large cages filled the area. I quickly learned where the angry creature cries were coming from. The cages were full of shadow beasts, some of which were completely mechanized.

No longer wisps of silky onyx shadows, their forms consisted of gears and bolts and pistons. Steam billowed out of their nostrils. When they roared, nothing but a high-pitched whistling sound erupted from their mouths.

The cages were constructed out of bone. A horrible thought crossed my mind. I wondered if the spirits I'd seen on the streets of Midhaven were used to construct them.

The scales on my arms bristled like fur, sticking up and thickening as my emotions got the better of me. Rage filled my body. I couldn't watch this happen to these shadow beasts, even if they didn't belong to me.

I grabbed one of the bone bars of the cage and crushed it with my hand. The second bone I grabbed with my teeth and crushed it to smithereens. The shadow beast inside the cage was so terrified, it cowered in the corner, tucking its scaly tail between its legs.

"Hey, it's okay. I'm not going to hurt you," I whispered.

But my words were quickly met with a growl. It spun, its onyx skin shimmering with scales as it rounded on me.

I recognized something in its deep hollow eyes. Something *wild* lived inside of this spirit, something that didn't deserve to be trapped in a cage—he needed to be *free.*

My chest throbbed.

The beast inside the cage was *me.*

# 29

# Victoria

"*Set me free, Victoria Crow, and you will know what it means to be mine.*"

"Ahhhhhh!"

I jumped at the sound of Dezmond's voice yelling from upstairs.

Lucy shot me a terrified look as she closed her grimoire. "What the hell was that?"

I jumped up from my seat. "Excuse me for a moment, would you?" I darted back upstairs, finding that Dezmond was sitting straight up in my bed. He was panting, and his face was beet red.

"Hey, what happened?" I asked as I approached him. I set my hand on his forehead. "Do you have a fever?"

He didn't look me in the eye. "I had a horrible nightmare," he stammered, gripping my bedsheets as he swung his legs over the edge of my bed.

*Knock, knock, knock.*

Dezmond tugged my blankets over himself as Lucy found her way into my bedroom.

She stopped at my side and folded her arms. "Look, I know my sister's house is haunted, but that yell was definitely *not* from one of her ghosts. What is going on?"

Grubs came floating into my bedroom as a butterfly, hovering above Dezmond like a brilliant winged orb. Little pieces of pollen floated down from his wings. "*We can sit here all day and argue about your nightmares, but an Earth Uprising is on the horizon. If we don't act now, I can guarantee that you will be witnessing far worse things.*" He landed on Dezmond's shoulder. "*Demon, put on some clothes. We're all going to Grace's greenhouse.*"

Lucy took off down the sidewalk ahead of Dezmond and I with her grouchy familiar, who continued to lead our group as a butterfly. The afternoon humidity clung to my skin. I really didn't want to go into Grace's greenhouse, where everything was going to be ten times muggier. Green and purple pumpkins sprouted out of the ground. Their black vines curled along the sidewalk, forcing Dezmond and I closer to one another.

I grabbed his hand. "I should probably let you know that both Amon and Krim are missing."

His fingers wove into mine, strong and sturdy, offsetting my anxiety. "Doesn't surprise me. I'm betting that Dad probably tagged along with them, too. This Maverick bloke is bad ju ju."

A summer burst of magic illuminated my periphery as my mother rounded the bend. She carried a bag of groceries in one arm and waved at us with the other. "Well now, if it isn't the best witch and the best demon for the wedding! I just saw Lucy and Grubs. She said something about meeting at Grace's greenhouse to discuss some magical business about an energy vortex in town? Why wasn't I invited?"

I laughed. "Mom, I don't know if you want to spend your afternoon sweating your mascara off. Apparently, Grace's familiars are hosting some summer solstice meeting. I have a feeling it's going to be muggy and gross.

Mom smiled. "Good point. Maybe it's best if I get to work in my kitchen. I'd hate to get in the way of one of her hedgehogs. They're very prickly about their opinions, especially Goblin." Her eyes swept to my boyfriend. "Dezmond, have you seen your father?"

"No. I was assuming that he was with you," Dezmond replied.

Mom shook her head. "He didn't show up for twilight tea yesterday evening. I have an *amazing* harvest this year. I am planning on bringing a fresh batch of summer solstice tea to the wedding."

Dezmond sighed. "Well, that's not good. Let me know if he turns up at all?"

My mother's blue eyes met mine. "Victoria, have you seen Francine? She usually stops by my place in the mornings to carry tea to my friends around town. This morning, she didn't show up."

"No, I haven't," I replied. "I also haven't seen much of her offspring."

Mom gave us both a concerned look. "Well, I'm off to prepare the tea for the wedding. Text me if you or your sisters need anything."

As Mom continued past us, her aura sent waves of light into the air. During the summer, when solar flares were frequent, her magic (just like her sisters), often created beautiful illuminations in the atmosphere.

The colors branched over the trees as we approached my sister's property. I'd never seen Grace's greenhouse so lit up with familiar auras before. The structure looked like a literal Christmas tree, only with a much brighter array of color. Oranges and reds mixed with purples and yellows, painting the entire structure in a brilliant display of the sunburst colors that reminded me of the lilies Dezmond had gotten me.

Lucy stood outside, with Grubs fluttering above the entrance. She turned to face us. "Something big is going on. But I can't get inside. There are too many pumpkin vines."

I tugged out my stethoscope and ran it along the greenhouse wall. Black pumpkin vines curled away from me as I inspected the surface.

"What are you doing?" Lucy huffed.

"Listening for the secret entrance."

"Wait, there is a secret entrance?" she stammered.

"Of course. Every garden has one, including Mom's. Grace just thinks she is the only witch who knows about."

The pulse of the plants became louder and louder, until the sound became so violent, I had to tug my ear buds out. "Found it!"

Dezmond set his hand on my shoulder. "You two go in. I'm going to hang out here. I'm not feeling too hot."

I faced him. "It's probably a good idea not to go into the humid death chamber I know this is going to be."

He nodded.

I set my hand on the wall. "I'll try and make it quick." Pumpkin vines curled aside, revealing the magical entry point her familiars used when they ventured out to mingle with other wild creatures in the neighborhood.

I crouched and scooted my way through the tunnel of woody plants. Lucy cursed something about *freaking thorns* as she followed. Once the tunnel thinned, I straightened myself and glanced around. The air was oddly *not* humid. There were no chirps, nor growls, nor the pitter-patter of tiny paws across the leaf-laden ground.

Skittles, one of Grace's jumping spiders, hopped from leaf to leaf before settling in front of the group. His eight legs danced on the leaf, making it tremble until he finally settled himself before the insects, mammals, birds, and reptiles that had all gathered at the base of the stump.

He tapped two of his front legs onto the leaf, quieting the chatter of the familiars before him. "*We are hereby prepared to commence forth our fur, scales, quills, exoskeletons, and feathers in the much-awaited event of the summer—welcome to the movement known as the Earth Uprising*!"

Lucy and I stared at each other.

A prickly ball of quills darted across the greenhouse. Goblin, Grace's green hedgehog (due to his seasonal allergies, his quills changed into a vibrant shade of goblin green, hence his name) came scurrying over to where Lucy and I stood.

"*Excuse me. We are in the middle of a very important meeting. No witches are allowed to interrupt*!" he stammered in his proper British accent as his quills stood erect.

I stared Goblin down. "Grubs here seemed to think that you and your friends could help us figuring out how to find a dangerous demon named Maverick."

"*I said no such thing*," Grubs grumbled in his grumpiest of voices from the nearby plant.

A munching sound followed by belch erupted out of the leaves, making the entire plant tremble.

"What *won't* you do for a snack?" Lucy scolded her bookworm, who had obviously tricked us into thinking he was going to help us, when all he wanted to do was fill his grouchy little tummy with leaves and flowers.

Goblin snuffed his nose at us. "*Maverick, hmmmm? Never heard of him. If he's dangerous, why on earth would you want to mingle with him?*"

"Because he's fucked with Dezmond, and therefore fucked with me," I said, startled at the sound of my own voice.

The plant leaves curled, withdrawing from me as hot, angry sparks surged out of my aura.

"*None of us are concerned with this Maverick fellow. Now, be off with you, before your magic contaminates our earthly business.*"

"You mean, an Earth Uprising?" I probed.

Goblin's body prickled. "*Again, this business is only to be discussed by familiars. Now, be gone*!"

"Before we go, can you at least tell us where Grace is?" Lucy asked.

Goblin snuffed his nose pompously. "*That witch spends most of her free time with her grumpy grim reaper at the bakery.*"

"*Ahem,*" Skittles began, waving four of his eight legs above his head. "*Goblin, we are about to commence forth with our discussion! If you wish to be part of it, then I suggest you stop chatting with the witches who have no business being here.*"

Goblin pinned his ears back against his head, trembled ferociously, then launched himself like a green missile toward Lucy and I's ankles.

"Okay, we're leaving! Sheesh!" I stammered as I jumped back, bumping into my sister before he jabbed his quills into me.

"What a spiky little grump!" Lucy said as she grabbed my arm to prevent me from falling.

I crouched down and began to crawl back out of the greenhouse. "Remind me to have a talk with Grace about leaving her familiars unsupervised. It looks like they're doing more than just starting their own commune. Why were they discussing an Earth Uprising?"

"Historically, familiars have created the movements when they sense a disturbance in the three magics. In an attempt to re-balance them, they draw upon the forces of the earth, hoping to correct whatever their instincts don't agree with."

"And apparently witches aren't allowed to be part of it," I grumbled as I straightened myself and wiped the leaves out of my hair. I was so frustrated with how Grace's familiars had treated us, I didn't seem to care that Dezmond was missing.

"Snooty bunch of bugs and rodents. Grace has spoiled them," Lucy stammered as she straightened next to me.

I stared at the greenhouse, ready to charge back in and give her familiars a piece of my mind. "You know what? We're not leaving. Francine won't settle for this. She's got a real set of eyes when it comes to scoping out familiar gossip."

I closed my eyes, sensing for her. But the warm, protective flares associated with my hawk's presence didn't return to my aura.

# 30

# Dezmond

I walked away from the greenhouse while Victoria and Lucy scoped out the situation with Grace's familiars. Lights illuminating the sky darkened as green smoke exploded into my periphery. Two men manifested beneath the giant oak tree. Both had reddish-brown hair, and were dressed in green tweed sweaters. Freckles dusted their wide, square faces. Their eyes were hazel, one of the two with a tad more brown than green.

I took a step back as the smoke cleared. The last time I'd seen a demon manifest unannounced, it had been one of Dad's adversaries from the demon council. As the smoke cleared, I squared my hips, ready to defend myself as necessary. I'd had enough of strange, unwelcome guests turning my day to shit without my permission.

"Oi! Dezmond! How have you been?" one of the demons asked. His voice carried an Irish tune.

The second, who stood a few inches shorter than his friend, waggled his thick fingers in the air. When he spoke, his voice mimicked the same spirited sound as the other. "Bring it in and give us a hug!"

I was jostled between the two as they ambushed me. "I'm sorry, who are you guys?"

"Didn't Eugene tell you that we were visiting from Ireland?" the shorter and stouter of the two said.

I squinted between them. "Wait a second. Uncles Oscar and Liam?"

Both began to chuckle.

"I'm Liam, and *this* is Oscar," the taller of the two said as he held his hand down to the level of his hip. "You were just a wee lad when you last saw us."

"Your father said it was okay if we crashed at your place," Oscar said as he cracked his thick knuckles. "He also said you were the best demon for Amon's wedding. We are super excited to start planning his bachelor party."

Liam ran his fingers through his thick hair. "We expected you to be at your apartment, not a bunch of stray kitties who like to beg for treats?"

I ran my hand through my hair. "Oh, about that. I've been at my girlfriend's place."

Oscar smiled. "We heard that Eugene is hitting it off with a witch named Cindy, and she might happen to have a couple of twin sisters who are visiting."

I chuckled. "Wow, you guys are just as bad as my father."

Liam's hazel eyes studied me. "Speaking of your old man, want to see what he's been helping us with?"

I jolted. "Wait, he's been hanging with you guys? We've been looking for him!"

Oscar clapped his hands together. "Well, what are we waiting for? Let's go get this Ravenblood party started!"

Before I could step away, Liam and Oscar's shadows erupted into plumes of green smoke. Without Pawz, Jawz, or Sniffer, I was helpless to stop them from taking me into the Summoning.

A gritty sensation filled my mouth. As shadows coalesced around me, my feet hit solid ground. Shiny black cobblestones glinted on the street. Dark brick buildings surround me.

Laughter sounded from the building with a giant wooden sign that looked like it was carved during another century. The sign read:

**The Shifter's Wild Spirits**

The aroma of woodsmoke met my nose. A backlit wall was lined with shelves that held bottles of spirits. A map of Ireland hung above the bottles. Kegs were stacked behind the bar. Liam helped swap the kegs as Oscar removed older ones out from beneath the tap pulls.

Liam straightened himself, readjusting his suspenders as he faced me. "Welcome to a *real* Irish pub, not any of this nonsense your Dad's had to settle for in the Midwest."

"When he showed us Paddyshack's, I almost shit myself," Oscar chortled as he began to dry mugs with a towel.

I sat on a stool in front of my uncles and propped my elbows onto the counter. "I assume you two run this pub?"

Liam grabbed a shot glass and set it in front of me. "We do. We serve a lot of demons who are passing from one place to the next."

"You mean, between life and death?"

Liam shook his head. "No. To places on the surface. And by the looks of it, there are lots of demon and witch folk who want to leave the coasts and settle somewhere in the Midwest. Oscar and I can't understand it."

Oscar began to stack the glasses. "Unless, you believe in the dragon vortex."

I snorted. "*Dragon vortex*?"

Oscar smiled. "You've heard of ley lines, or magical energies that all mingle in certain spots? It's rumored to draw demons and witches together like gravity. I think that Midhaven might be a location where these energies pool themselves."

I shrugged. "Magical vortex or not, I can tell you that you won't have Krim's bar as competition any longer. Maybe you should move your pub above ground and out of the Summoning. You know what Krim did to Shadow Daddy's, right?"

Liam shook his head. "Yeah. He disgraced his entire demonic bloodline when he settled for a bakery." He grabbed a bottle of whiskey and poured me a shot. "For now, we only serve demons. No mortals or witch-folk are allowed. By the way, I'm the demon officiating your brother's wedding. How about we give a toast to the best demon?"

I grabbed the shot and downed it. *Fuck*. How badly I missed the burn of alcohol instead of Krim's obsession with frosting in my throat.

Liam refilled my glass as soon as I slammed it down. "So, how are your shifting talents coming along? Eugene mentioned that Cindy's witch daughter helped you out when you injured yourself, and that your magic has gotten a bit beastlier in the process?"

I grabbed the shot glass. "Since when has my father been spreading rumors about how *beastly* I've become?" I blinked. I could have sworn that Liam's hand turned to claws before morphing back into fingers. A wolfish smile curled his lips, something I'd seen plenty of times in my father.

Oscar busied himself with hanging a banner below the map of Ireland with Amon's name on it. A reddish-brown tail bristled out of his pants. "I hope Amon loves his bachelor party."

"Who cares what Amon thinks. *I* love you both, for saving my ass. I've done absolutely nothing to prep for it."

Liam's nose wrinkled as a muzzle warped his face.

I glanced between them, noticing all the sudden canine-appearance in their features. No way was the alcohol already warping my perception. "Are you two *wolf* shifters?"

Liam and Oscar grinned, each displaying a set of pointed canines.

The door chimed as another demon walked in. Short, spiky blond hair fell into her face. She took up a seat a few barstools down and propped her elbows onto the counter. "I need your stiffest drink available. On the rocks."

"You got it," Liam replied.

Oscar busied himself with the bottles of whiskey while Liam grabbed a new shot glass.

I rose to my feet and approached her, biting back the anger as it swelled in my throat.

Sloane was slumped over at the bar. Her hand was wrapped around her side. Bandages bound her shoulder and arm. Her hand, too, was covered in blood-soaked linen.

I stopped at her side. "What happened to you? Did you get into some kind of fight?"

Liam set the shot glass full of spirits in front of her.

She grabbed the glass with a shaky hand, spilling a few drops of whiskey onto the counter. "If you want info on Maverick, I suggest that you don't treat me like shit right now." She downed it then slammed the glass down. "I'm going to need a few of these before I can share anything about our argument over the dragons."

"Wait, *Maverick* did this to you? He used that creepy voodoo doll on you, didn't he?" I stammered.

Sloane grunted as she repositioned herself on the stool. "That is no normal voodoo doll. Maverick has been using it to manipulate shifters into doing horrible, wicked things."

My stomach squirmed. "Did it bite you too?"

She glanced up at me, her red-rimmed eyes reflecting the same pain I felt when I had those shadow needles wedge between my ribs. "The Spirit of the Wild is a ravenous shadow beast. He won't be satiated with elemental runes or demon flesh—he's out for the blood of a witch from the Crow family."

My jaw clenched. When I reached out to grab her arm, she shifted, morphing out of my reach.

A fox manifested on the ground, snarling up at me. Her black ears pinned back against her hair bristling on her shoulders. "*If you care for the golden dragon, you might want to check on her.*"

A bell chimed as she leapt toward the exit, her bushy tail swishing through the door as she left.

It took me three seconds to rip my ass out of my uncles' bar and exit the Summoning. My feet hit solid ground. Gravel crunched under my boots as I tore toward the grove of willow trees where Torchie's mother lived.

"Willow!" I cried as I reached the barrier of green and yellow leaves that dangled like garland down from the canopy.

The air was thick with silence.

*Something is wrong.*

The branches were still, not lively in the breeze as they had been when I'd visited her before.

"Willow, are you here?" I asked as I dipped into the trees in search of her.

"*Dezmond? Is that you*?" she replied. Her voice was subdued, not warm and sun-like.

"Yeah, it's me. Is everything—"

"*—Victoria is going to be so upset*," she rumbled in an icy tone.

My foot splashed into dark purple liquid. Willow's golden reflection shimmered in it. A wound gaped on her side, spreading her scales.

"What happened to you?" I whispered.

"*A monster*," she said, not meeting me with her golden eye. "*I couldn't save her from it in time.*"

My stomach dropped. I recognized the placement of the gashes, and the precision of the marks. *I* had made these wounds when I'd tried to free the caged shadow beast in my nightmare. Sickened by the sight, I bent over, preparing to wretch. Branches began to spin as nausea churned my stomach.

*What is happening to me*?

*Am I possessed by this shadow beast called the Spirit of the Wild*?

Feathers were scattered on the ground where I collapsed. It took all of my willpower not to lose my shit after what I saw next.

# 31

# Victoria

Something was wrong. Francine had *never* gone missing for this long. Speaking of missing, where the hell had Dezmond gone?

Speak of the devil. Purple smoke burst into the air as he manifested.

Dezmond took a step toward me. “Victoria, I’m so sorry, but I found her in the willow groves like this.”

Lucy slapped one of her hands over her mouth. “Oh my goddess.”

My stomach pitted. A red-tailed hawk lay limp in his arms.

“Francine!” I cried, closing the space between us. “What happened to her?”

“Willow said a monster attacked her.”

I grabbed Francine’s frail body from him. I cradled her head in my palm. Her once vibrant eyes were dark, no longer filled with bursts of magical color.

My breath hitched as a sob escaped me. “No, please. Francine. Please don’t leave me.”

As I cried, one of my tears fell onto her head, and dribbled down her beak. My heart was broken. What was I going to do without my hawk of over twenty-five years?

Memories played behind my eyelids as flashbacks of our life together welled up from some long forgotten time. I remembered when Grace had shoved a handful of rolly pollies into my rain boots, which I squashed between my toes. Apparently, I could never forgive myself for accidentally murdering a bunch of bugs.

I'd been so mad at myself that I stormed into the field behind the farm, losing myself in my despair. Screaming at the top of my lungs, and finally ripping off my dress, I stood as a naked seven-year-old, staring up at a tree. My tears blurred the giant bird of prey gazing down at me. I still remember the fierceness in her eyes. I loved all creatures, big and small. I couldn't forgive myself for killing something, even if it was unintentional.

"*Calm your spirit, wild one,*" the bird said, her voice high and powerful. "*You have many creatures yet to befriend. But to do so, you must tame your spirit if you are to master the wild witch you will one day become.*"

A feather fell from the tree. I caught it, captivated with how it glowed with the magical colors of a sunset.

"Victoria," Lucy said, her voice breaking me out of my first memory of meeting Francine. "I'm so sorry. What can I do to help you right now?"

Salt stung my cheeks as more tears began to flow. Francine had been sent to me from some other wild force I had no control over. *She* was the creature who had first called me a *wild witch.* Why did she have to die for me to remember?

As tears dolloped down my cheeks and onto her, she began to glow. A silver light encompassed her, then quickly evaporated. All that remained in my hands were a few of her tail feathers.

Dezmond set his hand on my shoulder. "Look, I know this is a bad time, but I need you to see Willow. She got hurt trying to protect Francine from whatever killed her."

I locked my eyes with his green ones. Something wild and untamed reflected back at me.

*Wild witch.*

Francine's words filled my mind, stirring something ancient inside of me.

As I flipped my thumb over the feathers, what remained of Francine's magic was transferred to me. It hummed and bounced between my fingers, rooting itself into my palm.

"Victoria, sweetheart, did you hear me?" Dezmond said as he set his other hand on my shoulder.

"Willow got hurt?" I asked as I stroked Francine's beautiful feathers.

"Yeah, she's in bad shape. I want you to look at her."

I tucked Francine's feathers into my pocket. "What are you waiting for? Bring me to her." I faced my sister. "Lucy, I'm sorry. I need to go."

She embraced me. "Text me as soon as you can. I want to make sure we get even with whoever did this to your feathered friend."

Dezmond enveloped me so quickly, I barely had time to release my sister before I was thrown into his thick, inky shadows. My eyes burned even though I clenched them closed. Flashes of Francine's magic still lived inside of me. Even though she was gone, I could still feel her watchful gaze on the back of my head.

My feet hit solid earth. I unraveled myself from his arms and started to walk toward the willow trees.

He caught my hand. "Victoria, wait."

I spun to face him. I blinked, not wanting to look at his gorgeous green eyes. They had so much emotion and strength swimming inside them.

He tugged me toward him, taking my other hand into his callused one. "Hey, I feel fucking awful. But I know I don't feel as bad as you must right now."

"I don't want to talk about it," I said, desperately wanting to shove past him and fix what I could. Even if I couldn't save my hawk, I could still take care of Willow.

"All right," he said, not letting go of my hand as he walked alongside me toward the long yellow and pink branches that reflected the setting sun.

The moment the branches grazed my head and shoulders, Willow's exasperated voice filled my head. "*Victoria, I'm sorry. I know you must be furious with me right now.*"

I glanced up at Willow's giant golden eye. "Why would I be mad at you?"

"*Because I let the monster get to Francine before I could stop her.*"

"Was this monster the Spirit of the Wild?" I asked, rage cracking in my voice.

Dezmond's hand squeezed mine tighter, while Willow blinked, sending a massive tear splashing onto my foot.

Willow lowered her head. "*I cannot say for certain who this monster was. His magic was far too powerful, able to conceal his true identity behind the elements he mastered.*"

I tore away from Dezmond's grip and ducked between the drooping branches. "Look, this isn't my first rodeo. I've dealt with a lot of familiar deaths in my years." But my words were just there to cover up what I really felt. What was I going to do not having her annoying me with her shrieking fits?

And what about her offspring? What would happen to her fledglings if they didn't have their mother to continue teaching them how to hunt?

I needed something to focus on, to bury myself in. Taking care of Willow was exactly the medicine my soul needed. The gentle brush of the wind through the leaves helped to conceal my continued sobs.

"Tell me about this monster that hurt you and killed Francine," I said as I tugged my stethoscope out of my pocket and plugged in my earbuds. My voice sounded cold and distant, startling me.

Dezmond tensed beside me as I set the chest piece onto her massive scaly side.

Willow's scales shivered. "*Oh, that is cold. What is that device called? And what is it used for?*"

"It's called a stethoscope, and I'm using it to listen for your heartbeat.

Just like with Dezmond, I heard *multiple* rhythms bouncing inside of her chest cavity. Some sounded like waves crashing upon a shore, while others resembled the distant rumble of thunder.

I withdrew my stethoscope from Willow's body. "It looks like you are on the mend. I'll come back tomorrow and check on you. I also expect you to tell me more about this monster."

*"Or, I'll come to you, if that would be better. I know you have a wedding you are preparing for."*

I looked to my demon boyfriend, who was as white as a ghost. "Dezmond, can you please take me home? I'm exhausted."

His shadows embraced me before the sweet warmth of his voice met my ears, "Of course."

My house manifested as Dezmond brought me home. He lowered me onto my doorstep, refusing to let me go. "Hey, I'm sorry about everything," he said as he set his hands onto my hips. "Can I please comfort you tonight?"

I withdrew from his embrace. "I think it would be best if I slept alone."

I ignored the hurt in his eyes.

"Can I at least kiss you goodnight?"

"Sure," I whispered.

"Sure? Or yes?"

"You know, maybe I should just go."

"Victoria, wait, I didn't mean to—"

But I turned on my heel, emotionally spent from the day, and retreated into my home.

# 32

# Dezmond

After Victoria abandoned me on the curb, my shadows curled around me, bringing me down into the dark, dank alleyway of the Summoning that housed my uncles' pub. Sure, the pain of losing her hawk had destroyed her. But did she have to turn me away?

My brain became a thick boiling brew of confusion. Watching Victoria tend to Willow's wounds didn't make me feel any better.

How was I connected to this shadow beast Willow had identified as a *monster*? Better yet, why couldn't I fix this shitty situation for the wild witch I had fallen muzzle-over-tail for?

The sound of fiddles danced in the air. As I entered the pub, a demon folk band came into view. Oscar and Liam were dancing arm-in-arm, spinning one another as they traded places.

Dad's two spirit ravens darted overhead, purple smoke billowing out of their wings as they tore across the pub in a celebration I had no intention of joining. "Zeddy! Where have you been?" Dad called as he spun and faced me.

Both Amon and Krim were standing next to Dad. I didn't acknowledge them and headed straight for the bar. "What a fucking day," I grumbled as Liam found his way behind the bar.

"What are we drowning our sorrows over?" Liam asked as he took up a glass and set it in front of me.

I glanced over at my family. Oscar took up Amon's arm and began to dance with him instead. Both Dad and Krim made their way over to me. "Victoria's hawk was killed, and I had to be the one to deliver the news to her."

"Wait, Francine?" Dad grumbled.

"Sounds serious," Krim agreed. "I'm sure Grace knows by now. She said she had something pressing about a bird to tend to and couldn't join me for dinner."

I glanced down at my phone. Who knew if I'd ever get a text from Victoria again. I couldn't blame her if she didn't want to speak to me for a few weeks after what I had to share with her. "Yeah. Willow said a monster attacked her, then it killed Francine."

Dad set his hand on my shoulder. "We all know that Sloane and Maverick are shifters. Could it have been one of them who killed her?"

I shook my head, doubt knotting in my stomach. "I don't think so. Sloane was in this pub not long ago, and I'm pretty sure she was bit by the same creepy voodoo doll that bit me."

Dad shook his head. "Killing a witch's familiar is like murdering a piece of her soul. Victoria will feel that pain for the rest of her life."

I clenched my hands on the bar. Should I tell them about the horrible nightmare of the caged beast, and the cannibalistic spirits wearing masks?

Or the fact that *I* was a suspect?

Liam's hazel eyes settled onto me. "Your father just told me that he and your brothers have been prowling around. After that shady fox named Sloane came into our pub, Oscar and I also did some of our own sniffing around town."

He reached under the bar and tugged out another shot glass. An angular black stone sat at the bottom of it.

"What the hell are you trying to spike my drink with?" I asked.

Krim's eyes went wide. "It's a shadow pendant."

"A *what*?" I asked as I dipped my fingers into the glass.

Krim's shadow grabbed my arm before I could grab the onyx stone. "Don't touch it. The magic is very nasty to one's flesh."

"How come you can touch it, but I can't?" I argued with my grim reaper brother.

His bony fingers clinked against the glass as he grabbed the stone. "I'm the only demon in this family who has a shadow with skeleton hands, remember?" He held it in front of his face. "Uncle Liam, where did you and Oscar find this?"

"Not far from the pub," Liam answered. "We also noticed it had a little fox hair stuck to it."

I squinted at the stone Krim had called a shadow pendant. "Hey, there are markings on it."

"Let me have a look," Dad said as he lowered his face next to mine.

"It looks like one of the runes that Willow and Drake gave me and Victoria." I glanced at Krim. "Which by the way, what ever happened to the air rune I let you borrow?"

"About that," Krim said as he ran one of his hands through his hair. "As soon as I took it to my lab, it sort of vanished into thin air."

I ground my jaw. "Great. Now we have *none* of the runes Drake and Willow gave us. How are we supposed to unlock the magic inside of them if they're gone?"

Krim weighed the stone in his palm. "I think Sloane might have given us something to work with instead."

"I'm not following."

Krim squeezed the shadow pendant. "I think Sloane is leaving a trail for us to follow. Shadow pendants are known to leave traces of residual magic that can be traced back to a demon's shadows."

"Which means we can use it to hunt down this shadow beast called the Spirit of the Wild, can't we?" I suggested.

Krim nodded. "Historically, shadow pendants were created by female demons to help with manipulating shadow elements. Sloane is a female shifter, is she not? She could have been hiding the runes from Maverick by turning them into shadow pendants."

Liam, Dad, and I all stared at my grim reaper brother.

"Guys, don't look so shocked. It's basic shadow alchemy. While *normal* alchemy focuses on the principle of equivalent exchange, meaning nothing can be gained if you do not give something of equal value, *shadow* alchemy focuses more on the essence of void—a concept that revolves around the elemental space that connects all three magics. For shadows, earth, and the goddess to remain in balance, the elements of water, air, and fire must each be present."

"Since when did you get so poetic about alchemy?" I asked.

Krim's blue eyes lowered to me. "I learned from the demon council that shadow pendants are created by female demons by using shadow elements. *How* they are created is still a mystery."

I glanced up at Dad and Krim, sucking in a breath. "Guys, I've been a wreck, and not only because of Francine's death. I had this horrible nightmare, where I was in some shadow town version of Midhaven." I glanced up at my brother. "Krim, you and Amon were both in it."

Krim raised one of his eyebrows. "I hope we didn't do something awful to you."

"No, but the shadow beasts did something awful to the both of you, at least they did to your shadows."

Krim glanced over at Amon and waved at him.

Amon abandoned his dance with my uncle and approached the bar. The fiddles died as Oscar, too, followed.

"Hey, Zed. What's going on?" Amon asked as he took a seat next to me. "Sorry I didn't fill you in on what Krim and I's lead on Maverick. Neither of us could find any trace of him. Dad sort of just jumped in like he always does when he wants to help us, but even his ravens couldn't pick up a trail from this creepy demon."

I rolled my shoulders. "I'm the one who should be sorry. I haven't done anything to prepare for your bachelor party. I've not been a good best demon."

"That's what Oscar and I are here for!" Liam chimed in as he rummaged through his whiskey bottles.

I glanced at the stone. "Yeah, well. Victoria's pretty upset about her hawk. Right now, she doesn't even want to talk with me."

Liam propped his elbows on the bar, his hazel eyes sweeping to me. "Give her some time. A witch has a special bond with her familiar, but she can form an even *better* bond with her demon."

Amon shot Krim a look. "Did something happen?"

"Yeah. Poor Zeddy had to deliver the bad news that Victoria's hawk was murdered," Dad intervened.

"Wait, Francine? *Murdered*?" Amon asked.

"Yeah," I ground out, not wanting to repeat the same story a second time.

Amon's tattoos retreated up his forearms. "Dude, that's awful. Do you have any knowledge about who killed her?"

I swallowed, thinking back to the horrible, caged creature from the nightmare. "Willow said it was some kind of monster."

"Well, I guess I know what my bachelor party is going to be like," Amon said as he took up a spot next to Krim. "Putting this fucking asshole named Maverick in his place. He's got to be the one responsible for your bad luck."

Krim's gaze leveled with me. "Zed, what do you remember from the shadow town of Midhaven in this nightmare?"

I stared at the onyx stone in the shot glass on the bar, watching as swirls of color mixed inside it. "The windows had these creepy dolls in them, the same one that Maverick had."

"Were your own shadow beasts present?" Amon asked.

"Yeah, they were. But they'd been transformed, just like you both," I said as I looked away. "Their jaws, claws, and muzzles became metallic."

Krim's blue eyes narrowed onto me. "What kind of metal? What color was it?"

"It was yellow. I was pretty sure it was gold," I answered.

Krim snapped his fingers. "Creepy shadow beast dolls? Shadows turning into gold? We're dealing with shadow alchemy that involves *voodoo*."

Dad shot Oscar and Liam a look, while Amon kept his gaze on Krim.

"Voodoo shadow alchemy is considered to be the most dangerous branch of shadow magic, as its rituals deal with sacrifice."

My stomach swallowed. "Sacrifice, of *what*?"

Krim continued, "In order to find its true mate, the Spirit of the Wild sacrifices a shifter to the onyx flame that first gave birth to the Summoning."

"In other words, the Spirit of the Wild makes off with the shifter's mate, while the shifter goes bye-bye?" I ground out.

Krim nodded as he grabbed his drink.

My imagination ran away with me as images of the scaly beast I'd seen grabbed Victoria around the waist and tossed me into the flames. "Great, that sounds fucking fantastic. What happens if the demon tries to fight the Spirit of the Wild before he gets sacrificed?"

"He hopes that his bond with the witch he desires is strong enough to withstand the beast's ravenous appetite for his mate," a greasy voice sounded from behind.

Amon and I bumped elbows as we jumped.

I spun, finding a demon with a metallic arm and a top hat staring right at me, his upper lip curling in a grimace. "And as you know, Dezmond Ravenblood, wildness comes with a price."

"Maverick," I said, jumping up. "Why are you here?"

His mechanical arm made a horrible whining sound as gears began to spin. "I'm hunting down a fox who's left a trail of blood right to this pub. Turns out she's left one of her runes with the Ravenbloods."

Amon and Krim spun toward him.

Amon's tattoos slithered down his forearms. "Did this dumbass really just threaten the Ravenbloods on *our* turf?"

Maverick's metallic hand opened and closed, sending sparks into the air as his dark eyes found me. "What you saw in your nightmare is just the beginning of what I have planned for this crummy little town. Cindy and her vet daughter are going to feel the Spirit of the Wild's bite before long."

My father's spirit ravens tore through the air, their feathers igniting into a purple inferno as they surged toward Maverick.

"Eugene, stop!" Liam grabbed my father around the arm, while Oscar grabbed the other.

With a flick of his metallic hand, Maverick disappeared before the ravens could catch him.

"That fucker just threatened Cindy and her daughter!" Dad yelled, staggering away from my uncles.

Krim grabbed Dad's shoulder. "Settle down. I think we can use the shadow pendant to track down Maverick's creepy voodoo doll."

# 33

# Victoria

The rattling sound of my windows jolted me awake. I'd only just dozed off, still reeling from losing Francine. I awoke to the unsettling sensation that something very large was watching me.

"*I've been watching you since the wee hours of the morning, dear,*" Willow's voice burst like a fresh ray of sunshine into my head.

"That's not creepy at all," I grumbled to the mother dragon who was now sending me magical solar flares that cast my bedroom in golden light.

"*I hope you are in a better mood than yesterday. Your sister will be counting on you to enlighten her with fun and festivities.*"

I grabbed my phone from my bedside table.

*Fuck...*

Today was the day of Lucy's bachelorette party, and I'd done absolutely *nothing* for it.

Another obnoxious burst of golden energy came shooting through my window, blinding me as I stood up and attempted to dress myself. "Looks like you're a real ray of sunshine, Willow. I take it that your symptoms have disappeared?"

*"Oh, that magic isn't from me. There is an aurora hovering in the atmosphere."*

"Shit. Are my aunts here?"

*"They will be, momentarily, judging by the way the solar flares are taking to my scales. Only the magic created by the aurora can make them shine this way."*

After I grabbed a quick shower, I dressed and descended my stairs. Willow's golden light had brightened my entire kitchen, making it glow like a golden disco ball. The light made the vase of flowers Dezmond gave me sparkle.

Guilt wallowed in my stomach. Why had I been such a *bitch* to him last night?

My phone buzzed in my pocket. Holly was calling me.

As I prepped myself a cup of coffee, I answered. "Yes?"

"Look, I know today is Lucy's bachelorette party, but Rosie finally had a bowel movement and passed something I think was the source of her recent rainbow flare up."

I laughed. Only Holly would sound so excited about a serpent finally pooping. "That's great. I'm sure everything at the office is super colorful."

"What's wrong? You sound awful."

As I prepped coffee, three fuzzy birds flew by my window.

"I. . ." my voice broke as I choked. How was I going to break it to her chicks that they'd lost their mother? "Holly, I need to go. I've severely dropped the ball on Lucy's bachelorette party. Can you please ask one of the interns to take care of Rosie for me until I can come in later this morning? I think I have magical relatives coming into town and I need to get situated."

"Sure thing. Magical family is always something to get used to. Are you sure you're all right?"

"Yeah. I'm just stressed with everything going on with the wedding."

"It's going to be a fun day. It will be here before you know it! I'll see you when you stop by the office."

Thankfully, she ended the call, leaving me to grab my coffee and walk outside onto my back porch. Willow had perched herself in my tree, her giant golden scales camouflaging with the leaves as they shimmered in the morning sunlight. The only reason I noticed her was because I'd spotted her reflection in the pool. Her tail lowered from the tree, dangling in front of me. "*I'm here for my checkup.*"

"Why are you showing off your tail?"

"*A dragon's pulse is best felt in their tail, not their chest.*"

"Ah. I did not know that." I reached into my pocket and tugged out the same bewitched stethoscope I'd used on her the day before.

A similar thundering rhythm I'd heard of multiple heartbeats came crashing into my ear buds. "Can I ask you a personal question about Drake?"

"*Of course.*"

I glanced over at the pool, remembering Dezmond and I's hot, steamy night together, when supposedly our bond had formed. "The bond you have with Drake, you would consider it special, right?"

"Absolutely."

"Would you call it *fate*?"

"*Fate, as in our relationship was decided for us*?"

"Yeah. I've read a lot of renditions about what the idea of fated mates really means. But I can't help but wonder if there are certain rules that maybe creatures like dragons follow that don't apply to witches and demons."

Willow's tail curled, sending out yellow sparks into the air. "*Drake would say the elements aligned for us. There is a reason we connect with some elements more intimately over the others. And opposites don't always attract. But they are always needed to help us learn to grow into our magic.*"

"Well now, it's not every day you see a dragon perched in a tree," a woman's voice sounded from behind me.

I spun, finding the source of the aurora flares as they bounced off Willow's scales. Two witches emerged from my home, seeming to appear out of nowhere. While my aunts displayed similarities in their features, such as the same narrow, upturned noses, their hair, eyes, and outfits had striking contrast.

Millie had dark brown eyes that lit up with gold. Her hair was as black as night, and it draped in thick satiny waves over her shoulders. Dressed in a burgundy top with a black corset that was bound together with green and golden lace. Black leather boots dressed her legs, tapering just below the knee.

Tillie busied her fingers with a lock of her golden hair. It was shorter than her sister's and tapered at the base of her neck. Silky silver fabric clung to her arms. Instead of boots, tan sandals clung to her feet. Her toenails were painted a bright shade of pink. She also wore a bright ultramarine blue corset.

Both of my aunt witches had crows feet that creased the corners of their eyes, suggesting they had spent a great deal of their lives smiling. But instead of their wrinkles aging them, they both seemed to glow with the same youthful appearance my mother was blessed with. When I squinted, I noticed the lines framing their eyes were in fact the source of the aurora magic that made Willow's scales so luminous.

A snort and a burst of flame directed my attention to what Millie was holding. Torchie had his wings folded, a contented look upon his face as he dozed in her arms.

"Victoria!" Tillie yelled as she tossed her hands into the air in a similar fashion to how my mother did. "It's so good to see you!"

"You as well!" I stammered, still trying to figure out how long it had been since I'd seen either of my aunts. There was an awkward pause where I didn't know if I should or shouldn't embrace them.

"Has it really been almost a *decade* since I've seen you in person?" Tillie asked, seeming to have read my mind.

Millie rolled her eyes. "Sister, Victoria was always my favorite niece, because I could feel how untamed and wild her magic had grown from miles away." Her dark eyes settled onto me. "She will forever be a witch who has talents for unleashing the magic in those around her."

"I guess my temper as a kid will always be something that goes down in history," I replied, trying to take Millie's words as a compliment.

Tillie glanced between Willow and me. "Speaking of talents. How did you obtain the little scaly one? Are dragons normal inhabitants around Midhaven?"

I shook my head. "Not until recently. Willow is Torchie's mother. She and her mate entrusted Francine with hatching their little one, who you are currently holding."

My throat caught fire just mentioning Francine's name.

Tillie clapped her hands to her cheeks. "Oh, it's not every day you get to see a dragon using your pool as a bird bath!" She walked over to the water and lowered her hand inside, then withdrew a freshly shed dragon scale. They shimmered like flower petals across the surface.

"A *gift to the aurora witches who made my scales shimmer so beautifully,*" Willow cooed, her voice echoing into all our minds.

Millie glanced down at Torchie sleeping in her arms. "I was flying into town, and what do you know? A dragon comes soaring overhead, his tail nearly whipping my hat off! And now, he won't leave me alone."

I laughed. My two aunts were probably the only witches I knew who still traveled across the country on broomsticks.

Willow lowered her wing as my two aunts were nearly swept away by the gust she created. "*I'm so glad he finally went down for a nap. It's taken Drake and I over a week to figure out how to get him to sleep for more than a few moments.*"

"Drake must be your mate then, hmmm?" Millie asked.

"*Yes,*" Willow replied. "*He was thinking about dropping in to Amon's bachelor party,*" Willow replied as she sent another gust of wind over us.

"We can't let them throw a better party than us!" Tillie exclaimed.

"Who's talking about parties and not inviting me along?" another woman asked as she emerged from my back door.

I must not have sensed her aura due to the bright aurora flares encompassing my home.

My mother brushed past her sisters and made a beeline toward me. She approached with such force that had I not braced myself, we both might have gone for a tumble into the pool.

"I am so sorry about Francine. Grace told me what happened to her this morning," Mom whispered into my ear.

"Lucy must have already spread the word, didn't she?" I said, tearing up in her arms. I buried my face into her neck.

"What's happened to Francine?" Tillie asked as she too, suddenly embraced my mother and myself.

I broke away from them, but not soon enough. Willow's wing had branched around my mother and aunts, swooping us all into one giant wing-tight hug.

When she released us, our magic combined after too much time apart, creating a beautiful pinkish-orange halo around our heads.

Millie spoke first. "Your hawk of how many years is *dead*?"

"Twenty-five," I replied. "She was killed by something that possesses some dangerous, dark magic we still have no luck with identifying."

"*She was killed by a monster who lurks in the shadows,*" Willow added, lowering her head for the first time from the tree.

Millie and Tillie glanced at one another, purple and yellow sparks zapping into the pool, where they caught a few of Willow's scales on fire.

"Your aunts came to town at the right time," Millie said as she turned to her sister. "Cindy, do you still have that magical deck of cards?"

Mom nodded. "I had a feeling that you two were going to be asking for it. I currently have the deck at my house."

"Illuminating monsters who lurk in the darkest of shadows are just but one of our specialties. An aurora witch possesses talent for cleansing out the energies that have no purpose in a witch's life, especially one who has yet to embrace her wild magic."

I glanced at them. "I have no idea why everyone is all of a sudden saying that my magic is wild."

"A *wild* witch?" Tillie laughed high into the air. "Dear, we've known that about you since you were in diapers. Cindy has stories of how you could summon the wildest of thunderstorms, and even a swarm of mosquitoes with your tantrums as a child."

Millie clasped her hands together. "But before we get the festivities going, will you please treat a witch to this lovely, enchanted bakery in town? I hear they serve mushroom-shaped cupcakes that can make a witch lose her shadow virginity?"

I nearly slipped into the pool. "*Shadow* virginity? What does that entail?"

Tillie grinned. "That she'll find a demon to pair off with instead of a man."

Millie cackled maniacally. "Oh, Tillie. You need to get laid."

"Why did you think I flew all the way out here, sister? My broomstick barely does anything for me any longer, even when it vibrates."

By the time I arrived at the clinic, it was already mid-morning. Holly handed me my usual clipboard. A little pile of poo had been drawn next to Rosie's name at the top.

"I'm pretty sure she's the most active she's ever been since she did her business," Holly said.

I handed her back the clipboard. "This better not be a multi-colored scene like the one involving a sick triceratops from Jurassic Park."

Holly snickered as I walked past her and entered the room where Rosie had been quarantined by the vet techs. Rosie herself was not in her usual cage. Now I knew why the techs had put her in a separate room—she'd learned to escape her enclosure. She was curled up by the window, sunning herself. Her scales were all a brilliant iridescent rainbow.

Her tail twitched as she curled it around the rune.

I approached the window, reaching out to gather her into my arms. "All right, old gal. It's time to—ouch!"

I recoiled as she lashed out, sinking her fangs into me. "Hey, what was that about?"

Fire burned in my veins. For as long as I'd known Rosie, she had never *bitten* me. I didn't believe she was venomous, but from how badly the spot where she bit me burned, I was starting to second-guess.

As I glanced at the bite, a voice filled my head and said, "*Igniting the darkest places of our souls, fire burns through the skin, the flesh, and the bone. It reveals our pains, our fears, and our passions. Fire is the purifier, the lifeblood of our magic. Fire is both medicine, and a curse.*"

"Why did you *bite* me?"

"*Sorry, I had to strike,*" Rosie hissed. "*It's to help you build a magical immunity for the beast you will face later. The burning sensation should dull by the time you see him again.*"

"How do you know about the Spirit of the Wild?" I asked, shaken.

Rosie's tail curled around the rune, which was thankfully clean. "*I am a descendant of dragons. Their magic has long been forged in the elements that give me my colorful skin.*" She nudged the rune toward me. "*As for the rune, it will offer you protection. Make sure you keep it close to you.*"

The moment I entered the bakery, Lucy and Grace glanced up at me from a table by the window. I could tell from the flower arrangements that they were discussing decorations for the wedding.

Grace came flying over to me with her arms in the air. She pulled me into a hug. "Lucy told me about Francine. I am *so* sorry." When she released me, she had tears in her eyes.

"Seriously, you don't have to do anything for the party. I want you to be happy in time for the wedding. Mom said something about our aunts having something magical prepared for the evening."

A wave of exhaustion and relief swept over me.

As my mother took our aunts over to the counter to pick out cakes and pastries, Grace gave me one of the sprigs of lavender. "Smell this and tell me what you think."

I sniffed the flowers, which teased a sneeze out of my nose. "I must be allergic to Lucy's wedding flowers."

The little purple flowers began to sparkle.

"Okay, what's happening? Are your flowers bewitched?" I asked.

Grace beamed. "All of my herbs are bursting with magic! Lucy said something about you both visiting the greenhouse, and overhearing my familiars discussing an Earth Uprising?"

Lucy scrunched her nose. "Before your snooty hedgehog shoved us along, we overheard them voting on if they would join forces with the wild familiars when it came to participating in the Earth Uprising."

"That's just the beginning! You should have seen the dragons in Ireland!"

The three of us jumped as a male voice sounded from across the room. Krim and Amon sat at a table, mingling with two men I didn't recognize. Eugene beamed at my mother as she made her way over to where he was seated.

My cheeks heated when I spotted my boyfriend. I approached the table, eager to overhear what they were all discussing. The frosting decorating cupcakes and pastries changed colors as everyone chatted about the upcoming wedding.

Dezmond spun in his seat. “Victoria?”

His smile warmed me. I’d been so distant and cold to him. I stopped at his side. “Hey, I owe you an apology for last night. I didn’t mean to blow you off, and—”

He stood and pulled me into an embrace.

My body melted against his, and I was instantly lost in him.

He planted a kiss on my neck, then muttered something that sounded like, "*You can make it up to me tonight.*”

“Who needs to call the fire department?” Millie teased.

“I think we’re going to have to toss these two into the pool to cool off,” Tillie agreed.

Dezmond grabbed my hand and thankfully steered me away from our mingling family members. We stopped in the corner behind one of Grace’s dragon trees potted in the corner. The leaves made his eyes even greener as he locked his gaze with me. “About Maverick and Sloane. Last night, my brothers and I learned that both shifters are working against one another.”

“Really? How come?”

He shrugged. “No idea. But the air rune I let Krim borrow vanished into thin air.”

I reached into my pocket and tugged out the rune Rosie had given back to me. “At least we still have one. I still have no idea how Willow and Drake expect us to use any of them.”

His cheeks bulged. "Dude, has that been where I *think* it's been?"

"Want to know what's strange? Rosie *bit* me. Then, I heard this voice say something about fire."

"What did the voice say?"

"It was definitely a female voice. I wonder if it was Willow. She said something about flames being the purifier, the lifeblood of their magic. She said that fire is both a medicine, and a curse."

"I heard the voice too," Dezmond admitted. "She had something to say about both the water and air runes. She said water was the teller of truth, while air was the wind of change."

I propped my hands onto my hips. "Why didn't you tell me that you were hearing these voices?"

He shrugged. "I guess I just figured that it wasn't that big of a deal. I hear my shadow beasts in my head all the time. Maybe I'm too used to hearing disembodied voices to care."

"How did you find out that Maverick and Sloane are working against one another?"

"Sloane stopped by my uncle's pub, and I noticed she had the same marks on her arm as I did after I duked it out with Maverick."

"Wait, he attacked her with the voodoo doll too?"

He reached into his pocket and tugged out an onyx stone. "Liam found this stone she left behind. Krim called it a shadow pendant, which he thinks we can use to track down the doll. He also believes the voodoo doll could be the source of the Spirit of the Wild's magic."

Fire burned in my belly at the thought. "We need to find and destroy that fucking doll before it hurts anyone else."

He pocketed the shadow pendant and grabbed my hand. "Victoria, whatever this monster is, I can promise you that I'm going to get even with it. I won't let it hurt anyone else you care about, I promise."

I heated, thinking of how he was going to fight for me. "When is the bachelor party?"

"Tonight. What about you and the ladies?"

"Same."

He blinked. "You know, I really hated not being able to spend time with you last night at your place. I wish you would have let me."

My stomach swooped. Dezmond wanted to be there for me, through thick and thin. "One last question. Who are those two over there I assume are some family of yours?"

He glanced over his shoulder. "Oh, those are my father's half-brothers, Liam and Oscar. Liam is the one officiating the wedding."

"So, they're basically your uncles?"

He nodded. "They're both wolf shifters, and very fucking proud Irish."

"Who wants to place a bet that your uncles and my aunts are somehow going to hook up?"

A chuckle escaped him. "I hope your aunts like fur and fangs, because they're not shy about showing them off."

I grazed his stubble with my hand. "If they are anything similar to their nephew, I promise they will have a good time."

# 34

# Dezmond

I spent my afternoon helping Liam and Oscar prepare for Amon's bachelor party at their pub. Even though we were excited for a night of partying, all of us felt the weight of a tremendous shadow that seemed to lurk around the Summoning. The only shining light in this shitty situation was the fact that Victoria wasn't upset with me any longer. And she'd recovered her fire rune. But that didn't mean that I'd won her back. The wound she sustained from losing her familiar was soul-deep.

This fucking shifter named Maverick was going down after what he'd done to hurt her.

I hadn't told Victoria the details about my nightmare. She'd already gone through enough of one already. What I *could* do was figure out how to work with my family on how we were going to put this fucking Maverick guy in his place.

I walked up to Krim, who was sipping a glass of whiskey with his reaper. The two had been guarding the rune Sloane had left—something he identified as a shadow pendant. Every once in a while, a tendril of smoke would coil up out of the glass, where it would fizzle out with a gaseous *pop*! His reaper shadow sat across from him at their table, his hood drawn over his bony features. The two were discussing something quietly and quickly became silent as I approached.

I pulled up a chair and eyed his half-empty whiskey bottle. "Pregaming for tonight, I see?"

The earthy aroma of cloves and smoke burned my nose as he poured himself another shot. "It's time to put my grumpy grim days behind me. I'm considering popping the question to Grace."

I squinted at him. "Fucking darkness. Why does everyone have marriage fever? Am I the only Ravenblood who hasn't bought a ring yet?"

He downed his shot, then slammed his glass down in front of his reaper's bony hand. "You're a shifter. Your rituals are different when it comes to finding a mate."

I swiped the glass from his reaper before he could pour my brother another shot. "Hey, sober up. I need to know more about how these shadow pendants are created. I think it will help me decide on if I'm going to take part in this ritual or not."

Krim chuckled darkly, his blue eyes lulling dangerously to me. "There is no choice—there is only *fate* when it comes to the ritual."

I shook my head. "I'm not understanding. Are you saying the results from the ritual are already decided upon, regardless of my choices during it?"

"How much has Dad actually shared with you about the ritual?"

"Enough to make me wonder if it's all just a bunch of shit he made up."

His mouth twisted. "You've got some nerve, baby bro. The Spirit of the Wild is not something that exists in a demon's nightmares alone."

I snatched the whiskey bottle and poured myself a shot. "That's what I need your help with, figuring out how I'm going to go up against this wicked shadow beast that fucking *bit* me." I downed my shot and slammed the glass down onto the table. "Now, tell me about your hypothesis. Talk to me like I'm a kid. Don't get all philosophical on me."

Krim waved his hand, dispersing his reaper, then set his elbows onto the table. His bloodshot eyes leveled with me. "Look, I can discuss alchemical formulas all evening, but it boils down to one simple principle. You cannot domesticate magic and expect it to remain healthy, especially if it's wild to begin with."

"Domesticate magic? I'm not getting it."

"In other words, to *tame.* Goddess magic is the most powerful of the three magics. She is the ultimate creative and destructive force behind any magical ritual—a force that only witches can tap into."

A plume of purple smoke erupted in my periphery as Dad and Amon manifested. It was probably best that they appeared, because I was ready to ring Krim's tipsy neck.

Dad walked over to the bar, carrying a jar of tea bags. "All right, boys. Party's about to start. Dezmond, get your ass over here and help me with the tea kettle."

"I'm sorry, did I hear you right? We're having *tea*?" I asked as I abandoned Krim and made my way over to the bar.

Amon set the tea kettle onto the bar in front of Liam, who's mouth dropped open.

"This has to be a joke," Oscar grumbled over his flight of whiskey shots he'd prepared. "I thought we were going to get blasted and forget who we were for a few hours."

Dad shot his brothers a death glare. "Don't you *dare* insult Cindy's summer solstice tea until you've tried it." He grabbed the tea kettle and handed it to Liam. "Now, get this pot boiling and find us some teacups."

"Whatever you say, boss," Liam grumbled as he took the kettle and set it on a burner behind the bar.

I glanced around the room, noting just how full of shadows the pub had become. Amon with his serpents, Krim with his reaper, and Dad with his two boisterous spirit ravens who flit between my uncles as plumes of smoke while they busied themselves with preparing food and beverages. I seemed to be the only demon in the room who didn't have my shadows joining in. Pawz, Jawz, and Sniffer had completely abandoned me. The last time I'd seen them was in my nightmare, before I found the beast locked in the cage.

A shadow beast who was *me.*

*Or is the beast really this Spirit of the Wild that I am somehow channeling?*

Dad reached for one of the shot glasses full of whiskey, which was swirling with green smoke.

Amon grabbed his hand. "Hold it. Didn't you say Cindy's tea is more potent on an empty stomach?"

"Are you saying I can't share one shot with my firstborn son before he gets hitched to a witch?" Dad ground out.

Amon chuckled. "Dad, we all know you've kicked the habit. Let's not have you go down that lonely road again." He reached into his pocket and tugged out a bunch of brown sticks. "Besides, cigars are where it's at."

"Gross," Dad said, crinkling his nose at my brother. "I'd rather drink myself into the grave than inhale that skunky crap."

"Oscar and I will help you with those," Liam said as he extended a calloused hand.

Amon handed two cigars to my uncles and offered one to me.

I held up my hand. "No thanks. Like Dad, I kicked one of my addictive habits and have no regrets. I no longer smell like an ashtray."

Liam lit up his cigar with a lighter, then Oscar's, then my brother's.

Amon took one puff and began to choke. "Yeah, I think I agree with you and Dad on that."

My uncles puffed on their cigars like a couple of smokestacks.

Liam blew a purple smoke ring around my face. "All right, best demon. What do you have planned for your big bro?"

"It's not about me right now," Amon said. "I want to help Dezmond take down this Maverick guy who hurt him and my father, and now Victoria."

Amon's words, while loyal and kind, did little to calm the ache I felt in my bones. "I need advice on how I'm going to fuck up this shifter who messed with my mate."

Liam and Oscar grinned wolfishly. "*Mate*? Well then, it looks like you are getting serious with this witch."

The hair on my forearms bristled. I wouldn't have Victoria be anything *less* than my mate at this point. I couldn't bear to think what life might be like without her.

The tea kettle screamed as it let off a plume of steam.

"Let's start with a cup of tea, shall we?" Oscar said as he prepared the teacups, dropping tea bags into each one. "If Maverick wants to ruin someone's night, then have him crash the wedding. Right now, we're going to have some good old-fashioned fun."

"I'll do the pouring," Dad said as Liam retrieved and handed my father the kettle. "Cindy was very careful with how she prepared this. She said this year, it has a special potency because each and every one of her daughters has experienced a growth spurt in their magic. I like to think that's because of my sons." He tipped the kettle forward, pouring scolding hot water into each cup. The tea simmered and popped, sending purple and green bubbles into the air.

As he handed out the cups to my uncles, and to his sons, he held his up in the air. "A toast to the Crow witches and the Ravenblood demons. May our veins always overflow with magic!"

My nose tickled as bubbles colored like a sunset floated in front of me, then with a gaseous *pop*! exploded. Something floral, fresh, and windswept burst into my nostrils. My vision became blurry. A mirage appeared, distorting my family.

"Bottoms up, boys! Have a sip and tell me what you think!" Dad said, his voice far fuzzier in tone than it usually sounded.

I brought the cup to my lips. Bubbles fizzed and popped, filling my mind with memories of Victoria.

I remembered how good she smelled when I first met her at the clinic. Then, how warm her magic was when she patched me up. Like a movie, each infatuation I'd had with her played in my mind as one continuous memory.

I set my teacup onto the bar. "Dad, how long have you been drinking this tea for?"

Dad's lopsided smile turned into a shit-eating grin. "For as long as the love of my life has been giving it to me."

"Do you mean Mom, or Cindy?" I asked, knowing just how loyal he'd been to my deceased mother. Part of the reason he'd become so dependent on alcohol was the fact that he couldn't get over my mother's death.

"That is partially true, Dezmond."

I turned, spooked by the female voice that drifted like silk across my right ear. A transparent woman hovered in my periphery. She drifted in and out of my vision.

*Fuck.*

I was so far gone, I couldn't see straight.

The aroma of fresh fallen leaves mixed with that of flowers. The ghostly woman stirred my senses, settling a calm upon my panic. "Magic and medicine are not the same thing. But they are more similar in ways than they are different when love is involved."

My family's laughter died as the woman's smooth voice caressed my ears. A comfort I'd felt long ago nestled itself protectively around me. "Wait, *Mom*?"

Her smile answered my question. "It's been a long time, Dezmond, my youngest son."

"I haven't seen you in so long, I've forgotten what you *look* like."

Mom's dark eyes narrowed. "I don't have much time. The solstice tea will only open a window for me to speak with you for a few moments."

I glanced over at Amon and Krim, who were laughing so loudly with my father and uncles, that I could hardly think.

"Hey, guys! Get over here! It's Mom!" I yelled, waving my hands.

My mother traced her fingers in the air, creating a halo of sparks that fell over me in waves. "They cannot hear you. Focus on me."

A soft, silky texture brushed past my ear. Claws dug into my shoulders. And they were long and curved, far different from Torchie's stumpy ones.

A high-pitched *shreeeek* broke the silence as my father, brothers and two uncles glanced at the silvery bird who had taken up its roost on my shoulder.

I jolted. "Francine?"

Victoria's transparent bird arched her wings over my head and let out a terrible cry.

Mom vanished.

Dad, my uncles, and my brothers all stopped laughing and stared at the hawk perched on my shoulder.

Anger and Sadness flit over to where my father was staring, mouth open, at Victoria's bossy spirit familiar. She was far more silver than the brown I remembered, and her talons were twice as long. They pinched like a bitch as they dug into my shoulder.

"*Listen up, you rowdy Ravenbloods!*" Francine said, her voice a shrill cry in all our heads. "*Dezmond is my new owner. I'm adopting him as my demon in death. He will be helping me with revealing Victoria's Crow's wild magic.*"

# 35

# Victoria

As evening rolled in, I made my way over to my mother's house. High-pitched laughter erupted from her garden. The sound did not belong to her. As I rounded the path and entered her backyard, a cackling fit broke through the humid evening air.

My mother's garden was quite simply put, *stunning*. The aroma of roses, hydrangeas, and her absolute favorite, lavender, created a floral perfume that was sure to enchant all of us before the evening was over.

Tillie and Millie stood opposite of one another beneath the giant oak tree. Fairy lights were strung between its branches, making the bark and leaves glow a dull green. A cauldron bubbled at their feet. The source of the light beneath the cauldron was a mystery. There were no crackling embers, or smoke from a flame.

A black cat arched its back, bolting into the flowers as an albino rat chased after it. I laughed. My aunts were such odd balls. Even their familiars behaved opposite of how normal predator and prey creatures would act toward one another. The rat's whiskers sent out a shimmy of orange sparks, catching the cat's tail ablaze. I was convinced that somehow, their familiars were using their magic to heat the cauldron.

"Am I interrupting some kind of mysterious ritual?" I asked as I made my way over to my aunts.

Tillie clapped her hands together, sending a halo of colors spewing into the air. "Oh, hello Victoria. We were just preparing for your arrival! Let the festivities begin!"

Millie threw a stone into the cauldron, making the liquid inside *pop*! "We're mixing up an elemental brew. Come dear, approach the cauldron and watch how this is done!"

I took a seat next to the gnome statue that my mother's toads, Bloated and Pop, had perched upon. Their throats bulged as they observed the mischievous behavior shared between my aunts.

Fingers curled, Tillie tossed her lanky arms into the air and said, "Born from water, our magic grows. Water is the element of wisdom. Water always knows the truth, even when the mouth is too afraid to speak it. Water is the truth our hearts sing with."

Millie mimicked her sister, creating the same movements with her fingers as she added, "Carried on the wind, our magic travels far and wide. Air is the element of movement and change. Air always knows where to go, even when the body refuses to do so. Air is the movement our souls soar with."

Both clapped their hands as they said in unison, "Igniting the darkest places of our souls, fire burns through the skin, the flesh, and the bone. It reveals our pains, our fears, and our passions. Fire is the purifier, the cure. Fire is both medicine, and a curse."

Bloated croaked and hopped onto the gnome's head as the brew inside the cauldron sent a plume of green bubbles into the air.

I glanced between my aunts. "The voices from the runes came from you two, didn't they?"

"What voices?" Millie asked as she tossed a bundle of dried herbs into the cauldron.

"Dezmond mentioned he heard voices when he touched the runes of water and air. I also heard *exactly* what you said when I recovered this from one of my patients at the clinic." I reached into my pocket and tugged out the fire rune.

"What a marvelous item, a rune of fire!" Tillie said. "Let me guess, one of the dragons gifted it to you?"

"How did you know?" I asked, tilting the rune between my fingers. The symbol on it flickered with the same green light as the liquid in the cauldron.

Millie beckoned me with her fingers. "Bring it here, my dear. A little bit of flame is exactly what we need to get this party started."

I hesitated, not wanting to give up the last of the three runes. Rosie had instructed me to keep it close, and I didn't quite trust what my aunts were brewing up for the evening.

Tillie reached her hand into her cleavage and tugged out a tarot card. "Elemental magic works in mysterious ways, which only the Wild Card can decipher."

Millie tilted her hat up and pulled out another card.

My mouth dropped open. "So there *are* more Wild Cards. Mom always said there was only *one* in the deck."

Millie laughed. "Cindy said that to prevent her daughters from fighting over them, in case any of you discovered the secrets behind wild magic."

"What kind of secrets?" I asked.

"Secrets only this spell we've brewed can reveal. There are *four* Wild Cards total in the Three Magics Oracle Deck. In order to create the elemental spell, we need all four Wild Cards to be present."

"Excuse me. There will be *no* elemental spell casting on my property without my permission first," Mom said as she made a beeline over to the cauldron.

Grace followed my mother, stealthily avoided tripping over Bloated and Pop as they hopped over the garden gnome, and made her barefooted way over to me. "Please tell me that we're brewing up a cauldron full of crystal dicks," she said with a cackle.

Tillie spat out her tea. "A cauldron full of *what*?"

I snorted, thinking back to my last Halloween celebration, where I had, indeed, bestowed upon my sisters a spooky yet spicy centerpiece for my kitchen table.

Grace giggled. "You have no idea what I have planned for everyone this evening."

I rolled my eyes. Ever since the magic mushrooms sprouted in her greenhouse, my youngest sister's mind had jumped off the diving board and straight into the gutter. Most of her jokes about mushrooms had become exceedingly phallic. I hated to admit that I had been a prime influence behind her immature behavior.

My mother stood between her two older twin sisters. They complimented her brightness, offsetting her. Both Tillie and Millie set their Wild Cards on the tea table next to the deck.

The rune in my hand warmed as I gazed at the cards. There were only *three* present, including the one that had been in my deck to begin with. I could feel its sizzling magic even though I couldn't see it. According to Dezmond, there was a *fourth* that had somehow fallen into the hands of a shifter named Maverick.

My mind started to spiral. Seeing the design on the card did terrible things to me. I felt broken just by looking at it. I became consumed by the dread I'd felt every time I'd avoided the letters from the cancer clinic.

The flares of Lucy's aura bursting into the air announced her arrival. She walked into the garden with one of her other bookish friends, Alyssa. Alyssa was one of her bridesmaids, apart from Grace, and myself. I was so grateful that Lucy was an introvert and hadn't made her wedding larger.

I grabbed Lucy and pulled her into a hug. "I'm so sorry that I've been such a flake toward your wedding. None of this party was planned by me. Mom and our aunts deserve the full credit."

"Don't be. You've been through enough over the past few days."

"We never discussed the venue for your wedding. Did you two settle on a park?"

Lucy clapped her hands together. "Yes! We are renting out a gazebo at Willow Park. The trees are going to look so pretty this time of year!"

Hearing Willow's name made my stomach knot. While Lucy mingled with my aunts, I found a place to remove myself from the group. I needed to ground myself. My blood was boiling—either from the fire rune, or from my lack of confidence regarding the Wild Cards my aunts were obsessing over.

My mother's magical flares coiled around me, setting my anxiety at ease. "Victoria, is everything okay?" she asked as she slipped a bundle of dried herbs into my hand.

"Yeah, it's just been a rough week at the clinic. And I can't stop thinking about Francine."

I glanced at Lucy, who in a matter of moments, had become tipsy from the boxed wine. "Okay, who planned this pin the shadow sex toy on the demon game?"

Grace scoffed as she hung a picture of a black silhouette of a horned demon branching out of his head onto the trunk of the oak tree. "You told me I needed to get creative when it came to the games. Well, we're going to have a whole lot of fun." She pinned what looked like a black ring onto the demon's crotch. "Just wait until you hear about the infamous shadow ring."

Lucy gawked. "Wait, there are shadow *cock* rings?"

Grace grinned. "Sister, you have so much to learn about the magical things a demon's shadows have to offer you."

I stifled a laugh. I wondered if Amon or Krim had shadow beasts like Dezmond did. I was quite content keeping our animalistic shadow sex a secret.

As the evening wore on, and the festive energy grew, a few of Grace's college friends dropped in. And Lucy had a few of her buddies over from the library. I was kicking myself. I really should have invited Holly, as she loved this kind of social scene.

Millie grabbed the deck and flipped over a few cards. One was a Goddess Card. Next, the Water Card. And lastly, the Maiden Card. "Oh, looks like we might be throwing *you* a party before long too, Cindy," Millie suggested as she strung a clover garland over my mother's head. "By the way, who is officiating Lucy's wedding?"

Lucy squeezed herself between me and Grace. "Liam is Amon's uncle. He's officiating the wedding."

"Is Liam single?" Tillie asked as she tossed a stone into the cauldron, making the liquid inside hiss and pop.

Mom snorted into her tea. "Even if he was, I'm not hooking you up with him."

Tillie reached into her bag and tugged out a jar with something black oozing in it. "Lucy, your cousin Danika wanted you to have this. It's a gift from her bee farm in Colorado."

Lucy took the jar. "What is this?"

"Black honey!" Tillie cried. "It's bewitched with all kinds of mountain magic!"

As Lucy tilted the jar, a flurry of yellow lights went buzzing past her face. Bees hovered around the jar. Whether they were real or a spell, I wasn't going to argue. As long as they didn't go zipping out of her aura to sting the party guests, then we were okay.

As the crowd grew more festive and friends mingled, Millie and Tillie put on a show of magical sparks with the cauldron. It didn't take long for them to concoct a new plan for entertaining the guests.

"I know, why don't we perform a tarot reading on everyone?" Tillie suggested.

Before I could protest their offer, guests began to arrange themselves around the table where Millie began to sort through the card deck. As each of the guests lined up, my aunts got busy. Millie performed quick readings that lasted no longer than a couple of minutes each.

My heart jumped into my throat. What would mine say? Sure, I'd had the deck for years, but I had never tried to experiment with its magic.

When the time came for my reading to be performed, I glanced up into the tree. I could have sworn I saw the yellow eyes of my hawk gazing down at me.

I blinked.

*Torchie?*

"*Don't let your aunts know I'm here,*" he rumbled into my head. "*But pay attention to what the cards have to show you. Their message will come in handy when it comes time to face Maverick.*"

"Victoria, have a seat and let the cards work their magic," Tillie instructed.

I sat down before her table, glancing between the bubbling cauldron and her. Torchie had completely disappeared from the tree.

As she flipped through the cards, the fire rune heated in my pocket. I tugged it out, clutching it in my fingers as she drew three cards and placed them on the table.

Tillie drew a card from the deck and set it in front of me. "Ah, the Beast Card. Something we all must learn how to tame. The beast represents fear, anger, and blame." Tillie glanced up at me, her blue eyes sparkling with the light put off by the cauldron. "Are you blaming your fear on something or someone else?"

My throat went dry. "I didn't think I'd have to face that monster again, especially not without Francine."

"Victoria, what monster?" Lucy asked as she approached me.

I glanced at the bubbling brew in the cauldron. "Fire is the purifier, the lifeblood of our magic. Fire is both medicine, and a curse." I said aloud as I tossed it into the liquid.

The rune hissed and popped.

I could run and hide from my fear for as long as I wanted to, but not the blame. I didn't know how much longer I could keep my cancer a secret from my family.

# 36

# Dezmond

The smell of grease wafted into my nose. Thank the fucking darkness, because the aftertaste in my mouth was horrible. I opened my eyes, finding that I was in my apartment. Someone was in my kitchen, green shadows billowing out of their shoulders. A bushy grey tail swished behind them as they maneuvered between my counter and the stove.

"Rise and shine, best demon. Time for a good old fashioned Irish Breakfast," Oscar said as he walked over to the sofa and handed me a piping hot plate of bacon, sausage, and eggs. Beans paired with both black and white puddings, along with some fried tomatoes lined my plate. A pair of grey wolf ears stuck out of his hair, which twitched forward as he studied me.

I sat up from my spot and gratefully took the plate. "What happened last night? And where is everyone?"

"We all got blasted off that tea your father had us brew," Oscar said as he shoved a cup of piping hot coffee toward me. "It's going to take a while to sober us all up."

I grabbed my phone, wondering how Victoria had fared over her evening. It was already one in the afternoon. "Shit, how long have I been out?"

"Just a few hours. We didn't stop partying until about four in the morning. As for everyone else, Liam took Amon back to his apartment. He was too far gone to dip out of the Summoning. Krim's got your father at his place. He drank the most tea out of all of us. Apparently, Krim knows some alchemy that he's used for magical hangovers."

*Speaking of Alchemy.*

I patted my jeans pockets.

*Fuck.*

The shadow pendant—what had I done with it?

I rolled my neck, cracking a few vertebrae and rubbed out the soreness in my arm. "I vaguely remember talons digging into my shoulder."

"Did the talons belong to that?" Oscar asked, pointing his spatula toward my drum set. A hawk was perched on one of my snare drums, its tail feathers brushing past the cymbal as it explored my drums.

"Okay, so I *wasn't* hallucinating about Francine coming back from the dead."

"She hasn't left your side since we left the pub. I think she's your new guardian spirit familiar. Birds are hard to get rid of. Just look at your father," Oscar said.

*"Birds aren't as powerful as dragons, but you will want her on your side when it comes time to steal back the fourth Wild Card from Maverick."*

I jumped, spooked by the sudden thunderous voice that boomed into my head.

A pair of yellow eyes lit up from atop my kitchen cabinet.

"*Torchie*?"

Liam reached out, scratching the little guy under his chin. "He's been super helpful with preparing breakfast, haven't you, little dude?"

"*The Three Magics Oracle Deck can only reveal its power if all four Wild Cards are present. The Spirit of the Wild is trapped in the doll. The only way to free our ancestor from Maverick's curse is to collect all of them.*"

"Wait, there are *four* Wild Cards now?"

"*One for each of the four elements,*" Torchie added.

"Why didn't you just tell us that little detail before?"

"*My parents know far more about the ritual than I do. I only hatched a few weeks ago.*"

I jumbled my brain, trying to think of who had what. "I know that Maverick has *one* of the Wild Cards cards. Another is with the deck. Who has the other two?"

Cackling laughter erupted outside. I blinked as I swore a pointed hat zipped past my window.

Francine let out an ear-splitting *shriek* as two witches promptly dismounted their brooms and stared at me through my back door.

"Wait a second, are those Victoria's aunts?" I asked as one of them squished her face against the glass to peer inside.

"*Tillie and Millie are aurora witches. You should have met them at the bakery,*" Francine agreed.

"Yeah, but I didn't think they'd *follow* me." I sprang to my feet and opened the door. "Hi, I'm Dezmond, Amon's youngest brother. How did you know where I lived?"

"As Francine pointed out, we are aurora witches," one of them replied. "Tracing magical energy is our specialty. Your shadows are all over Victoria's property. It wasn't difficult to trace them back to your place of residence."

The other witch clapped her hands to her cheeks. "Oh, my. Isn't he just as handsome as the others?"

"Tillie, stop it. You'll scare him off," Millie said as she tossed her hair over her shoulder. "Can we please come inside? The alley cats keep trying to ride on my broomstick."

I moved aside, allowing both to enter my apartment. I closed the door quickly, finding that Anchovies's kittens had started to climb onto my deck. Millie was right about the cats, especially the young ones.

Oscar's ears perked, and a wolfish smile parted his lips as he glanced between Victoria's bizarre aunts. "Oi, can I make either of you an Irish breakfast? I'm just getting warmed up!"

Tillie shot my uncle a flirtatious glance, while Millie threw up her hand and said, "we've come for one reason only." She reached into her pocket and pulled out a deck of cards. "Take the deck to Victoria. She did not have a good time last night after we performed a tarot reading on her."

"Why not?" I asked.

Millie sighed. "I'm afraid the deck is lacking its full magic. When we performed our tarot readings at the party, we might have accidentally placed a spell on both the Crow and Ravenblood families by accident."

"Accidental spells are also known as *curses*, in case you didn't know," Tillie added as she rolled her eyes at her sister.

"What kind of curse are we talking about? Me growing hair out of my nose?" I joked.

Tillie snorted. "*And* he's funny. Is it that difficult to find a demon who has an actual sense of humor on the coast?"

I pondered Tillie's question. Apparently, demons who lived on the coasts were not as laid back with their jokes as the ones who lived around Midhaven. "Why are you giving me the deck?"

"Because only you and Victoria can fix the mess we created. Rumor has it that you two share some very powerful magic that has fated you as mates."

I took the deck of cards, and my hair stood on end.

Oscar approached us with a plate of muffins he seemed to have whipped out of nowhere. "Dezmond, go find Victoria. I think I can keep a couple of witches company for the time being."

I jumped on my bike and pulled it out onto the road. Francine kept her distance, hovering a few yards back as Torchie led the way to Victoria's home. As I drove, an unsettling sensation of being watched prickled the hair on the back of my neck. It wasn't Clawz trying to dig his way against my ribs, or Jawz gnashing his teeth, nor Sniffer sticking his snout into my ear.

The Spirit of the Wild was close. I could taste his breath. It filled the back of my mouth, making my tongue heavy with his desire for flesh. Sloane had said something at my uncles' pub that I should have paid more attention to, something that Torchie had warned me about.

"*The Spirit of the Wild is a ravenous shadow beast. He won't be satiated with elemental runes or demon flesh—he's out for the blood of a witch from the Crow family.*"

Every time I feared him, I felt his presence become closer. Was he preparing another attack?

I pulled my bike up to the curb outside of Victoria's place and parked. It was a Saturday, so she should be home.

Francine perched herself in the oak tree out front. The sensation of having her eyes on the back of my head was a bit unsettling. How my father got used to having his two spirit ravens watching his every move was beyond me.

Before I could knock on her front door, it opened, revealing a very red-faced witch.

I squinted at her. "How did you get sunburned?"

Victoria shrugged. "I've been burned by magic before. I guess I got too close to the cauldron in my Mom's backyard."

Her scent did something wild to me. I burst through the door, grabbing her around the center as she wrapped her arms around me. I ran my fingers along the hot skin on her shoulders. "You've done enough of tending to my wounds. I think it's time I return the favor."

When she didn't flirt back with me, I knew something was wrong.

She unraveled her arms from my neck and sighed.

"Hey, random question. Do your aunts like to just show up randomly?" I asked, trying to stir up a conversation that might make her laugh.

Her blue eyes found mine. "Yeah, they are pretty random individuals. Why?"

I pulled the deck out of my pocket. "They just came by my place and gave me this."

Victoria shot the deck one swift look, then turned her back to me.

"Sweetheart, what's going on? Did your aunts really cast some spell on your family last night?"

Another sigh escaped her. "There was more than spell casting that happened," she confirmed as she made her way into the living room. "I can't help but feel like I'm a curse to my family."

"How are you a curse to your family?" I asked, befuddlement breaking in my voice.

She busied herself with a few odds and ends, straightening her bookshelf. "I've been lying to my family about my breast cancer. Why can't I face this? Why can't I just be a good person and tell them about this monster?"

She slumped down, collapsing onto her sofa.

I sat next to her and grabbed her hand. "You know, that's the first time I really figured out that you see cancer as a monster."

She shrugged. "I know, it's stupid."

"It's not stupid at all. We all have monsters that we have to face, whether we like it or not."

She didn't meet my gaze, so I squeezed her hand. "You know what's funny? Sometimes we're so afraid of hurting those we love, that we forget that our pain matters to them." I glanced down at our hands, and how wonderfully hers fit into mine. "My Dad's a perfect example of that. He spent years trying to bury his grief over losing my mother with the bottle, whether he likes to admit it or not."

She glanced up at me, tears shining in her blue eyes. "Dezmond, the monsters you've shown me aren't like the one I've been running from. Your shadow beasts are nothing compared to the cancer I've been terrified of facing again."

My heart broke for her. "I've ignored my shadow beasts, trying to avoid their needs for so long because I've been afraid of what their desires might do if they take over. They've done so before, especially when I get close to someone."

She locked eyes with me. "How do you tame that fear?"

I blew out my cheeks. "Trust. You trust yourself, even when you are afraid. If you don't have trust, what do you really have, in any relationship? And I'm not just talking about the romantic ones."

She squeezed my hand as she leaned over and tucked her head beneath my chin. "I'm such an idiot. I should be able to face this. I should be able to tell them. But like you, I've hurt people I care about before."

I relaxed, inhaling her sweet scent as she found refuge in me. Victoria felt the same fears I did, the fear of not having control. Surrendering to something that could rip you apart at any moment was terrifying, especially when it could happen to someone you loved.

I tucked her against my body, feeling her laugh against my neck.

"Want to know something random also?" she asked.

"Sure."

"Did you know that the voices we've been hearing from the runes were really my aunts casting spells?"

I chuckled. "With how strange both of our families are, that wouldn't surprise me."

Her fingers caressed the calluses on my open palm. She leaned into my neck, grabbed my earlobe with her teeth and whispered, "I can't help but think that fate somehow brought our families together."

I leaned into her, until teeth turned to sucking and kissing.

*Sweet fucking shadow beasts*, how easily she could turn me on.

I lowered my hand onto her thigh and gave her a squeeze. "You know, I can't help but think that fate has made us mates. Do you agree?"

She tore her blouse over her head while I worked off my jeans. Our bodies jostled against one another, my hands groping, her breath hot on my skin as she kissed me.

I kissed her back, my breathing matching hers as she raked her greedy hands across my chest.

She grabbed my thigh. "Why don't you be a good boy and let your mate be the one to fuck you how you want to be fucked?"

I was sprung harder than a diamond in a blizzard. "Ride me like a broomstick, my wild witch. I want to watch that gorgeous ass bounce."

Her hair whipped across my face as she spun and straddled my legs.

I grabbed her voluptuous hips and tugged her down atop me.

"Dezmond, you're too big. I don't think I can take you," she said, amusement teasing her voice.

I grabbed a handful of her thick hair. "You're the only wild witch who can tame my dick. Now, make me a good boy and take it every inch of it."

She let out a moan, squeezing herself down atop my cock.

Darkness—I *was* massive—far thicker than I'd ever been. She teased her slick opening over my head, allowing herself to stretch. In and out. Fast and slow. Her moans became breathy pants. Her ass lowered further with each acceptance.

I released her hair and grabbed her around the front. My hands clung to her thighs as I bucked my hips. "Only you can tame this wild beast I've become."

She shuddered, and gravity took her down, down, *down.* I grazed my teeth along her shoulder. I tasted the salt on her skin, which made my desire for her primal. My clawless hand gripped her breast, while my clawed one grazed over her scar. "You are my mate. Tell me you know it."

"Yes, I'm yours. I'm your mate," she panted. Her fingers found my balls, which she began to squeeze.

I buried my face into her hair, inhaling her intoxicating scent as she bounced atop my lap. I surrendered to her softness against my hardness. Claws raked across my ribs. A roar ground in my throat as I inhaled the burning scent of her arousal.

*Fuck.*

My shadow beasts all wanted to claim her, *again.* Should I give in to their primal instincts and unleash their wildness? What if she couldn't take them?

I slapped her ass. Claw marks lengthened the fingers of my handprint. The swollen base of my cock began to bulge as my knot appeared. I was going to swell up and come any second. But my mate needed to come first.

"Dezmond, fuck," she whimpered. "I don't know how much more of you I can take."

I slowed my rhythm, shadows coiling out of my arms as I found her clit with my clawless hand. I made slow, rhythmic circles, focusing on *her* pleasure, not my own. Victoria would give and give and *give,* like me. We were both generous souls, but that didn't mean I should take advantage of her generosity. This was my opportunity to make this ritual about my mate.

I kissed the back of her neck, exhaling. Her walls curled around my cock as I slid out of her.

"What are you doing?" she breathed as I took her hand and steered her away from my lap. Her legs shook as I hooked her beneath her knees and lowered her back onto the sofa.

"Let me look at you," I said, rising over her on the sofa. Hot and sweaty, red with a sex rash, she gazed up at me. Her dark hair was strewn across the pillows, her skin glistening with sweat, she could have passed as a painting.

I knelt between her legs, grabbing one and kissing down her ankle. "Sweetheart," I growled into her thigh, burying my face into the redness where she'd taken my knot. "Right now, it's about you. I'm only getting warmed up."

# 37

# Victoria

A week and plenty of love bites from Dezmond later, I was pretty sure that Lucy and Amon's wedding was cursed. When the morning of September nineteenth finally came, Dezmond glanced up at me from my kitchen table with the most pitiful look I'd ever seen on his handsome face and said, "Shit's getting real. Amon just texted me saying that Liam has food poisoning."

I gathered our breakfast plates and set them into the sink. "If Liam can't marry them, what are they going to do? Do they have a backup plan?"

"I have no idea. It's going to take some serious magic to pull off this outdoor wedding." He glanced out the window at the overcast sky. "Let's hope that the weather holds off. Apparently, we're also under a severe thunderstorm watch."

Thunder rumbled outside, dwindling my confidence.

My phone chimed. Grace had texted me.

> **Remind me to never drink Mom's solstice tea again. She bewitched me with the plague.**

She texted me a picture of her hair. It had grown down to her knees and had changed into a vomit shade of green. She'd spent the week hiding in her greenhouse, leaving Krim to work alone at the bakery, hiding so she didn't have to be seen.

**You'll just go as a bewitched green fairy.**

**You mean a barf fairy. I can't be seen like this, absolutely not!**

**How about the bouquets for the bride and bridesmaids?**

**Flowers have completely wilted. I don't know why. My hormones are all out of whack, probably from the stress of this wedding.**

I pocketed my phone. "Everyone is dropping like flies, except for us."

Dezmond chuckled. "Krim just texted me saying that he's experiencing some intestinal distress. I really don't want him to elaborate."

"What about our parents?" I asked.

He smirked. "I can only imagine what they might be doing right now to prep for this afternoon."

I winced, trying not to imagine what Dezmond was insinuating. Sure, I was glad that Mom had, like myself, and all her daughters, found a Ravenblood to get close to. I wondered what our future shadow discussions about our demons might sound like.

Dezmond gathered our plates from breakfast and set them in the sink. "As long as the bride and groom are okay, this wedding must go on. Let's get changed and make our way over to the park."

We climbed my stairs and entered my bedroom. For the past week, it had become our den of late nights talking, takeout, and of course, having lots of sex.

As I undressed from my bathrobe in front of my dresser, Dezmond came up behind me and wrapped his arms around my center. "You know, we can't spend all morning on my sister's wedding day fucking around."

He nuzzled my ear. "I'm not fucking around, I'm fucking *you*." He caressed my shoulder with one hand, while the other remained planted on my belly. "Rumor has it there is a wild witch in town who knows how to tame a shifter's magic."

I leaned back into him, watching in my mirror as he removed a lock of hair away from my shoulder. A growl rumbled against my back as his fingers slipped into my panties. His hard length pressed against my ass, and I was brought back to that amazing time we'd done doggie style in my bed when all three of his shadow beasts attempted to claim me.

I reached up, grabbing a fistful of his thick hair. "At least let me dress, then you can decide if you want to rip my clothing off or not."

"No," he whispered, his teeth raking a scorching line down my shoulder. "I'm going to claim every inch of your body before you dress."

He grabbed my hand and led me over to the bed, where he slid my bathrobe off my shoulders and onto the floor. His fingers traced my jaw, where he cupped my face. With his other hand, he touched my chest, moving with tenderness across my scar. "Do you have any idea just how gorgeous you are?"

I ran my hands down the dark strip of hair bristling down the center of his abs as his boxers bulged. "Did you know that you are the first person, sorry, *demon,* to ever make me feel like a goddess?"

His mouth quirked. "If I ever stop worshiping you like you are one, then slap me upside the head and tame me like you've already done."

I laughed, lowering my hands to the elastic band of his boxers, releasing his hard length.

His mouth met mine, his cheeks and the skin surrounding his lips rough with stubble. We kissed, the head of his cock pressing into my belly as our bodies joined.

His hands dropped to my hips, and he thrust me backward so that I fell onto the cool sheets of my bed.

"Spread those gorgeous thighs, love," he whispered as he grabbed one of my wrists and pinned it over my head.

I grabbed his other hand and lowered it to my clit. "I need you to warm me up first."

He fell beside me on the bed, reaching for my breast. Clawing my way across his heaving body, I straddled him.

He grabbed my hips and tugged me toward his head. "Sit on my face, my wicked witchy woman."

I kneed my way up to his face and set my hands on the headboard of my bed. Before I lowered myself, his tongue thrashed against my clit, tugging a moan out of me.

"That's it," he encouraged, licking one slick line across my entry. "Make me your beast, love. Tame this demon until his shadow beasts are yours."

I gripped the top of my headboard with one of my hands and his hair with the other. "If you want to claim me, eat me like you want me."

Dezmond's tongue did something beyond the normal. Part of it curled inside of my opening, while the other continued to tease my clit, its silky, sinful texture driving me mad.

My body shuddered as an orgasm threatened to break out of me. I tore myself away from his forked tongue and fell beside him, heaving.

He rose to his side, wiping the back of his hand across his mouth. "You taste divine. Why did you stop?"

I grabbed his hand drenched in our desire and pulled him atop me. "Because no man, nor demon, nor beast, can truly claim me until he's fucked me."

His eyes lit up, the primal look in his gaze capturing me. He rose onto his knees, lowering himself between my thighs as I spread my legs for him. He rocked his hips against mine, and I accepted every inch of him.

Each time Dezmond made love to me, a new side of his beastly personality appeared. Today, I had a tender beast who satiated my emotional vulnerability as much as his claws and teeth did my body.

With my free hand, I grabbed his ass and dug my fingers into his skin. I closed my eyes, wanting this to never end.

"Victoria, look at me when you come," he grunted, his hair falling into his eyes. His face blurred, a fury of wild green embers, a beast hungry for something more than my body.

Goddess, I fucking *loved* this ritual we'd created. Magic or not, I could get lost in us. With Dezmond, I could *fuck* monsters. I didn't have to run from them.

Our breathing became a fury of elated huffs. The pressure built at the base of my spine, rising through my center. As I trembled, he pumped harder, bringing about his own release.

Breathless and sweaty, I raked my fingers along his back. "You're going to make us late."

He lowered himself, his knot still pulsing, inching me toward another orgasm. A smile curved his lips as my back arched. "I'm fine with that, as long as I'm pleasing my mate."

An hour and multiple orgasms later, we finally convinced ourselves to shower and get ready for the wedding. I retreated into Lucy's old bedroom, where I'd stored my dress.

I tugged it on, feeling the cool, silky fabric cover my torso and scar and breast, where Dezmond had left tender from his love bites. When I walked into the hallway, he emerged from my bedroom, wearing a button up shirt, slacks, and a tie slung across his shoulders.

He whistled, closing the space between us as he propped his arm onto the doorframe and leaned forward. "Holy fucking darkness on a cracker. You look *spectacular*."

I flushed. "So do you."

"I'm wild for you, Victoria. I'm going to sprout horns for you before this wedding is over." He grazed my cheek with his stubble as he planted a kiss on my neck. "Can I have you help me with my tie? I don't think I know how this works."

I grabbed both ends of his tie and tugged him back into my bedroom. A feather fluttered down from my dresser, landing on my bed.

"*Glad to see that your mated bond has finally made you two crazy for one another.*"

I spun, spotting a silver bird perched atop my dresser. My mouth dropped open. "Oh my fucking goddess, *Francine*?"

"*Victoria, why do you look like a tomato*?" Francine asked, her voice ringing shrill in my mind. "*And I'm glad to see that your mate told you that my spirit is still around.*"

He scratched the back of his head. "Yeah, about that. Francine showed up at the bachelor party before we all got blasted off your mother's tea, according to Uncle Oscar. I honestly thought I was hallucinating. That's why I didn't mention her."

Francine ruffled her silver feathers. "*Typical demon, putting his cock before his brain.*"

I snorted. "Francine, who killed you? Was it the Spirit of the Wild?"

She arched her transparent wings. "*A certain fox knows more about wild magic than I do, which is precisely why I'm taking this.*"

She dove, her silver talons gripping into the deck of cards as she took off out the window.

"Oh no, you're not going to fly out on me," I stammered, chasing after her silvery tail feathers as they fluttered into my bedroom. "Dezmond, will you do me a giant favor, and help me catch my sassy spirit hawk?"

He grabbed my hand, kissing the top. "Of course."

I tugged him toward the stairs. "Let's take your bike and see if we can catch up with her."

Once outside, Dezmond lowered himself onto his bike. I climbed on behind him and wrapped my arms around his front. The engine revved, and we pulled out onto the road. Francine had always been rebellious, and apparently her spirit was no different. Why had she swooped in and taken the deck with her? And who was this fox she mentioned?

I clasped my wrists around his center as he picked up speed. What felt like fur rubbed against my skin. His back arched, hardening against my chest.

*Shit.*

Was he shifting *again*?

A gust of wind nearly knocked me off the bike as a shadow descended over us. Two large wings blocked out the sun, casting us into temporary darkness.

A pair of claws grabbed my arms and lifted me off the bike. A belch erupted from above.

"*Torchie*?" I stammered, swinging my feet as I soared upward.

The dragon's massive claws gripped around my arms and swung me skyward. "*Hold on tight.*"

Dezmond continued driving, steering his bike down a dirt road. From what I could see, he was no longer following Francine. He was headed for the warehouse.

"What's happening to Dezmond?" I asked as another giant gust of wind blew past my ears. Buildings and treetops became smaller as he took me higher.

"*Something your bond has prepared him for*," Torchie said as he banked to the left and, and with another *swoop* of his wings, lowered himself down beneath the clouds. A familiar building came into view—the animal shelter.

My feet hit solid ground as Torchie lowered me down into one of the giant kennels outside the building. His wings settled as he folded himself behind me.

I spun, facing the tiny baby dragon I once knew. "Look at you! You *grew*!"

"*I know, I'm huge*," he grumbled, the scales on his cheeks burning bright pink as he blushed. "*All thanks to your magic, I'm no longer the size of a cat.*"

I reached my hand toward him. "Can I pet you?"

He nudged my palm with his nose. "*Of course*! *Just don't scratch the scales behind my nostrils. They're hot.*"

I ran my hand over his massive head, marveling at how smooth his scales were. They were no longer a purplish violet, but a gorgeous red with orange iridescence that caught the sunlight. "How did my magic do this to you?"

He nuzzled my palm with his nose. "*When you tossed the fire rune into the cauldron, you helped to release my flamable magic.*"

I jumped, realizing that Torchie wasn't the only creature standing in the kennel with me. A fox paced the cage, its yellow eyes narrowing on to me.

"Who are you, another shifter?" I asked as the fox sat on its haunches, its bushy brown tail with pink on the end swishing behind it.

The fox shifted, and a woman took over her form. Her short brown hair with pink tips fell into her face as she locked her yellow eyes with me.

I dropped my hand away from Torchie's face. "*Sloane*?"

Francine descended from the sky and perched on her shoulder. "Hi Victoria. I'm glad to see that you've helped Torchie to release his magic."

"Is it true that you're working against Maverick? And what about Torchie's parents?"

Sloane nodded as she removed the deck from Francine's talons and held it toward me. "The air and water runes remain with Maverick. Therefore, he remains in control of Torchie's parents. Dezmond is going to need your help if he's going to release the elemental magic from Willow and Drake. If you trust in your wild magic, you can break the curse Maverick placed on the Spirit of the Wild."

I swallowed. "How?"

Sloane's yellow eyes narrowed, catlike. "The Spirit of the Wild's magic gives life to the cards. You are a wild witch, someone who can reconnect creatures large and small with the elements." She offered the deck to me. "Now it's time for you to trust in your wild magic."

I stared at the deck, not wanting to get burned by it, or the runes associated with the elements again. But this time, *I* was doing the drawing, not my aunts.

I grabbed the deck and drew the top card—a card I had not seen before. A witch stood with her hands at her sides. Magic surged out of her fingers. The magic was free—*wild.*

The card shot out of my hand and spun into the air. Shadows burst from its corners as it settled onto the ground. The kennel rattled, wind ripping through my dress as a giant shadow beast manifested itself. The creature had Willow's golden eyes, Drake's thunderous voice, and Torchie's flammable breath. This monster was a true master of the elements.

As I gazed into its eyes, I saw my reflection. Shadows spread from my mastectomy scar, coiling around my other breast.

The Spirit of the Wild took a step toward me, quaking the earth as shadows spewed out of its nostrils. "Witch of the wild, I will claim you as my own."

As I gazed into the beast's eyes, memories began to flood my mind. The memories of my diagnosis. The hospital. The chemotherapy treatments. The loss of a sacred piece of my body. . .

My magic ignited, burning like a torch in the night. I no longer had to run. I could *see* this monster for what he was, and I was going to tame him once and for all.

I threw out my hand, sending sparks into the air. "Dezmond Ravenblood is my mate, not you. *Fuck off*, cancer. This wild bitch of a witch is done with you."

# 38

# Dezmond

"*Dezmond Ravenblood is my mate, not you.*"

My hands shook on the handlebars of my bike as Victoria's voice filled my head.

"*No,*" a much deeper voice ripped like hot needles through me. "*I will claim her as my own.*"

As the Spirit of the Wild's voice thundered through my head, pain shot through my body. My arms spasmed, and I lost control of my bike. I fell forward, tumbling onto the ground before crashing into the grove of willow trees.

Dust billowed around me as I staggered to my feet. I crouched on all fours, claws ripping, fangs dripping, with the ghastly aroma of exhaust from my crashed motorcycle burning my nose. "Where is she? Where is Victoria?" I grunted, struggling to regain my focus. "She's *my* mate. I will fight for her, you hear me? Show yourself, you fucking shadow beast!"

A low guttural rumble echoed through the clouds. Lighting zapped through the air, making the scales on my arms stand on end. I scented the air, trying to find the source of this shadow that was getting too close for comfort.

The willow branches didn't seem right. They remained slack, not drifting like they usually did on the breeze. The *clank, clank, clank* of a metallic hand broke my focus.

Maverick manifested before me, his top hat slanting sideways as he grinned wickedly. Clutched in his hand was the doll. Onyx mist spilled out of its hollow eyes as it observed me. The Spirit of the Wild was inside, lurking, waiting for me to make the first move.

My back prickled. I forced myself not to lunge for him. The last time I tried to pick a fight with this shifter, his fucking doll *bit* me.

I blinked, and a lone dandelion seed drifted in front of my nose. I scrunched my muzzle, trying not to sneeze.

"*Don't allow Maverick to intimidate you. Drake and I will give you the wind and the rain you need to break him. Trust the earth beneath you. Focus on the flame you and your mate have to offer—the flame you possess is the cure, dragon shifter,*" Willow breathed.

I swatted at the seed, knocking it down onto the ground, just as the skies opened. Rain poured overhead, dripping down my nose and onto the seed. A tiny sapling sprouted out of the soil, its green leaves illuminating the shadows that coalesced around the trees.

I had the elements that Willow and Drake had given me—air and water. But I had no Torchie—no *fire.* How could I possibly bring their magic to life without the spark of a flame?

Maverick tossed the doll onto the ground before him. It landed with a dusty *fwop* between us. Shadows billowed out of the doll, coalescing around the trees.

He laughed high and cold. "I hope you brought your deck of cards, because you're going to need all the magic you can get, Ravenblood."

I ground my jaw, preparing for my attack.

Maverick folded his hands across his chest, his metallic one clinking as it jostled against his good arm. "Don't you want to meet the beast you can summon? Don't you want to know his power?" Maverick asked, his gold tooth glinting.

"Not at the cost of the dragons. As soon as Torchie hatched, all three of them became *my* family."

His golden tooth flashed. "The elements separated from one another are weak. Only when they are combined with a shifter's shadows do they truly reveal their wild magic."

Another shadow appeared at my side. One by one, my shadow beasts manifested, tossing their heads into the air. But the beasts who haunted the corridors of my mind were no longer shadows—they'd completely transformed into golden metallic creatures.

"*Destroy the doll,*" Jawz growled as his tail thrashed around me. "*It's the source of the cage Maverick has used to trap the Spirit of the Wild inside.*"

Maverick reached into his pocket. He tossed his Wild Card out into the open. Rib bones arched out of the ground, curving up and around one another. Bones rattled against each other as the doll was locked in the cage.

*Shit.* How could I destroy it now?

Maverick laughed. "Nice try, Ravenblood. But I'm afraid your shadow beasts, like the Spirit of the Wild, are now mine. Soon, I will also have the wild magic of Victoria Crow to control."

A roar ripped out of my throat. *Nobody* threatened my witch, or my shadow beasts. I dug my claws into the ground. My spine buckled, and I sprung toward him.

Maverick's metallic hand extended toward me. I slammed my jaws down onto his wrist, tearing into the gears, ripping a few out as I tore my mouth sideways. The bitter taste of oil filled my mouth. I gagged, choking as I spit it out.

Maverick had disappeared, shifting away from my attack. A small black creature with a long skinny tail darted out into the open.

*Fuck*. He was a pack rat!

Dozens of rats swarmed out of his top hat, golden whiskers and eyes glinting toward me. Weighing down my legs, they climbed up my arms and dug their tiny claws and teeth into my scales until I was too heavy to move. Each scale the rats bit into turned into gold.

I swung my head sideways, sending a few of the rats flying.

One of the rats smacked into the cage, making the bones rattle. Shadows billowed out of the doll's eyes as another beast manifested itself.

The Spirit of the Wild towered over me, great darkness living inside of his hollow eyes—darkness I'd been avoiding that lived inside of me. He wasn't just a shadow beast—he was a master of the elements.

The Spirit of the Wild was a *dragon*.

He lowered his great head, shadows spilling out of his nostrils as he spoke, "*Dezmond Ravenblood, offer to me your sacrifice, or you will forever become the beast that lurks within my shadows.*"

The fighting would never stop. My shadow beasts could not be tamed, not when they were fighting for what they had always wanted for me—my *mate*—the same thing this ancestor of the dragons wanted as his own. One by one, my shadow beasts would fall victim to his shadows—the monster I had concealed deep within.

*Unless...*

I remembered what Victoria had said about the fire rune.

"*Fire is the purifier, the lifeblood of our magic. Fire is both medicine, and a curse.*"

My heart jumped.

*Blood...*

Shaking, I opened my mouth as wide as I could, then sank my fangs into my arm. My mouth filled with the iron-rich taste of my blood. As my canines dug into my flesh, memories of Victoria tending to my injury flashed before my eyes. She had shown me compassion when I was down. With her care, she renewed my strength by trusting in me.

As my blood filled my mouth, a horrible cry ripped out of the cage as the doll set on fire.

"No!" Maverick yelled, his pack rats all swarming the cage. As soon as they hit the bones, they were consumed by the flames.

The pain of a thousand sharp needles ripped through my ribs from the inside out. A thundering rhythm of my own pulse threatened to rip me apart. The scent of my blood burned my nose, filling me with flame.

Pawz and Jawz tore ahead, diving into the surging inferno as it consumed the cage.

"*See you on the other side, dragon shifter,*" Sniffer said as he dove into the onyx flames.

# 39

# Victoria

The Wild Witch Card sparked in my hand as a burst of magic erupted out of my aura. Shadows branched out of my fingers, reaching for the Spirit of the Wild.

The great beast shuddered, his head hanging low. His hollow eyes drooped, then closed. He fell forward, landing with a dusty *flop* onto the ground.

When the dust settled, a man wearing a tattered black biker jacket lay face down in the dirt. Claws jutted out of his paw-like hands. A wolf tail bristled out of his torn jeans. Long canines glistened in the corners of his gaping mouth.

"Dezmond!" I cried, running to where he lay and dropped to his side. No longer a demon, nor a beast, he was something in between. His arms and neck seemed to be covered in bite marks.

I grabbed his shoulder and gave him a shake. "Dezmond, can you hear me?"

Sloane dropped next to him and set her hand onto his shoulder. "He can't shift properly. Looks like you'll have to work your magic on him."

"Wait, did the ritual work? Did we break Maverick's curse?" I asked.

"Only time can tell," Sloane answered, a pair of fox ears appearing on the top of her head.

"*To the clinic*!" Francine screeched.

"*I'll carry you both*," Torchie offered.

Dezmond let out a groan as Torchie flapped his wings and grabbed ahold of him with one clawed foot, then myself with the other.

With a whirl of brown and pink fur, Sloane shifted back into her fox form.

A week later, I tucked the Wild Witch Card into my clipboard along with a stack of new patient intake forms. It had taken me a few days to recover from what I'd said to the Spirit of the Wild. As soon as I'd told off the giant shadow beast, somehow, keeping the card close to me gave me a little confidence about what to do with the new Dezmond.

I'd done one of two things by telling Torchie's giant shadowy ancestor to go fuck off. Either I'd cursed my family for many generations to come, or my magic would backfire. Either way, I was convinced that Dezmond Ravenblood would never be able to fully shift out of his new half-beast, half-demon form.

Dezmond's heart rate and breathing remained stable, but I'd made a point to check on him every couple of hours where he was curled like a dog in the back of an overnight kennel in our quarantine room. Holly was the only individual, other than myself, who was allowed to check on him.

Holly poked her head into my office as I took my lunch. The look in her eye told me everything before the words, "he's awake," escaped her mouth.

I jumped up from my chair with my clipboard in hand and darted down the hall. Deja-vu swept over me as I grabbed the door and swung it open. I wanted to see the Dezmond I knew from a few weeks ago, his bald head hung over, slumped between his shoulders. Instead, I found a pair of fangs sticking through the metal bars of the kennel as he attempted to gnaw the door open.

"Do we sedate him?" Holly suggested, hesitant to walk into the room.

I stepped inside, set my clipboard down onto the exam table, and approached the cage he was busy chomping on. "Hell no, not until I've spoken with him first."

Dezmond pulled his fangs away from the metal door and gazed through the bars at me. The green color of his eyes was far wilder than what I remembered. His pupils dilated as he spotted me.

"Can you even talk?" I asked, half-expecting him to growl.

I unraveled my stethoscope from around my neck and held it out for him to sniff. His head drooped sideways, nostrils flaring as he inhaled my scent.

I sucked in a breath, opened the kennel door, and took a step back.

He wagged his tail and crawled out of the kennel. In one swift movement, he stood on two legs, wrapped his arms around my center and embraced me.

"Please tell me this isn't a dream," he whispered.

"I sure hope it isn't," I said, trying to wriggle myself free from his grip. He was stark naked and getting hard by the instant.

Holly backed out of the room as he nuzzled my hair. "What happened to me? And what about the wedding?"

"Lucy and Amon eloped," I answered, slinging my stethoscope back around my neck. "As for you, I don't know. You've been unconscious for almost a week. You don't seem to be able to shift properly between a beast and demon any longer."

He held up his hands, which still had the residual claws that resembled those of a bear. "I don't understand. I destroyed the voodoo doll like Willow and Drake wanted me to, and *this* is what I get for it?"

I grabbed his big clawed hands. "How did you destroy the doll? And what do you remember before you shifted last?"

He winced. "I remember Maverick shifting into a bunch of pack rats, then me sinking my teeth into my arm."

I jolted. "Wait, you bit *yourself*? Is that where the wound on your arm came from? I thought the bite came from one of the dragons."

He nodded. "Remember the ritual?"

"I do, but I don't remember *biting* yourself being part of it."

"Willow and Drake's spirits were present when the Spirit of the Wild confronted me. I discovered that Torchie's parents represent the elements of air, and water. Torchie represents fire, but I didn't have him with me. Then I remembered what you said about the fire rune, *fire is the purifier, the lifeblood of our magic.* That's when I knew that my blood—the blood of a dragon shifter—would work." He squeezed my hand. "As soon as I spilled my blood, the doll set on fire. Thanks to you, I was able to torch that creepy doll and break Maverick's curse."

Sparks shot out of my stethoscope, lighting some of my paperwork on fire. I patted it out, then grabbed the card that thankfully hadn't gone up in flames.

"*Wild Witch*, huh? Did you know you had this card in the deck?" Dezmond asked.

"No, I didn't. Sloane told me that I had to use the deck to help you, and that's what I drew. Next thing I knew, I was facing the Spirit of the Wild." I bit my tongue. "When that monster said he was going to claim me as his own, I sort of told him to go fuck himself."

Dezmond chuckled. "I know, I heard you say that I was your mate. You must have meant it, because I've never been stuck between demon and beast form before. And I know how you feel about my wild side."

We both laughed. His sound and warmth set me at ease.

My phone chimed, which quickly stole the comfort Dezmond offered me. I tugged it out of my scrubs. "I have my appointment at the cancer clinic this afternoon. I'd be very glad if you went with me."

His green eyes swept to mine, and suddenly I knew I could face any monster I might meet later today. With Dezmond, I didn't have to face my cancer alone.

Dezmond tucked his tail into his pants, and he learned how to retract his claws. For the most part, he could pass as a normal-looking demon again. But he didn't have much luck with the new set of horns that sprouted out of his head the moment we left the clinic. It took a whole lot of will power on my part not to run my fingers through his hair just to play with them.

By the time I parked my Jeep in the hospital parking lot, my heart was in my throat.

Dezmond hopped out of the Jeep first and opened my door. He held out his hand, helping me down. "We're facing this monster together," he said, offering his arm to me.

I slung my arm around his and walked into the hospital. The sterile, artificial smell broke my temporary comfort. I remembered the countless weeks of coming here, being hooked up to chemo, not knowing if or how long it would take for my symptoms to disappear, if at all. Good thing I had a vice grip on Dezmond's arm, because I would have spun on my heel and darted out the door without him.

Not long after I checked in, a nurse brought us back into the patient rooms. The Wild Witch Card in my pocket sent sparks out of my scrubs as she opened the door.

We walked inside. A pair of X-rays were on display in the far corner.

I recognized the beastly anatomy.

*Shit.* Did someone at the hospital find out that I'd treated Dezmond's wounds without a medical license?

The far door to the room opened, and a familiar woman walked inside. She wore a white lab coat. Her short brown hair with pink highlights framed her angular face. A pair of yellow eyes darted between us.

"*Sloane*?" Dezmond and I said in unison.

Sloane's mouth quirked. "Please, have a seat. We have a lot to talk about."

Dezmond sank down, but I remained standing. "Okay, how many jobs do you work? First you're a shelter manager, then a yoga instructor, and now you work at the hospital?"

Sloane grinned impishly. "I'm a fox shifter. I shift my way into a lot of different roles, especially when rituals between witches and demons are involved. I happen to take great joy in studying their results." Her yellow eyes narrowed onto me. "Victoria, I sent you the letters from the cancer clinic. But your appointment today is not to confirm that your cancer has returned."

Anger surged through my body. "Why would you send those horrible letters to me? Why would you *lie* to me? Don't you know how terrible of a monster cancer really is?"

Sloane reached into her pocket, tugging out an onyx stone. "The only way to have you fully engage with the ritual was for you to face the monster, who you so eloquently told to fuck off when you faced the Spirit of the Wild." She offered me the stone. "I think you will find that by facing that monster, you've cured yourself."

I took the stone from her. "Even if my cancer *is* cured, how can you tell that our participation in the ritual actually broke Maverick's curse?"

Sloane pointed to the wall. "Take a look at the X-rays you took of Dezmond a few weeks ago. Tell me that you don't notice anything different."

"Sloane, I don't need to look at X-rays to know that I now have horns," Dezmond said as he touched the pointed tips barely visible in his thick hair.

Sloane smiled. "Horns are proof that a dragon shifter has become the alpha, the true king among his shadow beasts."

At the mention of the word alpha, Dezmond's chest swelled. "You mean my shadow beasts aren't going to dominate my life any longer?"

Sloane's eyes swept to me. "Not when you have a wild witch taming them."

My chest heated as Dezmond's green eyes landed on me. I was going to have way too much fun with the thought of him being an *alpha* shifter.

He squinted at the stone in my hand. "Hey, did you swipe that from me? I remember having it."

"No, Francine did. I asked her to bring it to me once she had given you and your family expectations at Amon's bachelor party."

He shrugged. "I still don't remember what those expectations were."

Sloane smiled. "You shouldn't have to remember a thing, not when elemental instinct takes over. I created this shadow pendant a long time ago, when Maverick and I were once friends. Over time, he became obsessed with exploiting elemental magic by trapping dragons. As a thank you for breaking the curse Maverick had placed on the Spirit of the Wild, I'm giving it to you."

I glanced at the stone and blinked. I could have sworn that I saw Francine's reflection staring back at me. "I don't understand. Willow said that a monster attacked her, then killed Francine. The only real monster that Dezmond and I faced was the Spirit of the Wild."

Sloane's yellow eyes narrowed. "Are you sure about that? You've been running from a monster for a long time now, one that you finally trusted in yourself to face." She turned to Dezmond. "As you know, monsters can wear many masks. The Spirit of the Wild is a shadow beast who represents our wildest fears. Both of you faced your fears together. In doing so, you've helped the offspring of Drake and Willow develop his own unique magic."

"Talents, as in lighting his own farts on fire?" Dezmond added with a grin.

I winced. "I sure hope not. I've already had to deal with an unbearable amount of flatulence at my clinic from a rainbow serpent. I don't need any more reptiles adding to the problem." I locked eyes with Sloane. "If the monster that killed Francine wasn't the Spirit of the Wild, then what *did* take her life?"

Sloane leveled her gaze with me. "Francine wasn't killed by a monster. The *fear* of that monster is what Francine decided to confront. She willingly volunteered her earth magic to bind the other three elements into one, as now seen in the stone. As your familiar, she chose to sacrifice her body so that the wild magic of her witch could live on."

My throat closed.

Francine had made a sacrifice for *both* of us.

"What do you want me to do with the stone?" I asked, tearing up.

Sloane flipped the light box off, darkening Dezmond's X-rays. "Take it to the dragons who relied on your bond. I'm sure they will be grateful for how you made use of their elements." Her yellow eyes narrowed onto me. "The bond you and Dezmond share is something us shifters all wish we can one day experience."

My chest swelled at the sentiment. Somehow, I knew that Francine's spirit wouldn't be far off, and that I could continue to look to her for guidance, mother hen magic and all.

# 40

# Dezmond

As soon as we left the hospital, my horns felt larger, more pronounced. A new sense of confidence swept over me as they spiraled like corkscrews out of my scalp. I felt good, *really* good. I wanted every fucking witch, demon, and shadow beast in Midhaven to know that I'd earned a demonic dragon crown of horns.

But was I really a dragon shifter if I couldn't do the one thing other than breathing fire that dragons were known for?

The prickling sensation on my horns intensified as we walked into the sun. The tingling feeling traveled down my neck, branching through my spine, until it settled near my shoulders.

I grabbed Victoria's hand and tugged her over to a hedge of bushes, concealing us from the sight. Claws extended, I gripped her around the waist and tugged her close.

"What are you doing?" she asked.

"I want to try something," I said, feeling that wicked *swooping* sensation in my stomach again. "Can I please have the pendant Sloane gave you?"

Victoria handed it to me. The moment the cool onyx stone touched my palm, scales appeared on my forearms. I sucked in a breath. On my exhale, two membranous wings ripped out of my shirt. The scent of wind and thunder burned my nose as I took Victoria skyward.

Victoria clung to my neck and let out a scream.

"Don't worry, I got you!" I said, grabbing her legs and swinging them around my front. I took her up and up and up, not stopping even when I hit the clouds. The wind filled my lungs, until drops of rain saturated us both. Victoria's scrubs clung to her body, making her curves ever more voluptuous.

"Where did you take us?"

I bucked my hips, teasing a moan out of her. "To a place where I get to claim you as my mate over and over, and nobody is going to hear you cry out my name."

"*Ahem, there will be no mate claiming up here in the clouds.*"

I jolted, flapping my wings until I swung myself sideways to face the thunderclouds brewing to my left. A pair of golden eyes met me, blinking as a giant dragon manifested before us.

"Willow? What are you doing up here?" I asked.

"*Teaching my son how to do a proper backflip now that he's grown into his wings. I see that you have also sprouted a pair of your own.*"

"*That doesn't mean that he knows how to use them,*" Torchie huffed as he poked his head out of the clouds next to his mother.

"Is that a challenge?" I huffed back at him.

Torchie swung his tail toward me, nearly knocking into my ass as I pivoted.

"Hey, not cool, little scaly dude," I grumbled, feeling my horns extend toward him. I reached into my pocket and tugged out the shadow pendant. "The first dragon to catch this before it hits the ground is the winner, got it?"

"Are you *kidding* me?" Victoria yelled, clutching me tighter.

I tossed the onyx stone into the air.

Torchie dove, disappearing into the clouds, belching a giant gas bubble as he went.

Victoria's legs squeezed my center. "Dezmond, wait."

I clutched her tightly around me. "Hold on. I'm not going to let him get away with being a showoff, not to the dragon shifter who helped him to hatch out of his egg."

Her fingers dug into my back as I dove after Willow and Drake's rebellious son. Down we went, bursting into a storm of elements. Wind and rain and lighting danced around us until we swooped down into the canopy of trees.

Torchie landed first. I followed.

"*Not bad for your first time spreading your wings, dragon shifter*," Drake said as he shuffled out of the trees.

Victoria still clung to my front. I grabbed her arms and unraveled them from my neck. "What did you think of that?"

"Flying is going to take me some time to get used to," she breathed into my ear.

Willow landed gracefully beside her mate, dwarfing him and her son. "*Spreading your wings for your mate is the best thing you can do to reinforce your bond.*"

I grabbed Victoria around the waist. "What happens next for you three? Now that Maverick and is gone, do you plan to stick around town?"

Drake's nostrils flared before he thundered out a reply. "*Our business in Midhaven is done. You've helped us to ensure that our elemental magic will remain wild for many generations to come.*"

Willow blinked, sending a few of her eyelashes drifting on the breeze. "*Thank you both. Breaking the curse is the best gift you could have given us.*"

Her sweet yellow eyes made my heart swell. "Where did your ancestor go?"

"*Back to the Summoning, where we are sure to join him before long,*" she answered as she lowered her giant head next to her son. "*Give the stone back to them. They've earned it as a gift from all three of us.*"

Torchie reared his head back and belched. A bubble escaped his mouth and rose into the air. When it popped, the stone fell out.

I caught it before it hit the ground.

"*We offer you and your mate an elemental stone,*" Willow said as she lowered her giant head and arched her wing over us. "*Use this stone with the Three Magics Oracle Deck. It will ensure that your bond will connect you with the elements.*"

My heart thundered alongside Drake's rumbling growl. Only now did I realize that Willow, Drake, and Torchie, were actually *leaving* us. How much I was going to miss Willow's golden sunlight, Drake's thunderous voice, and Torchie's flammable burps.

These dragons were my kin, my *family*. What was I going to do without them?

"*You worship your mate by offering her our elements,*" Willow's powerful voice echoed into my head.

My eyes stung as our three dragon friends vanished, their tails, scales, and wings blending back with the grove of trees where I'd first met Torchie's parents.

Victoria grabbed my hand. "I'm really going to miss them."

"Me too," I replied, stuffing down a hiccup.

She tugged out her phone. "Lucy just texted me. She and Amon are heading to the bakery. Sounds like they want us to meet them there."

I decided that I wanted to keep my wings a secret from my family, at least for the time being. Once I flew us back to the hospital, we hopped into her Jeep and drove to the bakery.

Amon and Lucy were sitting outside, laughing as Liam and Oscar tried to catch one of Goblin's hoglets in a flowerpot as it darted in and out of the tea stand. Cindy and my father sat at another table with Victoria's aunts as they watched Scythe hover spookily between the two witches. His silver tail twitched as he begged for cat treats.

Millie clapped her hands together the moment she spotted us and said, "Well now, here come the best witch and the best demon!"

"Oi, Zeddy! How was your nap?" Dad asked as he glanced up from his plate of pastries at me.

"It was fine. Victoria took good care of me."

Victoria's cheeks flushed.

Dad beamed. "Krim, how about another spot of tea?"

Krim's cheeks bulged. "I don't think I can look at tea for a while without becoming nauseated."

"Did you know that your brother can *fly* now?" Victoria asked as she took one of the pastries from his platter before Scythe could float his way over.

Krim chuckled, waving his hand to shoo his insistent ghost cat away. "All demons can fly with the help of their shadows."

Victoria shot me a wicked smile. "Not like your baby bro. I highly doubt any of you brothers or your father have *his* wingspan."

The magical sparks that erupted between us could have lit one of Krim's cupcakes on fire.

A dark chuckle filled my head, "*She has no idea what's coming her way.*"

I dug my finger into my ear. "Jawz, is that you?"

Another growl followed. "*Wait until you see our new form.*"

Their voices retreated into my head, leaving me to focus on our mingling families.

Victoria motioned toward Lucy and Amon, sliding her hand into my butt jean pocket so she could caress the base of my tail. "Look at them, freshly married, and we're freshly mated. What do you think the difference is?"

"I don't know. But I do know this," I said, wrapping my arm around her waist. "I'm going to spend the rest of my days finding out with you."

Grace bustled out of the shop, carrying a platter with a giant lone cupcake in the middle.

Krim cleared his throat nervously. "Everyone, apart from celebrating Lucy and Amon's elopement, Grace and I wanted to make an announcement."

Grace smiled gingerly at Krim before lowering the platter in front of him.

He grabbed the cutting knife with a trembling hand and handed it to her. "Love, you do the honor."

Grace grabbed the knife and pressed it down into the cupcake. She clapped her hands onto either side of her face as blue frosting oozed out of the center. "I'm so excited! It's a *boy*!"

Victoria rushed over to her sister. "Oh, my goddess, Grace, you're *pregnant*?"

"Krim and I just found out. Apparently, all my nausea wasn't from Mom's solstice tea," she admitted.

While Victoria and her sisters embraced, I walked over to Krim, who looked like he was about to laugh or throw up. "Wow, you're gonna be a Pops! How does that feel?"

"Like I'm the luckiest demon alive," he flustered. "Amon, I'm sorry if I stole your thunder, but we've been wanting to share this news ever since you and Lucy eloped."

"Don't be," Amon said, clapping Krim on the back, making his apron jostle. "I can't believe the luck we're all having with the Crow sisters. It's almost like fate made this happen."

When the excitement settled, I took Victoria aside. "I never quite asked you. Do you want kids?"

"As much as I've loved fostering a dragon hatchling with you, birth control is one of the most magical things ever invented." She squeezed my hand. "I'm open to having children, but I'm not in any rush, if that's what you mean."

My heart shuddered, happy with her reply. While I would always have a soft spot for youngsters and critters, I wanted to spend some time enjoying our bond with just the two of us. "Me neither. I have a feeling you're going to be an amazing aunt. I'm sure you'll teach your nephew about all kinds of wild magic."

# 41

# Victoria

**October 1st**

The Three Magics Oracle Deck sat on my kitchen island, awaiting the moment when I'd play with the cards again. Dezmond and I had made some changes around my house over the past week. Brisk autumn air meant the pool had been put away, and the scent of pumpkin spice wafted through my home. Plastic skeletons hung from a garland rope across my mantel, while every corner on my bookshelf was covered in fake spiderwebs.

Now was the time for my absolute favorite season—the spooky season of Halloween.

"*At least my tail feathers don't get stuck in those stupid fake spiderwebs any longer,*" Francine said as she hovered above my shoulder. The pot of tomato sauce bubbled and popped from my stove, which she'd been eyeing for the last hour.

I glanced up at my spirit red-tail, admiring her new appearance. "Francine, I need to thank you. Sloane told us what you did for Dezmond and I."

She ruffled her tail feathers like she always had before. Only now they were silver and far less intrusive of my thoughts. "*I have a message for you.*"

A letter floated down from her talons.

I caught it before it hit my kitchen table. "Who is this from?"

"*Open it,*" she said rather shrilly. "*As long as you don't start calling me a messenger pigeon, then I'll be around to deliver your mail to and from the vet clinic.*"

The back door swung open as Dezmond entered my kitchen. He brought in the crisp scent of woodsmoke, as he'd been prepping a fire out back where my pool had been.

He came up behind me and wrapped his arms around my front. "What's my favorite witch brewing up for dinner tonight?"

"Dragon scale stew," I answered as I sprinkled in a bit of salt.

He chuckled, then kissed my cheek. "Who is sending you snail mail?"

I ripped the letter open and tugged out a folded piece of parchment. My breath hitched. I instantly recognized Sloane's handwriting.

**Dear Victoria,**

**Francine has notified me that I did not live up to my part of the deal she made with me regarding the ritual. She shared that your vet clinic is in dire need of a magical expansion. In repayment for her**

**earth magic, she insists that you become the sole owner of the facility.**

**With your approval, I am surrendering full ownership of the Paws & Claws Animal Shelter to the Crow's Nest Vet Clinic. Please contact me with the next steps on how to relinquish ownership to you.**

**Sincerely,**
**Sloane Fox**
**Your Resident Fox Shifter**

My hand shook as Dezmond kissed my cheek again. "I can't believe this. Full ownership?"

"Woohoo! You hear that? You could be head witch boss vet at *two* clinics!"

I glanced over at the deck. "Why don't you gather the cards and meet me outside to celebrate?"

He squeezed me tighter. "Why do I have to celebrate with a bunch of cards, when I've got my wild witch right here?"

I giggled and gave my tomato sauce a good stir.

Francine let out a *shreeeeek*, spread her silver wings, then disappeared into my bookshelf and out of sight. She was likely off to pester her offspring, who had thankfully started to hunt a new population of pack rats and kept them far away from my home.

Dezmond spun me to face him. "Want me to take you up and prove to you that you don't need a deck of cards to experience a dose of my magic?"

"No," I stammered, setting down my wooden spoon. "Flying is not my thing. I'm a witch who prefers to stay grounded." I reached into my pocket and tugged out the elemental stone Torchie had given us. "I do, however, want to see how this is going to work with the Oracle Deck. Maybe if you're a good boy, we can have a little fun while we're at it."

Dezmond grinned, his canines elongating as he dropped his hands to my hips. "All right. You're the boss, witchy woman. But I refuse to touch the deck. You seem to be the only one who can tame the cards, let alone my magic."

"Stop being so scared, you're an *alpha* shifter now, according to Sloane," I teased as I grabbed a marshmallow from the candy cauldron and shoved it into his mouth.

He chewed, then swallowed, then kissed me again, this time on the lips. "I'll make a deal with you. If I grab the deck, then you are required to play with my horns later tonight."

I kissed him, then grabbed the deck, along with a couple of mugs decorated with ghosts and pumpkins. "Come on. It's cozy snuggle under a flannel blanket and drink hot cocoa by a roaring fire time."

As we set up our dinner date outside on my deck, the sun dipped on the horizon. We ate our dinner and boiled water on the flames to make our hot cocoa. Soon, the only light we had was provided by the roaring fire.

I set the deck onto the table between us, along with the elemental stone.

An ember jumped out of the fire, landing on the stone, which quickly burst into a puff of sparkling purple and orange flames.

"Oh shit, *no*!" I screamed. I threw out my hand, but it was too late. The deck sizzled and cracked as each of the cards lit on fire, then just like the rune, promptly disintegrated.

"Well, that was anticlimactic," Dezmond said with a laugh. "I was expecting something like, whoa. Check this out!"

As the flames roared upward, so did the shadows Dezmond was making with his hands. They became monstrous, branching upward and outward as they grew.

I jumped up from my blanket, startled as to how quickly the flames had transformed him. His horns were no longer a dull brown, but they were long, curved, and glowing. As the shadows reached around his arms and legs, they stripped off his flannel shirt and jeans, leaving nothing but a smoking-hot demon standing before me.

My breath caught. My dragon shifter boyfriend was absolutely *stunning*.

The shadow bear, lion, and wolf all spiraled around Dezmond, untamed wildness glinting in their eyes as each of them studied me. Good thing my backyard was private, because I'd never had sex with an inferno of shadow beasts, let alone outside under a blanket of stars before.

Dezmond grabbed me under the knees and pinned me against the wooden railing surrounding my deck. "I never liked those cards anyway," he breathed, his voice heaving with desire. He grabbed my leggings and tugged them down.

He lowered his face between my legs and teased me with his tongue.

"Dezmond," I breathed, grabbing his horns. I could control where I wanted him to go. When I squeezed, he went faster. When I relaxed, he slowed.

The flames kicked up, and Dezmond straightened himself. He raked his teeth along my chest, nipping at my breast and my scar as he bucked his hips, forcing his hard length against my opening.

As his shadow beasts all funneled beneath us, his wings siphoning away the smoke and ash as the magical flames removed my remaining clothing. There was nothing that separated demon from beast, or witch from the elements.

One cock sprung out into the open, followed by a much larger, veinier of the two. I grabbed the smaller one, which my fingers barely touched when I closed my hand around the thick base, and began to pump him.

His nostrils flared as I stroked his shaft. He teased my entry with the thicker of the cocks, a knot swelling at the base as he slipped inside.

My vision blanked, and I saw stars. He went in, in, *in*. He rolled his hips, sending me into a fit of pleasure. With each thrust he made, his cocks traded with my pussy. One was knotted, the other keeled with soft shiny scales. *Goddess*, this was the wild, untamed sex I had been waiting for.

With each flap of his wings, he brought me closer to the edge. I was jostled between beastly shadows and my double-cocked demon, their dark masses struggling to claim me as their own. I was bonded to Dezmond Ravenblood, and all his shadows, each and every one of them. Rolling my hips, I accepted every glorious inch of him.

"Take me, love. Take *all* of me," he growled, forcing both of his cocks deep inside. "I need you to be mine."

My back arched as I closed my eyes and embraced his wild side. The flames surged around us, burning bright behind my eyelids. Flame and shadow brought me to the edge, then released me into a trembling fit of an orgasm.

My fingers curled into his hair, while he relaxed against my chest, resting his head against my neck. He pulled one of the blankets over me. The fire returned to its normal size as we struggled to catch our breath. Shadows gone, I tucked myself against his heaving chest, reeling in his affection as he kissed my forehead. We lay silent for a while, the only noises being the wind, a distant thunderstorm, and the crackling flames as we synced our ragged breathing.

"I hope you're okay with a horny demon, because I don't know if these are going anywhere," he said, pointing to one of his horns that had shrank back into his hair. "Fate might have given me something I have no control over."

"If what we have is fate, then I'm keeping it forever," I said to my shifter as I kissed his stubbled cheek. "I'd call what we have something wild, and full of magic."

# Epilogue

**October 31st**

"Isn't it a little late in the year to have a Summerween pool party?" Grace asked the next day when I sat at a table sipping on my cup of Summer Solstice tea. My mother had given us all batches of our own to try out as she was starting to experiment with new herbal infusions that complimented the seasons.

I nudged my teacup toward her for a refill. "Today is Halloween. Dezmond and I have been bewitching my backyard with our wild magic, which apparently can turn the seasons in our favor."

She shot me a look of approval as she poured hot water into my cup. "That's my point, it's no longer summer. Wouldn't it just be a *Halloween* pool party?"

"Not when I promised my sisters a summer-themed one! Besides, Dezmond's band wants to play. Apparently, they renamed themselves from the Nematodes to something he said isn't as lame-sounding."

I'd gone all out this year decorating for my favorite holiday of the season, pool style. Jack-o-lanterns carved as dragons lined my back deck, casting a spooky atmosphere in an ominous orange glow. Coffin-shaped rafts floated in the water, and inter tubes bubbled with pink and green bubbles that foamed out of their centers. My favorite spooky decor was the Wild Witch Card itself. It floated in the air, saturating the atmosphere with a magical orange glow.

Grace and Lucy arrived right at seven. Both were bundled up in hats and coats, swearing under their breath. Lucy ascended the wooden steps onto my deck next to the pool where I sat preparing the last of the decorations. "Victoria, there is no way we're swimming. It's basically snowing."

I glanced up at the sky, where a few flurries swirled in the air. "Show me the bathing suits, my fellow witches. Then the real festivities can begin."

Grace folded her arms across her center, matching Lucy. "I think my tits are going to freeze off if I remove any clothing."

I grabbed my Wild Witch Card and tossed it into the air above the pool. It showered us in a wave of orange and purple sparks that instantly warmed the area.

"Playing card tricks now, are we?" Grace said as she removed a boot and dipped her toe into the steaming water. "Wow, it feels like a sauna!"

Lucy scowled. "Still snowing."

A shivering ball of green quills scurried to the edge of the pool.

"Don't even think about it, little prickly dude," I scolded Goblin as he sniffed one of the inner tubes. "Grubs is eating something that will probably make him sick later. You should go bother him."

He glanced up at me with his beady black eyes, nose twitching. "*Don't you like my Halloween costume?*"

"What are you, a *green hedgehog*?"

He snuffed his nose high in the air. "*No, my hoglets dressed me up as an avocado. It's Wilma's favorite fruit*!"

Ignoring his blatant attempt to cover his lame costume, I unraveled my robe and lowered myself onto one of the coffin rafts and flopped onto my back. Glancing up at the sky, seeing my magic burning like a hot flame around us was all the proof Grace and I needed to get in.

"Any ideas on where you and Amon are going for your honeymoon?" I asked Lucy as she braved the pool and joined Grace and I in our coffin rafts.

She flipped onto her stomach and floated over to me. "We thought about just going to some random mountain town in Colorado."

"Oh, that would be wonderful!" Grace chimed, her raft nearly tipping over. "Mom's been thinking about taking a little vacation too. I think it would be good for her to spread her wings a bit and see what other magical towns there are out there other than Midhaven."

I kicked Lucy's raft and made it spin. "Didn't our cousin Danika send you a jar of magical black honey from a town called *Timberhaven*?"

"You know what? She did! I also heard from Aunt Tillie that Danika is a bit of a bookworm like me."

On cue, Grubs came inching his way between paper cups and bottles of soda. A pair of Lucy's giant purple sunglasses sat atop his eyes as he nodded his head like an accordion-shaped punk rocker. "*Come on, witches. Time to get our magics on*! *The Ravenblood demon brothers have arrived*!"

Krim and Amon emerged, both bundled the way my sisters had been.

"I'm not getting wet," Krim said right away, standing beside the pool with a grumpy scowl that matched Lucy before.

Amon clapped him on the back. "Pretty soon you're going to jump into the deep end and be the next demon to propose to your witch."

Grace's magic bloomed out of the water, sparks taking the form of a massive mushroom that floated over Krim's head and burst into a flurry golden butterflies.

His scowl softened, turning into a smile as he eyed my mushroom-obsessed sister.

"Where is the Zed Man?" Amon asked as he reached out and grabbed Lucy's hand and tugged her close.

"Yeah, he was the one who told us about this pool party I never agreed to," Krim added as his hood fell over his head, casting his features into shadow.

I felt a little frustrated that my sisters both had their demons and wondered why mine had yet to show.

The flames in the jack-o-lanterns changed from orange to purple as a giant gust of wind swept over the pool.

"Cannonball!" Dezmond cried as he fell out of the sky and landed dead-center into the pool. Lucy and Grace fell into the water, while I remained on my raft.

"Hey, not cool!" Lucy stammered, splashing the pair of demon horns that rose out of the water.

"Seriously, you're going to have to be a little less dramatic with your entrance," I said, splashing him.

Dezmond was shirtless, tossing his fist into the air. "That was sick, little fire dude! We're gonna have to work on some more diving tricks like that!"

"Holy shit!" Amon said, ducking as Torchie shot a blast of flames overhead.

"Your dragon isn't *little* any longer," Krim grumbled as he shook away the water Dezmond had splashed onto his hood.

I grabbed Dezmond's hand and tugged him close for a kiss. When our lips joined, the Wild Witch Card showered us in a wave of sparks.

"Calm down you two, or at least get a room," Grace teased as a mushroom made of magical green dust bloomed over her head.

The only article of clothing Dezmond wore other than his swim trunks was a bandana. He pointed to his head and the new name of his band. "Guys look. We're no longer the Nematodes. We're the *Wild Elements*!"

"*All right, now it's time to party*!" Grubs said as he flung his sunglasses into the pool.

I lowered myself down from my raft into the water and stood next to my demon. "Everyone, I need us to join hands for this spell. I want to make sure no wendigos, evil mushroom sprites, or rat shifters cause mischief in our little town of Midhaven ever again."

Dezmond shot his brothers a look. "Guys, that means you need to get your asses in the pool, now."

"And that's my cue to leave," Krim said, but one little blast of flame from Torchie's nostrils made him turn around.

Dezmond grabbed Amon and Krim by their shirts and flung them into the pool.

They surfaced, Amon's shadows rising out of the water like an enraged sea serpent, and Krim's reaper tossed up his bony hands.

"Dude, not cool!" Amon grumbled, flinging his wet hair out of his eyes.

Krim's mouth gaped open as he flung back his sodden hood. "Yeah, what the fuck was that for?"

I grabbed Dezmond's hand on my right as my sisters both settled on my left. Grace grabbed my hand and Lucy's, and she Amon's until we finished our circle with Krim grabbing Dezmond's.

I sucked in a breath and closed my eyes, focusing on the magic we brought to the water. It lit up like a flame, each of us funneling our energies toward the center. "By the way of the goddess, the earth, and the shadows. With the power of wild magic, I ask that you protect our families as they grow together."

I opened my eyes. The water began to spiral as my spell stirred the elements.

Torchie reared his head back. With a plume of flames, lit the Wild Witch Card on fire.

As the ashes blew out into the snow flurries, a sense of peace settled upon me. Here we were on Halloween night. Three witch sisters and three demon brothers. A full year had passed since we'd first met the Ravenbloods, who would forever change our lives for the better. I was excited to see what would come of our new family's magic.

# Acknowledgements

Writing has been my way to explore and escape into characters and worlds for a very long time. It's constantly moving and changing, keeping me on my toes. My hope is that my quirky stories are something that readers enjoy and connect with. I could not have created this book without the help of many others. I wanted to acknowledge a few prominent influences in my life that continue to encourage me on this writing journey.

My mom and brother who have always supported my random creative endeavors, whether it be panting, drawing, or writing.

My father who is no longer with us, but still encourages me to write in spirit.

My husband Bill, for supporting me on this journey and for making me laugh with your feedback on my first drafts.

My critique group, who has put up with my stories for the past seven years. Carly, Debbie, and Ed, you've helped me to craft my character's voices as well as find my own author voice.

My friends Jordyn and Angela, for being two amazing souls who came into my life when I thought about quitting self-publishing. You have both been a light in the dark, helping me to keep writing and embrace the imperfections in my writing craft.

My amazing editor Sarah, my beta readers, and my street team for cheering me on when I had lots of doubts.

My readers, because you are what brings the written word to life.

My taiko group, Sun Mountain Taiko, for drumming with me and driving the rhythm behind my stories.

My local library, where I work in the family and children's department. To my fellow library staff who provide energy and enthusiasm for reading, art, and the community. Your energy is contagious!

The park where I work, providing me with the opportunity to connect others with nature. I'm so blessed to have the Colorado outdoors in my backyard.

Visit Amanda's website at www.amandacaseybooks.com to follow along with her writing adventures.

www.ingramcontent.com/pod-product-compliance
Lightning Source LLC
LaVergne TN
LVHW091348120526
838644LV00042B/604

* 9 7 8 1 9 6 5 3 7 5 0 8 2 *